THE GAME FOR REAL

THE GAME FOR REAL

Richard Weiner
Translated by Benjamin Paloff

Two Lines Press

Hra doopravdy first published 1933
Translation © 2015 by Benjamin Paloff

Published by Two Lines Press
582 Market Street, Suite 700, San Francisco, CA 94104
www.twolinespress.com

ISBN 978-1-931883-44-3

Library of Congress Control Number: 2014955049

Design by Ragina Johnson
Cover design by Gabriele Wilson
Cover photo by Gallery Stock

Printed in the United States of America

This project is supported in part by awards from the National Endowment
for the Arts and the PEN/Heim Translation Fund.

ART WORKS.
arts.gov

THE GAME OF QUARTERING

He boarded the Métro at La Trinité. – It was after midnight. After midnight on an empty, ordinary night at the start of the week. In the first class car, no one but us two.

He boarded at La Trinité. I won't say that he merely reminded me of someone, because I put my finger on it faster than that. He was just as alluringly unhandsome as the Spanish dancer Vicente Escudero, which struck me immediately. Who knows; maybe it even was Vicente Escudero. – Vicente Escudero, at his ease, looks like a man betrayed, standing over the body of the woman who's betrayed him (and in whose death he's played a part) and with his gaze, which is like a lead line, measuring how deep his hatred must plunge into vengeance to be appeased. And which determines that the lead line is too short for something as deep as this.

And Vicente Escudero is, when dancing, like an assassin amused by the thought that one can do just fine without a lead line, that one can plunge headlong into a bottomless hatred, and that this bath can be refreshing, if we only plunge into it without thought of return.

He was unhandsome. Broad Spanish feet, almost fake. And maybe they were . . . Words, which he would not have uttered for anything in the world, withdrew into the steep wrinkles that fell from the downturned corners of his mouth, and which were rather like perfectly conjoined scars. Vicente Escudero knows many, many words of this kind.

I don't know what prayer is. But, having seen him, I was quick to compose one. An ardent one. I prayed that Vicente Escudero would *not* assume the empty seat opposite me. (He had twenty-five to choose from.) I prayed, knowing that he would sit exactly where I was afraid he would: opposite me. I knew this with such certainty that my plea inadvertently became more ardent just as he was moving in the other direction, for I was praying with the certainty that I was praying in vain. And indeed, after two steps he turned around and sat down there, opposite me. Opposite me.

From his pocket he drew a program from L'Apollo and started reading it intently. He read with the unsettling interest of a spy. He paid no attention to me. He wasn't *not* paying attention in a provocative way, but with the kind of strained impassivity by which a misfortune is placed before us, a misfortune that is already at our doorstep, though not yet set in motion. I countered with an unspoken question. A question? Only from a twitch of one of those two scars, so perfectly conjoined, did I realize that I may have actually asked him something. It was a distinctly responsive twitch, if an inadvertent one. It was an answer to the question: "Are you following me?" – He replied (through that twitch of his scar-wrinkle) without looking up; he immersed himself in reading his program, maybe even more deeply than before. And suddenly there came a certainty that he would not get off at Notre-Dame-de-Lorette, that he wouldn't even be getting off at Saint-Georges.

At each stop he leaned out and read the station name,

which he happened to know by heart. This he demonstrated I no longer know how. He was reading the names of the stations, but it was directed at me. After Saint-Georges is Pigalle. That's a transfer station. So how did it sound—How do you think it sounded?—that unspoken question I posed to him as I was pretending to inspect my (trembling) hands? Perhaps it sounded like: "Get off at Pigalle!" – No, not like that, it sounded like: "Aren't you getting off at Pigalle?!"

The interest with which he was reading his program from L'Apollo now attested so cynically to its own phoniness that a chill ran through me. A chill, plus the certitude that he had understood (not raising his head) what I had been silently asking him to do. And, of course, he didn't get out. – After Pigalle is Abbesses. But the question "Aren't you getting off at Abbesses?" was so pointless that it fell away automatically.

After Abbesses is Lamarck. That's my stop. It's not the last stop. Vicente Escudero could still go three more! – But shortly before we came to the station the certainty that we would both be getting off at Lamarck took on an air of necessity to his will or my own, already so self-asserting that my considerate gesture—"We'll be arriving presently, see that you don't miss it, sir" (for he was reading)—broke off of its own accord. He looked at me. With a look as though in generous confirmation that, yes, this was no fantasy: of course he'd been sent, of course he'd been handed a mission.

"And sent by whom, and a mission to do what?" I said with a benumbed smile. And he replied with a smile as well. An exceedingly solicitous smile at that.

He got up. We got out. He walked beside me. The flamboyance (but was it flamboyance?) with which he didn't let me out of his sight from that moment on was equal to the flamboyance with which he had ignored me until then. When we stepped into the elevator (for there's an elevator) he paid me the same polite attention I had shown him in the car, stepping aside humbly and affably so that I might be the first to enter. – The building where I live is not far from the station. He walked beside me the whole way. He looked into my eyes as though they (these eyes) had been stolen from him. He matched my step. He did so with a kind of naïve and deferential ardor.

A woman was standing at the door to our building. She was wearing a checkered loden dress and green silk stockings. She was heavily made-up. She had even applied carmine to her nostrils, and with such senseless brazenness that it occurred to me that she might have wanted to say something particular by it, for example, that she had fallen into despair while making herself up, or that makeup is one of the guises of her desperation. She was leaning against the doorframe. He leaned against the opposite doorframe, waiting for the door to open. They did not converse, not with a look, not with a smile. But how to put this? They were from the same team. They were from some sort of team. Not only was this certain, it could not have been any other way. They were from the same team—not like spouses, not like lovers, not like friends, not like acquaintances, not like castaways on a raft, but they went with each other. – I know the building's residents. Neither he nor she lived there. Nevertheless, they were waiting at the door, just like me. The door finally allowed us in.

I stepped aside so that she could go first. I followed her, and once inside I swung around; no, not to check whether he, too, might have been coming up behind me, but merely to be sure to shut the door behind him. And now I see I am walking along with him on one side, her on the other. I don't know how this happened, but they'd gotten me between them. I say that they'd gotten me there, for it reeked of utter violence, without my being able to recall how they'd moved me into this position. Their walk, their gestures, their glances (which crossed like the arms of adults rock-a-bying babies) were synchronically symmetrical, as if these two were posable puppets mounted on a single shaft. But what naturalness, what ease! Could these really just be people, nothing more? I felt no fear, no alarm. Perhaps I was a bit curious, but with a curiosity that was disinterested, confident.

I called my name out in front of the porter's door, as usual. The sound of my voice was like a veil that had suddenly fallen from something. And it was only then that things took on the air of "something's not quite right." Panic weighed down so sharply and unexpectedly that my lower back completely buckled, my torso heaved. The word "help" started prying at my lips like a crowbar. Here, however, both of them gave me an admonitory wag of the finger, though they did so without withdrawing their eyes' and mouths' strict, if cheerful, watch. Needlessly: the panic had already settled down in the meantime, flat and unbleached, like a thread of jute. Yes, I strode past a panic already tamed. The admonitory fingers had done their work; now their symmetrically summoning hands expressed a mute and gracious "This way, please." I slowed a little and replied with a similar gesture. Thus, for a moment, we were playing a *très magnifique* scene of gracious and unpretentiously worldly gentlemen. We played it carefully, conscientiously, like in the theater, and it popped into my head that maybe that's what we were here for. They yielded at last to my gracious insistence: they took a small step before me, languorously hunched over, as though from embarrassment and an acquiescent desire to please. – When we'd gotten to my door, they stood again like they had at the building's entrance, one to each side of the frame. But it was no longer as it had been—out of the blue they were wearing a severe, hard look. Their mute appeal for me to open up was overbearing and threatening. I dug into my back pocket for the key, looking from one to the other. And still there was that confident curiosity within me. Their gestures, always so peculiarly simultaneous and symmetrical, became impatient and curt: now a finger pointing toward the keyhole; now a derisive and contemptuous jerk of the head; now an exaggerated collapse against the doorframe, like that of people who are waiting before a still-closed theater and affectedly pretending that they will surely never live to see the day; now tapping their feet angrily, if quietly.

A grotesque thought suddenly popped into my head. In the form of an absolute mathematical certainty, that is, that they wouldn't bear it if I, shoving the key into the lock, were to look them both in the eye, but at the same time. Sure, I knew this was absurd. Nonetheless, the comforting sense that this was somehow just possible did not abandon me. I found the key, I ram it into the lock, my gaze fixed before me, and now I'm faced with four eyes, each of them individually and all of them at the same time, as if mutually: two of them brown, two blue; one curious, one timid, and one sweet; the fourth said nothing.

The key turned.

I came home around one in the morning, went up to my door, slid the key in. –

How's that? What about those four eyes? The man? The woman?

How impatient you are! How impatient! Just let me get the door open.

You see: I came back around one in the morning, I went up to my door, slid the key in. I unlocked the top lock, unlocked the bottom one, leaned in gently. The door didn't open. Not that it didn't give at all, but it didn't open.

That means there must be someone pushing against it from inside.

Which is to say, as we do when things are falling apart like this, "a thought popped into my head."

A thought popped! And as yet it's no more than that huge juniper seed when the forward march of the litany of holy logic, recited on a rosary flicking whistlingly along, comes to a screeching halt. As it must: – The door gives, but it doesn't open. It's always doing that in spring and summer. The apartment is humid; the door swells and catches on the upper left corner. In summer, yes. But today? What day is it? It's the fifteenth of November. *That means* they've been running the furnace for fourteen days already. *That means* the door has already dried out. *That means* it opens easily. Yesterday it opened easily. Why is it catching today? Because something is blocking it. What's blocking it? Let's see. We're on the ground floor. The porter opens the pneumatic lock with the push of a button. A tenant enters, shuts the door, and, passing the porter's lodging, he calls out his name. He has to call out his name. And if he doesn't? Or if he calls out a fake name? The porter knows the voices and names of the tenants. If he has the slightest suspicion, he comes out to check. But the porter is married. Furthermore, his wife is plump. The children are already grown. And yet there are still some wild nights over at the porter's. The whole building knows this, and we know thanks to the porter, who brags about it. My door is not opening. *That means* the porter and his wife had a wild night. An hour earlier, two hours earlier, they'd heard the bell. Open up, by all means. But worry oneself over who called out and how they did it? Would you? Love really is the road to perdition.

My door isn't opening. Despite the fact that the furnace has been going for fourteen days already, that the door's already dried out, that it opened just yesterday. That means ... –

Here's the huge juniper seed felt along the forward march of the litany of holy logic: *"That means someone is leaning against it from inside."*

You have come to this point exhausted, terrorized, no longer remembering, incapable of stopping. A thought? Hardly! It's the outermost guardrail of composure, of sangfroid. Will that guardrail hold up against our blow? Or will we topple over it? Or will it break? Will it give? It won't give? A door that doesn't open? *That means someone is leaning against it from inside.* I know this beyond sure; I know this spectacularly. My litany of holy logic has prayed me into the certainty that "this makes sense." This makes so much sense that there's no miracle to chasten its arrogance. Hasn't everything conspired to confirm that the door isn't opening because someone is leaning against it from inside? So where's the miracle? That he's cornered? Helpless? So if I unjam it, what then? Me? I'll unjam it, believing. Believing that, despite everyone and everything, the door is resisting me not because someone is leaning against it from inside, but ... O terrified courage, come to me! Eyes, squint! O shoulder, my ram, come, have at the door ... It's opened! – – – – – – –

And now look at the guy who's doing it! – Who? The guy who was just leaning against the door from inside, of course. Let's take a look at him. Do you see him? He looks so on and so forth, right? But that's the point. The point is, namely, yes: Does he look the way we'd expected (for, *after all*, we had been expecting him)? We'll say it right off the bat: no idea. And let's tell ourselves presently just what it was we'd expected. Let's settle into our sangfroid, our composure, and behold: I come home late at night. I unlock the door. The door gives a little, but it doesn't open. I force it with my shoulder. I'm face-to-face with a stranger—let's say, for the time being, an intruder. I should be frightened; I should at least be astonished, and so what if I've foreseen this, for I did foresee this, after all. But everyone knows what it means to "foresee spooky things": on one side of the scale, there's the premonition; on the other, the hope that the premonition is false. The side with the hope is *always heavier*. By which I mean that premonition is never armor against dread. We always drive like a runaway train into what we dread—through the barrier of premonition. Foresee it or don't—what you dread, you will dread forevermore. But nay: I wasn't feeling dread because I encountered a stranger behind my door; I wasn't even astonished. I merely became conscious of the fact that I *should* have been astonished. But somehow the astonishment didn't feel like it. If you look into the mirror, and in the mirror—nothing; if you put a record on the phonograph, and there's no sound. It's the same way here: I know that I *should* be astonished, but astonishment refuses.

And so now we move on to this other person! Now that the miracle has worn off, let's stop calling him an intruder. The miracle has worn off; therefore, we are justified in calling him not an intruder, but rather a thief. Fine. What can a thief expect in someone else's apartment but to be caught? And so how does a thief, now caught, *normally* look? Every which way: he makes a run for it; perplexity, as they say, ensues; he braces himself to resist; he attacks. And yet who among you has ever seen a thief who, having been caught, starts bawling, and that's all? For this guy was bawling, and that's all. And so you're astonished that my astonishment and my shock remained out back. Isn't that rather like, instead of themselves, they'd only sent some duly authorized replacement, i.e., a dumbstruck question, from whose secret memory drawer an associative recollection leaped from this teary-eyed thief to the domestic fantasy of a boy whom his mother has caught with his finger in the jam jar? Do you know those tears of the jam-thief? They're not tears from any fear of punishment. They're tears set up long in advance: this boy—my intruder, my thief—was quaking to the core; he was quaking long before there was any reason to. This smartass, this tough guy was a quaking daredevil. How do we square this? Yes, that's the question: how do we square it?

So take a look at what he's doing! Look at the fists shoved into the clenched teeth, from where he'd love to cry out, but he's afraid. And those eyes, which moan for you right now, right now, to tolerate his tears; otherwise, they'll well up on their own, they can't hold back any longer—oh, this weepy thief, whose left hand is reflexively bidding us: "Come closer, don't be afraid. But don't beat me, alright?" his boyish anxiety adds, howling. "Don't beat me!"

What would you say to that?

I said simply, if just a little peevishly:

"What is it you want here? And why are you bawling? It's ridiculous!" – And I shut the door behind me.

And I go about my business. You know, like he isn't there. That guy right there! I know very well that he's behind me. That he's skulking like an obedient dog. You'd almost say: like a cunning bitch. – Please, just imagine it: a surprised thief, or something of that sort, and instead of the least bark, he's skulking behind me like a pinscher I've whistled for, and which has rushed in, wagging its tail as a sign it knows it's going to get a beating. And which doesn't have any idea that I only whistled out of terrible fear, that I was staking everything, everything on that whistling. A dog, shall we say, with fists to its maw, and with terror-stricken, teary eyes, and with that left hand comically bidding me not to be afraid of coming home, like I have nothing to fear. Home! Just imagine: a thief who bids me not to be afraid of coming home! And then, sure enough, something popped into my head. To wit: this guy is unspeakably *unthreatening*.

Like anybody, I too have a silly weakness for wanting to wedge myself into a spot where someone else is not. It was by chance that this occurred to me right after I'd made that move—I say by chance, for there was no reason why it should have occurred to me after that move in particular—when I had turned around, crowding him. Let's understand each other: "to crowd" suggests the notion of assault. Just this once, however, it merely indicates that I turned to face him, nothing more. I don't go after him; I don't preach; I don't reprimand. With the possible exception of reiterating with my eyes what my *mouth* had uttered a moment before, as in: "What is it you want here?" (Sounding neither threatening, nor overly curious!)

But look at him! Just take a look at him! For on my soul, this spectacle was worth it: the elegant pantomime of some deep, some unfathomable loss! The right hand at last pulled away from chattering teeth! The twisted right hand, away from which the cramp is slowly and incessantly drifting, and which is again mindful, which is again cautiously connected, which, under his coaxing eyes' crazed surveillance, is dragging itself forward, approaching, astir; whereas the left, heretofore so beseechingly outstretched, has suddenly gone slack, so helpless, as if felled. But that right hand *on the march* and its rebellious fist opening slowly, slowly, grudgingly, out of the superiority of some insidious enmity: you could call it a bud, but one that would admit under pressure that it is no bud at all, but a hard knot of little snakes wrapped in rose petals. – It opens so grudgingly, so shyly. But why? Why? If it doesn't even hold anything so foul?

O thief, my thief, what will you give me, then, for the key?

He is so afraid of me. Don't be afraid! But he's so afraid of me! Why are you afraid of me? You have the key—who gave it to you? You have the key. Thieves pick the lock to get in. This is a key. The real thing. Thieves don't have a key. They can't have a key. You have one; perhaps you're worse than a thief? – Show me. Glory be, the notched key. The lackey's key. Kept with the porter. It's no fake. It's the real thing. From where? How did you get it, whoever you are? Did you pinch it off someone you'd killed? Did you just steal it? Hmm? Nothing to say, whoever you are?

Then, for the first time, something flashed in his eyes, something other than astonishment, other than fright, other than pleading, other than lamentation. But perhaps it was an order above all orders, one regarding not people so much as things. A directive as follows: *for it not to matter that I get hold of the key.* And I obeyed. I loyally obeyed that it *not matter.* After protracted confusions, the first certainty. Oh, hardly a comforting certainty, hardly a negotiable certainty. But rather a suspiciously unfair certainty, you might say, kind of like someone sweetly talking you down while readying the straitjacket. It was a tricky, treacherous certainty, *but a certainty nonetheless.*

"Are we up to something here?" I asked. "Then let's be up to something, right? A drama, is that what we're going to have here?"

His eyes got ready to answer, but they changed their mind; suddenly, as though he had replaced them, they were again just the eyes of a frightened and pleading thief. I say: a thief—but who is this stranger behind my door exactly, of whom I should have been terrified but was not terrified, who assumed my terror *within himself,* and around whose corporeal being—for he is corporeal—I step with such stubborn indifference, as if around my own shadow? Who is this unexpected intruder into my bachelor life's daily rhythm who, all things considered, does nothing to spoil it? Under whose gaze, watchful yet remote, am I pretending to be disinterestedly inspecting my ground-floor apartment, my abode, where it's so easy for a stranger to intrude, no different today than any other (when I am invariably alone)? For God's sake, who is he, paradoxically present, a man so *rare* that it's almost like he's not here, and under whose haunting, haunted supervision I perform an array of passes suited to an inspector, after which I lie down *fully aware* that I could sleep peacefully, that I am alone, that I am still alone despite the fact that he's here with me? I'm not bothered, not at all bothered by this someone, whom I see and do not regard.

I throw myself into my rounds, beginning with the dining room. Pedantic, manic passes through the cupboards, the drapes. On my heels, he whom I take for no one. He's a shadow, more shifting aside than moving—a shadow, a nothing that delights in nothingness; a shadow, an amplified, unfathomed nothing. Can you heed the presence of someone incarnated only as if in confirmation that he's not there *for real?*

The hand outstretched with the turning key, the imploring eyes, beseeching me to take it, this, my key, all of it has the accent of an essence so paradoxical that it bothers me . . . What is meant by this ataraxia of the nerves, this eerie breakdown of all experience?

"Don't be afraid. Surely you see I'm not scared, and that I won't do anything to you."

He went over to the corner, put his hands behind his back—a petal flutters down, circles in darkness; a memory—rather like the way day laborers used to wait at Klein's, in the cobbler's shop, until work came for them. You could see into the workshop through the glass doors from the office, where Mr. Štajer, the *Vorarbeiter*, would measure us with a brown paper ribbon, which he used to tickle our feet.

The memory circled around, drained of color. It landed softly and, once landed, sobered up, and in so doing unwittingly betrayed where it was supposed to have been going: to the realization that I'd already spent quite some time, as they say, in an impossible situation. Yes, *because something really isn't right here.* The passive resistance of dumbness isn't okay; the boyish fright and impetuous distress of this certain someone are not okay. Everything is like it's inside-out, and that's not okay. If it was okay, this thief (or whatever he is) would behave differently. But this disconsolate, this shrinking, this unnaturally withering thief: none of this is okay. And how could it be okay that I can't manage, I can't even manage to be struck properly dumb by things I know should strike me dumb, in a position that so urgently demands my dumbness? Which I refuse. No: what refuses is something within me. How dumbfounding it is that I'm not struck dumb. It's dumbfounding! And behold: *dumbfounding*, the word, is like nightshade, like a blossom of nightshade, with which something that was supposed to be has also come into bloom; and barely has this flower opened before it flips over, like images painted across vertical blinds that, with a flick of a spring, are hastily and chaotically snuffed out, slat by slat, until, with the turning of the last of them, a new image appears, the image on the reverse. And this image means: fear. Nothing anywhere, and suddenly there's fear.

And yet again, it's already like he's going to snuff it out. Who? With what? From where? Or perhaps it's just the brightness from the crack under the door to the next room? Someone in there has turned on a light. Who? Why? – He knows for sure, for sure he knows, and I turn around quizzically. Meanwhile, how close my confidence has become with this person so reminiscent of "the fellow from Klein's." He's not the kind who begs the question; he's someone whom it's impossible not to ask. So I say, "I would bet...," stifling an explosive rage, but placated by the awareness of his having ferreted out my testament, "...that you've gotten yourself into a mess." For he nods like a boy who's been caught and reproved, but who has already ascertained that the incubation period for his lashing has already lapsed. – He nods, with gratitude for such magnanimity, and in agreement that he would come to earn it. – Good, good! If that's the way it has to be, let's also have a look at the bright crack under the door.

To the door! Let's get it open! Look sharp! Not the look sharp of distraught impatience, ravenous after a long and cunning play for the irrational hope that a fugitive experience is again lying in wait behind the door, that there at last we will find the key, the only true key... to the gates, then... the gates of hell... And who should open up—it's me who opens up—don't think he has the look of the damned, bedeviled by a yearning to "put an end to this." Instead, imagine someone like... yes, someone like a happy father returning home from work and impatient for his portrait of the family idyll, which he is already conjuring for himself in advance. Oh, that group of loved ones he hastens toward! He's bought a baggie of delectables on the way. Standing at the threshold, he is singing happily, jovially, grinning: "Guess what I have!"

I was impatient, too, but not curious. I, too, *knew*, opening the door, what to expect, though *unknowing* what I would behold. I, too, already *knew* that whatever I would see, I would see something from the world now poised, perhaps befuddled, within me: a smooth sheet of paper pulled out of a crumpled, squeezed, twisted—by me, no less—ball. I *knew* that that inside-out world where I had made my home till now would not end behind the door, and could not end. I *knew* the door would open and the mystery would remain intact, I was merely *aware*, and unwittingly, that I would find the mystery—now only tight-lipped, not twisted—and the question of what form the mystery would have no longer upset or irritated me. That's why it's not odd that what actually surprised me wasn't the woman lying on the sofa but her gesture, so peculiarly automatic, like the gesture of a sleepwalker, and at the same time as direct as a greeting: she tugged at the hem of her loden skirt, as if embarrassed about her exposed legs. It was a futile gesture, she had on a skirt short enough that you could see her green silk stockings almost to the knee—it was a gesture so nakedly futile as neither to provoke, nor to repulse. But she also abandoned it so naturally, so easily, and in the same way that she would abandon it every time that, in the naked silence that presently seemed to encircle the three of us, it announced itself anew. I say it announced itself, for this gesture was talkative.

I shrugged my shoulders and smacked my lips; not surprised, merely annoyed, and annoyed by the thought that the taciturn "fellow from Klein's" might have come in behind me. Might he be so indiscreet? I turned my head, and it was indeed a wonder that I didn't brush up against him. He was there, right up behind me, with the same old-woman's curiosity and excusing himself like a footman: the helpless flinch of the shoulders; the faint upward drift of the otherwise vertical arms; the awkwardly moronic smile. All in all, the sum total of his embarrassed excuse for a bad habit he was attempting in vain to suppress. I looked at him from an oddly skewed perspective, as if on a mound that was sagging; that is, he followed me so close that we were nearly attached.

Trickster! He was concealing the fact that they were acquainted, that they were playing their agreed-upon roles. In vain. I caught on in an instant. Her nostrils, nonsensically blushed to cinnabar; her long, mascara-caked lashes, no different from blinds brought down over a suspiciously demure gaze that transports explicitly outlawed goods! To smuggle them, to smuggle—what she wouldn't have given! That vision, sweet-and-innocent to the eye, gets at you. But the stereotypical tugging at the skirt testifies that it's all a ploy, hard-headed as a ram, to fool the guard. A ploy ultimately thwarted again and again. And with each new failure, there was this little display, packed with fierce forbearance—the enraged repose of an ant assuming a burden that will come to naught. Resignation shining with needles of frozen irony. The gentleman-servant, caught with his hand in someone else's pocket, a pickpocket dutifully admitting that it's checkmate, and who neither repents nor talks his way out of it, knowing with a comfortingly obdurate certainty that this will not be his last time . . .

That slyboots, that intelligent little bitch! She knew immediately that together we were playing, if not at life and death, then at truth and lie (how she recoiled as she came to the certainty that it was worse than life or death); she calculated her odds solely by squinting, and having inferred that she could not win, with feigned indifference she launched an effort to play for stalemate. Three times, five times, seven times she shifted in the hope of turning my attention away from her eyes, which were trying to sneak past to *him*; seven times, nine times, eleven times I caught her off guard with a sideward glance, and the ploy was thwarted. – She answered each of my displays with the foxiness of a servant coolly faking gentlemanly resignation to his fate, and again she would surreptitiously ready a new round. It was as if two bitter adversaries were butting heads again and again, fully aware that but for the referee's favor neither one of them would win. Our unbridled hatred melted our grimaces into the affable smiles of knightly adversaries—foul cunning pretended that this was less a matter of success than of *playing fair*. Her empty gesture of tugging at her skirt was repeated so frequently, steadily, and stereotypically that it eventually took on the character of a sort of secret means of communication. It was, consequently, a talkative gesture and, you would say, a luridly provocative one. It piled up like vile snowdrifts; I was unable to dig out with my eyes; they put up massive resistance. The sense of a peculiar world pointlessly besieged by terror persisted. I came to feel at home there. I was supremely aware that my uninvited guests were here because of some supernatural unrest; everything in this apartment was different from how it usually is, but the shape and form of things had not changed; the change was separate from them, as if it were their distinguishing feature, overlooked until now. Imagine that every day you eat from the same plate with a floral print; you know it so well that it would not escape you were it replaced by a plate with slightly different flowers. But one day you take a closer look and discover a tiny, heretofore overlooked flaw. Go on, try—how should I put this?—try to enthrall it; fix your eyes on it; a moment later, you're looking at a kind of intimate unreality: the one reality, irrefutable, since it's quotidian, remains solely this heretofore overlooked flaw; it's like the only discernible shape in a fog, only you don't know "where to put it." Or else try saying your own name over and over again. Suddenly, it's not that you're estranged from it; on the contrary, it's emerged as the last debris of the real—it's a name that has become a thing while remaining a name, the name of someone you don't know, though it's yours.

It was no different with my uninvited guests. They were strangers to me; they were estranged from me all at once, but not as much so as my own apartment, albeit still familiar and unaltered to my eyes. They were somehow more real than it was. They were strangers, unfamiliar, and yet theirs was an assigned unfamiliarity, promised; only I didn't know "where to put them."

And that pointless, telling game with the skirt, again and again! It was sort of like the rhythmic incantation of voiceless conversations. It was a measure; but this measure turned into gesture, and in turn the gesture was becoming eternal. This meter was unstable: at the outset, I would say, it was moving toward the key of shabbily artful ploys, then it passed unnoticed to the slower meter of a trapped pickpocket's indifference, after which it settled into the time of the woman's embarrassment. This embarrassment: it struck an irritating contrast with her makeup, with her posture and attire, but it was remarkably sincere; indeed, it was gripping. And despite her brazen eyes, which, no, did not cease their efforts to arrive artfully at an understanding with that other fellow. We were each playing a false card, but we didn't make a show of it, since each of us had caught the other and knew the false cards of his opponents. The alertness of us three, of which two would alternate as two against the third, created a homey atmosphere where one could breathe easy. We were frauds so cynically unashamed that we felt righteous about it. I switched seats— to her feet. I looked at her, to see if I could figure out "where to put her." I looked into her eyes, she into mine. Both of us so nonchalantly, so unsheepishly, as if we were each just an object to the other. – He would pace; he would stop; then he stepped toward us, smiled shyly, and shrugged his shoulders ("how silly of me to have been frightened by such a thing!"). He shifted boyishly to the side, turned on his heel, started pacing again. That boyish turn I found particularly striking, for he was no longer quite young. A stranger would have taken us for acquaintances who had overstayed, no longer had anything to say, and were sheepishly keeping quiet.

Out of the blue, I felt like doing something as yet undefined (her eyes, without turning from me, flickered under this caprice, as if seeking a balance they'd momentarily lost), and before I know it I'm seeing my own hand reach for her hair and tug at it feebly. He was standing right next to us. He caught sight of the end of that touch and turned to meet my eyes once again. Amiably and tactfully, he gave them an approving, impish, and encouraging smile. Pulling her hair, I heard and felt a weak snap. She smiled. She put her hands under her chin and raised it slightly. It was an obliging gesture that reminded me, I don't know why, of the gesture of a shopkeeper explaining how to work a toy you've purchased. Under that pressure, her head slipped out a little. It revealed on her neck the kind of groove you see on poseable dolls. When she'd shown this, her hands again withdrew, and her head fell with a faint click.

He, seeing this, slapped his hips like a man who's "having a laugh," turned my chin so that I'd pay attention, and seized the woman by the arm. She rose up, and when he let her go she fell with a faint click, just as her head had. The woman sighed, but as if she'd done no more than the thing with her skirt.

He doubled over as if seized by impudent laughter, which was bizarre, for his face remained impassive. Or no, it was rather sad. He doubled over like a good prankster who's pulled off a joke, then he performed a hasty "now watch" gesture and did a tumble like a little clown. His aspect, however, in no way fit this apparently boisterous move: it remained sad the whole time; in fact, now it was quite desolate. This lasted for a while. I watched attentively, stiffly, with interest, but like at a spectacle I'd deliberately come for.

Then he sat down on the sofa as well, at her head. He started to stroke her tenderly. I can't say how ghostly, yet in no way frightening, was the suddenness by which he passed to those tender displays immediately following that quiet and crazy footwork. So sensuous and chaste were his caresses! I saw him exactly in profile. It was the profile of an impenetrable ascetic. That's how it struck me. For until then he had always shown me his full face, whereas from that point on he had the look of an eager goody-goody—eager for temptation. Two different people. I was reminded of my friend Fuld, whom I hadn't seen for several months. Fuld's head, too, was a sort of Janus head (we ascribed this to the peculiar configuration of his upper lip). This one here was like Fuld, but it was not Fuld—it could not be Fuld. And it was just then, in the thought that it was literally "as if it were Fuld," though it couldn't really be Fuld, it was just then that I was chilled, and immediately after, I was chilled again, because that's when I first realized that the anxiety had arrived precisely with my Fuldian memory. But it was with that double trembling that I'd caught the trail of "where to put them." It had been so indistinct till then, who could say it was a trail. More like you'd woken up in a strange land, but on a road that suggested an almost overbearing certainty that it led precisely to where you had to go, though you yourself have no idea where that is.

It struck me how great an error it was to think that—as if all journeys end—and I smiled. Fortunately, however, no one would ever see that smile. I then caught sight of it unwittingly, in them, they'd suddenly become like mirrors. And my apartment indulgently resolved to return to the axis from which *he* had dislodged it.

Not for long. – I left them with a silent "goodnight" and made for bed. It was late, time to go to sleep. Yet, as I was crossing the threshold, everything was again knocked off its axis. – In the frame of the door, a kind of obstruction. I didn't see it, I didn't feel it, and still, an obstruction. Nothing to be torn down, nothing to chop through, nothing to vault over, and still, an obstruction. That is, something that demands that it be overcome. Nothing in the bedroom had been touched. In my mind, I repeated to myself: "And yet (I said 'and yet'), and yet nothing in here has been touched," and I quickly got stuck. I was stuck on that "and yet," and suddenly I understood how very ponderous it was. And I knew: I knew that that "and yet" had been dispatched by a heretofore underground impulse that had already revealed, though concealing it from me, that in the bedroom it *only appeared* that nothing had been touched. It wanted to conceal from me that the order I was seeing with my eyes was a momentary, desperate, slapdash order, the likes of which are thrown together in towns shattered by earthquake, so that the lord who has announced his tour of compassion not encounter devastation—unwashed, unbrushed, unshaven. Here was this bedroom, where it appeared that nothing had been moved. This ambiguous, evil bedroom, this stupid bedroom that wanted to deceive me with its Potemkin order. No change, then? Who are you kidding, you disaster smoothed over with hasty rakes of sham sympathy? You want to confound me! Me!

So there's this bedroom where nothing appears to have

been touched. – Order? By all means! – But not the usual kind. – Order? By all means! But after the revolution that broke out whilst I was sojourning far away, that triumphed, that, in the meantime, settled in and blocks my view of where it was really heading, what it has achieved, what its point had been. This bedroom had been my atelier, where I'd hack away my wasted days. – But this bedroom was changed, albeit without appearing that anything had been touched. Only now I know, now I know what that unfeelable thing is, that invisible obstruction in the doorframe—it is the cumulative resistance of all the wasted days to come: they've mutinied against the hack; they'll no longer allow themselves to be done up; they won't be a party to masquerades; they're resolved not to lie and not to be duped. They will strictly be what they will be. In the doorframe, there stood not future time, but future tense—it leaned on a knotty cane, for it was an old man, and asked not to be a party to my hack masquerades. And that resistance of the future tense had the shape and range of a truly immeasurable silence. Which, once I'd recognized it, drew aside, let me in, and I crossed the threshold.

And I entered chambers that whispered to me that nothing is also something. I was willingly convinced. Then it was as though their immeasurability gradually diminished. Slowly, slowly I came back to myself. I was somewhere that resembled my bedroom, at first nearly, then almost, and finally enough that it set the mind aglow. It was actually that a revolution had gone down here, and that it was hiding what it really wanted. – The whole time there was this great silence, though no longer hermetic; the sound of beingness carried in, as if from a far-off passage. More and more distinct. – And then, as if my millstone had been suddenly removed: I turned my head. I determined that yes, I was in my bedroom. It was different from before, but it was still my bedroom. – A bitter relief rippled through me. I started getting undressed.

I started getting undressed. The day, already departing for tomorrow, returned hastily and somewhat reluctantly, as it does daily, somewhat like a chastened child on his way to bed, who in the confusion forgets that he has to say goodnight. He's returned, the helpless little cripple, and he's sobbing into his elbow, "Look what you've done to me!" What a wretch! Day after day, the same story: I hear out his grievances, but absently; I argue with him, but without interest; I promise that I'll do right by him tomorrow, but my mind is elsewhere; I warn him to cut it out, but I warn without passion. Because that's pretty much it, my mind is elsewhere: on the harbor that awaits me. But where you enter, it seems to me, you don't sail out from again, so I'm making sure I keep to the buoys that lead the way: straight ahead, sleep. A line of buoys leads me there, they're quietly swaying on a very black, very languorous surface. The pilot plows through the water, which doesn't so much as splash. As if he were slithering over it. This pilot is silence. – Today, however, he doesn't quite want to be. In what silence there is, something is whispering. I listen in, attentive, unriled. It's nearby—those two over there. The kind of whispering before sleep, the whisper of considerate guests who are afraid of disturbing you. You can hear them removing their clothes: the absent punctuation to their whispering. Not long ago I would offer my hospitality to friends, to couples. We'd spend an evening at the theater. Upon returning we would converse for a short time longer, then I would leave them and go get undressed. Like today. Then, too, one could hear the call of things that had been put off: affable dots, accent marks, and semicolons set my guests' whispering to music—a whispering in no way mysterious, a whispering that told all. It was having a cozy time in the silent womb of my apartment, in the spacious silence. Here and there a distinct word slipped through the slightly open door, as if to assure me that I had a share even in that which I did not discern. Those words spun out like a rosary, dense at first, then less and less frequent. After which nothing but whispers and the chatty punctuation of things. – I pay close, but cool, attention. Yes, it's entirely like the other day, after the theater. The friendly idyll before sleep. – What am I saying, *like* back then? What a fool I am! *It is* the other day after the theater. Next door are my recent guests. That is, today is not so long ago, what with not so long ago having been today. We came back from the theater. We had a bit of conversation. That before retiring we might hit upon something. That we might find some pretext for falling asleep beneath a baldachin of laughter: we'll chat—chat like tossing a ball, any which way—so, then, what might we chat about? About the waiter, who got a bit tongue-tied; or how we laughed ourselves silly at the usherette who offered us the programs, displaying them like they were tablets of law; at our gesture of refusal she'd shrugged her shoulders as if regretting that we did not want to submit to the law, and worried that we might thus be risking our salvation. We solemnly vow that tomorrow we will go to such-and-such a place, and we go to sleep bursting with laughter, because we have unwittingly revealed to each other that we don't think it matters. –

Yes, but it was precisely out of this cheerful laughter that my fear prolapsed. It alerted me that they were cowering here somewhere. It alerted through the sweaty shirt sticking to my back. It was a strange fear: I didn't *have* it, but I was aware of it. As if it had appeared to me. I knew that it and I were face-to-face, so close I couldn't see it. So close *it* wasn't there to see. A peculiar fear. Unexcited, reflective, and imploring. Imploring me to shelter it within myself, to take it in. It looked so unhappy, it looked particularly unhappy. One evening—I was quite young at the time—an older man had stopped me on the street, and he said to me: "Take me with you." I looked at him, one would say, as befit the circumstances, well, with revulsion. He broke into tears: "Take me with you, no one wants to take me with him." I wasn't afraid, for I clearly saw that he was suffocating on the tenderness with which everyone was thrusting him away. I was certain that he wouldn't harm me, that he had nothing to harm me with ... I wasn't afraid, I say, and yet I was seized by horror, and I know precisely where it had come from: it was the horror of being infected with misfortune. With his misfortune, for this man was unhappy the way others fall ill. I took to my heels, but he came after me, quietly calling, "Don't be afraid, you big ninny, don't be afraid of being unhappy." But I fled, I fled, for unfortunates like these pose a greater threat to us than Jack the Ripper. In like manner was the unsightly and piteous fear that was confronting and courting me here not my own fear, it was beyond me, without my having actually beheld it; and yet I knew it was here, and I feared it as I would someone with an infectious disease: i.e., its horror.

I remembered that I had been scared in the very same manner already once today, it was just as I was inspecting the dining room and it occurred to me that I was not particularly astonished at the stranger behind the door, and that it wasn't okay for me not to be astonished. I recoiled at my not feeling horror. Who knows, maybe that's just the sort of horror that makes us sweat whenever, out of nowhere, we've run into ourselves, as I did today when I ran into my apartment; who knows, maybe there is *constantly* residing within us this sort of unexpected eternal visitation, from which we recoil only when it occurs to us that it's like we'd been looking the other way all this time. Only we seldom run into ourselves: we rattle the keys, we cough, we drag our feet across the floor, we do what we might so that the thief will make it out the window in the meantime. There's no merit in being robbed; the merit is in putting up with the sight of the burglar—putting up with him as if he were an old acquaintance.

At last, silence. Utter. It bumped up against one of those sort-of-fleeting rustles that jacks make when raked together, and then it spilled away, silent as a swamp. I identified it immediately, that rustle—it was *her* amber necklace tossed onto the marble mantelpiece. It, that rustle, was the threshold of voicelessness, but at the same time it was the wake-up call of her presence. It was like the click in a stereopticon just before the photographs are replaced; the "view" replaced by a "view" just as smoothly, fluidly, and with the same almost violent suppleness as with a "peep box," and no matter that none of the preceding images had announced this one, no matter that there was no precedent for this one among those past, no matter that it had clicked in as if sent down, here it was like something that could not be—it was here as the sole thing that was, indisputably, and upon which one had to gaze: the imagined "fine acquaintances with whom I had returned from the theater" had withdrawn and been replaced by the image of "these two, so strangely familiar." And the transcendent, unfortunate, solicitous horror, which I (without actually feeling it) caught wind of by feeling my shirt sweaty against my back, was absorbed by the picture called "these two, so strangely familiar," and faded markedly. – It might have seemed that the phrase "as a graveyard" should follow "silent," so deep was the silence that followed. But no. Rather, it resembled the silence that washes through an apartment wherein a harmonious family is at its ease. I was pierced with so powerful a sense of intimacy (with those two) that it formed a sweet knot in my throat. A muted light still shone in the living room. From that I judged that those two were not yet asleep; I got a cheery taste for playing host; I went out to them to see whether they needed anything.

When I entered, it struck me that they were both still dressed. That confused me a bit, and my bliss lost some of its depth. Admittedly, they weren't asleep yet, but they were already nodding off. He was sitting in the armchair under the lamp. I was turned toward him, which is to say he was giving me that face of a goody-goody gourmand, about which I have already spoken, and which reminded me so much of Fuld. His half-open eyes did dampen this impression somewhat, but it was still distinctly there. His head turned a little, his mouth slightly open, and his hands, which he had raised to his head (where they now remained) as if at the height of despair, aroused the impression that he would have long since cried out had it been physically possible for him to have done so (thus entirely different than if this cry were to have appeased his will). Despite this, however, he did not look like he was desperate; amazingly, he didn't even seem sorrowful. His features rather reflected, as it were, the animal irritation of people whose slumber is hindered by some physical defect. I understood that what ailed him were his upraised hands. I took them and slowly placed them in his lap. He looked up sleepily, with the grateful expression of a child when we've gotten him all nice and snug. All this time, then, *she* had been tensely watching what I was doing, and seeing how attentive I was being to him she smiled understandingly, you might say conspiratorially—with that indulgent superiority of older sisters who know their little brothers' weaknesses and urge a strange man not to think poorly of them and to indulge them as well. Against expectation, however, the smile ended by plunging into her mouth's left corner, which twisted. And it was as if this had thrown her into embarrassment: again, that tugging at the skirt, though this time in the manner of a movingly strange gesture. She sought to extricate herself from this new embarrassment, making as if she were awkwardly positioned and looking for a better spot on the sofa. I approached so as to fluff her pillow. As I bent down, I heard at first a whistling, a kind of admonitory rebuke, and right after that, words.

"Take him off my hands! I hate him. Take him off my hands."

I straightened up, surprised.

"Who?" I eventually muttered.

Was it because she couldn't stand my gaze? Was it a sign, her averting her eyes? Toward him, it seemed to me. I followed them, and they indeed came to rest on him. I got the sense that she was eyeing us uncomfortably. When I turned again to settle things with her with my eyes, she had already lowered her eyelids again and resembled a young lady who "knows how to sleep."

I went back to my bedroom to lie down as well. Once there, with one leg already in bed, I suddenly stood up again: all at once it had struck me that I was forgetting something. I thought about it hard. The sole outcome of which was that I arrived at a tautological semblance of a thought: *I won't remember what it was*; that is, the thought that "I've forgotten something." Today I write "tautology," but then, at first glance, it didn't seem a tautology. Only after I had constructed a rather subtle logical chain from one half-proposition to the next (a chain I'd hardly be able to follow today) did I succeed in satisfying myself with the conclusion that if I am not able to remember something, I *therefore* must have forgotten something, and only in this was there some hope that I might still recall *that thing* which I had forgotten. And, as a result, I immediately remembered that something, while also being aware that this was not yet it. That is, I got a flash of a certain act by Grock, the unforgettable king of clowns. He is aping his partner, who, having readied his fiddle, suddenly can't remember what it was that he'd wanted to play, so he turns, goes to the piano, and leans his elbow against it (his back to the audience), his fist to his chin, assuming the pose of a man struggling to remember.

But this is where I raised my head, having realized that the thing I couldn't remember was those astonishing, brief, and rash words of the woman as I was fluffing her pillow; with them, then, was the reason they had vanished—the words, that is.

So now I had remembered both those words and the thing that had overshadowed them in my memory: it was a disproportionately large space suffused with a sense of the incompatibility between the sounds by which I had judged that these two had gotten undressed—sounds that I had heard so clearly, so distinctly, and which were surely not mere reminiscence—and the fact that entering the living room I had found both strangers still quite clothed. But having raised my head with that recollection, I was at the same time confronted with the fact that I was sitting at my writing table, that is, with something quite unexpected. He on one side, she on the other. They were now in their pajamas. They were standing faithfully, the way I was just then imagining Grock's partner. Or no, they had already given up that posture again; but I inferred—I no longer know why—that they had given it up only just before I'd noticed them. And so it was actually as if I had been sleeping and was awakened only by their having given up that posture. Or else they had their fists to their chins the whole time, yet they contorted their faces symmetrically with mine. The smile that was playing on their lips was remarkable for the light it cast on the recent, albeit already buried, past. In this way it also happened that I again recognized, which is to say I caught up with, what had directly preceded this, that is, that I myself had recently settled into the posture of Grock's partner, and they had crept quietly in and were aping me *good-naturedly*, until finally, having readied a smile and turned their heads, they inadvertently induced me to look up.

This, however, is where I gave a start, for he spoke.

"What's that you're playing with there?" he said.

Far be it from me to say whether I started out of surprise or because he'd caught me at something I'd prefer to keep to myself. For it was only now that I realized that with my right hand I was massaging one of those pliable puppets they sell in the gallery of the Folies Bergère. If their arms were straight along the body, they'd just be nude, but they have them folded behind the head, which makes them naked; and they are so flexible that they gratify even the most lascivious fantasy. One of those dolls rests upon my writing table. That's her place. Of the reason behind this whim I can say nothing more than that it's more or less at the antipode of the reasons why others buy them. *However*, this time I had taken her into my hand unknowingly.

So I gave a start, and I thrust her away. And something so peculiar happened that my astonishment—if that's what it was—at the stranger's unexpected words, or my sheepishness at having been caught in so ambiguous a game (if I indeed regretted it), was all at once as if extinguished. It was oddly discreet; it was imperceptible. All around that modestly amazing phenomenon, however, it was as if everything had been piled up to foster the hope that it would bring about some decisive, universally desired answer that had, so far, been hanging in the background. That from this would come an answer to the questions, events, and matters that had arisen so remarkably this evening, and perhaps even an answer to those two, who surely had to know and, in truth, perhaps did (and thus, perhaps, that smile of theirs); everything, I say, turned toward the *sound* and listened intently to what would follow. I have said that, having been interrupted by the words "what's that you're playing with there," I thrust the young lady aside. Now, these toys are made of a flexible, very soft, yielding material. Imagine that a ball bouncing off a tabletop were to make a sound like that of a heavy, unyielding body. That's just what the young lady I'd thrust aside sounded like. I was so surprised that I automatically moved to console her—she weighed no more than before, and she was just as yielding to the touch as usual—but dropped her again. Once more, the same bang, like a Browning going off, you might say. I looked up at the strange woman: she was no longer looking at me; she was staring at the table and stroking her brow embarrassedly. I looked up at the strange man: he did not dodge my gaze. But the impish smile fell from his lips. He was still smiling all right, but in a sort of reproachful way, and he was shaking his head as if at a child who'd done something he shouldn't have, and it's a wonder he didn't get hurt. Without taking his eyes off me, he reached for that young lady himself, picked her up, dropped her, fixing me with his stare. Nothing. Not a sound. She fell the way she should.

"What's that you're playing with there?" he asked again.

I looked from one to the other, and suddenly it dawned on me that they resembled someone *collectively*. It wasn't like they each resembled a third, and therefore each other. It was as if their *combined* likenesses gave the likeness of a third, someone I knew. It's only with difficulty that something like this can be imagined, only barely. I, too, raised this objection, quietly, but in doing so I couldn't overcome the certainty that their features were merging into those of someone who in fact resembled neither him, nor her. Here it was as if something broke down, and I remembered that if I had been late in coming home today, the blame lay in the episode with Mutig, Giggles, and Fuld.

On that day—it was already dusk—I was playing Mozart's *Eine kleine Nachtmusik* on the gramophone. The main theme of the rondo inevitably arouses in me the associative image of a happy, carefree, and obstinate boy who does not appreciate the troubles of the grown-ups, whose experience he regards as a horrid and impenetrable nuisance. The adults advise him, they reason with him. He plays innocent and keeps his schemes to himself. But once they've quit their sermon and turned their backs to him, walking away smug and high-mannered, he sticks his tongue out at them and goes back to his prattling. And the theme confesses that this boy has not listened to them; he'd kept quiet as long as they'd encouraged him to, but he'd done so only out of a derisive superiority and because he is impatient—had he talked back, the sermon would never have ended. He is happily, carelessly, and obstinately impatient; he's racing toward the unknown, the menacing "what's ahead." This theme is the master key, with it I get through closed doors; it is the ladder to what cannot be believed; and the difficulty by which it unfurls like a vine loses the name of difficulty, and comes to be called desirability.

When the rondo's theme had returned for the third time, it whispered to me that if I were to wish to see Fuld today, I would see him, I need only try. For a moment earlier I had, in fact, felt a desire to meet with Fuld. (And thus we see that the rondo's theme is prescient as well.) I dressed and went to find Fuld at a café in Montparnasse. We had arranged nothing. He never went to that café. That's precisely why I chose it, for I felt like a meeting with Fuld as though with some unlucky star—I mean that, and not with a lucky star—and why make yourself out to be such a star in a place where such a star *cannot be*? Meeting someone we wish for like an unlucky star must be unlike any other meeting. Or else it's better not to do it. Fuld, of course, was not at that café. I was neither surprised, nor annoyed. My failure merely inspired me to look for Fuld at a café by the same name on the Champs Elysées. He didn't go there, either. But I was driving blindly toward Fuld: that is, I had become dependent upon him; in other words, I was proceeding methodically, and the most methodical of all is to proceed in the absurd. It was absurd to look for him in Montparnasse, even more absurd to look for him on the Champs Elysées for no other reason than that he had not been in Montparnasse. Great, then, was my expectation of finding him. It was a certainty. – I hailed a cab.

The taximan, who was already going who-knows-where, veered suddenly from a remarkably dark and quiet street into some artery, strikingly bright and busy. The shift was so jarring that I unintentionally glanced out the window to orient myself. But the motorcar had already come to a stop, and I got out. I was in front of an enormous house with glaringly bright, yet veiled, ground-floor windows. It was a massive house, but, for whatever reason, from the *côté cour* it gave the impression of a theatrical backdrop. Besides that, it struck me that the bustle on that lively artery was of a nature entirely its own. There were many carriages driving, many people walking. It's not that their movement was quiet or spectral. The acoustics were not at such odds with the optics. But immediately past its source the din, while quite distinct, was as if sucked away and carried off elsewhere. I had the impression of a waterfall. Or else, the more I looked at the house, the more powerfully it reminded me of a certain house up on Rue Lamarck, just below the Sacré-Coeur Basilica; the whole time it was reminding me of that house more and more, but not for a moment did it lose the certain optical accentuation that marked it as not being that house at all. There's a tavern there. Steps plunge long and steep from Rue Lamarck down to Rue Muller. I couldn't see them, but I had no doubt that they were here somewhere, for how else could one explain the waterfall-like din? It is true, of course, that at its higher end Rue Lamarck is quiet and at that hour of evening entirely empty. There was therefore reason to wonder at the unusual movement, but how could I wonder, when my budding amazement was suddenly deflected to an even more worthy phenomenon?

That is, I spotted a shadow on the curtain of one of those ground-floor windows, and I immediately recognized that shadow as belonging to Fuld. Not only did I recognize it, what's more is that I ascertained Fuld was listening intently to something being said by the silhouette sitting across from him. That was Mutig.

There was nothing particularly unnatural in this. I recognized both shadows (they were conspicuously sharp), since I know both Fuld and Mutig quite well. It was natural, too, that

I was also immediately aware that Fuld was listening to Mutig, and that he was listening to him intently and disapprovingly. Which is to say, I have often tempted Fuld into evil. And this shadow corresponded precisely to the posture Fuld assumed when I was seducing him into evil. Meanwhile, I would usually be sitting like Mutig was now, for evil is comfortable; Fuld would be standing. Standing at the table where we had been talking, and leaning his fingers on the table so heavily that they quite buckled. His head would be bent, and you couldn't get far beyond the tense, gloomily sad expression on his face: something was cooking in there, but what?

Fuld was *un incorruptible*. We had long been virtually inseparable, so he knew I was a libertine and a waster— "unselective," he would say. He didn't hold it against me, never tried to steer me away. He was disinterested, oblivious, and was equally so toward my debts—debts of every kind—when it came time to pay—never so much as a word of encouragement, reproach, consolation, much less a contribution or aid. Beyond that, I wouldn't dare say anything specific about our relationship. Once or twice, however, it has seemed to me that he couldn't get by without me. How happy I would have been had I managed to ascribe that clinginess to the simple attachment of friends; but something got in the way. That is, one day I stood at the very cusp of my undoing. It was within his power to save me. And he did actually save me, too—with a rough, curt, almost brutal, unspoken support. Without reprimand, but also without friendly counsel.

Looking at those two familiar shadows, I was suddenly seized—yes, seized—by the certainty that Mutig was seducing Fuld, as I myself had seduced him, and that Fuld was defending himself, but only feebly. What I will now say in brief occurred so quickly that there are no words for it but those that provide a rough approximation. But it nonetheless occurred in time, and in a continuous sequence. I was seeking out a reason behind this certainty of mine (that is, that he was being seduced and was, but feebly, defending himself). And I came to the realization that if I am seeing them both in profile, then they are facing each other. And it crossed my mind (as if for the first time) that whenever I attempted to overcome his supposed virtue, Fuld would always, and without exception, stand so that I could not see him other than in profile. Did he do this deliberately, or did his genius inspire him toward it unwittingly? Might he, too, have been aware of the peculiar conformity of his face, inlaid—were you to view it head-on—with a kind of provocative irony, something like a pledge of potential complicity, and affixed there as a spur toward increasingly arousing and lurid intimacies? Or else was this an unwitting defense of his purity—oh, it was almost angelic—against the treachery of a Satan who fed on that purity like a parasite? Was this treachery rooted on his lips, on his brow, in that semblance of a double chin? That's immaterial. What perhaps is material is the fact that he always defended himself against me, to whom he had never succumbed, sideways. Head-on, he enticed; in profile, he disarmed. I see his shadow from the street, and actually, much to my surprise, more than his shadow: not profiles traced broadly, dully upon the curtain, but it looked as if they were motionless, though not expressionless, organdy masks. And for Fuld's profile, there could hardly be anything more depressingly real: this ironic, wickedly lecherous feature with which he—if I am facing him head-on—invites one so perfidiously—might it be born from that ascetic wrinkle, which I know so well, which has been carved by remorseless and unpersuasive tears and, in profile, disarms my seductions? And that chin—which is as if really his own only when he muses over the unfatherly, severe word he would use to refuse and to shame—he was leaning it on two equally bony fingers; and the nose, too proud even to forebear but a hint of stench; and the brow, so sharp as to be a bulwark!

To seduce him while he turns his side toward his seducer—that is, to attempt to break a resistance so uncompromising that it no longer even tries to defend itself—and I, having foundered before that stronghold so impregnable and God knows how dearly bought, am just stewing in my shame, but I can be rather pleased with my defeat. Such is the sovereign power of purity, that it softens even the non-will of an evil that has been repelled. Here, however, he's being seduced by Mutig, who is facing him. Mutig is not held back by the hieratic mask so much as spurred on by the face of the disgusted debauchee, who resists only in order to tease and egg his tempter on.

Before the theatrical house, a banal parallel with the twin Janus head: who is Fuld? He who resists me so easily that I am not even worthy of his defense, or he who forgets to resist Mutig as well? Mutig's shadow is comical, tipped far across the table, his slightly outstretched arms gesticulating immediately above it: it's the shadow of a haggling merchant. – But the shadow lies. Mutig is not funny, Mutig is dangerous.

The shadow only comes off as funny. Mutig is urging Fuld toward evil, and Fuld is putting up only a feeble defense. If Fuld doesn't get reinforcements, Mutig will crush him; Mutig knows this. And he knows that I see them, that I've found the game out, that I might be dashing in. How will he hold me back? Mutig's shadow makes itself repugnant, foul, and funny. Mutig tells himself that no one is rushing to the aid of Fuld, who faces a shadow so repugnant, foul, and funny. Fuld takes no guff. With a creature whose shadow is repugnant, foul, and funny, Fuld can manage quite well on his own. A ploy, a mere ploy. Mutig doesn't know how to be repugnant, foul, and funny. He is wily and dangerous. Mutig resembles a doe, beautiful and evil, his shadow is only aping a nasty little hound dog, and doing so deliberately. Mutig! It's a shadow. But behind the shadow are your dark, somewhat squinty eyes, whose speech your mouth merely seconds. Mutig, how much fortitude you would otherwise have to have for your name not to be an ironic commentary on what you really are.

"Mutig is tempting him toward murder, and Fuld is succumbing," I cried out, not letting them out of my sight. Fuld succumbs to everyone he faces. He can only resist sideways.

Fuld's shadow turned. Now that organdy mask was facing me head-on as well. Behind their almost downcast lids, the eyes looked ashamed, flashing with gluttonous whims. The ironic smile was acceding to vice and now only sought the how and where-to-go to hide its consent, and at the same time it regretted being enslaved to its own hypocrisy. And if I didn't spot Giggles from outside as well, it was because her shadow broke before it reached the curtain; she was standing aloof. When I entered, however, she was the first to hail me. She was standing as straight as a candle, her arms hung down, her little head with its tousled hair twisted slightly to the side—such was her habit—and on her face that fleeting smile of a sorrow whose principal distress was in how to put on that it was a simple smile and nothing more. She was standing there like a puppet they were bargaining over, who knows she's being bargained over, but does not know how to express it, or cannot. All she knows is fear, a slightly theatrical fear, for she is a puppet who is counting on the fact that, should the worst happen, her famously powerful queen, Puppenfee, will intervene. Giggles spotted me, recognized me, but didn't stir. Fine; but she smiled, she smiled as though shorthand for her customary "Well, come closer, don't be shy!"

Giggles likes me, but Mutig, her man, despises me with a simmering disdain. He expressed this in the coquettish crossing of his leg and his affable smile, whose evil and untimely wrinkle he hastily wiped from his lips; he expressed it by laying his hands on the table, as if they were suddenly overcome with boredom. Fuld also made it clear that he had seen me, but only in that he bent his head ever so slightly lower, and his fingers, braced against the table, buckled. His knuckles collapsed and clattered.

All of this was in greeting. Here they were as if on stage, each with his assignment and in his appointed place. They were acting. A new act had begun with my entrance, they had known about it from their past rehearsals, they'd been expecting me. I understood right away that I, too, was acting, and I settled into it quickly. As if at the instruction of an invisible director I headed without hesitation for the far side of the table, where Mutig was sitting at one end, Fuld at the other. Thus I had my back to the window, with Giggles opposite me. She was standing back, but in such a way that one would know that she, too, belonged to the group. I mention this because the four of us were not alone in the place. From my position I had a perfect view. It was a spacious hall, with a vaulted ceiling, at the same time it called to mind a subterranean chapel (I thought of La Sainte-Chapelle de Paris, Assisi, and the Gypsy church in Saintes-Maries-de-la-Mer), the beer cellars of Munich, and a knightly hall. It would surely have been echoing were it empty, but now it was full of people. They were sitting at white-clothed tables. You might say they were the spectators at the Théâtre des Variétés, with their obligatory refreshment, yet these spectators had agreed not to order anything. For the tables were bare. This gave a solemn impression and was a bit unsettling. They were mainly men. It was as if our table were the stage they'd come to see, but it was apparent they were paying us no mind at all. They spoke, they clamored—literally, the same kind of din as on the street just a moment ago—as if we weren't there, though I had no doubt that they were mostly talking about us, that they were like the chorus of the play that the four of us were now acting out; that is, they were gesticulating about our every movement, about our every word, though somehow on the sly. It was discreet, and I found it excruciatingly annoying. Those people had a complexion that was at least olive, though often black, but only a few were of a genuinely Negro sort. As it happens, I don't know how I even arrived at any certainty as to this circumstance, since most of them had a sort of double-sided hood over their head.

What is just now transpiring, and what is soon to come, is a sort of one-off script.

Having described the "auditorium," I will depict the general situation on the stage. Each of us was, roughly speaking, as if fixed in the position he was occupying when the curtain went up. I don't know the cause for the relative motionlessness of my fellow actors, but I well know the cause of my own lethargy, which is to say that as soon as I had arrived at my place at the table (I've said that I had retired there as if at the instruction of an invisible director), it was clear to me beyond all doubt that I hadn't so much wound up somewhere as frozen into something. (And I apologize for that frightful, but unavoidable, turn of phrase, which is the only one that fits.) I knew that I was with the other three in a closed system—as if we had grown into a transparent cube, cut off from the ordinary, phenomenal world. The slightest individual attempt at a turn, a step, a movement was in communication with the entire construct, which would then swing (for it was suspended).

In other words: we had not been completely deprived of the ability to move, but whatever any of us undertook, his position relative to the others remained unchanged and was as it had been initially, that is, when "I took up my role." This is just to explain why, for example, I had no luck in seeing Fuld and Mutig other than in profile, and it follows from this finding that these two were invariably face-to-face. – Giggles is no exception: not for a moment did she cease to be that puppet I'd spotted when I came in, a puppet incapable of expressing whether she was suffering or rejoicing, an awfully timid puppet, yet counting on the power of her queen, Puppenfee. All I want is for the reader to picture it like she was constantly, if almost unnoticeably, swaying, like she was charmingly floating, like she was in the grip of some music that no one else but she could hear, though she might not be able to say who was playing it for her, whether it be the words, the atmosphere, or my own unconscious desire. I would want the reader to picture Giggles a bit like a leaf that submits to the will of waves just a hair before it has circled down upon them, perhaps in the naïve hope that they would have mercy upon it for its having "obliged" them.

The supernumeraries—that is, the guests of this sanctuary, which is both a tavern and a knightly hall—won't let us out of their sight for a moment, though they're careful not to make a show of it. I don't know how it was for the other three, but as far as I was concerned that circumstance contributed decisively to the impression that we were acting before what one calls fate, which also likes to pretend that it's a disinterested observer.

Once I had assumed the place indicated by the invisible director, Mutig—as if issuing an initial rejoinder—grabbed something from the table and tossed it lightly; it fell like a heavy object, let's call it a Browning; I looked: it was the rubber girl from the Folies-Bergère; it was as if all holes, patches, and stitches.

Mutig: ... were we then to eliminate duration ...

Fuld: Pardon! Let's be precise: eliminate, or refute it?

Mutig: Eliminate it. As a concept. Naturally, as a concept. By refuting it we would pose the question of its reality, and the question of its reality doesn't enter into it, for what matters to us, let's say, is ethics. After all, you understand what negating the concept of duration would mean in an ethical system! Don't you?

Fuld: Perhaps an effort to furnish responsibility with an alibi?

Mutig: Responsibility! A nasty word, and less than a word: the utilitarian formula of moralists. A hindrance to emancipation.

Fuld: But a concept that does not rule emancipation out.

Mutig: Naturally, for we are opportunists. How does that strike you? To exclude the notion of emancipation from the ethics that is its foundation? Which is therefore the ethics of the strong. Who then take precedence ... Are you laughing?

Fuld: Pardon. On the contrary. That's just how I look ...

Mutig (tossing his head carelessly): But someone here is laughing. (Which is to say, I had smiled.) Not only is emancipation my right; it is my duty. It is my duty to come into being. (Pause.) Our adversaries don't understand a whit of our ethics. To them it's irresponsibility, self-will, the unleashing of a fundamental evil! But we are not evil, we're just simple.... – Giggles, am I evil?

Giggles: Oh, you and your evil! You're merely awful.

Mutig: We've eliminated duration. First implication: the act has no genealogy. The act is independent of what precedes it; it is free, alone; thus it does not know; it does not diminish. Only he who pays duration no mind can submit to what he encounters unreservedly, can serve it unreservedly...

Fuld: Serve at this moment...

Mutig: Naturally, at this moment. (His beautiful hands flickered over his head like white flames.) At this moment, naturally. How then, I ask you, to submit unreservedly, if not to what things there are in this moment, and nowhere else? Where else, if not in this moment, would you seek that which is? – Giggles, aren't you happy?

Giggles: Oh!

Fuld: Are you really happy, Giggles? Despite...

Giggles: Oh! Why ask if I *am* happy? The verb *to be* is not an auxiliary verb. I say: I am. Simply: I am. I endure.

Mutig: What are you, Giggles?

Giggles: Oh! What does it matter, when I am through you?

Mutig: Which is to say, Giggles is heroic, Fuld, you see? Giggles knows and doesn't doubt that at every moment I am really entirely what I appear to be at the moment. What more could she ask for?

Fuld: And if at that moment you are really entirely unfaithfulness, repulsion, contempt, hatred?

Mutig: As if it would come to that!

Giggles: Oh, it won't come to that!

Fuld: Giggles, if he were to loathe you, he would leave you.

Giggles: Oh Fuld, of course. But I am Mrs. Mutig. I cannot and do not wish to be anything but a Mutig. So then why should I gripe if at a given moment Mutig is an unfaithful Mutig—repulsed by me, contemptuous of me, hating me?

Mutig: In short, entirely Mutig. Unspoiled. Giggles has caught on to something that you haven't. Giggles gets that those who have died away within us will not be resurrected by our sorrow, nor by our pity. Giggles gets that the sole honor we can pay the dead is not to drag them behind us. To bury them quickly. (A loving glance at Giggles.) You see what it means to apply our ethics practically? Giggles, where is the happiness in being loved by me?

Giggles (like a schoolgirl): The happiness in being loved by you is in the certainty that I make allowances for you, and that I fade away.

Mutig (like a teacher testing a good student): What allowances do you make, Giggles?

Giggles: I allow, and in doing so lighten your burden, that you are not omnipotent.

Mutig: Good, Giggles. And if in *one moment*, if in one moment the only way to ease my burden were—a mere supposition, you understand—to ease it, that is, to deceive it, were only (his words collapsed with a mournful violence) if you, because it's what I wanted, were to slit your own throat?

Fuld: Let's say, "If you were to take your own life."

Mutig (curtly): If you were to slit your own throat...

Giggles (with a happy laugh, into which there crept a timid horror): Oh!

Fuld (repentantly): A supposition that... (Faster and faster.) Your suppositions are bloody. Mutig, my dear, too gory for a supposition, too figurative, my friend (and suddenly, as if he'd signed and, under some kind of unfamiliar pressure, automatically appended his initials): *my dear friend*.

Mutig (professorially, but with a touching, youthful awkwardness): To abstract from duration—and why else would we exclude the concept of duration, if not to proceed practically, as though everything in the given moment were always complete? For you, Fuld, and for a great many others, to abstract from duration would mean to turn irresponsibility toward your maximum life potential.

Fuld: That objection...

Mutig: You wanted to say that that objection is no objection at all, my dear friend, true? We do not refuse responsibility for our deeds, of course, naturally. We refuse responsibility merely for what we will be in the next moment. Next time.

Fuld: Only that the thing you do next will be a function of what you will be in the next moment. And in that next moment you might be someone who denies responsibility for the consequences of what you just did, when you were different. Therein lies the catch, in my opinion (he said "in my opinion"): for whatever responsibility is, isn't it responsibility for consequences?

Mutig: My fine friend, we have settled, have we not, that our ethics and our current morality are two separate things. How, then, even in our dreams, could people such as ourselves, living upright, arrive at the thought that we were answerable to someone other than ourselves? Ethics is not the Napoleonic Code. You are perhaps haunted by the idea—allow me to put it like a "man on the street"—that our ethics would not prevent us from leading—as they say—our fellow man unto misfortune, and to leave him lying peacefully on the roadway like a motorist gone mad? It doesn't stop it. Naturally. – Our interlocutor, for example, is now surely thinking of Giggles. (He turned sharply toward me and was very beautiful.)

Fuld: Naturally.

Mutig: If I say that we do not refuse responsibility for the things we do, this means simply that in the given moment we would consider it a shame to undertake anything so as to evade the natural repercussions of our action.

Fuld: Naturally.

Mutig: At last, then we are agreed! – The only people who can eliminate their regard for duration are those for whom catching fire and living are synonyms, and such people cannot help but eliminate duration. The *raison d'être* of flame is the verb: to burn; nay, a substantive: that which burns. Is that clear, sir?

I: Giggles!

Mutig: Leave her out of this! Giggles listens to me alone. Don't bother yourself! She listens to me alone, and only when I address her directly. Otherwise—to her good fortune—she's deaf. (Expertly.) But since we are speaking of this subject—subject: Giggles—isn't our ethics a sign of hope for creatures like Giggles; that is, for creatures called upon solely to make allowances?

Fuld (eagerly): Explain. Please, explain.

Mutig: Gladly. Let's suppose that they've died within us. Let's suppose that Giggles here is, for example, at this moment, dead. Dead within me, that is, for herself and in general. Giggles, who knows me—who has been allowed to know me—won't say, "Mutig has repudiated me," so much as . . . What will you say, Giggles?

Giggles: I'll say, "Mutig *still* hasn't come back to me," "Mutig *still* despises me."

Mutig (with triumphant glee): Did you catch the nuance? – And what else, Giggles?

Giggles (reciting): Mutig doesn't know, but he remembers. He remembers that I have made many allowances for him; that I was making allowances as I faded away; that he endured it, and thus he loved me; that there are many creatures that must allow, because that is the law; that there are few creatures that allow as they are fading away, because that is a rare credit; that is to say, he made me this way; that is, I made myself this way out of love; that it is therefore to my credit; that I may therefore give in to the hope that Mutig has not tired of me as his sla—

Mutig (he waved his hand and snuffed out the last word): You're golden! That will do! (To Fuld:) And do I recall that it wasn't so long ago that she wanted to jump out a window because I had cast her off? – What did I teach you when you wanted to jump out the window?

Giggles: You taught me that with you there was hope, because you had repudiated the word "forevermore."

Mutig (he corrects with playful pedantry): Because, taking no account of duration, I make no distinction between "now" and "forevermore." Inconsequentiality is a great virtue. Inconsequentiality is the holy name of the act without genealogy. – It's odd, but doesn't it seem to you that our allegedly cynical ethics is wondrously similar to *caritas*?

I: Givers of death and life. Depending on whether you accept or reject your loved one as sacrifice.

Mutig: My dear, that's rhetoric. Just remember how much stock was put in Yahweh finding the sacrifice *pleasing*.

I: That was God.

Mutig: And we are the givers of life and death; that's why we set afire; that is, we burn. –

There was a silence. It had the flavor of a prearranged silence. An entr'acte, you'd say, and we were switching the scenery. All at once, and as if on command, the spectators drew fat cigars from their breast pockets and started to smoke. They whispered, pointing their fingers at us, though their heads were turned away. A moment later the expansive space was filled with smoke. I felt a light breeze. The smoke started to accumulate. Bands started to form, they trailed toward Giggles, they circled around, enveloping her like a mummy's wrappings. Giggles smiled. Then everything went quiet again, the spectators straightened up in their seats, assuming dignified poses; many of them folded their hands in their laps. Thumbs twiddled.

Mutig: Fundamentally evil, that's what they call us. But what, in point of fact, is the fundamental evil of moralists? Nothing but divine oblivion. That's just our point: to become oblivious—like God. We unfortunately have far yet to go. – We have so much further to go that we still—still!—are pleased to manufacture proselytes. Candidates for divine oblivion, meanwhile, have a utilitarian craft: they teach altruism . . . –

I: You!

Mutig: Giggles understands me. But what is this understanding? She has the key. But turning it—eh?—that's something else. Giggles is a teachable pupil. Giggles knows, for example, that the loss of love need not be fatal. Giggles understands why I refute duration.

Fuld: Was that a slip? You don't refute duration, you exclude its potential. If I've heard you right. You exclude, you don't refute.

Mutig was taken aback, he glanced among the spectators, he greeted them here and there with an actor's venal smile. Then he scowled like a shamefaced sham-artist, jolted himself, turned to Fuld, and covered his mouth theatrically with his hand the way a simpleton does.

"Did I say that I exclude it?" he posed at last.

His hand shifted slowly from his mouth to his temple; Mutig rested his head and contemplated; when he emerged, a peculiar smile emerged as well; it proceeded impudently across his lips; his hand collapsed inertly on the table. Mutig looked up.

"No! Not exclude. Refute," he said. (To Giggles, casually:)

"And why do I refute?"

Giggles: You refute so as to learn to live without support.

Mutig: That's it! – And now, please, if you can, square this circle: Giggles gets that one must do away with supports, and Giggles cannot imagine how she could live without holding on to at least one support.

Fuld: Which? Come on, which?

Mutig: It's all the same which. She needs, let's say, your respect. Only yesterday she said to me, "Oh, you know, so long as Fuld thinks I'm merely a wretch, and not damned, I haven't lost everything."

I glanced over at Fuld, more or less the way Horatio looked at the fratricide gnawing away at Hamlet's plot. What was I to do! Fuld's deep wrinkle, I alone could see it from where I was, how it thirsted for sparkly tears, whereas Fuld had forgotten his tears long since. Yet what provocative trigger might Mutig have spotted for him to exclaim so triumphantly:

"But this is what I said to her! This is what I said to her: 'Is that what you're counting on?'"

Fuld (in a voice bolstered by his guardian angels, drawing on their last strength): You had no right to that. You lied. – Why did you lie?

Mutig: Because I can't forget that she was dear to me. Because I want her to be strong—like me. Because I have a duty toward her: you see how little I'm able to forget still. We—myself and those like me—of course we'll manage to live without support; we rank, however, among the chiefs. But not yet as strict as we'd need to be, not yet as oblivious as our duty would have it. We still—still!—look after even those whose destiny was fulfilled by our having exploited them; we still look down on them later, too, when they've served their purpose, when we've already cast them away again; we look down on them; we shouldn't. Imagine it, Fuld: I, for example, would honestly wish that Giggles, too, if only Giggles, could live without support. I'm conducting a dangerous experiment, I know that. But it's necessary. – Giggles is so very miserable, you know!

Fuld: Have you lost your mind?

Mutig: But I've already told you that she doesn't hear unless I am addressing her directly... Giggles is so very miserable, you know, and if you were to snatch the very last support from under her...

Fuld (in a voice that sobbed with a cowardice that had revealed itself as wicked): Come, Mutig, a man of your caliber doesn't mess around with logomachy, does he? Are you forgetting that there is *truth*, eternal truth? What would be the point in saying I've lost my respect for it when I haven't?

Mutig (with a slowness so willful that what he was saying was more visible than audible: a boa uncoiling into an entrancing slide): But you *have* lost your respect for it! And how could you esteem a dame who'd just as well "slit her throat" for me, though she knows that to us she's lower than a footwrap?

Fuld: To all of you?

Giggles: I hear you, my dear, I hear you. Have you erred, since I hear when I shouldn't hear? Oh my dear, oh my dear, don't make such cruel jokes.

Fuld (leaning over the table and speaking as if he were reading an invisible inscription there): Giggles, who shouldn't hear, hears. Giggles, who shouldn't suffer, does.

Mutig: But she doesn't hear, it only seems that she does. – Less than a footwrap—to all of us, to all of us, to us who are the meaning of her life, as she says, you know? (Quieter and quieter, and leaning so far across the table that he touches it with his chest): We are having such a beautiful game with her—an innocent game—for her benefit, you know! *Voulez-vous jouer avec moi?*

What will come next is *con sordino*. It's a potpourri of what I know and what I saw, a potpourri *con sordino*. – A new and dizzyingly rapid change of scenery. The spectators, all of them together, have quietly stood and are leaving in a slow and orderly fashion. At the exit, spectacular demonstrations of courtesy. The hall has emptied out. The air is suffused with ozone. It is no longer so much a hall as a spacious room. It is empty, and a low stool, like that of a shoemaker, has been brought into the middle. There's a blackamoor sitting on it. He's almost squatting, his knees spread wide. His teeth are shining, he's giggling quietly.

Mutig: For her benefit, you know, however much it may seem otherwise: for this game, one might say, is cruel.

At these words, the black man has stood. He's picked up the stool, he's moved over. He's stood next to Mutig—giggling like that all the while—he's put the stool down, but he hasn't sat on it again. Mutig puts his arm around his neck like a buddy, and in a tone of light conversation:

"Giggles! What she really is is a corpse, you know. And I can't drag a corpse through life. It disgusts me, and she terrifies me. And anyway, there are better things to work at than dragging corpses. I have better things to say, by which I of course mean vanities merely of a more splendid variety. – What, she doesn't quite strike you as a corpse? Then you still don't know everything. You couldn't imagine how we treat her, my friends and I. She doesn't even react anymore. That is, she reacts in her own way: she interprets our scorn merely as a difficult test she's being put through. Perhaps it really was just a test at first. Not something she was supposed to suffer, the dummy.

She was supposed to hold herself high. A test we've consented to—oh, the little lamb!—a test we've consented to becomes irrevocable, eternal; it solidifies. It's the solid eternal (now you understand why I refute eternity?), an eternal that is more and more solid. Giggles had nothing left, nothing. We stripped her of everything. That is . . . There was one support, one hope. Just one. – As I told you: 'As long as Fuld doesn't think I'm damned . . .' Are you beginning to understand what I need you for?"

Fuld: I'm hardly a professional killer, am I?

Mutig: And who says that it's therefore inevitably *you* who'll do the killing?

Fuld: If she's crossed you so bad, you'll knock her off. Knocking someone off! It's not so hard. (Hastily.) Are you a Christian? It's not like you're a Christian, is it? So then why the pussyfooting around the people we've put a button on? You're too noble. She's dead, so she's foul. But you, Mutig, are disproving yourself by remembering; you remember that this dead girl was living through you, right? You don't want her to be foul, or a dead girl, either. Aren't you looking for a way to provide her with an opening for rehabilitation? Because she's *your* dead girl, right? Killed by you, right? You're not perfect yet, Mutig, you really aren't.

Mutig: Oh, you're a sharp one! Yes, it's a matter of her rehabilitation. I'm not pretending to be better than I am. Maybe I want it out of cynicism—her rehabilitation, that is—so I wouldn't have to feel ashamed that I ever mistook a woman capable of falling so low as worthy of myself. Take all of her hope, including the last she has left, her hope in you, and she'd gain her freedom—get it? Do you follow me? Then there wouldn't be anything left to hold her back, there would no longer be anything to use as a pretext for tolerating a scorn so difficult and (in a whisper) eternal! Maybe then she would be rehabilitated again in our eyes; maybe she would be truly happy again. – You see, my friend, it's actually for her that I'm praying. If only she could react not in her own way, but the way we, her alleged gods, expect her to!

Fuld (a long time before he responds): React. – Sure... react. – Just what do you mean by that?

"I don't know exactly," Mutig answered lazily and somehow affectionately, "I don't know. Maybe that—seeing how it's the end of everything, everything—maybe that she'd leave— that she'd retire—move on to greener pastures."

Fuld (with a focus that, after sort of roaming long and tenderly, suddenly reared its head): To greener pastures? – To greener pastures. (With feigned joy at having solved a tough riddle:) That she would leave you? She, you?!

Mutig (to the blackamoor, to his face): Yes, that she'd leave me.

Fuld: In other words, you want to win, but through defeat. What a stoic!

Mutig: A stoic! – Oh, to greener pastures—but you know.

Fuld (quiet, he looks askance).

Mutig (affably): Naturally. – Giggles is lower than a foot-wrap. Imagine, for example, that she were killed. She'd be rehabilitated by it.

Fuld (slowly and reflectively): But does Giggles's death matter... She can't hear us, right?

Hardly had Mutig given an offhand "But of course she can't hear us" when he jumped up: "What now, Giggles, have you lost your mind?"

Giggles's head had fallen to her chest, an invisible hand had swept the life from her little face, but it forgot to do away with the smile. Giggles collapsed. But Mutig took her and set her on her feet like an ill-supported doll.

Fuld (continuing as he watched with indifferent attention): If Giggles's death is up to me, then what's there for you to brag about?

"Pardon me, sir," Mutig replied with an imperious smile, "but all the same, we who now struggle are but five. My friends and I. We are not so petty as you think. The power over lives is indivisible, a sixth is like the whole. Is that not enough for you?"

"How do you proceed?" Fuld asked, as it were, expertly.

Mutig's hand pondered for a moment. Then slowly, like a leopard, it started to stalk across the table. It was the genuine stalking of a leopard ready to pounce, and then it did. And once it did, it darted. Mutig's clenched fist was its maw, and in that maw—a rubber puppet; vertically, terribly. – But Mutig's mouth, slack, pronounced: "*Jettatura.*"

"Jettatura," the Negro repeated, eyeing the puppet closely, as if spying its sclera. He and Mutig turned fully toward each other, embraced like old friends, and the word "Jettatura!" which they spoke to each other's faces, drained the color from their cheeks and the lips that had pronounced this word, as if in doing so they'd forever lost all memory of what it was to smile.

"Don't think me crazy, Fuld. We had no wish to enchant by black-magic practices, though there might have been something of black magic there. Our aim was for a pure result, from our non-occult powers. This doll here? A mere record of our achievements, let's say. A sort of book of work to be done as well: we have committed to demolishing every single part. So let's get down to work, and no excuses, right? – I'll explain it to you. – Here, for example, we have the eyes. They're transfixed. Why are they transfixed? Because there's no point anymore. Because they've lost their power. Giggles's poor eyes!

To think how they once reigned. – At the time of our *first* love, they were promise-grateful. There's no other way I can put it: promise-grateful. You would have sworn they couldn't give enough, and that in their thanksgiving there would forever gleam a spark of agitated regret at not having expressed all there was. They were steadfast in their promises, these eyes, defiant and proud in their gratitude. Already back then, this runaway *figurante* from the Folies-Bèrgere could see she was heading for disaster, but she saw it with such steady rage that the horror passed her by. – Fine. After our *second* love, too, they were drowning in iridescent fluid, and they were promising, and they were giving thanks. They were honest in their promises, but like a banker before a no-fault bankruptcy, when he doesn't know whether he'll actually be able to keep them. They were recalling the defiant and insane promise from before, they were comparing, *they were realizing*, they were calculating the possibilities and my insatiable demands. They were trying to look honest, which is why they looked stupid. And they gave thanks. But sometimes one gives thanks because it's shameful to beg. I might have overlooked that if, after our *third*, they weren't just pleading. I didn't yet suspect that I was *already* her master, and her pleadingly grateful eyes now gave her away. After the *fourth*, she disbanded all her armies; but what did she have to begin with? Words are a dame's reserves, but they can't manage them. She said—I'm ashamed to repeat it, it was so banal—she said: 'I can't live without you.' And that's how people dig their own graves! I'll explain it to you. It had evolved into a game—evil, innocent, I don't know, but it had dropped right into our lap. People accuse us of hatching a plan to drive her methodically to suicide. A laugh.

"I'll explain it to you. One day we're sitting—Andrew, Paul, John, Peter, and I, you know we're like brothers, which is to say we're predestined for each other—a quintipartite singularity. We're sitting one day, it's getting dark; we blend, so that we've already lost the sense of physical distinctness; that's how it falls when the gloved hand of evening holds the reigns, as it were, of five minds running together; we were quiet for a long time, and in the silence there slowly hatched the thing we'd all been thinking of; I had a good sense that it had to be christened, and I knew its name: The Story of Giggles's Eyes. I started The Story of Giggles's Eyes; we got into a rhythm; they kept me going, God knows how, maybe by the way the others stretched, the way they shifted in their seats. When I got to the words 'I can't live without you,' to me they sounded not like they were mine, but rather as if Giggles was saying them, and saying them as if she were pronouncing sentence on herself.

"'I can't live without you': banal words, you hear them a hundred times a day, but you know how it is with banalities, a hundred times they're nothing, the hundred-and-first will open up suddenly, God knows why, and they're full of meaning. – Was it the light, or something else? In short, barely had I said 'I can't live without you'—we were sitting in a circle—than we caught each other's gazes; our gazes locked at a single point, and so precisely that it made a spark. – We were a circle, and its center was a spark. Was it perhaps our collective thought? If it was a collective thought, we belonged to it, not it to us. We didn't make a peep, not then, not any time before, not after. Was it this quintipartite thought that had popped out and made the spark? The center was shining brighter than ideas usually gleam. Was it something else, then? What?"

Fuld: *What?* (And a jousting of thousands of words rushed into that "What?" and shattered within it.)

Mutig: Hold on. That's not what's important. – Andrew was playing with this puppet. This one here. Do you see it?

(Mutig lifted it and showed it around.) He sat it prettily on his knees, and just like that: he plucked out its eyes. God knows where he got the nail from.

"It's blind," he said.

Mutig leaped up: "Giggles, now what are you doing?"

Which is to say that Giggles had shouted "Jettatura" and toppled over again.

"So then why did you promise that you'd be smart, Giggles? What kind of way is that to behave? As if you'd been listening in the first place. Party-pooper! As if you haven't known all along that nothing is going to change."

Giggles now resembled a doll so perfectly that I really couldn't tell . . . Mutig grabbed her—she was as though in two pieces, and sagged across his arm—he sat at the table with her and caressed her.

"I'll keep you on my lap. Just like at home, when we have our little doll lessons: what does the cross over the mouth mean? what does the dimple in the little forehead mean? etc."

The Negro was caressing her from the other side. Giggles was tearing up, and she said, "I'm not blind. I see you just fine." (Giggles was tearing up, yet there were no tears in her voice.)

"But you don't perceive," Mutig added gently.

"Oh, I know, I know."

Mutig continued, "That's all there was from Andrew, 'She'll go blind,' he plucked out her eyes and passed her to Paul. 'She'll go dumb,' Paul said—the cross over the lips—and passed her to John. 'She won't figure things out,' said John— the dimple in her brow—and 'she won't stumble upon things,' Peter added, slashing the ever-so-beautifully-curved shoulders beneath her little head."

Mutig adjusted Giggles comfortably on his knees with the lovingly worn-out motion of mothers whose laps have fallen

asleep beneath their tike. For a moment he seemed to be looking for something, after which he turned, half-jokingly, half-
imploringly, to the blackamoor. "How about we just show him?"

The blackamoor puffed out his chest and bared his teeth.
It was a broad, strapping chest, a real cabinet, something like a
wire manger that the flame of an oil lamp had given a blond-
ish cast. A canvas banner from edge to edge, and in big letters:
GIGGLES: BEGONE. This stage was so exceedingly "like it
was real" that it was poking fun at reality. Never before have
I seen a more dastardly caricature: imitating slavishly, it exaggerated. The stage cynically represented a sincere salon. In the
foreground, on the tall cushion of a pouf, sat Giggles. She was
looking in such a way that one glance would tell you she was
calling for heavenly aid. She was making an effort at the casual
and fetching smiles that bloomed so naturally on the carmine
lips of dames who know how to pass by. (For there were a lot
of dames in there.) But the smiles she attempted were falling
into her lap like tears. She kept producing more and more;
they didn't want to hold. The salon was bustling. The men were
standing in groups and debating. There were clean-shaven
youths with lacquered hair, their fresh faces betraying what
they would be when the time came for their beards to sprout;
and there were bearded men with disheveled coifs whose whole
dignity lay in their self-righteous whiskers. They all hated
each other; thus they all agreed. The dames, with that casual
and fetching smile, passed from group to group and stopped
briefly at each. They'd stop, their gazes wandering somewhere
where they could not see, and having thus trespassed they'd
walk away; promises of assignations remained after them, and
the group was momentarily enfrothed and without airs; soon,
however, the brows furrowed again, the furrows converged into
clouds, and the men hated each other again, a bit more grimly,

agreeing still more harmoniously than before. – Across from Giggles sat Paul. Giggles was reasoning with him insistently. The talk was flowing, but it wasn't making a dent on Paul. He walked it dry-shod, like the Jews through the Red Sea. Giggles knew it; Giggles didn't want to know it. Still, once she'd managed to penetrate Paul's eyes, she hunted for a place where she could drop anchor, and there she posed some anxious question. But the eyes were not listening. Paul turned to the redhead beside him and spoke with her quite respectfully; behind this respect there cowered an old tryst. Again, Giggles started to speak. Now, Paul didn't let her out of his sight. His affable smile hissed like a spiteful verdict. Giggles finished her question even more timidly than she'd started. Paul took this question cautiously, but he didn't answer. He carried it to the redhead next to him; he reshaped Giggles's anxiety into a gallant ritornello and placed it at his neighbor's feet. She promised him something with a long look, and Paul returned to Giggles. He returned with an inquisitive look that placed too much emphasis on the lie that his attention and engagement had not wavered, not for a moment. Giggles went on, urging him still, and finished with her hand resting timidly on Paul's shoulder. Paul endured Giggles's gaze for a long time. Now—now it seemed he would answer her amiably, but here, with a phosphorescent jibe, he let slip that his was the gaze of an executioner. His eyes, looking somewhere toward Giggles's horror, were chanting that Giggles saw nothing at all, that Giggles heard nothing at all. Then Paul gently freed himself from Giggles's hand, rose, and moved away. It was like a tragicomic caricature of a fair judge—lo that he leaves with heart asunder—that his higher sort of fairness always prohibited him from heeding the distress of the condemned man writhing at his feet.

"Because she'd let herself go, because she was staring so,"

Mutig stressed mournfully, and the palm of his hand slid down the blackamoor's chest, in which things went dark. But he immediately brought up the lights again.

He presented the moribund backroom of a suburban tavern. At one table sat Giggles. She sat there mournfully and was smiling indescribably. Across from her, John. They were eating with broken-tined forks and nicked knives; they ate from chipped plates. "Why hasn't Mutig arrived?" Giggles asked. – She spoke with that light conversational tone that, like a somnambulist, heads straight for the trap of sobs where she will drown. John swallowed a morsel and smiled. The smile of a bearer of bad news who is ashamed at being just that. "Have you seen Mutig?" Giggles asked. "I have," John said, smiling the whole time. "Is he coming?" "He can't," John said, going stern. To himself he was saying: *Let's drop the friendly mask.* Giggles leaned in slightly. Warmly: "I don't know what it is, John, it seems as if my life were drifting away from me on the sly. I feel like it already did a long time ago. What do you say to that?" – John's gaze transformed into a noose; he took it and tossed it at her anxiously. "Perhaps," he said. – "You think so? Maybe you didn't understand?" – "I understood perfectly," said John. – "What do you think?" – John let it out with a discomfiture that only Giggles believed. – "Nothing. Life is drifting away from us all ... That's the standard fate of mankind." – "John," she pronounced, almost inaudibly, "so what do you think for real, that I've gone mad? So why are you steering me away from a truth that I feel?" – "But I'm not steering you away from anything," John said with strained compassion.

"Why did she let herself go? Why was she staring so?" Mutig spoke with mournful emphasis, and his hand slid down the blackamoor's chest, whereupon it went dark.

But the lights came right back up.

The stage as in the first image, but with a partition dividing it in two. One could see Mutig, Andrew, Paul, John, Peter, two ladies with unobligatory, fetching smiles. Giggles was there as well. She was standing as if in shame, off to the side. The seven were having a lively discussion. They were speaking as if they were stenographers: each word a chapter heading, and even their most fleeting glances were crammed with as much content as there was in an instant of dreaming. They were a gathering of the enlightened. But behind their mirth, their laughter, their gestures and words, there stretched a sardonic line, like periods at the ends of incomplete sentences. None of these seven was evil, but the sum of their kindnesses came to grudgingness. But who among them minded? I sought it in their eyes. Giggles's were filled with a skittish, guilty conscience. The group coiled into a knot, hardening so much, by all appearances, that it held their irritation in check; some unwelcome presence was irritating the group, the way a wet diaper irritates a small child; it didn't know how to acquit itself of this oppression; it tried by exuding a grudging scorn. Thus was the atmosphere poisoned. Giggles was forced to breathe it in. It corrupted her blood; the corrupted blood budded upon her in the form of an unattractive case of ringworm. Giggles was becoming more and more dilapidated because of it, and she was eventually so wretched that even I was disgusted. – Finally, Andrew broke off from the group, crossed the partition, and retired to the rear half of the stage. There he found some kind of album and started turning its pages mechanically. After a moment he called out, "John, this is interesting." This was a ploy; it reeked like burning sulfur. John went to join him. Now they were looking together, with mournful disinterest; the sulfur burned on. John approached the doorframe. "Renée, have you seen this?" Renée looked up with such nonchalance that it wafted of an unfulfilled contract.

She looked up silently, with prearranged surprise. Now there were three in the back half. They formed an embryo of a group, blithe and aggressive. The mass in the front half, dealt a mortal blow, was rotting. It held on, but it was done for. It was waiting for the signal to fall to pieces. The only point of its holding on now was the draw of the embryo expanding in the back. "Paul," Renée called at last. Paul left, withdrawing as though on guard. The group behind the partition swelled, it swelled with a lively will to harm that alien thing still standing in its way. It was smothering it: Giggles was somehow shrinking the whole time; she was less and less a nuisance; the group sensed it; the group was suffused with a satiated hatred and was rejuvenated by it. In front of the partition there were now only individuals. They were wracked with nostalgia. Their eyes wandered back behind the partition. They stole away, they trailed off: Peter, then Giselle, looking back like thieves. They leaped through the partition's breach as though from a burning house into a safety net. – In front there were now only Mutig and what was left of Giggles. Mutig picked up some bibelot and was weighing it in his hand. He said, without looking up, "Giggles, if you'd like, today you can sleep with me." – He served her the word *today* as if on a golden platter. "Of course," Giggles said; something jerked her hard; she went to the window; she leaned her head against it. Mutig looked up sadly, and upon noticing that Giggles was not looking, his guilty face brightened; now he's stealing off on tiptoe toward the others. – Giggles has turned around. – She sees she's alone; she's waiting for them to call for her. Nothing. – Past the partition, past the divide, the group is regenerated. It is complete. Is anyone missing? Anything? – Nothing and no one. The group is pleased with Giggles's regret, it feeds on it, it suits it. The group becomes aware of having a *raison d'être*: it is; therefore, it is against someone. It is happy. – Here and there, a sidelong glance at Giggles. Giggles waits. Nothing. Nothing. Finally, she is plucking up the courage: two steps forward, one back; again; and about face; again . . . Now she, too, is at the partition. She proceeds quickly, like across a blazing line of fire, and stealthily, like a leper. – A moment. The conversation dies down. Andrew has broken off and is moving forward across the partition.

"Enough, that will do," Mutig announced impatiently, "why did she let herself go, why was she staring so?" And the chest went dark.

But the lights came right back up.

But this time one needed to strain one's eyes, for it was only a false twilight. There was a sort of torture chamber. Five friends sitting on low stools formed a circle. In the middle: Giggles. No one spoke. Nothing. Nor any movement. And unrest germinated. They turned quizzically toward one another. Their gazes wandered, and they all strayed toward Mutig's face. There they found the answer to some enigmatic "why," knowing only that it was because of *him* that there was this wedge of awkward oppression that had slowly inserted itself among them. There they found the answer, and they immediately cheered up, for they learned that they were headed for something that would be ritually decisive. Mutig consented mutely beneath their convergent eyes. Giggles noticed this, and she attempted a kind of very moving gesture whose purpose I did not ascertain. But an attempt it remained. The five friends stood. All at once. Giggles sat down obediently on one of the now-empty stools, raised her head, turned it back slightly. All of this had an air of carefully contrived ceremony, yet above it there dwelled an accent of tragic improvisation, so much so that there was a chill. It was a comedy that had imprudently crossed a forbidden limit and become something real, somehow, as real as catastrophe. They withdrew, except for Andrew, who came forward. "If you think," he said. "... If she wants," Mutig elaborated. Andrew blinded Giggles.

"Why was she letting herself go? Why was she staring so?" exclaimed Mutig—exclaimed Mutig with mournful emphasis—and this half-light, too, went out in the blackamoor's chest. But the lights came right back up.

The stage as in the first scene. No one, however, except the five friends. They were dejected.

"How did we ever come to this?" Andrew asked, staring gloomily at the ground.

"Why was she letting herself go? Why was she staring so?" Mutig asked despondently—not this Mutig at the table, but rather the one in the blackamoor's chest. Peter stood and placed a brotherly hand on his shoulder.

"Let's be more humane. We'll let her go. We'll give her her freedom."

"She doesn't want it!" Mutig blurted, almost desperately.

"It's kind of sad, being someone's god." (This was Paul.)

Andrew stood; he took a sure step toward Mutig and, harshly: "And if she did. Now that she's ours ... How would you set that up?"

"I don't know. How would you?"

"It's so seductive, being a god," they answered as a single voice.

"Enough," Mutig exclaimed, and the lights went down in the blackamoor's chest.

"I never told you," he continued, "that we didn't ever reach a resolution, did I? Is a game without rules still a game? Isn't it rather fate? Why was she letting herself go, why was she staring so?"

"And what part of her were *you* supposed to demolish?" Fuld inquired, eagerly borrowing from Mutig's naïve terminology and covering for his own servility, of which he was ashamed, with an insincere, ironic tone.

"Actually, there's nothing left for me. I was merely a place, the burning bush where . . ."

I: ". . . God gave his orders . . ."

Mutig: "So be it. – And if you like, just think that I'm saying this out of foolish pride."

Fuld: "There's nothing left for you, but to me, who is only the sixth, you offer a portion anyway?"

Mutig looked up, amazed.

"A misunderstanding," he said, like someone who has noted that his speech was in vain. "Or do you assume that we would have worked her over *so hard*—the five of us—if we hadn't recognized her as damned?"

"Well then, if she's damned . . ."

"Of course she's damned—but she has to agree to it, she has to consent to it. Only then can she still be helped; for let us not forget, please, that this is actually for her own good. Pay close attention: she can't *not* agree to her own blinding, for she looks up to god, that is, to us, in vain; she can't *not* agree to her dumbness, for we do not answer her; she can't come to terms, for how could such an incorrigible simpleton comprehend that the worst outcasts are the outcasts whom no one is driving away! That one might not be driven away, but is still excluded? She won't get there, for a god's wrath proceeds without leaving any footprints."

"God's wrath?"

"Ours . . . – "

"I hear, I hear," Giggles choked, but she was choking without tears.

"Is she unhappy? Is she ever! But she presumes she's

innocent. One can live a long life that way, and quite tolerably. So then how would she guess that there are hangmen who perform their executions—how to put this?—who perform their executions cleanly? Who have no need to clear their conscience under the pretext that the condemned man deserved it? They don't execute him because he's wicked; he's wicked because they execute him. She won't figure this out, no way, but if you rub her nose in it—pardon my putting it this way—what choice will she have but to believe that it is so? But this is why she loves me! Gifting evil to our loved ones does not spur them; it doesn't seem clean; it smacks of denatured vengeance; but she did not, does not, love you with love. Were you to exile her as well . . . You, her last hope, I want to say, the last impediment to her rehabilitation . . . Look, here's a little pin. This won't hurt much. There . . . in her left breast. As a sign that Giggles deserved it, because she's wicked."

"She doesn't hear you?" Fuld asked, leaning in.

"But of course she hears me. So what?" And after a brief silence, "It was you who guaranteed that she would, just a moment ago."

"I'm the one who guaranteed it?"

"Remember, after all, those pastures. That the only thing she really wants is to withdraw to those pastures—liberated."

"You were saying that she heard us," Fuld spoke calculatedly.

"Certainly. And so what? Would you boast of being a gentle executioner?"

"That's not the point. – But if she hears us, she knows you've been leading me astray. Let's assume that I really do think she's wicked. If she's heard you leading me astray, she might think that I'm doing it for payment; for example, because I feel like that sixth part . . ."

"What sixth part?"

"Of the power over life and death."

"Giggles," Mutig said, turning to that almost-puppet (the Negro had not stopped stroking her hair). "Giggles, do you think that Fuld is two-faced?"

"Fuld, two-faced!"

She sat upright, exerting herself fully, and threw her arms around his neck.

"Giggles," Mutig said to her jovially, "you don't really believe that you deserved it, if we've treated you so poorly? We! Us!"

"I do."

"If you disgust us, if you look stupid, worthy of our scorn; if we deceive you, make a fool of you; if we no longer want anything to do with you . . . Do you think you deserve it?"

"I do. I've earned it with my stupidity, my ineptitude, my pride, my prickliness . . ."

"With your wickedness, you strumpet, with your wickedness."

"Oh no, not with wickedness. How could I love you . . . *despite everything*, if I were wicked? Fuld, am I wicked?"

"Um . . ."

"Um . . . oh, she doesn't get it. She doesn't get that wicked is not a synonym for bad. She doesn't get that to be condemned to love the way she loves is a curse. She doesn't know—Giggles—she doesn't know that there is also a wickedness free of blame. The basest of all.

"Redeem her," and he made a show of handing Fuld the doll.

"Unhappiness is demoralizing, a plague. I cannot stand to look at unhappiness," Fuld said suddenly, he said it very quickly, and his eyes were popping out at Giggles, as if he were trying, albeit in vain, to take her in visually, as if the span of his universe had suddenly become Giggles, and Giggles alone.

He was looking at Giggles; he was looking at her so extortively that he finally wrested a smile out of her; he was like Job, smiling with the hope that showered upon him, though he knew it was in vain; the smile of a child who dreads a blow that has already fallen, but who, even afterwards, doesn't let go of the naïve hope for the miracle that would divert that blow from its course. It was a smile that burst through dread ten times every second, though it was restored each time.

Fuld's posture, which hadn't changed for a moment since my arrival, was only now reminding me of something. It struck me, that is to say, it struck me as a yelp in the darkness. It struck me that Fuld's posture was the standard posture of an examining magistrate, it was so pure in its curiosity that you didn't know whether it had turned sadistic or was merely stern. That's the posture. But the face, which, try as I might, I could not manage to glimpse but precisely in profile—oh, that face, sorrowful, for real, unto death!—when it was then lit up by the words: *Giggles, might I shoulder the rest of your burden?*

And the hand of that sadistic examining magistrate with the redemptive face slides slowly along the rubber doll that Mutig is languorously proffering. And toward that hand another is sliding, Giggles's—: it is holding a fancy needle plucked from the little bonnet (she'd fished it out so smoothly, as if merely fixing a mischievous lock of hair), and behind this needle there creeps an untrusting, almost playful, oft-disrupted and reconstituted smile, dragging along three heavy words: "With what, then?"

In the meantime, the auditorium had filled up again, I don't know how. The members of the audience sprawled comfortably in their seats; there wasn't a piehole not gnawing a thick twist packed into the corner of the mouth. Before me, in neat rows, hordes of eyes snooped over my head. No! It's a single eye: the eye of a fly. I see myself in it, multiplied, but is it actually me? It looks like me, I'm that I, yet somehow topsy-turvy. It's my worry, it's *my* regret, I'm buffeted by a "now or never," and my teeth are chattering, but the answer I get from the fly's eye is a tidy mosaic of unfamiliar gentlemen (for the most part me, topsy-turvy), and it convinces me it's my mistake, that there is no worry, no regret, no caritas, nothing but the curiosity *to see* multiplied to the point of inhumanity, to see what this almost redemptive profile of Fuld's would give us were we to see it from the front. This curiosity grows and grows, it's already too great, I can't handle it, I see it, it's sprung forth from me like a finger puppet from a magician's box, it has the eye of a fly. It sways on a wavering nudge, it sways forward, back. It has the knavish smile of a scoundrel who's nicked the wire beneath the acrobat and is delightedly awaiting the consequences; the short, splayed paws of a welcoming little devil from limbo, along with his wicked joviality. He knows he's bewitched me. He knows, and he's smiling. He sways more and more, he smiles less and less. And having reached full tilt, he has stretched his arms out like a happy little jester getting into a tangle with a gendarme; the smiling was done; in the fly's eye, now so near, a tidy mosaic of unfamiliar gentlemen paralyzed by a curiosity that has no name. The nasty biceps of outrageous weightlifters sprouted behind the short paws: curiosity, as burly as a drunken stockboy, jolted me. Something twanged, crunched, and creaked beneath my feet; I fell on something; for a moment it put up a rough resistance, but all of a sudden it went slack and yielded disgustingly; something awkwardly jagged was left in my arms. The blackamoor vanished; Mutig, livid with furious regret, stood back and carefully examined his lacerated hands;

in my arms—Giggles. Facing me head on, however, and, as always, in the posture of a sadistic examining magistrate—Fuld. Fuld? No; something hideous; an expansive, sweet-toothed grimace, like that of someone inexpressibly good trying to polish off everything but his smile, someone as though barely a shadow, who, having realized the pointlessness in due course, has fled, covering his face and bidding me toward this empty disharmony.

"Are you nuts? Who gave you the right?" I tore the rubber puppet away from him and hurled it far, far away.

Fuld dropped his head to the table; a trio of sobs, then silence; tears rolled like peas from Mutig's eyes; they left an emptiness, and a grief whose way had been barred till now took up residence in that emptiness; hesitantly at first, but soon in an impatient stampede, like a startled herd. In long processions. Giggles's arms slid from my neck; she snapped and hung down across my own; the glass shards beneath her feet were a fine dust. I dragged myself and Giggles over to Fuld and stuck my free arm under his belt. I hauled them toward the exit, making hard progress. I had to get by Mutig. He feigned an empty gesture of forestalling me.

"You think it's fun being a god, when all you are is human?"

"A god? All you are is inhuman."

"You think it's so easy being human when you're some-body's god?"

They hung across my arms; their heads were swinging; they swept the floor with their arms. They were heavy. A café's Sunday din pecked into the spacious room. And Mutig—and why isn't he helping me?—was now pulling himself back together, leading us with the ceremonious step of a host. He opened the door for me and stepped aside.

"In spite of everything, thank you," he said. "But do take care of them, Mr. Successor."

I put them down at the curb and went to look for a car. The street had gone dark in the meantime. Presently I saw quite distinctly that I was here today for the first time. I didn't know the place; and not a street sign to be found—that got my goat! The whole time there's that traffic, as if it were being sucked out just past its source: but now it sounded like nothing more than a weir off in the distance. – I had barely gone a few steps when I spotted a hansom cab moving toward the place where Fuld and Giggles were lying. I recognized it at once as the cab that had brought me here, and I thought this natural—secure, perhaps, in the knowledge that I hadn't even looked at the driver earlier. The driver smiled; the one before (but how would I know?) *also* had that smile of the consecrated. But consecrated in what? I jumped onto the footboard, like lobby boys do in the rain when they're trying to stop a car for their clientele. (I envy them that jump, for they do it as if out of privilege—the privilege of youth, and I, now making the jump myself, am a little embarrassed at having presumed something to which I no longer have a right.)

"It's as if I'd foreseen it," said the driver.

"Foreseen what?"

"Sir," he said, "I'm not saying that I've foreseen anything, but that 'it's as if I'd foreseen it.' A sentence where 'it' has a conventional function, which is to say none at all, and where all the emphasis is placed on the condition 'as if I had.' I don't know whether you, too, have objectless premonitions. That is, premonitions that we recognize only after the object they were premonitions of has been fulfilled."

"Naturally," I said, intending sarcasm, but maybe coming off as just angry.

"Your 'naturally' attests to your suspicion. I'm not to blame if, through your own fault, circumstances rouse your suspicion that I'm pointing indiscreetly to your personal affairs. A driver is discreet by his very vocation. Unless I'm asked, I never take any notice of a person's affairs. I strive solely for so-called 'general thoughts.' Take, for example, my 'as if I'd foreseen it'; all I'd wanted to say was that the aspect assumed by premonitions once the event has come to pass is perhaps not from retroactive suggestion so much as like a lamp behind a banner. That banner is the objectless premonition, and the event itself is the light that shines through that fulfillment—only then do we see that it really was within. The event within the premonition, that is. – So it's to Rue d'Astorg, is it?"

A question so unexpected that it took a moment before I placed it, and I called out in surprise, "What, do you know this man?" (It happened that Fuld lived on Rue d'Astorg.)

The driver shrugged his shoulders.

"I'm the driver, after all, who chauffeurs gentlemen who've been through the wringer. Each of us has his destiny. There are people who float along from start to finish like advertising balloons: future angels have fallen for them, and they happily take them under their wing, so very far, where man is forbidden to go; there they are passed to the next angelic shift. – On the other hand, there are the people who spend their whole lives shambling out of pits. There isn't a man damned to hell who hasn't run into those oafs on the way down—it's like the only reason they were created was so that beggars would feel better, and to guide the way for marked beings. – As I've said, gentlemen who've been put through the wringer are set aside for me; gentlemen who've been put through the wringer are no different than timid gumshoes. They hold out against evil for much the same reason people bury a pheasant: to get it all wormy. And once the evil's teeming with worms, they have to leave it anyway, for it turns their stomach. Their hunger is eternal. Those are the most dangerous people of all—like people who haven't eaten their fill."

"And they all live on Rue d'Astorg. Of course!"

"My dear man, no. They don't all live on Rue d'Astorg. But they are all mine. I know them. Didn't I tell you they've been set aside for me?"

"Set aside for what?"

"To be carted off—if, after all, it happens that they've alighted upon the place they'd been sniffing around, not daring to get all up in there."

"So you're Charon."

"Right—across the Lethe of swill."

"And what about the lady?"

"It's not up to the dead."

"You really think they've killed her?"

"In a certain sense, of course. It's only *that* sense, however, that decides the misfortune. The little lamb that hands the butcher the knife he'd forgotten is a dead little lamb twice over. – Where should we put it?"

"What?"

"You know, the stiff!"

With great effort, Giggles rose and planted herself on the curb. She was staring at her beautiful legs.

"I hear you," she said mischievously, "I hear you, but he's lying..."

"For now, drive to Rue d'Astorg."

"No stops?"

"No stops."

We settled them into the corners, where they more or less stayed. I sat in the middle.

"So they'll be more secure," the driver said after taking their arms and placing them around my neck from both sides.

That neighborhood had the malevolent flavor of the Parisian neighborhoods outside the city gates, where majestic and bungled apartment blocks provide useless lessons in hygiene to the hovels, which see right through them. The embittered quarreling of spouses who have decided on divorce and are seeking out pretexts. I didn't know precisely where we in fact were, but it was easy to anticipate that the closer we got to Rue d'Astorg, which is contained within a single quarter, the more touchy Paris would become in its fixedness. Up till now, the opposite had been true: the farther we had gone, the more plebeian the landscape had become in its rambling. The tidy houses seemed to approach increasingly greater misfortune, and the sheds, flophouses, saloons, and ill-treated pavilions, more scattered than sparse, were becoming an ever-more-stringent rule; they pretended to nothing but an ambition to inspire Utrillos. The farther we went, the more gracelessly were we confronted by yards filled with scrap iron, jealous of its own better days and as prideful as a hidalgo; heaps of lime and charcoal that no one ever starts on; piles of junk that didn't belong to anybody, that belongs to no one and nevertheless revels in its place in the sun; the brickwork of Minotaurs lowing for liberators to lead them out of the labyrinths where they'd been hardheadedly thrust; and then those sulky and conceited little vegetable gardens, whose sole care is how to get out from behind their neglected palings and give the slip to the gardening equipment, with its efforts on their behalf so fair and so pointless. – In short, I noticed that, instead of getting closer to Rue d'Astorg, we were getting further away. I was, remarkably, of two minds as to whether I should bring this to the driver's attention, or else to take the detour in its natural course, and it was only when I'd decided that it suddenly occurred to me that Fuld and Giggles, lifeless till now, had come to. Their still-languorous eyes groped around for mine, the same question scurrying around therein. I was aware of it before I even needed to look, whether at him or at her: it arose right in front of me, as distinct as an iceberg in the sun, and I responded with all speed: "No, no, there now... Mutig's not here. You're safe, you're safe."

"Too bad," they answered, as though in a single breath.

The roadway was like a cord. The driver turned and asked, pushing aside the barrier glass, "Rue d'Astorg, isn't it?"

"Doesn't matter. Wherever the three of us go together, it'll be deserted anyway."

"The three of you?"

"The three of us! – Without our seducer."

"Without your seducer?"

"Without courage."

We were now in entirely free territory. Like someplace where nothing had yet been decided. A place from back before the waters were separated from the land. Still a dry shore, but already approaching the waters and rushing after their fragrance like a dachshund hot on the trail. The soil was getting spongier. The road, till now like a cord, negotiated the moors' beginnings, went around them, begging them for passage— moors are jealous and stingy. We were sent down long detours that, on this crude flatness, seemed like foolish and expensive jokes. We drove fast. On sharp turns Fuld would suddenly fall across me, then Giggles. Again and again I was required to right them, put them in their place. Each time they collapsed as if quizzically, with the incoherent, insistent, and uninquisitive questioning of drunkards. They were hideous to the touch: he, limp the whole time like empty packaging in the tentative shape of the object that's fallen from it; she, like a new, jointed, as-yet unworn doll. But though they were rather lifeless things, I took notice of them from one moment to the next, the way they were conversing behind my back "with their eyes"—asinine and somehow scattered, plotting something, but not yet knowing what. This unsettled me, or, rather, it twisted me out of shape, but so as not to compromise myself I pretended not to see. – Meanwhile, it had gotten late. It was the full moon, but the darkness was getting the better of it. The sky was full of stars; they shone so much it crackled; you'd say they're shining, knowing why: they communicate with each other across the systems; there is among them a simple, if voluntary, if coercive fellowship of an unfamiliar nature, and they've resigned themselves to it. And I felt a bit of shame that the three of us, though pressed so tightly together, have nothing in common but for our polluted secrecy. Perhaps the driver alone knew precisely what had brought us down—his innuendos, his almost irritably indifferent liberty at the steering wheel—but astonishingly, he was just the one I had unwittingly excluded from our depraved fellowship. It struck me, I no longer know how or why, that it might only be through a demon's incitement that we introduce so many unknowns into our equations, whereas it might suffice to dig out reserves that are long since calculated. Our prides, however, seem too minute for so noble a task, for what are we to do? Would we then want to finish calculating the mystery of life with these largely unfamiliar equations? – I had started to get it: we were driving along the Seine, downstream. I recognized the hillsides near Saint-Cloud, though they weren't actually hillsides so much as a sort of horizontal projection of them. That must have been the square beyond the Pont de Saint-Cloud, where there is so much dust in summer. But today it's all turned to mud. The tavern where the artisans' wedding parties head to was still there, but the background—the city—forfeited perspectival depth, as if it were a poorly painted theater screen. Le Pavillon Bleu, on the river, was, one would say, enticed irresistibly by the water. The path behind it, leading past the barracks to the park fence, commenced with great care, as if it were particular about its authenticity (anyway, it was authentic): it anxiously avoided the theater screen in the background, whose touch would have enchanted it, and ended in a sort of tunnel. Through the tunnel you could see the garden by Le Nôtre, but the gate by which one enters had disappeared; the garden, too, was merely a projection of itself, and incredibly simplified, summarized somehow. We hadn't encountered anyone this entire time, and yet we were never free from a sense—how should I put this?—a sense of nearby person-ness. Nor was there anything to be afraid of. I don't think I was even a little taken aback, having already seen from afar that the tunnel was bustling. Here and there I made out campfires whose glare was reflected in the arch, and where—it seemed to me—halberds glimmered. When we drove into this tunnel—for a long while now, besides their giving each other the eye, Fuld and Giggles hadn't exhibited the slightest sign of life—I was seized by a powerful, really quite powerful sense of something I had seen once before. And with all speed, as if it had long since been readied within me, I had also already identified that memory: that tunnel, it was the long whitewashed tunnel that led from the park in Písek to Heyduk Street, only it wasn't pure, but rather—if I can put it this way—mixed up with the vestibule of the town hall in Arles that I had read in the evening papers was used as shelter from the rain. (The tunnel in Písek likewise provided shelter from a rain-soaked promenade.) In no way did I marvel at that symbiosis, for I know Arles; it's just that

I was somehow bugged that that wound hadn't healed sufficiently well, that is, as I have said, that it provided so unkempt a mixture. Only now did I notice that the underpass was not solid; it broadened in the middle into an open rotunda, and it was just in this sort-of-courtyard that these campfires were blazing, with squires bustling among them. Those squires gave the impression of extras in the theater, awaiting the signal to move onstage, and passing the slow time by pretending that it really was their duty to keep order in a crowd of modernly dressed civilians who were giving off an impression that was the complete opposite of theatrical. Those squires surrounded us—I quipped that they'd been expecting us for a long time—and we understood there was no way to go further. The driver, it seemed to me, had already come to an agreement with them. When I asked why we couldn't just keep going, they didn't want to say, but what seemed strange to me wasn't so much that they didn't want to say, but the definite ostentatiousness with which they refused me an answer! So, I told the driver to turn around. He, however, folded his arms, while the mercenaries and the crowd started shaking their heads no: a quite tolerant no, but a resolute one. All of a sudden it seemed to me that there would be nothing simpler than to carry Fuld and Giggles through the passage and the grillwork, which was closed (now you couldn't see anything past the grillwork besides the self-assured darkness, which couldn't be anything but a black curtain), though the only thing that occurred to me to do was to ask why and where. The squires helped me. When we approached the fence, it turned out there wasn't a curtain there at all, but rather a gate, and quite a heavy one by the looks of it, but one that yielded as easily as the slatted doors to American saloons. We passed through it and found ourselves in a land that was at once garden, flooded polder, and oyster pits. These pits stretched out of sight and, oddly enough, didn't overflow. Narrow grassy dikes turned them into a kind of chessboard. Despite their being so narrow, trees had taken root in them here and there, and not just little ones, and some remarkable feat of engineering had managed to run a meandering yet negotiable road along the way, without violating the landscape's chessboard regularity or its aquatic monotony. Those pits didn't appear deep, and their water was murky. On the whole, the sense they exuded was rather mournful, though by no means inconsolable, and, as far as that enigmatic road was concerned, it beckoned me with its peculiar, gentle power, which surely stemmed from the now-distant bend in the road, beyond which it then stretched again, straight, ascending conspicuously. Conspicuously, because the land's contours, so it seemed to me, didn't correspond with that ascent, and as a matter of fact it was as though the road detached from the ground and led its own upward existence. I decided that we would set out along it, and I felt that this decision of mine was a legitimate countermove to the recent refusal of the crowd and the squires, a countermove that was just as tolerant and resolute. The only thing that confounded me was how it happened that these parts seemed to me to be negotiable, let alone passable. It was all the more astonishing that the road had an altogether dreamlike quality, whereas those low dikes stood out for their almost conspicuous realness. I told myself that the only way to get far there was by vehicle, that it would not do to go on foot. The image of my having to trudge with those puppets along the grassy dikes, among waters that weirdly did not overflow, gave me unbearable vertigo; I must have known that the hollows were shallow. But fortunately, just past those saloon doors in the form of heavy gates, there was a bit of dry space, with the distinctive texture of something that has shunned the rest of the aquatic landscape and formed a whole only unwillingly, when compelled. But to lay the lifeless Fuld and Giggles there without getting them wet was a delicate enterprise, and Fuld actually did slip away from us and fall into the water. I saw that he was aware of this involuntary spa treatment, even if he in no way showed it, neither by opening his eyes, nor with a twitch of the limbs, nor with a grimace. This awareness of his, exhibited by nothing, and of which something testified—perhaps a magnetic current from him to me—was even touching. I had to go into the reservoir after him, the water hardly came up to my knees; I felt its chill, yet none of its wetness. At last, Fuld and Giggles were on terra firma.

Two squires stood guard over them, as if at my command (true, no such order had even occurred to me), and I went back to the courtyard. When the gate had once again shut behind me, I hesitated in my response as to whether I would actually go find a wagon or not. That is, I really had gone there for a wagon, already knowing beyond any doubt, however, that I would find neither a wagon, nor the squires, nor the crowd. And, in fact, the courtyard was empty; all that remained were the campfires, smoldering away somehow, as if they ran on the coming dawn. And face-to-face with a prediction so magnificently affirmed, I was forced to search my conscience, knowing that I would have to answer the question of whether I had somehow deliberately deluded myself into going for the wagon, knowing it would not be there. – The courtyard was deserted, but again there was the ineradicable sense of human-ness, nearby and all-embracing, just as when we were driving into Saint-Cloud. I turned back toward the watery landscape, accepting as quite natural that there was no aquatic landscape, nor Fuld, nor Giggles, nor soldiers in armor; in short, that I was walking through a so-called living dream, a quite truthful reality, and thus, as they say, a zone of truth, where there is nothing with which to deceive oneself, that what this is here is an entrance to the Métro, which I, descending the staircase, in fact also quickly recognized by its red lights.

So I was descending the staircase, and I was feeling so embarrassed about the answer as to whether I was still shuffling along the zone of truth, or else had already popped out of it, that I decided to establish what was what, come what may. I paid for my ticket with money that would require the cashier to give me change. I determined not to pick it up. If the cashier alerts me to it, that will be proof that I'm awake; if she doesn't call after me, I'll know that I'm dreaming. I conducted the experiment, even if I was aware that it was actually a sham: I knew in advance that the cashier could not *not* call for me, *for such is the custom.* And she actually did. And because I made like I hadn't heard, she went so far as to send an assistant after me. An inspiration passed through me, that the constant confirmation of my prediction simply means there's no point looking for safety. For where there is only an inch of room for doubt—perhaps in the associative hint of a slight dry spot in an aquatic landscape—certainty is merely a word . . . and who knows. – The train arrived, I got on, the train moved on.

He boarded at La Trinité. My first sense was vexation at not having foreseen it. But was this really my only cause for regret? How was I to regret not having foreseen something—that is to say, his boarding at La Trinité—that had so convincing an air of originality? His boarding did not arouse memories of some event in the past. If I foresaw it—despite the fact that things that are being prepared will be a faithful analogy of what has occurred in some "back then"—I foresaw it in no way through some concrete experience, but rather only the way we sort of foresee the da capo in a minuet.

Were I to hold fast to this event, I wouldn't be able to do otherwise than retrace quite literally the beginning of that very game. But what for, if I can simply refer to it? Very well. –

Nevertheless . . . : The stranger, even if he was *utterly* human at the outset, didn't, in fact, seem a stranger *completely*: through the likeness of the Spanish dancer Vicente Escudero, or rather beneath it somehow, I just now recognized Fuld. But against expectations this discovery did not excite me in the least. The bizarre reality that Vicente Escudero was Fuld, while nevertheless remaining Vicente Escudero, was a matter of such indifference to me that I undertook nothing to identify him further—with my ears, say—except with my perhaps faulty eyesight. I did nothing to move him to speak, not even a single word. Here I was as though before something that I had absolutely nothing to do with, despite my being utterly secure in knowing that this was Fuld, when a three-note motif suddenly inserted itself between us. Yes, three notes, which you could hear—it might not have been possible to say where from—and which, once they'd subsided, nevertheless carried on, this time somehow objectively. I can't say it any other way than this: they carried on in the manner of a monkey wrench operating on large threads, a wrench that had been inserted between my fellow traveler and me, and now promptly extended itself, parting us irresistibly, one from the other. I turned in on myself noticeably, enough so that I was, at length, alone in an oppressive, yet light mist. Then the three-note motif rang out again, but this time with an emphasis that announced that something was beginning. At the same time, it sounded like a warning that it would be recorded as an injustice on my part if I were not to recognize it, this motif, but this warning was superfluous, for the very reason I had come was for this passing scrap of rondo from Mozart's *Eine kleine Nachtmusik*, and to sit at my own table. I would say I recognized that I was *still* sitting at my own table were it not for the hazy impression that between "before" and "now" a sort of fissure had inserted itself, one that I seemed to have slept through, though I was now back on its trail. I say "slept through," although I rather recollect something along the lines of a submersion, from which I am surfacing again—more than sleep. Memories of spicy yet thin air, and wafting within it but a hint of some amusing realness (the sort of thing that clings to the variegated decorations of national operas), and with which I am ultimately finding myself again, for within it sinks that now familiar, double, good-naturedly mocking travesty of Grock's posture recalling his partner, which I am just now caressing with my still-blinking eyes, left right left right, as I surface.

Their sideways smiles say symmetrically, from that side: "We're indivisible!"

From this: "We're bound together!"

These smiles, because they're sidelong, intersect right in front of my face. There they ignite a hotpoint: admittedly, I find it scintillating, but I see past it. Behind it, there's a strange hand; it is sparingly twisting a doll that some other hand is toying with; I surmise that that playful hand belongs to me. The doll has fallen out of it; there's a thump, as from under some heavy object, a Browning, let's say, and just then I also hear: "Are you just going to keep playing forever, then? A person might say you're dodging the bill that way."

I rolled a glance across his visage, it wound around to her face and rolled across it as well. And again that peevish unease:

Who is this third, this third, from their common likeness? The road leads there, but it's blocked; in this bare blockade wall, however, there's a crack, and through this crack dribbles a sort of meager certainty that between those two, Fuld and Giggles, there is a mysterious, yet definite, relationship. Yes, the man-stranger and the woman-stranger are Fuld and Giggles, but they are Fuld and Giggles, as it were, across mountains, across rivers. It's them, through unheard-of forms. Now there can no longer be any doubt. He, having smiled, twisted his head: this sweet-toothed grimace that someone has inexpressibly, but importunately and quite vainly attempted to finish into an austere smile!

"*Escudero!*" say I.

He: "Escudero!"

But barely had he said it than he turned to face me and drew up so close that there could be no mistaking his intention to let it be understood that what would now occur would be—as I would say—utterly exceptional, for my sake, for me, as a sort of honor: and it was off with the mask. But with the locution "off with the mask" I'm not capturing the nature of what happened. For the change that came about was not, verily, as though he had tossed aside his mask or put on another; on the contrary, the new face that replaced the preceding one *showed up* with the same somehow swift accrual by which living-room magicians exchange their various neckties. Actually, it was more complicated: a whole array of visages were exchanged on his face (if one must put it this way), but so swiftly that I couldn't manage to identify any one of them but the last; they flipped by no differently from pages of a block calendar quickly thumbed through, and in that nimble turning of the pages/faces dwelled, motionless, a pair of fixed, burning, almost inquisitorial eyes, somehow as if they were gradually burning through the top layer of those contemplated pages. But heavy lids suddenly fell upon those eyes, and the hard-braked contemplation blew over into a face that was so calm, so collected...

But the fact that I was face-to-face *with myself* was not the eeriest thing; eerier still was the ardor with which my thought was trying to persuade my hesitating senses that this was no delusion; eerier still was the certainty that my senses—at just this moment my sight—had begun to live outside of my thought. What's with them! They were looking to make a break for it, they were devising a way to explain away, that is to say refute, what was evident. But thought, like a gloomily overjoyed sheepdog, drove them back to the flock, and having discharged the time-honored office of bringer-of-reason, it persuaded them that they were deceiving themselves while believing the deceit, and it increased the panic.

I looked around for the woman, but she was deliberately turning her head away and tapping on the table. And, God knows how, that indifferent bearing of hers expressed a command so definite, so imperious and uncompromising, that my eyes again turned to the place they'd only just cowered from like worn-out, terror-hunched dogs, toward the eyes of that one whose collapsed eyelids were more bewitching and more sighted than the most fevered pupils. We were again facing each other—I and I—so closely that the waves of embarrassment got the better of my fear and led me toward an unwitting, overfamiliar gesture: I passed my hand across my face, but hardly had I done so than I was on my feet. Not my hand's sense of touch—for it did not remember that touch would have prompted it toward that suspicion—not my hand's sense of touch, but it was somehow another of its senses that caused alarm.

I was on my feet, a step before the tall mirror over the

fireplace—I say before the tall mirror over the fireplace, knowing with sun-like clarity that I'm in front of the mirror—which, however, didn't respond to me. And again: eerier than this betrayal of me—who, despite an unspoken but age-old pact, did not issue forth from those depths—was my ardent, gloomily high-spirited thought trying to persuade my startled senses not to be afraid, not to run away, that there was nothing to worry about, that this empty mirror was a correct mirror, *that this was how it had to be.*

Did I cry out? I don't know, but how else, except as a cry, could that sudden thaw work its way out, as copious and roiling as the fear that preceded it had been miserly and desiccated? I was standing before the mirror, I knew that the mirror I was standing in front of was eerily parched, yet I sank my gaze into its extinct waters just as assuredly as a fisherman, before the appearance of the auspicious full moon, plunges his nets into the teeming waters. All I did was point a plaintive, if unfearful, left hand at the unfaithful mirror, and I said:

"He stole my face; he stole my face."

"Which one?" she asked with a condescending indulgence that she had prepared to express with a still-smooth gesture when she was suddenly wracked as if by stifled anger, in which the lithe movement snapped. "Which one?" she repeated, having caught hold of the table's edge, so as to overcome not yet so much her anger as the buoyancy of her rebellious pain. "Which one?" she said for the third time, in a tone whose sloppy, conversational superficiality struck an incredible contrast with its unchecked revolt.

"What, don't you recognize Giggles?" she continued, laughing as if at a sly joke, but so excessively that I started to catch on to her intent, and in no time I had also actually discovered that this was her attempt to turn my attention away from the empty and, as it were, crumpled spot that was the only thing that testified to what had only just recently been the presence of him who had appropriated my face (and who knows if that's all). I won't soon forget her ever-so-splenetic aspect when she ascertained that her gambit had failed; but it was merely a fraction of a second. Like a person who, in the midst of a momentous operation that has been entrusted to him, has let it be known that he's overheard the flippant rogue, and now regrets it, so too did she shout down her own disgruntlement, and in fact, when she stretched her arms as if to part a curtain that didn't happen to be there, she allowed herself to depend on the slightly naïve pomp with which she announced her having come to do what she was just now performing. Having thus parted the imaginary curtain, she stepped back as though not to be in the way, and with the admirably fake gesture of criers at the town fair she called upon me to watch.

"You must pay close attention," I hear just then in a voice that rings a bell somehow, yet is not the voice of this one here, but rather somewhat shaky, sing-song, slightly protracted; a voice that extends no further than absolutely necessary for it to have somewhere to go, with a multitude of *fioritura* as lightweight as washed watercolor; the kind of voice ground out from a thick shell of time; but again, a voice now refined and domesticated. And I see that it had in fact issued from the woman who had parted the curtain, but who had gone from being the Giggles "from over hill and dale" to Giggles the ur-familiar—intrepidly timid, in the wondrous démarche of her queen, Puppenfee—the trusting Giggles from the tavern up on Rue Lamarck.

"You must pay close attention," she says after her usual fashion, that is, playfully threatening with her forefinger and hunching over slightly, "because Mutig hasn't shown you everything."

"Mutig..."

"Yes, up on the hill, in the blackamoor's chest. Mutig is magnanimous, the only one he snitched on was himself. Nothing about anyone else. Look...do you see?" she cried, pointing with the little finger, which had gone from playfully threatening to autocratically menacing.

And I, perhaps knowing that what I was watching was again just my own apartment, and seeing nothing there besides familiar objects, was nonetheless as though plucked out, as though in spite of everything, and the blinking flaxen light of the wiry nativity scene started up, just as it had up there in the blackamoor's chest, and just then Giggles was entering, *the Giggles of the other evening*, an evening already settling down nicely, it leaped fretfully into the luminous rectangle of the door, upon which Giggles was sort of caught. But having leaped for it, it realized its mistake and reeled back, for it had burnt itself on Giggles's pain, which was so great that it emanated from her soul, creating a bright aura. Like in the monument to Marshal Ney—yes, like in the monument to Marshal Ney—of which it is said that the hand gripping the saber *captures* the entire action of unsheathing, so too did Giggles's drooping hand, holding a hat, encompass the action of destruction, and thus in seeing Giggles I was also seeing how—a minute before—she was rushing to my stairs and snatching off that hat. And this, the caught-up-with past of a grotesque drama on a spiral staircase and its still more grotesque shadow, which the gaslights passed from one floor to the next as crudely as a gang passes the hussy they've snagged, again contain all those crumpled, dust-covered, shabby, as any-old-as-to-be-unsellable little tragediennes from the blackamoor's chest, those unmoving, prolonged-unto-jaw-dropping-tedium tragedies, who, when they'd had enough, even treated the tragedian of this community theater like dirt for having taken them literally. Yes, Giggles plays well: it's to a tee, as it had been the other evening, when Mutig treated her like dirt; when, not knowing up from down, she made a break for me. Yes, so too had she entered, hat in hand and in the aura of the overflowing pain upon which the fretful evening, which had settled down and mistook it for light, had flung itself. Yes, so too had she left the door ajar behind her, so too had she fallen exhausted against the wall—oh, such a good imitation!—and it was in that same spinsterishly gaunt, unsightly grief that I twice heard that "je n'en puis plus, je n'en puis plus," so too was my heart in my throat, so too did I now...

... so too did I now feel bad for thinking, *Poor, poor Giggles, she's standing there like a community theater actress playing Niobe, if only she had a real wall behind her instead of a screen*; for being unable to rid myself of these slanderous thoughts, for being her admittedly woeful, yet powerless, yet tense viewer, so too did I now...

No, so too nothing. There's no point. This time the foul thought of mine did not arise, it did not arise with the squeamish gesture like unto the disgraced, that I not dare; and this time Giggles did not...

"But Giggles, no," I shout at the stage, "what's gotten into you, have you forgotten your part? That's not how it went. What are you pointing your finger at me for? And why out of the blue? And the velvet darkness all around you, where's that from? And the way you're looking at me? Stay there by the wall, don't come any closer, drop the raised hand, Giggles, I don't want..."

"What's your problem?" I hear right in front of me, "can't you see past your nose? Wouldn't you perhaps be afraid?"

The Giggles from Rue Lamarck was menacing the Giggles on the stage.

"I was scared, Giggles!"

"What about them?" and she pointed back with a bubbly cackle. "You have to forgive her, she's forgotten her part. Anyway, I've just put her on notice. Now she knows.

"Now she knows," she repeated, and she held out her arms as if closing a curtain, and again it was just the two of us (we were perhaps fewer than two), "now she knows that you double-crossed and deceived her then, like you killed her, and killed her horribly.

"That's not allowed," she threatened, and she coaxed me into the seat that stood right beside hers. "No cheating. No hope, either. That wasn't nice, luring her to hope when you knew there was none. You're older than she is, more experienced. You must have known there isn't hope for everything. We unfortunates, sinners, we damned, you know, we're so gullible, all it takes is for you to smile at us and we already believe someone's shown us mercy. Providing us hope, that's a trick, and there will be no trickery.

"Really, none," she repeated with mock pleading. "Or perhaps you would deny having seen what I was all about when I came in—just now, back behind the curtain (she explained, pointing with her chin)? You didn't?... But you've been telling yourself in your head the whole time! 'She looks so sinful you'd sit somewhere else. She looks like an outcast. She's an outcast.' But then how could it be any other way, I ask you; after all, didn't I deify a human being—Mutig?

"Oh, for one person to deify another..." she sighed comically. "For that matter, you've been watching me for a long time already, don't you see? Oh yes, you've been watching! I know everything... now. For a long time you've been eyeing me, to see when I'd fall into my own crime. A dovish crime. But crime is crime. No such thing as a free ride. I was overgrown with such sworn misfortune that you said to yourself, 'Give her one of those small lady's revolvers with mother-of-pearl, and at the same time squeeze her hand with silver-tongued warmth: adieu! And that's it; it'd be a Samaritan act *inédit*.' Yes, that's what you told yourself... as I was leaning against the wall... *as I was leaning against the wall like Niobe from the community theater...*"

"Giggles!"

"My God... we're still having... a calm discussion. All that is in the past. And I know everything... now.

"And you were right," she patted my knee with godmotherly emphasis, "you were dead right. Just be a dear and tell me," she threw in inquisitorially, "why were you deluding me with hope? That's not right, you see, that's not right; it's not nice. Instead of hastening me out the door, out *that* door, you were saying... too bad, after all, we could have just played it out, it would have been more lively... you were saying: 'Giggles, it's not for love, all that suffers is your pride. If you were suffering for love, you wouldn't be opening up to me. I know you. Isn't it perhaps out of willfulness that you've capitulated to Mutig?' Pride! Like people would tear their hair out and bang their head against the wall for pride. And as if it were a matter of forsaken love—oh! forsaken love—and not at all of my devastation!

"I'm asking you... me! A little creature being vivisected. My fear was only waiting for him to say his piece. How could you have missed such an opportunity, you, who are ever so curious?

"Curious, curious, curious," she started saying stubbornly, "it's only out of that damned curiosity of yours that you consoled me; out of curiosity over *what would come of it*. What would come of the furious hope of a little creature being vivisected, what sort of vileness might she be talked into...yes," she said, suddenly curt, "without you, sir, I could have passed away in beauty.

"So now we know, without you I could have passed away in beauty. So I am the way I am...I happened to find myself a god. Now that's something. That, sir, is worth dying for! A god is a god. A god is according to what we deserve, and not according to his own perfection. But it's a god every time. I found him, you see. I'm the one who deserved to depart for those pastures. You thwarted me just as things were going good. 'There are other ways to god,'" she started aping me, "'than vanishing within him. For example, there's the dignity of life, and besides: Mutig is not a god.'

"Dignity of life! Mutig is not a god! I deified him, I think that's enough, huh? Dignity of life...is that what you traded me to Fuld for? Or was it to find out 'what would come of it,' Fuld and me, me and Fuld? We were supposed to shed some light for you, one on the other. We *interested* you, that's what. You wanted to test out what kinds of disgusting poses the dead would consent to if they were bought off with hope. O hope, hope," she caricatured, drawing out the *o*, "who, then, I ask you, will be taken in by it more than the one for whom there isn't any left? Why didn't you send me out to...to those pastures..., as befits the dead?"

"Giggles," I said, "I had it all thought out. I swear to you that in spite of everything I had it all thought out."

"What are you defending yourself for?" she responded jovially. "I'm not holding anything against you, I'm just telling it like it was. You're not to blame. I know you had it all thought out. It's not your fault you think *better than you act*. It's not your fault that you, too, are the dead among the living; that you, too, think that enduring is everything. You, like Fuld—you're no longer a weakling either, nor a coward—you're nobody, too. Between the abyss and the fire even a weakling will somehow make a decision, but you wouldn't get killed one way or the other, neither leaping, nor burning—you'd go for some wry 'I don't know up from down.' It's a good thing you looked into the mirror; wherever you'd find yourselves faces, you and Fuld.

"But I didn't beg you, you see, and I'm not knowledgeable about what the dead are capable of. – The dignity of life! What could be simpler than loving cads, what could be more pure! They were bad, but cluelessly. Mutig took my glory upon himself, and Mutig took my murder upon himself. With him it was easy to be dignified: to live when there was a reason, and to die when the living was done. You brought me down. To life? Where! To enduring. What for? Maybe so I'd prove something that way? What? I'm asking you. What would it prove?"

"That the one who wins is the one who doesn't run away."

"God willing!" she said, and she leaned sculpturally on her chin. "But I have always loved! I loved *him*. I loved Mutig. Don't you know that love is a dead end? And one that *always* leads to glory? No matter where it leads? Why did you hold me back? Why did you, in all your curiosity, ever hand me over to Fuld? Oh, because I was on the street and Fuld wanted me, I know. Those guys were as sharp as cactus needles and as bitter as wormwood. They abused and they tortured. But their scorn had edges and limits. I like things that your eyes can move along. They tormented and humiliated, but it was out of an earthy taste. But Fuld has a double face," she continued in a trusting whisper. "You know? A double face. Whether he was making an offer or speaking ill, everything that came out of him was the same slime. He's a glutton for problems. He has coarse tastes. He sets people on divine paths—you know why?" (And in a timid whisper:) "For the spectacle of vice and misfortune. What would he do with people who'd found their path themselves?" She turned toward me slowly, and, giving me a compassionate wink:

"You've been seeking each other a long time. You belong together. You're no good at taking things either, taking people, of weighing them and telling them hopelessly: 'You're following your own path.' You, in your pity, you don't know, either, that the main thing is to follow your own path. And there's nothing that can be done about it." She shrieked hatefully, "You only force them into detours. What you're running is purely a game!

"Fuld? He doesn't trust anything that's simple and positive, just because it's not confused and negative. Love, virtue, truth? It's not like he didn't believe in them, you know? But he's no good at dressing people in them. No one, no one in the world. He's a person so dissolutely suspicious that he thinks everything is dissolute if it's not perfect. Miserable people, miserable people, don't you know that there's no way for us to tempt the saints too much? You're worse and more intolerant than God. Maybe the devil will hold up against you; you'd bring an angel to ruin.

"Let me go, put me out to those pastures," she said suddenly, with bracing heartiness, "come on, hurry up, don't you hear me?" And she assumed the position of a kitschy allegory of Echo, winking at me that she knows what she's doing and how it looks.

And again that three-note motif, which this time I recognized immediately, and which, before blossoming, drew itself out, separating us. But when she was already quite far away, as though behind numerous veils, but always curiously visible, that taut motif suddenly slackened, brightened up, and began to spin off into the helix of a tango, toward which the rondo theme from *Eine kleine Nachtmusik* ascended like a tendril. And Giggles, her finger on her lips, smiled, and then she declaimed, "The rondo of cheerful lads, the rondo of luminous thieves who rob people who've formed from the shadows, so as to serve that *beautiful* justice, according to which one must take from the poor even what little they have, that it might then be handed over to the rich.

"Do you hear?" she added from far off. "Do you see? Do you remember?"

And I understood that she meant that bar I'd dropped in on several days before. That tango was playing. There was dancing. Mutig danced, too. Quite openly, and with the tilted head of someone calculating distance.

But what Mutig was calculating was the span of time that had been granted to his dance partner. She knew it; why else would she press herself to him so urgently, pointlessly? The tango crept up behind Mutig like a lasso primed for action, but each time it was flung toward him on a heavily stressed beat Mutig's evil flared up and burned it away. He glittered with guileless cruelty—it suited him like dignity. It was on that day that the words were born on his lips: "You think it's fun being a god?" They would soon ripen anew, and Mutig, weeping, would revive himself on them, on them and the devastation of today's dance partner, whose dovish crime grows and grows. May she be more fortunate than Giggles, may she not meet her savior.

Giggles entered the bar and made straight for the bartender: "Have you seen Dédé? He didn't leave me a message? Dédé?" – The bartender slowly set aside his shaker, folded his arms in a sober and lordly manner, and said with a courtesy behind which skulked a pink slip: "Giggles, you don't work today. You have the best days: Saturdays and Thursdays. Don't you think you should scram? Dédé! Of course Dédé was here. But he's a guest, and you belong to the house: on Thursday and Saturday. Today's Wednesday."

Giggles walked away obligingly. – Mutig danced past her. "Hello there, Giggles," he called. She lowered her eyes, squinting them as though from light, and slipped past like a shadow. – Later, Mutig told me, "You see, I don't harbor unfriendly feelings toward her. But she died out in such a way that even her suffering brought her shame. If she at least despised me, if she at least couldn't despise me, but no: she doesn't *dare* despise me."

"Do you see, do you see what you've accomplished?"— I could hear it from far away, but such that even if Giggles had already disappeared, I had no doubt as to the smile with which she spoke. Literally as if I was seeing it, that smile of the propitiatory sacrifice: it crossed her lips like a late-arriving guest, without whom things can't get started, the same smile with which, on Rue Lamarck, she had passed that long needle to me across the table.

And this scene arose before me in such hallucinatory earnestness that I unwittingly called out, "Again, Giggles? Why? Haven't I already killed you?"

"Yes, but poorly," I heard, but with such inappropriately sparkling laughter I couldn't stand it and bolted in her direction on the off chance of catching up with Giggles, for I was beginning to suspect that she had withheld something significant from me, that she'd deceived me. So I ran out—oddly, I don't remember opening any doors as I was running out—and ended up on a long, straight street, which I ran down with a speed that I myself remarked as the insistence with which that street urged me to err, casting around for why, to such an extent, nothing here rings a bell. Then I oriented myself better; I was running through the same place I'd recently driven through in the cab with Fuld and Giggles, everything was again as it was then, only somehow more cursory. Thus I ran as far as the theatrical Saint-Cloud, this time for the most part abandoned, and sped through that aquatic landscape, relishing how skillfully I plotted my path through those narrow, grassy balks between the waters, for I sought the shortest way: the one toward that bend in the road that had so enticed me the first time, and that now seemed to me a truly imperative goal. When the bend again revealed itself to me on the horizon, I felt at the same time the surfacing of the thought that I had not, in fact, ascertained whether I might have already gotten my face back, it unsettled me a bit that this thought had arisen swiftly upon my spotting that damned bend in the road, but I drove this unsettlement away again relatively easily. I felt around my face, or around where by right and justice it should have been; touch ascertained nothing unusual, but I recalled that back when my face had expired, touch had betrayed nothing then, either, it had been some other sense of the hand that had pulled the alarm, a sense that in no way registered now. So I said to myself: "According to touch, everything's back to normal. But what does that prove?" – All the more did I put on speed, and I wasn't the least bit amazed when, having run up to the bend, I ascertained that that's where Paris began, and that's just the beginning of Rue d'Astorg; that is, the street where Fuld lived (it occurred to me that I hadn't seen him in several months). Paris begins at Rue d'Astorg, which begins again at Fuld's building, which is otherwise halfway down the street. This didn't confuse me, and actually, as I started running to the steps, I recognized it instantly, and thus I recognized that I'd come to the right place. My ring was answered by a swift "who's there," and when I said my name it was answered, swiftly again, with "that'll do, come in," and they opened for me. I should actually write that "the women" opened for me, since it was mostly women in the apartment, in thick black veils, and it seemed to me that there were far more of them than an altogether small apartment could reasonably accommodate. Altogether small, I say, and still it was a long time before I'd run as far as Fuld's room; I'd almost say farther than from my place to here, and one of the women, in whom I recognized Fuld's sister, escorted me along a line of the rest, speeding along with me.

"We've already removed him, he's in his coffin, we've been holding the funeral until you came to receive what he's bequeathed you."

"So what did he bequeath me?"

"He's bequeathed you his face."

"But which one, since he had two?"

"Oh," she said, slightly offended, "you mustn't choose. Take the one that's there. You'll make do."

"But how am I supposed to take such a bequest with me?"

"We've already inquired about that. All you have to do is kiss him."

At that very moment we ran into Fuld's room. He was, in fact, lying in a coffin. It was an amazingly unwistful, unmoving sight. And everything happened so fast, like it was on fire. I leaned over and gave him a sort of kiss, like picking up a parcel forgotten in haste, and returned for in greater haste still.

And I galloped back out again, marveling only at how indifferent I was in my soul, and with a thought to nothing but my running.

I stopped in front of the building, as if this had been arranged, and in fact now the streets and roads, the city, the buildings and landscapes had broken into a canter. I stood there waiting for my building to run by. I already saw it from a distance. But the closer it was, the realer everything somehow became, and the spectacle of the world's becoming-real—if I can put it that way—was quite thrilling, quite absorbing. Most absorbing of all, however, was the question of where that notion of becoming-real had emerged from within me, to whom everything past already seemed equally real, but I didn't dwell at all on the question of its reality. "Is there something more real than reality?" I made quite a point of saying "than reality," as opposed to "than an apparent reality."

At last our building ran by—and verily, the convincingness of the phenomenal world reached such a level that there was no resisting it: the "it's true" that I said to myself I said sort of in the way one probes the thing that is most beyond doubt—not to say the only thing beyond doubt—like saying, in certain instances, "I love." – At last, then, our building ran by, it was morning, the porter's wife was standing at the front door, she was shaking out the mat. I greeted her and walked past. She called after me:

"And where, may I ask, are you going?"

"How's that?" I turned.

"I'm asking, where are you going?"

"But Mrs. —," and I kept walking.

"Joking aside," she said after me. "Where are you going?"

So I took up the ironic joke and said with a bow:

"To Mr.—'s," and I said my own name.

"Mr.— is not at home," she replied.

Under such circumstances, life is no plaything.

On top of that, at the last minute we learn that Fuld, whom I have not seen for several months now, has died.

(November 1929–March 1930–March 1931)

THE GAME FOR THE HONOR
OF PAYBACK

He had already covered such an infinitude that the one that lay before him was no cause for alarm. From the futility of the effort he'd expended he drew comfort for the futility to come. He was swimming through a subterranean tunnel and against a foul current. He was struggling with a courageous and resolute crawl, not against the flow—for it was a slow sewer—so much as against its, as though material, nastiness. The archway lowered so much in places that he had to immerse his head to swim through. Repulsive things touched his face. He was disgusted with himself and grew angry. After all, no one had instructed him to look after his own skull. Why, then, did he keep worrying about it? The only thing they'd directed him to do was to swim against this reeking stream; nothing more. He was supposed to be content with this. Like a laborer disabused of enthusiasm, he promised himself that next time he'd no longer worry about his head, and, what's more, he was done with this work. For he hated his head, he knew it's a workshop for manufacturing poisons to counter counter-poisons. But as soon as the lowered archway posed the next threat, he immersed his head again. He was somehow figuring out why, after all, even in this filth with no end in sight, he felt like remaining alive for as long as he had strength to. It was out of curiosity, which he despised. And the more futilely he checked it, the more he despised it: he was curious about what it could be, the twinkling point of light the size of a pinhead somewhere in the distance before him, this pinhead that seemed to have grown each time he surfaced, though he denied that it had really grown. But the curiosity was stronger than faith, stronger than loathing, and when he weighed it out he was compelled toward the bitter admission that, though he despised it, he could do nothing but swim, despite his spite. He got as far as denial: there's no twinkling pinhead; he was swimming through darkness and into darkness. But hardly had he denied it than it grew markedly, and he inferred that it had grown so much merely because he had placed so much hope in its growth. One more powerful crawl, one more dive, which he so detested, just a little more, a little more effort (what's this, against everything he has already overcome?), one more little half-stroke—oh, light!

Someone's eyes have opened. Timidly at first. But then enough that, between the still half-caked lashes, a ray of light got through. The eyes, rolled back beneath their lids, tasted it. And having ascertained that it was a ray of light from the actual day, they smashed through the barriers. The emerging sun was throwing the bed into disarray. On the bed, a man. His eyes were open. You could see that they were longing for that brightness, that they were enchanted by it, that they clung to it greedily. You could also see that they were shyly, silently suspicious of it. Keen observers such as yourselves would miss neither that enthusiastic greed, nor that dusky suspicion. They would have discerned that it was an old suspicion, a suspicion that had been coddled, weaned on a subtle flaw and fattened on it; overfed on a flaw burrowed deep like a tapeworm. Keen observers such as yourselves would discern that that look says to the sun: "You're cheating on me, too, *because* I love you."

That's you, the keen ones. He, however, is not keen. He has only joy and, for that reason, fear. But fear only smolders. In the meantime, all we have here is a roused sleeper who's gained his sight. He'd gained it quite well, for the first thing he'd spotted was the king bird-of-paradise with the iridescent and alluringly curled tail. The broad-shouldered palm frond—upon which the bird is perched so lightly that it seems as if it were holding itself up—is aware of the lovely spiral of the bird-of-paradise's tail and has grown beautiful for it, God knows how. That spiral's musical loveliness pursues the neighboring bird along a pink liana; it also inspired the branch of "little hearts," a vestige of the mercy (let us say, of the good fortune) that alighted upon the embarrassment of the artist who designed this wallpaper. There's the bird-of-paradise, there's the liana, there's the branch of little hearts, but there are such throngs of them, and their relations are governed by a rhythm so inexorably regular, that a universe arises within the universe. The new, encouraging, personal, and exclusive universe of a man only just awakened. And it happens that disinterested gravitational laws had just then felt like pouring brightness into what was nothing more and nothing other than a metrical universe of birds-of-paradise, lianas, and little hearts. Everything else is still in non-being. The cheap wallpaper, however, *is*, significantly and unproblematically.

On the bed lies an isolated person, a nameless person. And rightly so, since his name is Shame, and that's no name for a human being. But he doesn't know yet what his name is, for he's hardly woken up. That means that, regardless of the fact that he's already forgotten the land he's returning from, where people never have any shame, because the only thing they have there is the high-minded wisdom of animals and objects, he hasn't yet thought back on himself. It's no longer, and not yet, real; it's the most beautiful moment he could ask of waking.

He had gone to sleep late, and after a day of robbery. For precisely this reason, and having waded through a dream that was, as always, merely a more pronounced sense of the preceding day, he wakes up with the sun. The window of the family boarding house where he has been sleeping faces east. He is the first and silent witness to the luminous bloodletting between the day, which has struck all of a sudden, and the night, which is no coward. The light has not triumphed, but triumph it will. The darknesses cover themselves in twilight, but even this rearguard is already losing hope; it, too, is turning to flee. The light is still struggling; its empire is not, as yet, getting old, for it is still struggling; it is a dominion only just founded, unsteady for now; it is imperious and skittish like a youth to whom decline has not yet given a thought. It is a brief light, undoubting and kindred, as only that which is from us can be. The awakened man wakes in that dream on the edge of waking, toward which sleepers wade, those who have nodded off beneath the open sky and have been struck with a spike of sun nearing its peak, a spike as slenderly efficacious as a mosquito's proboscis. Just as it is for them, so too is it for him, that he doesn't wake up so much as he revives: he's the one who revived the birds-of-paradise, the lianas, and the little hearts before him, before him the darkness and its rearguard are fleeing. He is himself the triumphant light, for it takes his side as zealously as one should only side with oneself. He is a light within which this somewhat absurd land is sinking, but it's a land that is naturally and invulnerably absurd. It's an impossible land, but it's truly, indispensably, and reliably impossible. He knows it from somewhere already. It's the same one that recently washed him ashore, and which he'd already nearly forgotten. Now that he's aware of it, he is also aware of why he hadn't been aware of it till now: he hadn't been aware of it because he'd been identical with it. He knows he is happy.

He is happy. But because he has become aware of it, he's already less so. He recognizes it by a sort of disappointment that has broken in to rob him. He already knows what this disappointment is: that he won't get to go back... back somewhere. But where? Where? He'd be glad, at least, to see that far, but how can you see as far as somewhere that can no longer be visualized? What one can no longer visualize... What else is it—but how natural! And still how slowly it dawns on us nonetheless!—what is it but that which he hasn't recognized? Now he's on the right track: what he hasn't recognized, and where he nevertheless has an urge to go back to, is that perfect happiness of which one is unaware. He feels like going back to where he was unknowingly happy. He isn't afraid for his happiness, but he's aware of it; he's capable of sizing it up; he is— so it isn't an infinite happiness; so it's an endangered happiness. If he starts measuring it up, he'll get to its limits. He's afraid of this, but a proprietary instinct is stronger than fear. His hands, till now folded beneath his head, have shifted—they slide, they grope, they stretch. They've jerked, righted themselves; they were pondering. They've sensed, as it were, a new, unknown state. It was strange; it was an awakening. It was the recognition that he, who until now had not known anything about himself beyond that he is, had also already been, and would yet be. It was him discovering duration and sequence, it was the discovery of past and future. He had reached into a tangle of little snakes. The screeching birds-of-paradise, swaying lianas, and beating "little hearts" went quiet and froze, like magic. They went quiet under a shadow so unnaturally sudden and dark that the awakened man shifted his head to ascertain its cause.

What did he see that was so god-awful that his extremities, envenomed by a hideous, rushing spasm, now lie so mortally limp? I know, for this man is my affair. But do you understand, you whose name is not Shame? – This spasm of his extremities, this terror—it was because, having turned his head, he recognized that the day, the day beneath the heavens, was unspoiled in its ardor; that the shadow that had fallen had not crept in from there. From where, then? Where, then, did this purgative of colors and cries come from, of birds-of-paradise, lianas, and "little hearts"—where, if not from within him, this person?

He saw the blaring day raised on a fiery baroque pillar, but he was waking up in the rattling daybreak that rouses the condemned and ushers in the day he has feared for so long, hoping and despairing of hope, and that is, faithfully, as he had feared: ashily authentic, with hands dejectedly folded.

"...but then maybe Zinaida didn't believe it after all. Zinaida surely didn't believe it for a second. So what if it seemed...She didn't believe it—it can't be!—she didn't believe it."

Zinaida was a name that hadn't just popped up here. Fine, then, if it has already appeared, he knows where to put it. He isn't embarrassed about it. The name Zinaida is pliable and bent, like a tendril—a tendril so deliciously curved that the eyes can't resist it. They descend along it slowly and cautiously, as though down a trail through wilderness. The eyes are making good progress down it; their faith in it is steadfast. The name Zinaida is worthy of such faith. It leads, knowing precisely where to, no matter that it feigns indifference as to where it leads.

At first, lying there, he noticed the name; then, sitting up and hugging his knees, he stared at it; and a moment later, looking again at the cretonne wallpaper and realizing that he was now looking at it, he caught on that he'd gotten here by Zinaida's name, that it had led him here. The birds-of-paradise, lianas, and "little hearts" had now snuck out of the shadow again, things had cleared up, but quietly, like a legend that no one tells anymore. Something is replenishing it, dragging it out, he'd overlooked it till now: to the universe of birds-of-paradise, lianas, and "little hearts" there now also belongs a Chinese pagoda with two small figures. One of them is Zinaida. Luck. But maybe it's not merely luck that the pagoda with the little figures, all of them together, form, as it were, something tantamount to a name. That name: Zinaida.

The many things that can come of the name Zinaida! Now, now it has become so transparent that it is as if nothing. You see through it.

Through it you see yesterday morning; through it you see how he had gotten up with newborn ardor like that of newcomers, when they've awoken somewhere they've never been before, and where they'd only just arrived the night before in the dark. The yard of the old mill between the dense willows and the millhouse; the slow, rich stream that crept down beneath the shed, where the dismantled mill components loll about. A stream that fades away, that is, that leads astray; beyond its subsequent fate, which seems mysterious and is merely smallish: a meadow with a horizon beyond our sight, and the mill pool, before which the stream has slowed in the meantime, and where it will momentarily laze. In the yard, its black, furtively flowing water looked out over nothing more than the layabout lounging in the verdure; it issued a vague, noncommittal, rather suspicious promise. It was on just this promise that he had set off for the meadowlands. He was thinking of taciturn hobos who've grown so accustomed to their stride that even their stance is as if in motion, and being seated is merely as though another way of walking, indifferent to where, and yet still not without need: they, too, drag those alluring and admonitory promises behind them, like fluttering veils. – You can see (see through the gauzy name Zinaida) how he'd come to the pool, removed his sandals, pulled off his pajamas, and dipped his legs. Before him, a maple shrub like a straw basket, with birdsong. You can see him sitting between two little birches. The youths in Jan Preissler's paintings, too, sit beneath birch trees. You could see that he is a beautiful youth, for in such dawning it's a short way from *was* to *is*. Along the grassy trail—velvet—a girl walks with a pail. She's arrived at the pool, said hello, readied herself to gather water. He's shifted, for he'd been in the way. He's lifted his head, for he'd ventured to think that from *was* to *is* it's a short way for real, and this notion has given him courage.

"Please, sir, don't trouble yourself. Did you sleep well?"

The word *sir* was not only a word, it immediately transformed into a cloud that you could see. But it was a light cloud, artless, unembittered, since it was a cloud for play-acting. Not much more had happened than the distance from *was* to *is* had grown slightly. He was no longer quite a Preissler youth, but you could see him better: sitting on a fairy-tale-white, unsaddled horse, holding it by the mane, he was naked. The white horse stamped at the maple shrub, moved off, softly disappeared. It left a virginal silence, it inserted the possibility of regret, that is, it also inserted memories, that is, the past. The present had washed away all imaginary boundaries. He had the silence to thank for that. It occurred to him that what he had just experienced happened to wise men all the time.

"Would you like to do me a favor? Don't call me 'sir.' Talk to me naturally. I don't call you 'miss.'"

"As you wish, sir."

"Not 'as you wish, sir'; 'as you wish.'"

"As you wish, then. – But if I'm to talk to you naturally, then you have to do the same with me. They call me Zinaida."

"A name for a princess."

"Around here, for a country girl."

They looked into each other's eyes, he sitting, she from above.

"No sir has ever ordered me to talk naturally before."

She drew out the "sir."

"But Zinaida—I'm not ordering you, I'm asking you."

"How… Darn!" (And quickly:) "How odd you are."

She said no more. But everything she did next, be it gathering water, walking away, or balancing herself with her left hand at arm's length, was different from what it would have been were he not here. He was sure of it. It was precisely and pleasantly according to a rhythm of which he was the sir, and the rhythm was that of the circulation of his blood. Even the fact of her having stopped halfway toward her departure— she'd stopped for nothing whatsoever—of her having turned, of her having smiled, was according to that rhythm's will. And when she'd again gathered the pail and gone further, her distanced left hand swayed to that rhythm, to the rhythm of his blood. – – –

That person is sitting on his bed, hugging his knees; a person sitting on a bed like this is a person awakened with a ready-made faith. The disinterestedly languid look of the person awakened with a ready-made faith has come to rest on his feet. The person has given his forehead a fleeting pass, bitten into his bottom lip, and said, scolding:

"But no . . . it's not true. Why say something that isn't true? —
Again: one more time!"

He stretched his left leg, propped himself on his left arm,
sat a bit to one side. He was sitting sort of in mid-leap. He
again stared into Zinaida's name. Having firmly resolved to see
beyond it . . . "No cock-and-bull," he said, "only what's really
beyond it, that and nothing more."

Everything as it was initially: You can see him sitting by
the pool; you can see Zinaida coming to fetch water. This time,
however, he doesn't make room for her.

"How did you sleep, sir?" the girl asks.

This time, no Gesslerian "would you care to do me a favor,"
this time only the formally democratic: "Sir? You know, I'd
rather you spoke to me naturally—simply by my name."

"As you wish," the girl answers through her teeth and
almost shyly.

"I don't know how to exteriorize," the person sitting on
the bed says bitterly, and he fixes his disappointed gaze on the
sheet, "if I wanted her to speak to me naturally, I wanted it out
of a fervent human need," (he said "out of a fervent human
need," was ashamed for having said it, and relished his shame)
"and look, it's a wonder I wasn't peeved to arrange it. Why
peeved? As always—out of shame for my most noble feelings."

Here, however, a grimace so overcame him that he released
his right knee, too. He lay back down. He hissed, "But why am
I lying? Again! I arrived the day before yesterday, in the dark.
I got up. The window opens out to the meadows." (He turned
his head: the window really did lead out to the meadows. He
turned his head away again, reassured.) "I was looking out the
window. I saw the trail, the pool. I didn't take the footpath; I
wasn't by the pool. Why would I have said I was by the pool
if I wasn't? I didn't meet Zinaida there. She didn't tell me that

her name's Zinaida. I know because it's what they said when they called for her. When she first brought me lunch, I said to her, 'Thank you, but you've forgotten the bread, Zinaida.' And look, that's how it was. So much for the idyll by the pool!"

The name Zinaida coiled up. It's just a name. Not even that. They're just letters of the alphabet.

To fix the future—alright then: let's fix the future. Legal self-defense. For Christ's sake, where would he draw his strength from if he couldn't tell lies, if he were never allowed to lie to himself... for instance, if he couldn't lie to himself about plundering, about how he lives amid desolation, and this desolation can't be dislodged.

Where would he draw his strength from were he never allowed to take a break from the certainty that if a dead-end street tapers so much that you can no longer even turn around on it, that if on that street, over and over, he must constantly confront this irrevocable, this hideous thing that lay in wait behind him, then it is he himself who is barring his way, with his deeds, with his selfishness, with his hard and wimpy intolerance. To spin a yarn about the future, fine: self-defense. But to do it with the past—cowardice! Not a yarn, a lie. But what a durable lie it is. It takes so much work to really tear it down. Who would have said that lies have such solid foundations? As though they weren't even lies anymore. Maybe they're just alternative truths? Truths that have been squandered. He sometimes knows simultaneously both how it was and how it ought to have been. But he only knows. He doesn't recognize. What if what ought to have been was more real than what is? This eager, quiet, poetical youth by the pool! Why did that squandered potential have less of a right to be believed than an imposed necessity does? Either everything is questionable—and then questionable, too, would be the fact that he himself is—or else there is at least one reliable entity: him; but then he is both in his own fancy and in his own truth. Then nothing is in vain.

Not even the fact that in this numb awakening, that with the first frosty announcement of yesterday, he'd wanted Zinaida *not to believe* "it." Which Zinaida—for are there so many, were there so many. . . ? The one that had laughed at him by the pool? But come now—that one's been gone a long time, he'd finally, fearlessly, broken up with her.

Which Zinaida, then? Another one, an entirely different one: the sinister Zinaida, the one no one would steal away from him; the Zinaida of early evening; the Zinaida shuffling toward the table where he is waiting for his supper; the Zinaida carrying a writing pad, and on it an inkwell, pen, and registration form; the Zinaida whom he asks: "What's the hurry? Right before supper?" The Zinaida who is standing with her back to him and answering in a rasping voice: "Yes—yes—a hurry—the master said right away, sir"; the Zinaida with those slightly bowed arms, which she twitches; an animal, you'd say, on an oppressive chain.

The person on the bed bared his teeth and angrily nodded his head.

At last, he'd grasped the *true* beginning. Now post-haste, yes? Now post-haste.

And for starters: how could he drop everything and go out to the yard? A beautiful excuse: he couldn't, it would seem, surmise . . . Ridiculous! He surmised quite well. Still, he was at the point where the first little flames of alarm flared up. And yet, he was the only one there. The sole outside witness. The fact that he loathed the ostentatious manners of the Steels, is that any excuse? Those extravagant manners of theirs! Only he would have to watch himself with these extravagant manners!

It's not so certain that he had loathed these people immediately upon seeing them from the table, as they were driving in. It's quite possible that he had been utterly indifferent to them. That they hadn't had extravagant manners whatsoever. It cannot be exluded that he is now, yet again, reaching out for some "mitigating circumstance." He knows them, these jolly old mitigating circumstances of his, his supplementary moral alibis. He would have to watch himself; he knows how things go with these deceits: they're as indispensable to him as a snare to a poacher.

The person on the bed understands, but let's be careful, let's really watch ourselves. Let's not insult him, let's not exaggerate; let's be fairer than he is himself. Let's follow his thinking impartially and accept that, however nice it would be "that he had loathed them immediately as they were driving in," he is forestalling his wish not to be this thought's father—let's say he's at least making it as tough as it could be . . . For he well surmises that if he so wishes "that he had already loathed them then," it's because later on what happened was . . . the thing that only happened later. Or else he's seeking whatever alibi is available, but he'd settle for any of them—oh, how poorly you know him! After all, the alibi has to be a *little* likely. Sure, our good sir is a liar, but the gourmet kind; a crook, but a refined one. Excuse himself, sure—but make excuses, of all manner besides—not at all! Really: if he must be objective, he'd prefer to say, after all, that they, the ones driving in, were all the same to him, rather than loathsome. It is equally certain, however, that he had already begun despising them before the alarm, even if the little word "despise" might be a bit much; let's say that, already before the alarm, he'd come to hate them.

"Very well, my dear fellow," he says, the man on the bed, but he had come to hate them perchance just when, and only when, the innkeeper pattered up to the table where he was waiting for his supper and said, *in a most courteous manner,* "A gentleman has arrived with two ladies. A couple, and the wife's sister. The young woman is unwell, they would like her room to be next to theirs. I do have two rooms, only not next to each other; yours is between them. *Would you be so kind* as to let them have it?" – Might it have been just then that he'd started to hate them? – Hmm? You'd have let them have it. – How did he respond to that courteous "if you would be so kind"?

He who was sitting on the bed hugging his naked knees slowly turned his head and spotted himself in the mirrored dresser. – Well, no, he didn't flinch—nothing that would attest to fright, no straightening, no crouching—he didn't shoot faces at himself... Nothing... Why, then? The image in the mirror wasn't hideous. Of course it revolted him, but he got used to it. For that matter, I'm not betraying any secret if I whisper to you that he *wanted* to be revolted by it. Oh, willingly, yet so quietly as actually to be inadvertent. Having caught sight of that one there, his eyes got stuck on him. He saw someone who was unwelcome; he was, however, expectedly unwelcome. A foreigner. He sized him up with tepid animosity; he judged him with gestures and facial expressions. That one there performed them with him: both of them ironic, but with an irony so unsuspiciously innocent that it was disarming. A hand, sullen with a sullenness that lacked substance, ran across ashen stubble; squeamish fingers unearthed the degrading vegetation of the sparse, coarse hairs sprouting all the way up to right beneath his eyes, and the irritated flash in his eyes reproached them for this meddlesomeness. – The sitting man stood, stripped naked, approached the dresser closely, saw his entire self in the mirror. He stood in profile, for he felt like a look, and to get a good look at the bloated belly he was stroking with disgust. But because he wanted to have a *good* look at that *sign* (that's what he was thinking: it was a sign), he was required to turn his head slightly, and so it happened that he unwittingly *came eye-to-eye* with himself: he caught sight of a rotund runt of a man wearing an accusing look. He scowled at him, and the little person paid it back to him so faithfully that neither of them dared pull his eyes away: for they hated each other, and they were on their guard to avoid anything that would mutually entitle them each to take the other for a coward. This made for an awkward spectacle, but they wouldn't have fled from it for anything in the world. They looked themselves over with chivalrous superiority; they got so very sick of each other that the sickness inadvertently expressed itself through a kind of negative indifference. They saw the curdled face with the moronic, short beard, they saw that it was their collective face, but each was recriminating the other with his eyes: "How hideous you are," the eyes were saying to the eyes, "how can anyone be so hideous!" Then a hand appeared, the right hand. Two symmetrical right hands. The hands lifted eyelids that had collapsed into over-deep eye sockets! "The human eye should be *just so* round, *just so* free and deep, it's not shy, it doesn't hide," they hissed at each other. "And the hand? What about the hand?" the eye shot back. "Yes," the hateful doubles' bashful eyes confessed, "even your hand could have been spry, captivating, maybe beautiful, if only..." That's it: if only someone hadn't betrayed it. "Who?" thought he who was looking into the mirror. "Who?" replied the indifferent image, but one "who?" was the answer to the other. They comprehended at once—and through this recognition they were reconciled— that by questioning they had found, within their cleft insides, not just the question, but the answer as well, an unexpected answer, yet by no means amazing. Actually, it wasn't even an answer to that double "who?"—for the words that streamed simultaneously within them sounded like: "Hallowed be their names." And yet still, it was surely a kind of answer; perhaps an answer to a question still more binding, and therefore quieter, than those "who's" had been, so that it rendered them ugly cripples, for these unexpected words swiftly imparted to them remarkable and still more unexpected courage. The courage to quit that double self-torture. The hands fell, and the looks, which followed ashamedly behind them, meanwhile assumed so much restraint that, having incidentally brushed against the short legs and outturned feet, neither rebuked them, nor punished them.

He arched the small of his back, turned away, and was now sitting on the bed again. From there, again, onto a last brief and careless expedition to the mirror. That other fellow had been there the whole time. Their gazes brushed against their bald chests with disinterested severity, then they lifted.

Yes, it had been his fault. "I was accused unjustly, but not spitefully; things looked bad for me; I shouldn't have walked away." He took pleasure in succeeding to be impartial even in his own suit; he assured himself of it and softened. Just let someone come forward who would dare rebuke him for self-flattery! Just let someone speak up who's misheard that he assigns the responsibility for that misunderstanding to himself, and to no one else! Maybe then he could expect to be believed now as well, when he maintains (he raised his eyes) that, admittedly, after the first alarm he made off at the wrong time, but with an innocent heart. Yes, he ascribed no meaning to the episode with the bracelet. So how could one foresee the consequences—right? He had gone down to the yard because he was really hungry. The time for supper had already passed; no one can deny that. Even so, he can say that he had been hit with a hunger that was not only physical, but spiritual as well (he stroked his chin): he had begun to miss a book he'd started reading and had left downstairs on the table. And when he went back down—believe it or not—he got so into it that, for a moment, he forgot about that episode *entirely*. He still remembers how he had looked up, having been interrupted by the swift shutting of the kitchen door, and how, having noticed Zinaida, he pushed the book away: this made room for the bowl of soup, for he was as sure as water is wet that she was bringing soup. What a surprise when, instead of the steaming bowl, she placed before him the pad with the ink well and the pen sticking out of it! A surprise, yes; but how unsuspicious! How could he have missed such conspicuous things, words, and gestures, and so many of them, he marveled at it only a moment later, that is, when the lid's last clamp had been twisted shut, and when, suddenly gasping beneath it, he somehow retroactively ascertained that the methodical forging of that lid had begun precisely upon Zinaida's arrival. He was astonished and did not comprehend how he could be so absurdly unobservant. Maybe he was unknowingly following some ban on comprehending. And it was just then that she had come with the registration, at such an unusual moment! Only, how could he have missed that it had been intentional? And when he came back around from his pure (yes, pure) surprise and said sullenly, "There's no hurry; I'll fill it out after supper," how could he have missed that Zinaida's reply was as though filled with stubborn silence and spiteful rigidity?

"Well, then, Zinaida, go get me my soup."

Then, with her back to him, and with that peculiar movement of her slightly outstretched hands (this in particular was lodged in his memory; "as if she'd torn herself from some oppressive chain," he says), she, curtly:

"It's police orders. The master says, sir, that you've already been staying here for twenty-four hours...That it has to be right away..."

And this time, too, he did nothing; this time, too, he still felt like teasing. (Teasing!)

"Sir, Zinaida? Has a *sir* been staying here? What about our agreement!" Yes, and all the while he was staring ravenously at her bowed neck—in the already oblique sunlight flaxen down was *prattling* there. (And it was a shame for him to admit that he'd actually said "prattling" to himself.)

He's sitting on the bed, like at first. With his chin on his knee, willingly obedient to the strict auto-prohibition against looking into the mirror. And to this suspicious willingness to sweep up after yesterday's awkward misunderstanding (saying "misunderstanding," he twists his lips, but without being aware of it, and in particular without being aware that he is twisting them with the same violence he'd just used to coax the little word, "misunderstanding," from himself) for which he himself had been responsible. But the sticking point—even if it's merely a trifle—the sticking point is in the sweeping up. He's thinking clearly, he's thinking very clearly, he knows himself well, he knows where he has prepared stratagems for dodging the question, or pawning it off, and being aware of them, he bypasses them. It's odd, really, that his excessive willingness to trivialize the event is somehow a sticking point, and that it sticks by merely a trifle. For if he hasn't known till now just how tiny of a hitch it is, he knows the hitch is tiny. The fact of his having fallen into innocent suspicion now amounts to little—to nothing—for the suspicion has been removed from him. But that Zinaida also... For Zinaida *also* believed it—oh, surely, she surely believed it—and that she also believed is just the thing that makes you wonder. Makes you wonder, for three reasons. For three, also, are the reasons why, if all the others were gullible, Zinaida didn't have to be: first off, for the idyll by the pool (he knew that there had been no idyll by the pool, but he leaped over this lie like an escaping thief over a fence, without looking back); secondly, that she alone had seen him as suspicious with a suspicion yet to be manifest; thirdly, that she knew better than anyone how indiscriminate false suspicions are, since, before him, wasn't it she who had been suspected—hmm?

But the willingness to trivialize is a sticking point, and it sticks "by a Zinaida." It's stuck on the fact that Zinaida also *was capable* of believing it. In spite of everything. That's it! Now's he's got it: *she was capable*. Capable? Why not just say she believed? No semantics, please: she believed, or she was capable of believing—two sides of the same coin. But the only thing still winking toward semantics is: if even Zinaida was capable, then we might suppose that, in spite of everything, she had a reason. But if, in spite of everything, even she had a reason to believe, then we might suppose the reason to believe *was*. – Semantics? Hold on. Let us recall, point the first: *there was a why*.

Again his eyes fell upon the cretonne wallpaper. Strange that this time no one gave up: the cretonne wallpaper remained cretonne wallpaper; the memory of the sham-pastoral by the pool remained mere mechanical association. No matter! That morning had begun with a fairy tale out of a Preissler painting nevertheless. Now he knows what it meant: that's where he had been fleeing to unwittingly, from a humiliating yesterday, even before the memory had drifted back to him. He had been fleeing into make-believe. Why, if not from genuine shame? And if he had been hiding behind that fellow there by the pool, behind that fellow whom he had never been and could never be, now he knows the why for that as well: when in need, we are nostalgic for our antipode. The one by the pool whom he wanted to be, and for whom he'd invented the devoted Zinaida, was his antipode: one of those people *who are untouched by shame.*

Of his having stolen the bracelet? Look at my hands; turn out my pockets—nothing there! Innocent! You can see it, after all, if someone's innocent! Zinaida couldn't *not* see that he was innocent—oh, she couldn't! Yes, suspicion had fallen upon the innocent, but might it have fallen by chance upon a person *fit for ignominy?* But someone whom ignominy fits—you can see that, too. Aha! Suppose that Zinaida saw it as well. That he was innocent by chance? Just that: by chance! Accuse a proud man – – he'll rise. Within the marked man, you churn the settled dregs. Zinaida wasn't deceiving herself; she well saw how ignominy fancies him. *But how blindly he'd walked into it!* Shame had arranged it so beautifully: he took to it like a mouse to bacon fat. What cunning work ignominy had made of him!

Initially, it played it haughty: "Yield my room? What a nuisance, moving, when I've barely settled in," it whispered to him. Then, generously: "So be it, I'll yield my room. But you people move my things yourself. I don't want to know anything about it. I'm weary." Was that all? No, not yet. Ignominy turned itself into petty unease: "If you don't come help, your things will go missing, your things will get mixed up, maybe they'll even be stolen." His ignominy had turned into a perfection- ist; his ignominy rebelled; it held out; he was embarrassed to submit to this pettiness, but ignominy invents it: abracadabra, and the old-lady fear for one's allegedly endangered effects has already found a pretext to come to their aid "with head held high." Oh, with head held high! ... In his dregs, there were always pretexts galore. It was enough for him to close his eyes and stir them a bit. Does he hear? Ha—like he wouldn't! Ignominy feigns nobility: "Maidservants toil enough during the day as it is. Now on top of that they're to move your things! Run and help them; it'll be kind of you." Did it end there? Not even close! Ignominy really outdid itself that evening: when he finally got up, and went to oversee his effects (to help, he said), he would have sworn that he had been spurred "by some convivial-sounding affability." This master of two-faced-ness, and of the hardest sort: being two-faced with yourself.

They'd set it up superbly, superbly! Hardly had the ignominy gotten through its lie than the whole world lied itself to pieces. Except that the ignominy pretended it was lying for his sake, and that the world was just lying... purely. But with such conviction that it out-lied the truth.

And yet he was right there when the burning match fell into the powder: "Honey, I left my bracelet next door on the washbasin; be a dear and go get it for me." Misfortune sometimes enters so modestly, a world-weary old woman: "Just a moment, good people, to warm myself by the hearth, don't trouble yourselves." You'll only flash it an unwitting glance, no differently than if you were offering it an absent greeting. – "Honey... go and bring it to me, it's next door, on the basin." No more than a skip and a jump, from one room to the next; and yet how everything came to hinge on its not being hindered in its movement. No one noticed it at first, not the servant girls, nor Mr. Steel, nor his sister; nor did Mrs. Steel suspect whom it would actually let in.

"Honey... go get it for me." Misfortune snuck into the room behind him so innocently, just as he was closing his duffle; so innocently that he glanced toward it; he glanced at the basin; that's right, just like that, where he would have suspected...

"No, it's not here, you're mistaken." Mr. Steel came in right behind the unwelcome little saint.

"But it's there. I'm certain of it."

Then our man had another look at the basin. Today, he'd almost say that he did indeed notice something there this time: a double-dealing wallflower, still crouching, but now only still crouching... Today... Only, today is not yesterday.

Yesterday it wasn't the wallflower standing there; it was Mr. Steel, and he was looking in vain where there was nothing.

"Ridiculous! It's not here." And the words "You didn't happen to see a bracelet, did you?" were more to take him for their witness than to ask him.

That's just when things started to get ugly. That is, today he might almost say that things had started to get ugly just then. But today is not yesterday. Yesterday it was "merely starting to get to him." Mr. Steel's passing from room to room was working on his nerves; the alternating "I'm certain it's there" – "I'm telling you it's not" – bore into him like an auger; the wretched repetition of "a nasty business" was as irritating as an old woman rattling off her rosary. But he clenched his teeth and, despite this not being his fire to put out, he helped rummage: he poked around in his linen, his ties, he even opened his already-closed duffle and dug around in there. At last he exploded, "A nasty business, yes, and especially for me. This is the thanks I get!"

That's right! "This is the thanks I get," he said, the moron. What could have compelled him to say "this is the thanks I get"?! That's how to get in with them. – And he nevertheless managed to drop the whole thing immediately and go outside. Weird. – Weird? And what's weird about it, if you please? Might he not have a clean conscience? He'd had quite enough of this. Had he acted rashly? Sure. And what of it?

Yesterday it didn't look like he'd set a trap for destiny. (Oh, destiny has something up its sleeve.) Yesterday it looked merely as though he were fleeing an unpleasant marital scene that had nothing to do with him. He was stricken with blindness, just like that—like anyone who should be destroyed. Had he not been stricken with blindness, how would he, now sitting again at the table and waiting for his supper, have overlooked the disorder visited upon him? Stricken with blindness? I should say so! How else would it have escaped him that things had gotten off track? And he, meanwhile, was as if in a trance. It's true: he'd been stricken a bit by Zinaida's having stopped speaking naturally to him. Yes, but it had struck him in his naïve and unsuspecting mind (yes: he literally says "naïve and unsuspecting"). But how did it happen that he was able not to sense that tremendous breakdown, tarrying all by his lonesome in the garden, so long and so late? Nothing doing; not even those three old perfectionist schoolmarms... How's that? Not even the schoolmarms? Argh! But all the same, they came; all the same, he saw them come back from their walk, sit down, beckon toward him; he thanked them, after all... God, how to confront the fact that he saw, he saw with his own eyes, when the maidservant ran up, when she whispered something to them... that he saw them hastily stand up and *trot away*... that he saw them ally themselves with the prattling little circle in front of the kitchen.... How to confront the fact that he saw everything as though not seeing it?

He caught a heavy aftertaste; not, it happened, on his palate, but by some importunately new sense he surmised that he was entirely within it, within this aftertaste, and that it was the aftertaste of yesterday. Not from the iniquity, the calumny and injustice, so much as from the pestilent circle of disdain that had wreathed him yesterday in the garden, and from how unctuously simpleminded he'd been in allowing himself to be wreathed in it. Weird! Yesterday, nothing. He tastes this pestilent taste of contempt only now that he's been cleared again, now that they've asked his forgiveness. Weird? Yes—if they've cleared him rightfully, asked his forgiveness, if they've rightfully regaled him with a glass of champagne (for when it was "all over," they regaled him with a glass of champagne). But what if it wasn't rightful? – And he immediately beheld, like it was an exact, like it was a sharp drawing—graphically, somehow, devil take it!—that he was depraved, blameworthy, worse than blameworthy, because he had been cleared through deceit. He saw it as a hazardous footpath by which, with courage, he would surely get where he had to go, where he would be relieved of "it all"..., but that was just it: now the lonely view upon this footpath, from below, from its very base, gave him such vertigo, such massive vertigo, that he bent his head as though before a blow. Only it was him! He, such a virtuoso at circumventing tough roads! He who excels in the art of concocting easy detours, and, in an art much tougher still: that of assuring himself that those highways laid down at someone else's expense are actually more difficult than the trails leading to... Well, no, he won't say where, he won't! He might as well just throw himself into the abyss.

The window was wide open, the cock's crow waning, the hens were harassing him. Only the lark's song, a song as conspicuous as a custom-made, valuable treasure, strove to be worthy of the new day and the gurgling of the stream, which was answered by nothing besides its own quieting at the verge of the pool (that pool), like on a Sunday; and it was, in fact, a Sunday.

"Depraved, blameworthy, and worse than blameworthy! The pestilent aftertaste of contempt! As though stricken with pestilence!" – "Really? Really?" he pokes fun at himself.

And why, I ask? – Because the old schoolmarms had *scurried off* in fright? He strokes his knees. Scurrying old schoolmarms! Maybe they had a poor old woman's terror of being infected by a marked man . . . Retrospective condolences for your past terrors, respected ladies! What a fool he is! A moment earlier he'd been running down the whole litany of yesterday's iniquities: that they had all come to ask his forgiveness *afterward* he'd somehow forgotten to mention. How funny it had been, their rash flight from "the unclean"! Or else the shuffling innkeeper! (Zinaida had hardly left with the registration card.) But of course! The victim of all these *faux pas* was actually the innkeeper. Poor man, what a situation! To convey *such* a message! How he'd forced it out of himself! How comical he was in his fidgeting short pants, and that finger with which he traced his bald spot! "A nasty business, a nasty business." "What business is that, then?" "The business with the bracelet, sir. The lady's bracelet has gone missing, sir. 400,000." "400,000?" "It happened as things were being moved. From your former room to the new one." "The one you forced on me." "You were there." "To help. There were others there as well." "The servants were there as well, but we've already searched them." "Too bad." "Yes, sad, since it wasn't them." "All the better." "All the better for them, yes. If it wasn't them . . ." "If it's not them?" "A nasty business, nasty. If you would be so wise . . ." "A moment ago you were saying 'if you would be so kind.'" "If you would be so wise, you'd ask me to search you before the gendarmes arrive." –

The wrinkles of the person sitting on the bed fade away, one after the other; his bottom lip has again flattened its mean fold. Who would say of that slovenly, impertinent nose that it belonged to a sleuthhound? The corners of his mouth turned upward—oh, barely enough to notice—the upper lip puckered, the eyelids rose afresh, the outstretched arms moved slowly from the ankles to the thighs—you there, boy, rejuvenated, how'd you get in here?—and look, here's the smile, here's the *person*, the one who was thinking:

"You unfortunate innkeeper! You *cheated* innkeeper!"

"You *cheated* innkeeper!" was the fresh, enterprising thought that required no more than a flick—it flipped over, and on the other side was: "I've had a look around the washbasin." When this thought was flicked in turn, it withdrew as well, revealing a third, in which one recognized, God knows by what, that it was the correlate of the thought "I've had a look around the washbasin." To wit:

"I left the rooms and went down into the yard, and there I passed a lovely moment by myself."

Between the thought and its correlate a broad land stretches, overgrown with seductive realities. The fairy tale of meadows with mills has nothing on it. Strange that he doesn't rest his eyes upon it! If he were to lean over slightly, he might see it even better. So he leans his entire torso. The hands resting on buttocks recalled the beautiful walk a moment before: they feel like taking another one, in the opposite direction, and slowly move down toward the ankles. If he had seen himself, he would have been pleased. His back had grown younger; his scapular muscles twitched nervously: you'd say it was a person sunning himself after a swim. So he's sunbathing.

Somewhere around here there's some overly seductive possibility, and it's pestering him. He had brushed it off rudely at first. Oh, just for effect, as a test: to see whether it would turn its back on him after having been brushed off; for if it turned its back on him, it would mean that it was quite a seductive possibility, but a false one. For that matter, he has no fear; he knows in advance that it will not turn its back on him, not at all. For that matter, you can see it so distinctly, this possibility, that it's not only surely true, but it is the only true thing.

"Where is my head!"

"Where is my head!" – in a woman's voice; he hears right: a woman's voice. Feminine, not masculine; but just before that "where is my head," which sounds like a calm corrective to something riled-up, something else had been said. But what? "Where is my head" emerges as though from a phonograph spinning backwards. So the beginning is still to come. And here it is: it's a femininely alarmed "my bracelet!" – This "my bracelet" sounds so familiar and natural that the person sitting on the bed doesn't resist; insofar as one might say "doesn't resist" of a gesture that's actually automatic. Look at him, he's whipped his eye upon the washbasin, and just when he did so the phonograph went kaput. It's quiet for a moment, but so impatiently that you can hear it wearing thin. Yes, it's a provisional quiet: the transmission just barely makes it across. Yes. Now, at last, the disc is turning again in the proper direction:

"My bracelet! Wherever is my head? Bring it to me, dear, it's next door on the washbasin." Yes; now it's spinning properly; now, at last, you can see it properly as well: he happens to be in his room, in the new one assigned to him, the one where he's only just woken up. A short time ago he'd transferred his shirts here; he's kneeling in front of the dresser, he's putting them in, he's alone. You hear: "My bracelet! Wherever is my head? Go get it for me, dear, it's next door on the washbasin." At the words "it's next door on the washbasin" he turned his head. The washbasin was within arm's reach. He felt for the bracelet, he slipped it into his pocket. It happened so fast—yes, it must be said this way: *happen*; it happened; impersonally— so that this movement startled even him. So what had gotten into him? – But just then steps resounded in the corridor; that's not it, steps didn't resound; there'd been no time for "resounding"; there'd only been two of them. The rooms were right next to each other. Mr. Steel entered and headed straight for the washbasin.

"Nonsense," he called out, "it's surely in our room."

"I'm telling you that I left it next door on the washbasin. Don't you remember me washing my hands?"

"*Nom de Dieu, nom de Dieu, nom de Dieu!*" Mr. Steel sings to himself.

The whole time he's kneeling in front of the dresser; he hasn't turned around, as if there's nothing to fuss over. He didn't even know that Mr. Steel had gone back out. He only realized it from hearing the words "that's impossible" coming from the adjoining room.

"It's most certainly next door on the washbasin."

So what had gotten into him? Beg your pardon, if we should stick to the truth, we'd rightly have to admit that it actually hadn't gotten into him to ask what had gotten into him. For that matter, how does one ask, and why, in that complicated euphoria in which he was as though suddenly drowning? Such rollicking fun with those conceited bourgeois! If only Tiemen could have seen him! Tiemen! It was as if he'd just stumbled upon that name. It had surfaced unexpectedly and uncalled— that is, it was just the thing that was called for. Tiemen and his expertise: legerdemain of votive candles, breaking into church collection boxes, pilfering apples from grocers' carts, snatching smudged, dog-eared detective novels from cartons of used books on the riverbank. They caught Tiemen once, but it was settled at the station. Tiemen! A drifter-dilatant, but he had connections. He was so very young back then, and he was trying on the role of the ingenious, and therefore spoiled, child. Not that he would have considered himself a genius; it was his friends who took him for a genius; he didn't want to spoil their pleasure. Spoiled, and therefore ingenious, children were all the rage back then. – "So, let's just call it kleptomania," the commissioner sighed, hanging up from his conversation with the prefecture, where the "connections" had intervened, "and off you go!" "Me, a kleptomaniac?" Tiemen protested, priding himself on the systematic deliberateness of his most minor thefts. It was out of them that Tiemen, doltish-looking wiseacre and *sensitif*, gentle executioner and smartass dreamer, constructed his jealously guarded tale of the "simplified simpleton." – He wanted to be locked up; they had to kick him out of the station. – Fine. So that was Tiemen. But now it's Mr. Steel's play again, yesterday's Mr. Steel, Mr. Steel enflamed by Mrs. Steel's eternal "I forgot it on the washbasin."

"*Zut alors!* It couldn't have just disappeared. You haven't seen it, have you?"

The question arrived as though she had wanted expressly to help him stand up; for he was just now finishing straightening up in the dresser and was rising. ". . . If only Tiemen knew," and it was all he could do not to burst into laughter at this capacious notion.

"A nasty business, really a nasty business. I was just checking the dresser to see whether it might have fallen in there by accident. I perhaps don't have to tell you that this is still much more awkward for me than it is for you."

"More awkward?" Mr. Steel said irritably. "Perhaps."

He hadn't known that he was capable of bluffing so casually; a spiteful joy was just then at play within him. Maybe it was even visible. Mr. Steel straightened up suddenly, maybe for just that reason, and having first assented with only an absent "yes," he changed his tone: "Yes! – And what's there in your linen?"

"Nothing."

"On the bed? The case had been on the bed." They pulled up the sheets.

"I'm telling you that I left it on the washbasin."

Mrs. Steel had hardly entered when she'd set a snare and caught him with it; he, however, stepped forward, and oh how quickly she released him. Released? No! She recoiled, as though she'd touched a red-hot stove.

"It can't be anywhere but on the washbasin, and it's not on the washbasin. It's not here."

She was, in her suspicion, as if on a chain, which she was tugging angrily, but she did not recoil.

Mr. Steel was reciting, "But this is an unpleasant business," and he had faith in this as in an incantation that might put him on the right track.

"And what of the girls, then?" he ventured at last, suspicious, having determined beyond all doubt that they suspected him, "they were helping, after all."

Out of the blue he noticed not only that he was no longer alone with Mr. and Mrs. Steel, but that he had not been noticing that he had not been alone with them for quite some time already. He learned this, and from this he coolly inferred that he was somehow not himself. And hard on its heels, there was already a second alarm: he recognized the innkeeper, he recognized the maidservants, the cook, Mrs. Steel's sister, and several lodgers, and all of them distinctly; they were so conspicuously themselves that they were no longer in fact themselves; they were so disproportionately themselves that it had estranged him from them. Both the people and all the objects domesticated in the last forty-eight hours had been coated over, as though in a tight, translucent membrane. And the mayday rang out now for the third time, with the sudden authority of the light of day: it disagreed with the late hour. And the fourth notice: the thought-provoking memory of Tiemen sort of suddenly leveled off; it went ambiguous . . . And hardly had it split in two like this than a shiver ran through him; that is, he discerned that he was keeping his left hand in his pants pocket, and he remembered that that's where he felt the bracelet . . .

All at once he was at the stairs, not knowing how it happened that they'd allowed him to get that far. The only thing he remembered—and backwards somehow—was that he had made a point of walking slowly, and that, despite some unmaterialized barking that unnerved his calves, this had worked out for him relatively well. So he was at the stairs and descending, one foot in front of the other. "Could I be whistling to myself?" He no longer remembered whether he had been whistling or not, but his right hand was now flying instinctively toward his lips to stop up his compromising mouth. "Whistling to yourself! What an idea! As if they hadn't long since discovered that the only people who whistle to themselves are those who are afraid." He turned around, the weight lifted from his shoulders. No one there. From upstairs, a hue and cry like knocked-down bowling pins, but it was derailed at the bend of the stairs and made it no further. On the stairs, no one; on the stairs, nothing. These stairs inspired such confidence—he was already on the last step, from which one had a view out to the yard. There, too, nothing but three hens pecking around: an existence somehow so rarified that the emptiness of the yard was overcome by it. The light had pressed close to its hour, as if you'd taken the smoking lamp back down: it was a natural twilight.

"Only to want, only to want," he said to himself, walking slowly through the yard, and his raggedness was becoming whole, causing such metaphysical pleasure that he didn't resist the casual temptation to attack it willfully (he knew it wouldn't work out): "Only to want? But you never wanted. It happened. Happened. Impersonally. A moment ago you were still relishing how it wasn't you who'd done it, that it merely happened." – "But all the better, if it happened beyond me," he countered obligingly, "it happened through me all the same. If I had considered . . . who knows . . . Deliberation is the enemy of action. If only Tiemen could see me! But there is something to that: gesture sets you free."

The tables had already been set, but there was no one around. From the open kitchen you could hear butter frying; nothing more than your hearing told you there was no one in the kitchen, either. A sort of heartening security was wafting in from there. – The stream ran along the southern side of the yard like a hem. He knew that at this very moment it would already be pitch black, and that the water's specific gravity had suddenly risen remarkably: material materializing—so seductive; black blackening—so tempting. He walked past the shed, which was open to the yard, past the defunct millhouse. There was an automobile parked there. Their automobile. It was parked on the threshing floor. An automobile on a threshing floor is lovely; a threshing floor beneath the tires of a powerful sports car is lovely. And one with the other is beautiful, like an incomprehensible, occult conciliation.

He stopped in at the shed. He penetrated the reproaching shadow. The awareness that he was not the one who had done something, so much as that through which something had happened, incarnated; actually, it had assumed an incarnation. It was standing next to him, it was struggling: it was stripping him, scrubbing him. Stripping him of function, scrubbing away his individuality. As a make-up artist does to an actor when he's finished his role. It was a degradation, admirable; a degradation during which his chest unwittingly swelled. Not with pride, but with the certainty of a strange, unselfish freedom. He caught sight of it so clearly that he was dazzled by it, but with a bedazzlement he couldn't tire of, that what merely is—and thus him, too—is nothing; being is only that which *happens*. – He felt the bracelet in his pocket; he withdrew his hand. What had he actually stolen? Is it valuable? Is it plunder? It matters little. He hadn't looked, and he wouldn't. He narrowed his eyes, he let the bracelet fall; with his foot he felt that it had dropped next to the running board. He turned, looked around; over the empty yard the last flakes of mica swept up that evening were twinkling, there was quiet all around. He went out, sat down at the table, turned to his reading. He read for a while, then clapped: "What about supper?" – – –

But hold on, hold on, something's happening. Let's get our wits about us, let's not lose control. There had been euphoria here not long ago: he was becoming absorbed by it, he was flailing around in it. It had been like this (he showed how much of it there was), now its level had dropped a bit. Oh, delight that is starting to drain away, you'll know it in an instant; we're as sensitive to it as to a lukewarm bath that is likewise draining away. Fine. Suddenly things are a little less fine by him than they'd only just been. Why? And above all: why had it been so fine by him a moment ago? Why, because he was reveling in his reminiscence of yesterday, "when he had triumphed over the innkeeper and the Steels." When he had triumphed so gloriously over his slanderers. He reminisced about it and saw it. He reminisced about it and saw it precisely, as starkly as if he were looking through the untinted crystal of the beatitude he'd attained. And the thing he was reminiscing about so precisely corresponded with what he was simultaneously seeing so starkly. It corresponded so accurately that it aroused a tranquil, calculating delight. Aha!—he'd just said it: he saw as though through an untinted crystal, and this crystal immediately—how to express this?—became sort of smoky. That's not it; that doesn't put it quite right. Not like the starkness had been blurred; no; more like the *covering* had been shifted. Yes, the memory of the beatified yesterday and its optical transcript had split apart somehow, just like an inscription beneath birefractive calcite. That's why the bath flows with delight—hee hee! But where that birefraction came from, which is waxing so much that between the memory and its vision there's now even a – – – but of course! These are the meadow and the overgrown banks of the stream and the alder groves, from which several village rooftops peer out . . .

Oh, let's just say it for him, for he can't see it clearly, he doesn't recognize it yet. Let's say in his stead that into his rapture over yesterday, "when he'd triumphed so famously," there flows a chastening reality. But he doesn't know it yet—he, not knowing why, is merely unsettled by it. In spite of himself, he who *wants* to summon his rapture alone is also summoning those meadows, that stream, that alder, and the village rooftops, and now he's also summoning a thin column of smoke rising from a chimney, and he's summoning it like a fiber of the start of day—a fiber caught in a time-spinning wheel that has started whirling and reeling and spinning out its finished skein of indistinguishable days, hours, and seconds already past.

The chastening reality is pouring in, but he's still holding out against it within the run-down redoubt of his rapture, and now he's giving in to it—oh, it'll be a routine capitulation, a capitulation no noisier than the collapse of a sandcastle until he catches on that he's looking. And he does catch on, enough that his retina absorbs the group of those three people on the white lane winding beneath the wooded hillside, and it evokes an image that had overslept, that had fallen behind and is now pulling up afresh, until he catches on that there's no way around it, and now he sees only that which is (and nothing more)—that which is, that is, that pipsqueak of an innkeeper, who "will present to you" his domain, his kingdom, who will present it with the sweepingly inattentive gestures of a tour guide for foreigners: our man sees Mr. and Mrs. Steel, doltish tourists who, oddly enough, don't take the shopworn, well-rehearsed lecture as a personal tribute. How funny they are, his slanderers from yesterday, "over whom he'd triumphed"! He is so delighted to assign them a poor grade, knowing that it serves them right, and that they'll pay for it. Oh, to be on the highway, to look down on them from far away and then get moving, eagerly, to pass them by, thrash them with a look, one after the other, to cut short the braggadocio of cowards pretending that *it* had already blown over...Oh, so as far as you're concerned it's already blown over, has it?! Oh, so as far as you're concerned it's like last evening didn't happen?! So you're going to make like an ostrich?! So you...but after all, of course! The longer he watches that group of three, the longer he sees them, the more he catches wind of the God's honest truth that, for them, it *has* blown over. For real, they're not making like an ostrich in the least; for real, as if none of it ever happened at all; it's natural, for real, and despite that, for real, it's so unsteady that a modicum of insolent pluck would suffice, courage would suffice to deny it – – – but that's just it!: *he's in no position*. It would suffice to say "they couldn't have forgotten," and it would amount to the same as their not having been able to forget; it would suffice to say "no!" and it would actually be "no"... The only thing is that he, he doesn't measure up to that "no way"...

"What is it?" he asked, as if compelled to return something he'd appropriated improperly.

And the voice that answered, "mail," from behind the door sounded as though it were contemptuously tossing returned valuables. It was Zinaida's voice. Our man had "Slip it under the door" on the tip of his tongue, but instead he stuck his head out a little and raised his forefinger; just then, however, it was as though he'd remembered that that's how morons make a show of hitting upon "an idea," and he scowled repentantly.

"Wait a moment, Zinaida, I'm opening the door." And now he had. Zinaida handed him a bundle of newspapers and a postcard. She turned her head and left foot as though she were already leaving; how could she spell it out for him more explicitly that, as far as she goes, she'd rather slip the mail under the door and leave before he "would have to" see her? Can you be so sure that even he understood this?

"How did you sleep, Zinaida?"

He'd said it too late; after Zinaida, who, having given him the bundle, could at last do what she'd have rather done right away: leave. He was saying it *after her*, all the while with a foul bitterness in his mouth; he was saying it looking after her, quite meekly and without the slightest hope that she would answer him, when, getting ready to close the door again with mortified desolation, he was amazed to discover that the girl sort of hesitated after all, then slowed down. She slowed weirdly, and he recognized it and was intrigued by it, she slowed with the unwitting *ritardando* of a person in whom "it's working." He made out that what was working was anger contending with . . . that's it: what was hampering Zinaida's contemptuous anger?

"Perhaps grief," he said, testing it, but she suddenly turned her head and set off, once again quickening her pace.

"Why didn't you smack him one?"

She said it in such a way that he immediately jumped back

and slammed the door behind him. He reached for his face. Zinaida's "why didn't you smack him one" burned like a slap.

The postcard was from "the gang." The first thing that struck him was Tiemen's signature. But it was only after he had read the card a third time, a fourth—now like he's near-sighted, now like he's farsighted—that he caught on that what he was reading had come from "Montfort-l'Amaury." He read the signatures one after another, he said Montfort-l'Amaury to himself again and again, trying in vain to detach the names from the steadfast place that was somehow inappropriate here, to detach them as though from a word-canvas that the rest had been embroidered into, from the blurred word underneath, which will never, never fade beneath the rest, until at last it shone through more clearly: "They have already forgotten. They have already forgotten."

They've forgotten the affair with which he had been sleeping unawares, as with an infected dame. He had been sleeping with his own shame, and he didn't know, didn't suspect. They'd woken up so run-down from that monstrous intercourse that it had given him a moment's peace, it let him doze a little. Oh, the idyll by the pool and the legend of yesterday sung in verse *ad usum delphini*: the briefest delay, the tiny indulgence of the demanding monster *they* had mated him with yesterday—they who have forgotten. And what was there for them to forget, actually? What? *We* haven't forgotten yesterday's farce, which we attended only to digest our dinner, and so we'd have some-thing to kill the time before supper, we don't forget something that lasts only through its extension in time; we don't forget that which was not there.

But if the bracelet had actually been lying on the washba-sin, if he had actually taken it, if he had actually gone out into the yard and actually dropped it in the shed, and if what had then actually transpired had occurred regardless... Hold on! Now he has more riding on an answer: would Zinaida then have had a reason to say to him what she'd just said? Hold on! – No, she wouldn't have had a reason, for then yesterday would have run its course the way it had, *except for one thing*: he would sure as hell have *delivered the slap*. Mr. Steel would have gotten his slap; Mr. Steel's good cheer, his tribute to the summertime way of being, would have skipped over today. And why would this good cheer have left? Because yesterday he would have gotten slapped. And why would Mr. Steel have gotten slapped yesterday? Hold on! Because he, the one now in his room, would have had the guts. And why would he have had the guts? Because, once he'd chucked the bracelet, he would have been sure that they could keep looking until Doomsday and still wouldn't find anything: not on him, not in his dresser, not in his bed, not in his linens. Because knowing that he'd chucked the bracelet he wouldn't have been dying of fear that his slanderers had found the bracelet in the meantime and slipped it into his things so they'd "be right," so they wouldn't have to retract. Oh, how he would have stood up to them, he, who well knows that he's already just equivocating again, that he's already just faking again.

Come on! Why does he say "if I had pinched it," "if I had chucked it" ...? Why does he say this when he knows that in order for him to pinch, in order for him to chuck, he would have to be ... precisely: not himself, but rather a fundamentally different someone – – – He'd have to have been the hero of the idyll by the pool, the one from whom shame backs away, and not the one who was hiding behind that other one. – – – The cowardly him, him the coward, for he is cowardly, and the best proof that he's cowardly is that he's incapable of even imagining himself as a thief. – And look, look what the heroic variant of the bracelet he had stolen has transformed into: a paradise from which he has been expelled, and toward which he dolefully turns. He is fleeing, fleeing, but what a tough flight this is, through all those "as thoughs" and "ifs"...

As though, once I'd chucked the bracelet... – ... if I'd brushed Zinaida off... – ... if I'd only answered the innkeeper, what would he have heard in response to his...

Yes, in response to his "*you would have to allow yourself to be searched*"! But how had he actually responded? Tell them how you reacted, sir! Were you outraged? For a moment ago you were all set to be outraged! Scoundrel! Walking crooked highways and making yourself out to be a mountaineer! Let's be frank for a moment, okay? There was no outrage. Horror! The horror that in the meantime they would still find the bracelet on you; the horror that they might even set it up deliberately to "find" it. And how, sir, do you handle the noble, martyr-like heroism of spurned innocence? But that's just it: there isn't a trace of the noble heroism of spurned, martyr-like innocence in you; in you there's only a shimmer.

At last, then, he has touched the end of the proper thread! He was so proud of this that it cheered him up, even though he'd already foreseen where this thread would lead him ... So then how did it happen? How did it happen?

First of all, there's him, innocent as a babe, who knows that the Steels are searching upstairs for some kind of jewelry, he who had been there when it had gone missing and had left in a huff, regardless of the fact that he had a feeling, and precisely because he had a feeling, that "he was somehow behind this business." – And there's the innkeeper, that pipsqueak of an innkeeper. And there's the "you would have to submit to a search" from the Lord Innkeeper, who in no way anticipated that with his "you would have to submit to a search" he would sire a Zeus from whose head, hardly having shaken himself off in God's world, sprang beautiful Pallas, in beautiful armor.

"My name is horror, you big shot, and I'm coming for you. So you no longer seem to know what transpired back there (she pointed upstairs), when you were thieving. Ah," she whined, "you thought you were in the clear, right, that no one caught on...ah! Ah!—haven't you looked at yourself? Don't you know what a sleepwalker looks like when he's shuffling through a throng? No, you don't know! No, you don't know that it's impossible not to notice a pilfering thief—no, innocent-as-a-babe, you don't know. So let me help—I'm a good helper—I speak the truth: you steal, with a thievery so inept a state prosecutor should make a speech about it. With a thievery so inept they froze. Of the lot, you're the only one still going. The others—look!—tragicomic statues; only the heads still move, writhe, one after the other, after you. You're on the steps, you're in the yard, you're waiting for your grub, you're luxuriating in your reading—and there (she's pointed at the window) the whole time, the cast of *Sleeping Beauty* have their heads toward the door, let's say, following a mystical wisp. How long will this last? How long will the living stand there playing the roles of pillars of salt, if it's not the doing of magic? Sooner or later, and sooner rather than later, something will come of it: a voice above all, some kind of voice, and it's already been raised, too. What would you suppose it says? What else could it say? 'It's obvious he's the one,' the voice says. A sentence like the mineral irritant in a supersaturated solution, from which all kinds of things now precipitate; oh, all kinds of things, and with haste, I assure you: a bit of hypocritical mob anger, a lot of general scorn, and a thick druse of sadistic pleasure that's looking forward to something. Pleasure is the etchant of collective consciousnesses. The group grants its prisoners their freedom. It's given them their civilian packs! Freedom! Freedom! Once again we can be wicked according to our own individual genius. Only to remain momentarily lodged in motionless rapture over the powerful reflectance of the cast in ruins. Ah, reality, unleashed by interconnected forces, will unfortunately not reach that in which it delights: no, too bad, the thief will not be quartered. We will settle for a suitable stupor; for a stupefying conviction. Ah, a stupefying conviction! The argument—a mace. No, the thief will not be quartered; they don't do that anymore. But he'll get the club. Beautiful, too, is the image that he might slide into the trap himself. And maybe he's a masochist! Oh, the image of a public confession—Russian style! But first of all: shouldn't we telephone the police station?"

"And who is he?" asked the neurasthenic young woman from the room opposite.

"Well, he still hasn't registered yet."

"You'd better hurry up with it. As the proprietor, you could have some official unpleasantness."

"Watch out," the horror says, the beautiful horror in armor, "watch out, you're going to have a hard time." The group's mineralesque cruelty is relishing the phenomenon; the corroded group tears it into instances. The "stealing phenomenon" had been mesmerically beautiful; instances of stealing are merely interesting. You were that through which something happened; now you are merely that which has carried something out. Watch out, you're going to have a hard time. Mr. Steel, the out-of-shape athlete, has made the supreme pronouncement that you are a thief, and that's that; Mrs. Steel is about to have a hysterical fit at the obsessive thought that you're a communist rather than a thief; a sprig of doubt has shot up in the ailing sister; scraps of charity have stolen into the faith of the neurasthenic young woman ("he's a thief"), a charity drilled into her in her youth. The herd has to be grappled with, but how do you get people to understand you?

The herd had been put through "the case"; it disintegrated into people, and they were judging it. Watch out, you're going to have a hard time. The herd was dense, you could grab hold of it by something. But what can you do with a mercurial tangle of enemies? For that matter, where have they all gone? They've dispersed, like savages into an ambush. Extras being unnecessary for the time being, they've attentively withdrawn to the wings.

While you're filling out the registration, while the innkeeper is serving you the ruling of the herd that has long since gone (he is serving it up as coyly and cagily as he would his own scorched vittles), the Steels are searching. Automatically, not in earnest, maybe with a scrunched memory of catechism at Sunday school, but under the imperious and rheumy gaze of civic "honor." Now pay attention, you heard right: "it's here" (it's the gentleman's sister); "*it's here*": something like a stick hitting a rock, and rapidly. Yes, now also a spluttering waterfall of the panicked words "Only how could we have forgotten it!" – "Gina gave it to me to hold so that it wouldn't slide off her arm." – "We've treated him unfairly." (Let's not forget: we're talking about a sick woman, a delicate woman.) – "What now? We must give him satisfaction! He's innocent!" – You heard right, yes, but don't count on it. On the contrary, watch out all the more, things are going to get tough. Have you forgotten the rheumy gaze of civic honor? Have you forgotten the out-of-shape athlete who declared you a thief now and forever, and that's that? The gentleman's delicate sister cried out; Mr. Steel, who anticipated it, makes do with a whispery tantrum, but that, too, is a blow against the rock, merely a blow that enshrines the quiet.

Do you hear? "Quiet." Mr. Steel's tantrum is a whisper: "Quiet." – You see? You see how he grabbed for the bracelet?

"Shhh. Give it here! We will have no scandal!" says Mr. Steel. "Lord knows what he's capable of. We don't know him. He has a foreign accent. Didn't you hear? A *rastaquouère*. In for an inch, in for a mile. If he's in it, let him be in it."

Mr. Steel opened the wardrobe: he felt for an overcoat, the one in the back, the one furthest back; he unfastened its pocket; look! The bracelet's in there, that's where the bracelet is.

"But you won't accuse a person who . . ." (Let's not forget: we're talking about a sick woman, a delicate woman.)

Mr. Steel, however, has a persuasive "shhh!" Mr. Steel has a masterful "shhh," produced with a finger to his lips.

And a cynical "pfff!" by which the women's mouths are sealed for good.

Lovely Pallas in lovely armor changes visibly into an atrocious hand puppet from a fairground Pandora's Box. "I have come for you," she cackles, "flee, if you can." And she rocks on the swaying spring of the words "you would have to submit to a search"; "flee, watch out, for you are innocent, flee, watch out, precisely because you are innocent, for you are also that to which shame gladly adheres; the impression is against you, Mr. Steel has charged you, he's charged you falsely and knows it; Mr. Steel is strong, Mr. Steel will hand you over, for you are innocent."

Such was the speech he heard from the horror that grew out of the words "you would have to submit to a search," and barely had she finished speaking than he made a break for it. He's running. Four steps at a time. Behind him, a vampire; before him, catastrophe. There's a target, he's an arrow aimed at a target; inevitably, he hits it. And what if he doesn't? And why would he have to? Are there no such things as miracles?

Horror is hot on his heels, and hot on the heels of horror is the spry thought of a miracle. Hip! hip! Get going, little mouse. And the little mouse gets going, the little mouse is outpacing horror, oopsy-daisy! Now horror senses it on her back, its small, pink, ticklish snout, but how heavy it is, it's heavier and heavier, and what's with that whizzing that's become of its amusing mousy squeak? "A miracle? A miracle? You're where miracles go to die!" – And the rat is heavier and heavier, it's not a rat, it's his chafing affliction, it's damned Saint Christopher's mounting burden.

"I'm where miracles go to die"; does he feel, then, the head of cattle led to slaughter, and does he feel that infamy all his own?

He barges into the room—they're here. Even today he can still hear how miserably he shrieked "out!" rummaging through the dresser. Rifling through his pockets. Each time he sank a hand into a new one, he wished with an absurd sort of hope that it would not be in vain. At the same time, he was both a feather, extended so far it hurt, and its sheath, which knows that it can allow the feather to go no further lest it break, and which dreads that moment, knowing it won't outlive the feather. But the feather's frenetic yearning to be let loose, and the panicked fear of the sheath, which knows only destruction can bring relief, were cracking with shared impatience, for things to ease up already. The yearning; the fear; a limit; a fall that has no end. – Only it wasn't found, there was nothing in the pockets. He turned around. How must he have appeared that Mr. Steel, who was standing here with his hands stuck haphazardly in his pockets, *allowed himself* to say: "Don't look there, surely it's not there!" Yes, what kind of face had he made? Perhaps it's enough to say a let-down one. We can't exclude that he looked let down. How, too, to respond, and what to say, if you're fascinated by the chest of drawers "where it might be as well"; the linens, now strewn about again, "where it might be, too"; the built-in dresser with ties, papers and books, nooks; and what about the wallpaper—might there be a tear in it? – And so many more, so many more potential seats of betrayal?

"So how did I look? So how did I behave?" Only now, in reverse somehow, does he see Mr. Steel's mute and rhythmic "no's." This repeated negation was surely an answer... But an answer to what? After all, he knows that he hadn't said a word, that he hadn't asked a thing.

He is sitting here on the chair. He's dropped his left hand, the one with the "mail," dead; the right, the one with the "chin," is propped on his knee. Before him, yesterday; he's looking at yesterday, and out of the blue it's as though beneath something that's a filthy brown. After a moment it dawns on him that that thing, sort of like a canvas, portrays the fleeting, present moment when they're foraging in vain, to which Mr. Steel's mute "no way's" yesterday seem to apply. Now he knows! He'd ransacked the wardrobe to no avail; he'd turned to face the room again; he was sorely let down when he now suddenly realized what potential snares there *still were* here; and a new hope germinates within him... He sees himself as though doubled: he sees himself as a moron, and how he is *betraying* himself, looking at Mr. and Mrs. Steel and at the possible hiding places and pointing with his finger here, there, over there. Which is to say: "So did you slip it into the linens?" – "No," Mr. Steel remarked. – "Under the mattress, then?" – "No way!" that slanderer smiles.

No way, says the person sitting with his back to the window and gloomily resisting something he knows quite well: that nothing will come of his resistance, no way, the negating twist of the head didn't apply to the querying index finger. It did not apply, for Mr. Steel didn't know that I was asking specifically for what I was asking for. If he had merely suspected, he would have ... "He would have what?" he retorted to himself, riled up with comical haste, "he would have what?"

But the answer that barged into his mind was so odious that, regardless of his actually now having answered himself (it sounded like: "He would have slapped me."), he discovered a still more odious strength within himself; the strength to sequester that answer after the fact. He whitewashed it, word for word, with a question already carefully poised for ambush a moment earlier. It was the question: "How would it have been, then, had there been no negation?"

Actually, the person sitting in the window deferred that incredible object. Having answered the mental question of how it was appropriate to answer, it was as though he immediately forgot the answer, knowing nonetheless *that* he had forgotten and why he *had* to forget. Did he forget it? No, he merely embargoed it. The way alarming newspaper reports are embargoed at critical times. "Even the ones that are true?" Even the ones that are true. "But doesn't their truth go on regardless?" Of course, their truth goes on regardless. "So then what have you gained by the embargo?" Time. You might gain some time.

He knew that there was something within him that still had to be kept quiet, that if his slanderer had understood the mute question he would have slapped him. No: it was still much, much worse than that: the seated man knew there was something within him that still had to be kept quiet, that his slanderer would have been allowed to slap him without penalty, that he wouldn't have defended himself, that he wouldn't have been able to retaliate, that by then he would already... This *by then* especially had to be kept quiet.

By then? What does it mean: "by then"? Why is he saying "by then"? What's the point of saying "I would have succumbed to him by then" when, after all, he never succumbed to him? There hadn't been any reason to. And, after all, you don't even succumb unless there's a reason! So why is he saying "by then"?

Nor does a Secretary of State say, "Gentlemen of the press, don't push it, I can't say anything." – The Secretary of State sinks back into his armchair, purses his lips (he wouldn't have to, but the secret cramps them), lights a cigarette, and starts talking about something else. – He's lit a cigarette. He's attempted a smoke ring. He's brought it off; it's grown and faded away; it faded away because it had grown without suspecting where this would lead; it faded away over the house of cards that is the certainty that there was nothing in the clothes, nothing in the chest of drawers, nothing anywhere. Now let them come, yes, just let them come close (in fact, where did all these people come from all of a sudden?). Just let them relish the sight of how in love he is with his catlike vengeance; would you have said he was capable of such a thing?; it's the kind of pet that nuzzles up to him, it whispers to him, they get on like nobody's business, just wait for him to get on with it, just wai . . .

The cigarette between his lips has slipped a tiny bit, the left hand, which went after it, has collapsed onto the armrest: that's as much as his alarm showed when he found that his vengeance had gone off the rails.

Arsonist! Conflagration! Where did this come from? From these glimmers. From the guilt-ridden glimmers that were as though of no concern to them. They're not even hiding; oh, they're not hiding. After what they've committed, they're still frolicking! They have no qualms. Three nimble little snakes, three coiling little words: "I'm a gentleman!" . . .

Hands raised... "Assholes!"

He had obscured his eyes (or did it just seem like he had?). He shielded them, not so they wouldn't see the conflagration: who cares about conflagration! He shielded them because he couldn't stand the gazes upon him—so that all there was for him to do was double himself!—upon the theatrical gesture with which, like a bumbler, he made a break from his silkily mute vengeance-cuddling. (The outstretched index finger!)

"Get out, the lot of you! All of you out!"

Strange, strange that even now, *in spite of everything*, that ever-so-subtle triviality still sticks in his memory: that in response to his "get out, the lot of you!," of all of them Zinaida was the only one to shudder, and with a look so incomprehensibly grateful. The kind that might—ostensibly—lend one strength, even upon the scaffold. Such a look, and it did him no good! Thus he surely no longer had...

Censored.

It was in this room. In this room where today, in the summer morning, he *is allowed* to play whatever he wants (God only knows whether he'll abuse it): the innocent accused; the avenger of the righteous and the weak; the public prosecutor; the good judge; the magnanimous man who has taken on the worse bit; the desperado who soldiers hopelessly on; the downtrodden man who smiles for no reason but to give heart to those nearby, though they are less unfortunate than he; the lamb who has assumed others' guilt upon himself; the angel who begged for his own banishment... He's allowed, but by whose will, by whose power?

He knows all about what he's *allowed* to be. What who *is* he?

It was in this room where he, innocent, honest, offended, unavenged, identified his slanderers, not one of whom even stirred.

Mr. Steel, who this entire time had been swaying, light as a feather on his tiptoes, turned his head nonchalantly.

"Have you placed the call?" he said to the innkeeper.

The innkeeper didn't answer in words, only with the obliging and satisfied look of a miniscule mortal looking up to a larger-than-life idol.

The missus was fiddling with her necklace, "One who has a clean conscience will therefore not make a fuss. It would have been better for you if you had handed it over."

This stabbed him with shame as though with the flame of a blowtorch, and beneath the shame a retaliatory thought crumbled within him: "She's picked that up in cheap theaters: the contemptuous gesture of high-society ladies."

And Mr. Steel's patronizing, "It really would have been better for you; in that case I would have smoothed it over before the gendarmes—loss, discovery, that sort of thing..."

Recalling everything they were saying so precisely, and knowing of his own words only that they resounded in falsetto, stumbled, tripped, and picked themselves up like an old man: worn-out runts, dead-tired buffoons, swept away by some brisk broom before anyone even paid them any mind. No, there hadn't been such an utterly pointless spray of words after all. He recalls further: he'd hurled each of them more or less as though it were a stone into water; after each, a circle; with each, a bigger circle; a round space filled with emptiness, growing wider and wider; a crowd drawn together by a circle of misfortune on the street, eager for a spectacle, and nevertheless withdrawing: not out of fear; not out of irritability; not out of sympathy; out of the squeamishness of the living when it comes to the dead.

And again we have the conflagration and the first guilt-ridden glimmer, and it's nuzzling up nimbly so that he won't spot it. And with such cuddly importunity:

"I am a gentleman."

"*Bon*," said Mr. Steel, and he was about to leave.

What he would have given to have been able to stomp on the little snake! What happened was a pity—he'll bear the pity. The pity was his fault—so what! But to be allowed at least to forget that it was his own fault that was mocking him: "I am a gentleman!" – As if "I am a gentleman" didn't have a fixed reputation of its own! As if there wasn't a soul who knew this was the last gambit of con artists. – "I am a gentleman"; there's such shame for him in these words it's as though he'd appeared before them in his nightshirt. What he would have given to be able to forget.

And what he did was speak, speak, speak...

Suddenly he caught sight of the innkeeper, from a sort of dizzying proximity, a little fellow so small that he had to look up even at him, who was not tall; he caught sight of the innkeeper and also something like a crude remorse; both in one. Yes, the thing he could not resist was that crude remorse. He overheard:

"Mind yourself: raise your arms, let us dig into your pockets... Alright then, what's the big deal? If your conscience is clear!"

A second guilt-ridden glimmer slipped alongside his right foot, he stomped after it, too late...

He raised his arms and spread them apart. And what came of it? Yes, what came of his having raised and spread his arms? To what degradation would he subject himself at the hands of bandits, just so it would all be over and done? But others would raise their arms and spread them apart as well. Enough already with that hateful bias in his own favor. What was the point? Let's just consider cool-headedly what this was really about.

A person has gotten into a trumped-up situation; hysterical dames and bullies have hurled themselves at him; there's no way out besides a ransom—as ransoms go, is spreading your arms out really so dear? He even manages to envision a joker who has spread his arms for fun and is already feasting his eyes on "what comes next": next, when they won't find anything... Next, when he'll get them back for "it," and right good. Yes, he sees it like it's live: they're searching. It doesn't matter that they're merely "frisking." That's why the pulse of the man being searched hasn't yet missed a beat; it's not even a fraction of a second off; with plucky good cheer it's moving toward tomorrow, toward joys, toward love. The search is over, nothing has been found, of course. Is there less of the man who was searched? But how could there be? Afterwards, as before, he is *complete*. Yes, complete: this is the right word. He shakes his head; no different than a drenched poodle—no different... why all the fuss over a bath?—he shakes his head (Tiemen is an example: just now he sees how his mop of hair whipped around at the same time), and says: "And now for the hats in hand, you beasts; get to it!" And he says it in such a way that the protest would think better of it before the "hats in hand" would even register on the ear. What a feast of vengeance! What fun! What fun, most of all!

So he spread his arms. – He felt the innkeeper's paws upon him. *He could* spread his arms. He could. He could...

But yesterday had imparted something to him after all:

To think that he had just succeeded, during this flanking sortie, to amass a brief moment of freedom (a second? a minute? an hour?), the likes of which he had never experienced! What the others would have given for his discovery from yesterday! The freedom, that is, when in the sudden unlit brightening he recognized himself beyond what was subordinate—and everything that occurred in that moment, everything he noticed in that moment, that he got wind of, everything that at that moment he could reach with his senses, was in fact *merely* subordinate—that is to say, he was all alone with duration. Or maybe in duration? Or else maybe beside it? Today he no longer knows precisely, only that (for how could he forget it?) yesterday, and it was just yesterday, he had penetrated to where time had an appearance. An appearance, hard to say of what. Maybe something sort of like space, but a space that knows itself, externally; a space marveling at itself and disengaged from itself. It was weird, a weird moment, when time *let him go*... Yes, that's how to put it: time let him go.

If he thinks that the moment has come for him to notice, I'll say notice for real, something that he had forgotten in his past, forgotten in time, and that he has arrived at the point of being *allowed* to arrive there—he remembers: the innkeeper had just been digging around in his pockets—that he could bring it back to himself: the past to the present. The piercing cry from the yard, which he heard while knowing with dazzling certainty that it was a cry that had already subsided, this piercing cry with which there resonated something admittedly merely incidental, but that was firmly protesting that it had nothing to do with what was going on here in the room: Blanche (the second servant girl), whose shoulders started at this cry (this is also the past transposed); Zinaida, who, as if it were a signal, quickly left; heads lifting toward the sky, one after another, but so weirdly, so otherly. Somebody's bellowing, it's somewhere in the corridor, the powerful slam of a window, and immediately after that a stumbling cascade of other windows closing quickly (he said: "The windows have been reprimanded"); the imperious entrance of an unforeseen tidal rush and its even more unforeseen abatement (he said: "They've squeezed it in the door"); and outside, a stifled groan (he said: "Abandoned orphans, paid off with some great sweeps of a broom") and the frolicsome thieves' lanterns that had shone on this payoff. It was precisely with these lanterns that he started to get his bearings: these lanterns told him that the lackeys were bustling behind them preparing for the storm. And then he also got his bearings with regard to the storm's *having* burst, that within it the solitude around the mill was increasing threefold, and with it there was a threefold increase, too, of the self-assurance of his threefold tragic position; the mill, in its God-knows-how-many-fold, downpour-wired cage, was where he would have to hurry up and work out a brand-new, slightly operetta-ish constitution for the storm: for himself, with all the bells and whistles.

And he who was closing in on all these events, and then having closed in on them was hastily sorting them out, quite calmly took into account the quite quotidian phenomenon (for it *was* a quotidian phenomenon) that everything he was seeing and hearing was projected into the present from the past, where it still partially lingered, which is to say that it was storming, but that it had already been storming a good while without him suspecting it, and it occurred to him that between the revolution, which legitimated the operetta-ish constitution of this "state of exception," and the episode with the bracelet, there was perhaps some relation. He seized upon the notion that they were perhaps both the clumsy joke of fellow diners who'd overindulged, but hardly had he seized upon this than he'd already brushed it off, just like a drowning man holding fast to the edge of a dinghy, whose knuckles they beat with the oars.

So he brushed it off, he brushed it off with a gallows "now I'm in it." It was like a ransom to the racketeer, and the racketeer was his dread. He was behaving like a desperate, drowning man, without having fallen into the delusion that he might actually drown; yet he was still getting hopelessly soaked; he was dissolving, melting into the muddy, nattering shapelessness of the earth's saturated, humiliated crust, which had to put up with it, too, which was also struck by it, which was also defenseless. Out of the blue, he had become fascinated by the image of the puddles into which the downpour blasted, puddles pitted as though with smallpox dimples and puddles *fundamentally* unclean because they are neither only water, nor only soil. They harass the operetta's empire, closer and closer, they're all around, the mill is retreating from their unclean contact. But how else can one retreat before the concentric encroachment of a flanking circle than by flattening out? The mill is flattening out, it's flatter and flatter: now it's actually just two-dimensional. Where, within the tissue-paper thinness, was there room enough for his shame, and for the spitefulness of those to whom it was spectacle; where will he fit here with his robbing, on which he has swelled like a toadstool after rain? Where could one find in here everything the scum had robbed him of, which they knew they were robbing from him, and by which they nevertheless succeeded in appearing indistinguishable from the righteous? How did that geodetic surface accommodate so many earthly events and things so convincingly three-dimensional: now, for example, him, a person, and now his misery, and now his ignominy?

He caught sight of the innkeeper from such a dizzying proximity (he was so short that he had to look up even at him, who was not tall); he caught sight of the innkeeper—yet no longer so much his crude remorse as his moronic helplessness. But he, instead of fuming, instead of striking him, strayed right back into the dread and humiliation with which they were chasing him, and because he had, after all, been driven off those bitter lands he was surveying them so appreciatively and with such servile fondness (he saw himself; he sees himself) that he detested himself. For he knew, he knew where that gratitude and fondness had come from; the fact that he was increasingly certain that the moronic, helpless innkeeper *had not found it*, that he *had not slid* the long-since-discovered bracelet into his pocket. The innkeeper dug into his pockets honestly; the innkeeper really had suspected him; what a superb person he was. Why disparage him, why strike him if he was so kind and ... didn't find anything ...? How affable, how friendly a base suspicion appears to be when the jig is up! But he whose name has been cleared feels someone tugging at his sleeve; he whose name has been cleared closes his eyes, so not to see; if only he could plug up his ears as well, so not to hear, and his mouth, so to be incapable of a reply:

"Why would he have thrust the bracelet into your pockets deliberately?" – "To convict me in spite of everything." – "How could he dare?"

Is he whose name has been cleared able at least to not reply to "how could he dare"? – He is not; he is not. Except that he ventures a whisper so quiet that no one else would hear it. He, however, hears it himself (so then what good is whispering?), and he swallows some saliva.

"Because he knows me. Because they know me. They know one can do that with me."

But the innkeeper, such a pipsqueak that he had to look up even at him, who was not tall, spread his arms wide and spluttered, "That's odd; nothing!"

"Eh?" says Mr. Steel.

"Nothing. It's not here."

And he runs around like a lapdog through his own filth.

He had obeyed. Up to this point, only like a Doubting

Thomas. Maybe they were merely playing with him? But a fleeting, circling glance was enough to set him straight: "No, they're not playing. This is for real." – But was it possible that they were doing a poor job of their search? Might they have skipped some pocket? – He started digging around himself. Feverishly. A sort of ticklish and unfamiliar delight was passing through him like an inductive current. He understood: he was infected; he now suspected himself. But he didn't find it, either, and the current as if melted away. It left an emptiness, and for a long time nothing filled it in. This emptiness, as though a glass sphere: so thin-walled that it wasn't actually there anymore either.

"What will invade me?" the emptiness frets.

And all of a sudden, a break, a catastrophe so unostentatious that it's less a catastrophe than a previously agreed-upon change of antagonists, a rapid and smooth rending of something unseen. The third dimension now overwhelmed the flat, operetta-ish empire, and the confusion, the strangely logical confusion that had reigned within it till now, became cloudy with dust—as if it were a dream deferred, flushed with a bright, yet unilluminated, radiance. This was not merely a subjective impression; all the others, too, looked around, bewildered by this new reality; he saw it. This new reality? A dead deluge (as he'd caught the beginning of the storm not long ago, only when it had already been raging for a while, so too did he now *come to know* that the deep, nocturnal quiet which suddenly struck his fancy had been delighting him for a while already, before he was aware of it), and footsteps. And the footsteps in particular: for it was they that had awakened the new reality, it was growing behind them, it built itself up of its own accord from booming footfalls planted all in single strokes, like ashlars. And the steps, whose acoustic reality grew into that booming as though into their own super-imaginary real-ity, with these steps the imagery filled in with an actuality so convincing that everyone, without looking (it was pitch-black outside anyway), *saw* two uniformed men marching along the road, each with a rifle *en bandoulière*, that they had extin-guished pipes, that a few minutes earlier they had still been talking about the aftergrass, but that now they were moving in casual silence, each along one edge and in such a way that it was as though they were miming a reunion with each odd step and a farewell with each even. You could hear that they were walking rather quickly, but this reality was also overgrown as if with its own esoteric actuality, and so to those listening it was like the gendarmes were sauntering, despite their ears telling them that they were walking rather quickly.

All at once he was left alone with the Steels. He realized this while seeing the innkeeper leave. As far as the rest were concerned, he was prepared to accept not that they had simply gone so much as that they had miraculously disappeared. Mr. Steel was walking around the room and fiddling with keys. Mrs. Steel was seated, on the alert, and something about her hand at rest, caught on her necklace (but for that the hand would have fallen into her lap), recalled how a short time before it had still been fiddling with the necklace. Someone said "the lot of you!" – He was certain that someone said "the lot of you," yet he doubted that he had actually heard it, too. He had started to suspect himself (as to whether he had said "the lot of you"), but he couldn't be sure. But surely "the lot of you" had been spoken, for it was only for that reason that Mr. Steel came to a halt, and it was only for that reason as well that the hand of Mrs. Steel awoke. Nothing more. – He's mistaken: there was something else after all: those steps out-side had stopped. If he had anticipated that the night's quiet would set in as a consequence of their sudden stopping—still more hollow before it had set in, while those steps resounded within it as though in a baby's rattle—he would have been disappointed. If he had anticipated that the steps in the baby's rattle would be replaced by specific, coarsely processed, and incomprehensible "voices in the night," he would have been no less disappointed. It just happened that he anticipated the very thing that happened: the steps stopped as though smothered by the rhythmic whisper of the voices, which he heard not so much through them alone, but through the punctuation provided by the trees, which were drizzling.

Then the footsteps again, but this time on the stairs. They were the footsteps of a single person, but already upon the first listen they were the footsteps from one of *that* pair. Because they lacked the comrades' syncopated procession, they sounded hard and impoverished. A gendarme came with them, ascending compulsorily and treading like a seaman. So too, in fact, did he enter. He was projecting, God knows how, that he already knew; he was even projecting that he knew this as well: "...only we found nothing, neither in his room, nor on him." It was clear as day that the gendarme coming in was of the "called-for-no-reason-whatever" variety, but this gendarme, deprived of magic, went right up to our man with an official, overcast air.

"So it's you then, is it? Your papers."

He felt a dry ache on his calf as if from a chop of the hand. "Officer..."

"Your papers."

He knew where they were—they were in order—he dug around in his scattered things, and all at once he sees. He sees some straightforward, simple, definite thing that was liberating itself from something else, and what it was liberating itself from was, by chance, the very nostalgia for something straight-forward, simple, definite, the nostalgia that dwelled within him without his actually being aware of it till now. A peculiar, liberating look; a look/repose. – He stared again, still, he felt he had to tilt his head to see better, to revel in this pattern the way he should, and here, look: he sees that he's guilty. – He sees that he hasn't pilfered the bracelet; he sees that he has evaded the snares, all the snares; he sees that *nothing more can happen to him*; in particular, he sees that he is guilty. But it isn't enough for him to see that he is guilty. He's searching for a why. He looks still closer. Might he spot that why as well? And, in fact, he has already found it: he sees that he is guilty for just the relief of the certainty *that* nothing more can happen to him.

He stood with his back turned away, but the new, mute breakdown commanded by the affair at his back entered with such pussyfooting brutality that he got wind of it even without seeing how deeply it had deformed faces, things, and atmosphere. He *knew* this breakdown, in fact, still sooner than its cause, that is, it was the voice that shot from the yard and fell immediately at his feet.

"It's been found! It's been found!"

How quickly it happened then: The person bringing the bracelet had already run in ("In the shed. – Under the running board of the automobile." – "It must have slipped," a gendarme's ill-tempered baritone added authoritatively), but our fellow had not, as yet, turned from the dresser. He overheard some strange, shrill shouting (this time he didn't search long for its source: he immediately knew that it was him), in which he found the words: "And you had the nerve . . . ," and he found them right alongside his cool surprise that he was standing right next to Mr. Steel, not knowing how so sudden, so close.

Afterwards he remembers it better:

The gendarme, not letting him out of his sight, stepped back neutrally.

"And now? What say you now?"

Mr. Steel looked.

"You are obliged to say something."

Mr. Steel looked.

"You have nothing to say to me?"

"Me? No," Mr. Steel said.

He extended his arm. He remembers it well: he extended his arm with the intention of striking, but at right that moment he caught sight of himself, and somehow of himself as a person who's, of course, standing there with his arm extended, but not to strike so much as to gain his balance: under one foot it was as if the ground had suddenly gone slack, literally like a folding table when its latch slips, and it was as though that latch were Mr. Steel's "Me? No!" – Thus he was flailing for balance, and into this struggle, which had soured into deranged fury, there fell:

"You shitass!" he heard, having also sensed the gendarme's vulgar assault.

"You shitass!" he heard again, and this time with the tallow-solidified amazement that it was Mr. Steel who'd said "you shitass"; but the eyes that sought Mr. Steel suddenly fell as though through a chute to the gendarme's eyes, and his face was lashed by a hot and acidic, mercenary "Mum's the word, is it?"

It was only through the increased distance between himself and Mr. Steel that he comprehend that the gendarme had thrown him to the floor. He saw the gendarme lying with Mr. Steel in a sort of comical, heartfelt embrace, thus a thing so unbelievable that he unwittingly rubbed his eyes, convinced that he was suffering some grotesque day-blindness; but, having rubbed his eyes, he realized that he was seeing right, it was just that his interpretation was faulty; that embrace was nothing other than the friendly tussle of Mr. Steel on the offensive with a compulsorily impartial gendarme, who issued a paternal reproach:

"There, there, no, we can't give him a thrashing, what are you thinking."

And Mr. Steel disentangled himself; he did so with a seething glance at his paternalistic antagonist, and you could see how the tamed offense within him was obediently and submissively abating: like a person who, having wrestled in darkness, has realized his error, that he had been wrestling unknowingly with his friend, and he said, "No? But just take a look at him."

"Right," said the gendarme, "but when it comes down to it you have no proof."

The words "but just take a look at him" are seductive, like a precarious path. They lead to the mirror. As he is again gazing into it, he somehow sees himself the way we see ourselves at the end of a road we have chosen for ourselves. He clashed with his own image as with a stranger with whom we have agreed to meet, and whom we recognize at first sight, surprised without the surprise.

"Right . . ."

The gendarme's "right" has the appearance of something full, of something that has gorged itself on revolting food. It has to be overcome to not be thrown up, to not blurt out, as if pulled from a bulging sack of cryptogams, something along the lines of "we all know he's a shitass, Mr. Steel, of course he's a shitass, but the law is the law: we're not allowed to say it."

"The law protects me," the image says, concealing it

skittishly; in its eyes, however, was lodged a relief so base that he shouted his image down.

"Shitass," he repeats in his head, having broken into the bulging eyes of a gentleman who has been caught in indiscretions, and having cuffed him so brutally that the eyes didn't so much as dare to blink. Having broken in and thus hedged his bets, he lowers himself into some unnamable depths. A few things hinder him on his descent; he runs into obstacles, weird obstacles! Obstacles that obstruct out of a Samaritan impulse: "we won't let you go further; you wouldn't be able to stand the sight of it; you're weak; not hardy enough; maybe later..." – But the iconoclastic hatred through which he has spotted, as though in a sudden luminous rupture, something he takes for his goal, for an attainable goal, relieving and direct, bedazzled him with a suicidal euphoria and endowed him with undreamt-of strength. Some things hindered him, other things compensated with a path to a place—but he knows—he can't *not* discover, and he breaks and crushes the obstacles, brilliantly on the verge of something that's heading for disaster, and more and more dizzyingly so. He breaks, he crushes everything, everything that urges him to believe, with pure intent and after due deliberation (he doesn't doubt it), "that maybe it's not so bad for him after all." A terrible and liberating path, but nevertheless a sort of enviable impact at the bottom when, having denied outright everything he could have taken root in, he saw himself growing out of mold, rot, and muck.

He stood up and approached the mirror; he was growing over with a disheartening happiness—a creeping, atrophied scrub pine. Thus he was face-to-face at last with the villain he'd been pursuing for so long, the villain who coaxed him, beguiled him, deceived him; now he has him, now he's bewitched him, now he won't get away; he'll feast a bit upon his splayed hatred before...

Before what? Might he secretly long to allow himself to go soft again already? With these tightly, albeit not forcibly, closed lips of the large and, one would say, decent mouth, which keeps quiet so proudly? With these eyes, which it isn't like they are standing up "for their rights," on the contrary, they acknowledge that the statute of limitations is up, though not on all hell breaking loose; on human hell? With these hands, which push him away, which are terrified of him, but with a grip that at the same time as though impeded the assault of the stone-throwers and said, "just a little more patience, there might still be something out there to exonerate him"? He won't be coaxed. All done with his perverse mania for deliberately stacking the deck, so that he would lose. He won't be coaxed. And then: his one shot is for him to harden himself against himself. He knows it well, this human inclination to deal cleverly in contraband: to condemn himself to the deepest hells, but to reserve a purgatorial corner even there. He'll cut himself out. He won't count on his mouth, his eyes, his hands: exculpatory witnesses? (He'd round them up if he wanted: don't you hear them clambering behind the door?) – Judges are advised to be strict with exculpatory witnesses in their own litigation: you're getting ahead of yourself, you're a bit impatient, gentlemen; suspects, suspects! – Let's discuss instead the witness as is—as is, for example, Zinaida's view, or the words "why didn't you smack him one?" – They're witnesses, after all! Haven't been bought off! Unbiased! And actually even too forgiving, for is Zinaida then aware that with her "why didn't you smack him one?" she was actually providing him a back door? Put properly, the question would have to be: "How is it that you were able *not* to smack him one?" – To a question put that way there's no stylistic frippery, no equivocation. If we ask someone who was behaving the way he was behaving—if we ask him, "How is it that you were able *not* to smack him one?"—the answer's well within reach: concise, firm, unambiguous. For that matter, it's been given: "You shitass!"

Keep looking, please, keep looking, in case you find a false plaintiff who, having been convicted of perjury, would vomit at the accusatory word "shitass." – The world isn't perfect, but the flip side isn't, either. Irrespective of immanent justice. As he is standing here, he is boasting of his faith in immanent justice. No, he's not boasting; he believes in immanent justice. It's a faith-support. A support, I say. Did you suppose perhaps that he would betray it because today it happened to be testifying against him? Because it happens that it's his own skin at stake? And it would be pure metaphysical politics! How's that? – That's really what you were expecting? What an outrage! Who would have said, who, that we would get to the point of being so overly suspicious of ourselves!!! And why, I ask? Because, I'll answer, some crook tossed "you shitass" in our face. As if we didn't know that crooks are cowards. What, then, does the crook's "shitass" amount to? Everyone knows that no one senses a dangerous advantage more keenly than a coward. A coward is insolent only as far as his insolence pays off. Can you imagine a coward who would say "you shitass" to someone who's at least his equal? Never!

And so? So?

He was seized by a weakness so blustery that he reeled. He raised his hands: it didn't prevent his tumbling into the mirror; it only softened it. He and that other one, their foreheads were now almost touching. The unpleasantness of the face he beheld came on so brutally that he was already repudiating himself, without the least regret, firmly, like a sworn enemy, humbled at last—when here, as if they were spilled flowers, the carpet of words spread out before him: "blessed are they who endure wrongs."

And all at once, as though he had been meekly begging for it, he started to feel happy. His appearance started to appeal to him with an appeal so unconceited it was as if it were others who appealed to him. He lifted himself up; it didn't matter that he doubted whether his legs would already bear him again, and when, feeling strong, he saw himself standing without support he nearly came to doubt it. It was a strength better than the bodily kind. In particular, it was the kind of strength that commanded him inexorably to turn his face to the window. He had never before complied so willingly, and so he collided with the light, with morning, with Sunday. He collided with them literally as with corporeal beings that had heard of his plight and set forth in a double-time march to vouch for him. He went to meet them, slowly, gratefully, in no way meekly, as one meets an ally merely fulfilling his honorable duty. He leaned out the window; they were standing below, looking up. He saw Sunday morning. It didn't coax, it didn't persuade; with a sweeping, ever so simple gesture, it established that he had to assume his place, and that it was his by right and no worse than the rest. The meadow glistened like an army of lancers; they clambered all the way up to the horizon, where they scaled the rampart of a spreading stand of trees. From the treetops they roused the village, harassing it with arrows whose trajectories seemed more real than the winged point flying that way, and the village's primary concern was to send word to the day that it's awake, that it's not afraid. It was sending that word through vertical and twisting columns of smoke from dry timber, and if it was still visible, it was wavering impatiently so as to get up there already, somewhere where it would dissipate, that is, coalesce with everything else, there where everything just happens.

He finished getting dressed, he went out. Walking past the mirror he spotted himself once more—but this time involuntarily. He passed by; but after two or three steps he was stumped: he had to recoil again, and again he stood before the mirrored dresser, in profile. He stood there, strikingly alone, as alone as if he were looking upon himself *without* what he thought with, without what he perceived with, deprived of them both, as though he had abandoned them in the place he was recoiling from. But he was not spiritless. Something within him was presenting itself; something for which he was merely a place, for its origin lay at a great distance. He was not spiritless; he *was*, even though he neither thought nor perceived, and was like a drawer, still immaculately tidy a moment ago, suddenly thrown into... not yet disorder, but the now as if as-yet undaring *threat* of disorder. In that brief moment, that other time when he had been standing before the mirror, he had made little more of his eyesight than the image of his temples going gray and a short revolt against the unwelcome furrow that had intruded between his nostrils and the corner of his mouth, to which he had never paid any attention. But still, he'd started to miss the trustworthy protrusion of his zygomatic bone: it had apparently been eaten up by that tumefaction that had also infected his face and double chin. In short: he hadn't recognized himself. No: it wasn't like that. He'd recognized himself, but with a distaste he hadn't experienced before. He was seized by a terrible fear, but he mustered all his forces and stifled it. (Really: he wrung its neck, and with a madness, with a hideousness no different from how he had once wrung the neck of a chicken.) – Yes, he raised his head, splashed himself, straightened his tie, and eyed himself, hissing, "What have you done to yourself?" and stepped out. It was a specious stepping-out, which he compensated for with a jerk of the shoulders and a painfully slow turn: now he was standing there, facing the mirror, and looking himself straight in the eyes, as if this were a matter of how to hinder them in their accelerated blinking; he said, having shaken his head mistrustfully: "Such hatred!"—and left.

The yard—he already knew this—opens out from a spiral staircase, just when one had gone halfway down. He knew this step, and he was descending, scraping against the wall, and the more slowly he did so, the closer he got to the step. He stopped right when the first outline of the outdoors appeared; and, with it, legs. He spotted six legs; they were legs lying in ambush. Sure, it's funny to talk about feet lying in ambush, but what do you want, they were feet lying in ambush. They jumped the gun like it was no big deal, hardly three steps from the door that went out to the yard, but that didn't help them: you could see them stand up deliberately, because they knew that until he got to where he was going he had to go close by. He ordered himself to go not only close around them, but as close as possible (at the phrase "as close as possible" he clenched his teeth), and to size up the people to whom those feet belonged—for he didn't have the slightest doubt as to whom they belonged—to challenge them without haste, in the proper order, one after another. And he ordered himself under pain, not only that he must face up to them, but in doing so hurl an insult in their faces. But here his directive—the disorder that threatened the tidied drawer—had started to make a move, was already flipped: it wasn't a matter of going around them, sizing them up, and hurling an insult in their faces, but rather of *not being able* to go around them and not being able to size them up *without* having hurled an insult at them. But because they were standing in such a way that he *must* go around, the insult he would hurl at them didn't bow to his will. He *must* hurl it at them, not because he wishes it, but rather because he *must* wish it.

He stood on the threshold. He looked around. The innkeeper and the Steels were standing with their backs to him. And he made an unexpected discovery: he was wrong; his calculation was off; in no way was it essential that he pass close by. With a bit of caution it was possible to get out to the yard before they even noticed him. But before he could even delight in this discovery, the innkeeper turned around, and the Steels' heads followed this gesture. Had they spotted him? The apodosis of ". . . and over here was the servants' quarters, which we turned into guestrooms" knew nothing of him. Yet he was still sure that just as he was standing on the threshold of the house, he was also standing at that apodosis's doorstep. He, insulted, unavenged, stepped inside this clause without so much as leaving a ripple. He entered like a shadow. The insulted, the unavenged didn't exist.

". . . And over here was the servants' quarters, which we turned into guestrooms."

The innkeeper punctuated it with a pithy period. A period as if prearranged. A period/assembly point for an excursion to big fun, a period/rest stop.

"I am a gentleman!" – The outspread hands. – "Just take a look at him!" – "You shitass!" – "Yes, but do you have any proof?"

Before him who *must* pass by, *must* hurl his insult, there stood three illuminati, who knew that he must but can't manage. They were standing majestically, with dignity and aware of a triumph so perfect that it set aside the rather burdensome responsibility.

His head drooped; he stepped out; they were standing in his way; he didn't see them; he only saw the gate, and this, too, only as though through conjecture, it led to the road; he tried to walk slowly; he was blind, but he heard as never before. – Three coughs in chorus, as if a handful of sand that they'd derisively thrown at him, then a guffaw of non-speech; the non-speech choked on the guffaw and died at the words "... next year we're installing electricity."

When he was making things out again, he saw that he was on the road. He was alone. A wooded slope ran down to a shallow, grassy ditch. He fell upon the grass; the finger he was biting had no taste, but the chill of yesterday's rain still dwelled therein.

He was lying on his back. He had an urge to touch his eyes. They were dry. Not that they might have gone dry again; no, he had learned, not knowing how, that they hadn't gotten moist to begin with. And for this stubbornness on the part of his eyes he hated himself just a bit more. – He squinted and noticed a clump of bellflowers. They were luminously blue. At the same time, he also noticed everything that had transpired since yesterday; at first glance, it was compellingly material, but in this blueness that materiality as if melted away markedly. He immediately sensed that, really, "the weight had lifted off his shoulders." How his creditors had hounded him! And all at once, after all the quarrels and threats, after all the badgering, and when he least expected it, they offer him a reprieve. – It's paid off! All of it, with interest.

Lunch is served in the yard, at small tables. His is right next to the stream: he's got it covered. He's visible to every-one, and everyone to him. It's a table, and more than that it's a hideout, an impregnable hideout. He'd be happy to see someone dare rise, approach, and address him: "Sir, I've had enough of you, get up, scram." – He would say, standing with dignity and leaning against the covered tabletop: "This table is rented, sir. I've paid for it, the payment was accepted, so I am here by right." – Rent is more reliable than ownership, safer, more secure; property can be expropriated, declared unpaid-for, criminal, ill-got, but who has ever denied someone's right to a rented seat at a theater? – The call to lunch will come in a moment; he'll settle into his theater seat; he'll have a good view; he'll let them have it one after the other, one after the other. He'd be happy to see who would dare harass his paid-for, rented hideout! No one can deny him his right to the table! What a sense of power! Of safety! At his own table, there's a taboo. Would the fellow over there defy his gaze? Should we find out? Let's bet on it! – He sees it as though it's already happened: he fixes his eyes upon him, him there. The table is like an electric switchboard, he paws at it: is the fellow over there resisting? Push a button: aha! The resistant eyelids are lowered. As though he'd cut them down in a line. Just let them dare to come to his hideout! Poor them! – They don't suspect that it is he who is generating this dangerous current—now that he's finally understood where Shylock drew such great strength from: He'd paid! He'd paid! – You there, do you know how to get the better of this current? And with what? With words, really: words? But which words? There's the rub: there are innumerable words; the point is to find the one among them that inoculates against a legal rejoinder. Aha! I say against a *legal* rejoinder. But what is a legal rejoinder? We'll explain, we'll explain: Suppose that a hardened provocateur steps forward. One who would keep his eyelids fast. Who would meet the gaze behind the hideout with the lance of his own gaze. *Bon!* But now tell me what this provocative look could say other than "you're the one who had been suspected of theft yesterday"? – And so what? – Suspected—haha!—suspected! And what about the proof? After all, will he waste his time mentioning that there had actually been proof? Aha! But it was proof of his innocence; ah, of his complete innocence! – Fine! So we've found someone who provokes. Fine! But how could he provoke, except by lying? So what do we do with him? Still, no explanations, no proof? We'll skip it. – Here is the look that doesn't want to be averted. Fine! So then what lying slanderer will withstand two certain syllables? These: "Riffraff!"?

"Riffraff" is a lovely word. Its sound and appearance would merit better content than has been consigned to it. Gold is poorly distributed around the world. – "Riffraff." – Such a winsome word, and what has it been condemned to! – "Riffraff." – Such a sonorous word! Say it to yourself once, twice, and the scowled tinkling that hatches through the distinct layers of the midday shimmer immediately looks different. And what is that sound, anyway? It doesn't have the cheerful quality of bell-ringing, it has the crabby stress of a call to labor. It's the midday gong consigned to the housemaid Bela. She's hammering it with an acrimonious thought toward the most disagreeable moment of the day: serving at table. – He gets up; he says to himself, "Riffraff! Riffraff!"; he's delighted by what a corrective and winsome word it is; it's a surprise he doesn't say it to himself in a marching rhythm. – Now here's the last bang on the gong; he's slipped through the gate he'd hobbled to after the impossibly narrow and uneven footpath, along which he is also now embarking in the opposite direction. Here's the yard, the tables are bare, they're gleaming. He lifts his head, as if he were taking someone for his witness, but he already knows the testimony beforehand: it's started to drizzle; it's drizzling. – Lunch, under special circumstances, is served under the roof.

Here's the glass door to the winter dining room. It's as unyielding as an old miser; it can be coaxed just barely a bit, if you've tilted your head in a certain manner, then it grudgingly lowers its resistance: from it you'll deduce that the interior is a kind of white point without it being possible to figure out its whole; and there's the gliding of human shadows rather than the shadows themselves. They'd eaten in the winter dining room the day before yesterday as well. Farewell, hideout, farewell, stream that watches his back and lends him courage! He'll be forced to sit between *any two*. I guess we take a bowl from somebody and give it to somebody? How do we look someone *straight* in the eye if we're sitting next to them? And if he answers "riffraff!" with a kick to the shin, how do we ascertain who'd kicked whom under the table? And then: he doesn't have his *own* place at the table, no magical isolation—the crowd and the crush.

This rain! Like a teammate playing outside the agreed-upon rules. If he were now to say "I'm not playing," who would hold it against him? But let them: this round is admittedly different from what had been agreed, but he'll push through it anyway. He'll pass to them. He swears that he'll pass to them, but he swears to them no longer as an avenger, but rather as a captive, on his word of honor. There are a few other people sitting at the table, and across from them—nothing... They'd already come to him yesterday, they'd sympathized with him for the awkward misunderstanding. If it just happens that he's forced to dine with them at a shared table, he knows what behooves him: no provocations with looks; he has no right to disrupt the lunch of people who've done nothing to him... But what then? Eat with one's nose to the plate? Receive bowls with an exaggerated "thank you" and pass them on with a humble "thank you"? – And it would be the sort of thing where he couldn't stick a slightly decorous and "biting" irony into his "thank you" and "please"; where he couldn't enjoy a nice sprawl in his armchair during dessert, lift his head and say while chewing, "*Alors?*" in such a way that everyone immediately knew to whom it was apropos? – Now, for example, until he comes in... It's just that he's late, just about everyone's sat down already, he's the last... It's just that he'll have to get through the entire dining room, through the brambles of the sudden quieting, if not along the black ice of Mr. Steel's unctuous voice, he who *will not take him into account*...

Someone passed by. The late boarder jumped back, supposing that he was standing in the way, but so clumsily that he rammed right into the person he'd been dodging. That was Zinaida, carrying the soup. He swerved again, but just as ineptly; he inadvertently ended up right against the door. Zinaida reached for the handle.

"Here, hold that! Now wait a second!"

She opened the door, went in, and slammed the door shut with her foot.

He turned red, puffed up like a rooster. Fury was strangling him so much he had to open his mouth. But he didn't get anything out of it, not a peep. For he beheld a kind of large open space that he had to get through alone, without help, at the mercy of malicious stares feasting on his dizziness, and he beheld *that it could no longer be helped*. He was so unconditionally walled up in that "I can't *not* walk into the dining room" that he inadvertently recalled the first time he *had to* scramble out of the trenches. Now there wasn't even an order or necessity or duty. But who says there isn't duty? Only it's the duty of Newton's apple: to fall to earth...

Yet when he reached for the handle the door opened again, and he was face-to-face with Zinaida.

"Excuse me, please!" she said, as if underscoring the sudden quiet that had broken out from the dining room in her wake. But she closed it behind her so slowly that he wondered, he wondered whether that closing wasn't the mournful and ashamed retraction of the rude "Excuse me, please" a moment before, and when he looked up he noticed that Zinaida was not only not avoiding his eyes, but it was rather as though she had been waiting them out. They were standing there saying something to each other that neither of them understood. He, nevertheless, knowing that they were saying something to each other that he would never hear again, that no one would ever displace with anything, and that they could both deny later. Then she looked him over slowly from toe to head, and when she arrived at his eyes a simpleton's smile took up residence on her lips.

"Oh, it's you? Would it be a bother if you were to take your lunch in the kitchen? You're the last, there are no more empty places."

"That's not true."

She didn't lower her eyes; on the contrary, she set them on him. (Someday, later on, he'll tell himself, "she set her eyes on me still more Christianly.")

"No, it's not true. But there I'll lay your table *myself*. Nice. And you'll get more."

She took him by the hand and led him, submissive. But at the threshold she stopped.

"For Christ's sake, why didn't you smack him one?"

It sounded different from before. No longer just contemptuous; helpless.

"Is there a beautification society in town?"

"There's a beautification society in town."

"Do they keep apartment listings?"

"They do keep apartment listings."

"Is it possible to hire transport from town?"

"It can be arranged. – Do you want to go on an excursion, sir?"

"Draw up my bill."

"Are you leaving us, sir?"

"Could you telephone for my transport?"

"Are you not pleased with us, sir?"

"Telephone for transport."

"It could be here in an hour."

"My bill."

"I agree with you, sir. When something like that has happened..."

The innkeeper was preparing to burn him with a look, but all he managed was the word "*pardon!*"; he saddled himself upon it and rode off. – – – The luggage was already on the driver's box. It was well-situated. The innkeeper knew it was well-situated, he had been all the more eager in arranging it.

He who was in the carriage at length discovered the coveted sensation that he had reserved for noon at his *own* table, and which had ultimately stood him up. Now he was sitting in his *own* carriage. He leaned out:

"You should be ashamed... If I were to sue... If there weren't three of them, and they didn't have a car..."

The innkeeper lowered his head; with his right hand he was sort of crumbling something to the hens... Suddenly he stepped back, two paces, three, four; he stood and lifted his eyes; they were empty.

"Excuse me?" he said, and his sunken eyes were again made whole; he gulped:

"So you think it was only because they have a car...?" Even though his chin was quivering with terror, he plucked up his courage and let him have it with a look. But it was only for a second, as a test, but once the second had elapsed the innkeeper knew enough that he started to dare to open his mouth; the fear was God knows where.

"Right, but now I remember I forgot to charge you for the phone call." –

The carriage got going. The innkeeper was watching it leave and took two steps away; suddenly, he squatted down and slapped his thighs:

"And nothing for the servants either? You beggar!"

A narrow road beneath a wooded slope, along a little river, which it clung to anxiously. Groves, small bridges, abandoned mills, pools, the quiet of old settlements. Everything steady, more or less. He paid it no mind. – They drove past a sumptuous, operetta-ish tavern. He'd asked about the prices three days before.

"For a lousy ten francs' difference . . ."

He waved his hand: A shopkeeper shooing away the memory of the store that seemed like such a great idea, and that he's paid off at last. – He waved his hand. Glumly. Just like that, glumly, and he sank into a corner. As though he were chewing something over. His teeth started to hurt; he'd come to loathe them. And having come to loathe them, he arrived at a sort of path set down as though with a ruler, it went straight . . . When he got there, he was so amazed that his eyes popped out: he had arrived upon an indigestable revulsion.

They drove into town. He said to himself: "Traitor"; and he said to himself: "Where did that association come from?" They stopped in front of the office of the beautification society.

The street was called "Bel-Air." In the walled gardens, the jasmine and lilac had long since passed their bloom, and the tannery, having no one to quarrel with, added its own stench as well. – One entered the room through a glass door, straight off the street. Besides that, there were two windows; it was gloomy nonetheless, with a peculiarly defiant darkness. After he had unpacked, arranged, and hung, the time could be counted and calculated down to the minute—he knew he could count on it—when he would at last have faith in this room: today, at this very second, when he would pay the landlady what he still owed, when he would pack his things back up and hear the idling engine of the cab that had stopped.

"Have you come far?" the lady asked.

He didn't catch it, without having not caught it. – He shoved his hands into his pockets, strained, crowded right up to her, and with his chin resting imposingly on his chest said, flirting mischievously with the precise certainty that he was funny, "I advise you to keep everything locked away from me."

"Sorry?"

"I'm thinking that since you're checking me out."

"You must be joking," she said, stepping back.

"I must be...Where am I coming from? From the dale. From Benedictine Mill. Should you wish to ask...It seems I stole a bracelet there. Four hundred thousand."

When he returned that evening, he noticed, unlocking the door, three whispering crones. They'd jumped into a blind alley around the corner (the house stood on its own). One of them peeked back out a moment later. But because he was still looking in their direction, she quickly jerked away.

Rue Bel-Air was one of the three that led from the square toward abrupt ramparts. The square boasted the aggressive health of a beet farmer, and it *had been* a town. In the middle, on a brick terrace, six rows of chestnuts. They called it "lover's lane." In the day, it was strewn with greasy pieces of paper, at night a pitchy darkness. A statue of Marshal Vauban stood on a plinth at the head of this vice, excusing it. Yet he had a dirty conscience. Where Rue Bel-Air suddenly broke off there stood a Romanesque church. Its tympanum was the sole thing of consequence to have happened in the shameless town in eight centuries. The estimable family jewel on the goiter of a trifling and miserly governess. What there was beyond the church was connected to the town solely by its not having a leg to stand on. Oh, to break up with the *parvenu*, to disperse among the forests of the Morvan, to vanish beneath the ivy! The gloriettes, pavilions, terraces, the mascarons; the mallow, begonias, dahlias, and wild grape; the red cedars, sycamores, and fruit trees: this cascade of thickened southern beauty, strayed north and by the north wantonly mistreated. To repel down the cliff, to float down the little river that flowed around it, and "*planter là*" a deceitful town that exploited it as a decoy. But the courage had become paralyzed.

When he went out the next morning and headed for the square, he knew, even before he locked up, that he was no longer there: he had been replaced by his legend. A legend without beginning or end, a narrative as yet illegible, but therefore almost more credible than him, than the banal mediocrity of his impoverished existence.

He walked the street; he walked the lane of bitchy old broads. Broads of every age, broads who were somehow black—here a pleated jabot, here a skirt of mourning, here some black cockscomb, and all of it black with a sort of insatiable blackness into which the remaining color collapsed, as if through a trap door. Broads who were already decrepit—the sort of clumps of nettles they're waving, they'd happily lash you, but they can no longer pull off anything more than a curious pawing. – And that one there with the short, black crutch with the India-rubber end, which, having detected him, gave the agreed-upon signal, tapping on the slabs of the dusky sidewalk to the witch's kitchen. And her, cursing, with cold-sensitive hands beneath a black knitted cape, whose forgetful eyes, once they'd met his, took to bemoaning their having forgotten to slip away in time. And that old broad, empty as a gutted fish, who you would say was chewing, chewing on aphrodisiacal herbs. And that old broad hurrying along, with the full, pallid, still full-moon face of a mother of six, wherein sit her eyes, dead but flammable like cinders, with which she berates from behind a lily-white curtain...

When at last he turned around...

And what to do with that nosy, tardy, retarded and scurrying old broad who nevertheless couldn't even get it together to let loose a heavy pearl of the chilly black blood of the old broads from Rue Bel-Air and have it fall as casually and apathetically as a potent malediction!

The café had a terrace, and the terrace was on the corner of the main street and the square with the "lover's lane."

He saw *him* already from a distance. He was walking like someone who knows that nothing will stand in his way: swaggering with the prickly shyness of someone whom life has taught that obstacles would be swept from his path not because they feared his strength, but because they detested him... He was walking quickly, as though with purpose, and all over the place, like one who, having no aim, is afraid lest someone else catch him at one of his potential purposes. He was beautiful, with a beauty so violently specific that it shouted "en garde!" even from a distance; he was beautiful with the false beauty of an ill-formed fruit, which one's gaze graces but shyly, afraid of discovering the morbid flaw from which this accursed beauty rises.

He saw him already from a distance, and having caught up with him from behind, he looked him over with a certainty that would tolerate no protest that that other fellow was fleeing from Sodom toward him, who would not be caught. – The young man drew closer; before him, like a king's guard, the impudent consciousness of his own beauty; behind him, like an uncalled-for crying fit, the certainty that he was just a little boy, and that his beauty would sour and curdle, and that nothing would replace it, not even the declamatory braggadocio of old-timers who have acquiesced to being old-timers. He was encouraging this rottenly ripening beauty with a harvest of smiles that feigned indifference and fished around for someone to whom they might hungrily appeal; he was disdaining it with a lattice of long, groomed, pasted eyelashes that denied the presence of lust no differently than a valet who's been slapped around denies the presence of the master with a guilty conscience. Eyes on guard: whether against an unexpected challenge jumping out at him head-on, or against a creeping swear word slipping decently away. He was thirstily drawing closer, and with a prideful hopelessness. On his unclouded brow, a charming lock with an impudent nod toward the open secret that it hadn't fallen there by accident, but as a favor to the fingers, so that, in brushing it away, they might have a pretext to flaunt themselves; as a favor to those spindly fingers, so slender you wouldn't know whether to think them the touches of a harp or those of lewd intent. –

It seemed he wasn't from there, for he was still keeping to the street he was on, but they knew him, for hardly had the shoppers and shopkeepers detected him on their doorsteps than their eyes swept after him as though sweeping away anonymous letters that, arriving daily, no longer perturbed them.

He saw him already from a distance, but when the other fellow spotted him, he flared his nostrils, already just as much on the scent, but till then indecisive. But now they were certain, and from beneath the shadowy eye sockets an unabashed, masterfully aimed harpoon had been hurled; it sank into the pupils of the seated man. Its thrower was drawing near; the rope with the barbed hook was being reeled in, and because of it that fellow there was *looking* faster than he was *walking*—it was more and more provocative. To get loose! Free himself from that taut and disgraceful attention, which he is resisting forcefully, but which is pressing him all the more boorishly. That's how it goes with force; that's how it goes with violence; oh, that he can't break away of his own serene will! Oh, that he can't break away without immediately having the urge to find out what he thinks about the disposition of the coerced contract, he who's suddenly arriving at so assuredly deliberate a pace ... He who, having impudently examined this embarrassed ruse, was now lurking with a harpoon that was even less embarrassed, even more prophetic, that he might use to hit the panicked and naïve inspection of his ostensible superiority right in the pupils. – And because the strider was arriving right at the level of the sitter, there was nothing for their entwined gazes to do but veer one after the other, veer under torque so powerful that it even jerked their heads. Now it's like this: the strider, who till then had been looking in the direction of the square he was walking toward, turns his head toward the road already travelled, and the fellow who had thus far been staving off the one drawing nearer latches on with a gaze that is hateful and enigmatic even to himself, but he must, he must follow him whose person he already knows. But himself? Does he then know himself? Does he then, at least, know the enigma of a look that despisedly summons the despised?

The youth—how peskily beautiful he was, and how wonderfully his obstinate wickedness succeeded in aping the contemptuous disregard, the draped toga, of dignitaries betrayed,—the youth, having arrived, at a deceleratingly hurried pace, at the corner, from where he was supposed to *flit* across the square, stopped. He stopped, having preceded this with three embarrassedly apologetic little steps, the third of which was the first on the serpentine course of the hope he denied. He turned to face the seated man: he unfastened his pupils from him and harnessed them to the mystery of the café's green window boxes of rhododendrons. He didn't dare step forward or walk away. His gaze, which knew another's was lying in wait for it, hunkered down beneath the shrubbery, as if down a vertical scale whose regular segments it was now slowly creeping along all the way to the upper end, from which it was now just a blind leap, one that it will sure as hell make if it is cunningly aimed. From the right corner of his mouth, an uninterrupted pyrotechnic display of bashful smiles; they fester on his lower lip into an ironic disillusionment that dribbles dolefully downward. But the eyes proceed, and the line of sketched smiles thickens markedly. As if they suspected that they were passing by without leaving a trail. Someone amazed, someone whose eyes see while no longer having to look, is devouring these smiles. He is amazed at the mind that has already surmised the harm that has been inflicted, at the blood that is still resisting faith, at the senses aroused by a heretofore unknown prickling. He has studied the deceit of mendacious eyes; he knows full well that it's not alluring eyes, but merely proffered eyes, that deceive; he is not misled by the proposition's frightened hypocrisy, so while it might irritate him, while it might cause him shame, he suspects that both his ire and his shame were in league with that other fellow and against him in whom they had been kindled. Now! At last! Again they are eye-to-eye. All momentum was concentrated in their gazes: the bodies stiffened; but the eyes were like lunatic ants on a ruined anthill. They remain in each other's eyes, hypnotized and so alert that they manage to answer questions that haven't even been uttered yet, and ask questions for which an answer has long since been ready… The youth's face has turned to stone; hurl the harshest insult at it and the hieraticized injuries will fall numb upon this mask; the beauty, prostituted, made-up, yet triumphant over the morning sun, bedazzled in its triumph, is on the lookout for its own gender, which no longer applies. From the corners of his mouth, lizardy smile upon lizard-like smile. From the eyes of the one seated, frantic shot after shot, in vain: the lizards fall, and there's no fewer of them.

In the door out to the terrace from the café stands a waiter: the hands folded behind his back are waving a napkin; he inspects the points of shoes worn of their elastic; he casts a glance here and there; his puckered lips vacillate between contempt and petulance.

Opposite, across the street, there's a jeweler's. The proprietor is on the doorstep. He's turned toward the shop. (A few words.) A woman is surprised by a man taking her around the waist, her eyes were moving along an asymmetrical imaginary triangle: from the doorstep to the seated man, from there to the youth—who, as if chasing after himself, was already walking away again—and from this manifest, triumphant Sodom, so alluring that she suppressed her derision and reprimand, toward the nape of her husband's wrinkly neck, where she smacked a kiss that undresses.

The following morning, when he arrived for breakfast, the stranger had already drunk half his coffee. He was reading a newspaper and ferreting around. And having ferretted him out, he immersed himself tenfold in his reading.

He went in and ordered. – The waiter's original intention

was a half-turn away, but something very strong and evil stopped him halfway.

The waiter extended his index finger, despite its black nail, and the index finger indicated a table that was already occupied.

"Would you like to take your repast here?"

The guest's eyes popped out.

"No!" he said, and he added more quietly: "Why?"

The attendant brought a small plate and a glass. He flung them upon the table without a word. – And it was a good while before he returned with the coffee pot. He poured with his back to the youth; and as he poured:

"I thought... Given what happened yesterday... And that you're both always alone..."

He was saying this as if to himself, well aware *that* the new guest was looking. But that didn't confound him. Yet, when he had finished pouring, he put down the carafe, leaned his hands on the table, picked up the service key, and said, this time actually to him, "You are the gentleman from Benedictine Mill, yes?" whereupon he gathered up the coffee pot again, and, going back inside, stood momentarily on the doorstep with his torso twisted in such a way that it almost hurt, with these two words: "That's right!"

He disappeared; just at that moment, however, the young man sort of came to. Having wandered the environs and ascertained that they were alone, all alone with each other (even the street was abandoned), he turned his face toward him, so permissibly that it might be that we're only looking at our brother, at that beloved brother whom we have sometimes allowed, with a mute look, *always to tell us who we really are.* And this face was inundated with a smile; a smile-flood.

"I knew it..."

But there are dams against flooding. Sometimes.

"Excuse me?"

"Oh, *pardon*," the youth said, "I see that you're a stranger here, as am I . . ."

But he wasn't averting his gaze. He wasn't! On the contrary, he started staring like a fisherman at a line when it has begun twitching. And this look, even though it was as though irremediably stuck, was attempting an appropriate retreat. It had, after all, been suddenly, astonishingly satisfied, and it moved on.

The smile slipped out again. A smile that was no longer afraid, for it had grown skeptically curious and haughty. A smile that suspected that the word-lair, from which no one would now drive him, the gopher, away, was nearby.

He was waiting, encouraging discreetly. And the waiting was over.

"As you can . . . How does it strike you?" – But neither the words, nor the gesture, nor the look that he found threatening drove off that *confident* smile; they fell like poorly-thrown stones, somewhere toward their goal, and he knew that he was tossing out of fear that he might not happen to hit his target . . . Our man dug around in his pockets for change; he was seized with panic; he glanced around surreptitiously, as though for a malevolent beast that would leap out if you stayed, and surely would if you attempted to flee. The confident smile came to trust in familiar address, and while he was in fact using familiar terms with the apples of his coked-up, motionlessly nagging eyes, his mouth, so small that it was disheartening, was lewd, having released its corners and these words: "You silly! Why are you against yourself?"

After the initial quick steps, nearly a flight, he stood as if nailed there, not actually knowing whether he had stopped because he didn't know up from down, or was it at the call of the mysteriously explosive, unexpected memory of a small sycamore terrace on ramparts, of its bench, of the proud, impassive shabbiness of such places, of the view into the dale, of the facing slopes where shouts fluttered from tennis courts like bright flags unfurled all at once. A memory, and at the same time the intrepidly massive ringing of an open, enthusiastic affection for those places, as though toward a living being in whom he, all of a sudden, held an inexhaustible trust.

But as he was running past the Romanesque church, he was confronted by several bars of *portamento* on an organ. It really did confront him, albeit only with a timid warning, albeit only as a begging street vendor offers his wares: with such aspiring subtlety, and making sure that he's swept himself from your path even before you've shown your intention to pass with disdain. He couldn't *not* stop, and standing there he started to listen. He caught a Gregorian chant, and he heard it as if he were looking at a heavy, yet hovering veil that sweeps farther and farther away and waves with a mighty, regular, and tranquil breeze. And this breeze was again just the panting of words whose sound was at the same time, astonishingly, also the incarnation of their sense, the words "vanity of vanities" in the form of the vain pulse of the sea, in the vanity of which is nevertheless also its fulfillment.

"Vanity of vanities": not a threat, not a preacher, not a giver of joy, but rather an equals sign between extinction and origin, life and death, beginnings and endings. Unifier of the empire. – He didn't think this, he saw it: like a white-hot heat that does not burn.

But with this glowing calm, as sudden as catastrophe, there were two waves from below, two mutually antagonizing, and yet coordinated, hatreds: a hatred toward the flattering, lazy, and lying reconciliation by which he had allowed himself to be led astray even before his dishonor had been redressed, before he could even attempt revenge, and a hatred toward himself, that he is unable to allow himself to be led astray, that he *has to* oppose reconciliation, that there is nothing he can do but long for revenge, knowing that he's the one paying for it. Two hatreds, equally strong and antagonistic, yet still they add up: to senselessly enraged self-pity, to pitiable, bloodthirsty rage at everything he could possibly lean and rest on, to a savage wail of hope that is secretly counting on what is shouted to finally just drown it out.

The chant was as though felled, and the passer-by, not doubting that he has already, once again, murdered one of the obvious signs of desecrating mercy, entered with a suspicious hope that the dead might still rise from the dead . . . A blinded *legato* fumbles through the yielding cathedral gloom, like a perverse, wrinkled angel whose magnificence has not yet burned out completely. Four forgotten old ladies in indigo cretonne skirts have already forgotten even what the withered hope was that they carried here daily. In the apse, a sacrilegiously embroidered cope is decaying, and the horrors of a metaphysical comedy are playing out. Two ruddy ministrant's surplices are thinking only of the fleeting kiss a neighbor's daughter had planted on one of the acolytes last evening (in the darkened passage where only one of the two gas burners was burning, and filthily at that), and they aren't thinking of anything else. One of the boys reaches for the open Gospel to bring it over, and has to reach up on tiptoe. *Our fellow* sees the hypertrophic ankles of a child and the calves of a future footballer.

"You silly, why are you against yourself?" – He is fleeing. The street. Shops, a candy store, a stationer, a large bazaar, a motor car for hauling. Stock boys are loading goods: one astride on the freight bed, the other handing up from below.

Their frostbitten ears haven't shaken their blue, not even in summer. They speak in monosyllables, and each word is a condensed boyhood event behind a gate or on a bench, and behind each, two chummy adolescent coochie coos at some dame, coochie coo at hoochie-cooch. Their bared elbows are like knobs and clearly say that the day has twenty-four hours, eight hours of work and sixteen hours of what the blood incites, which either you listen to, and then you live a little, or you don't, and you get pimples. – A heavy country woman is walking in front of him. She might be thirty, and she might be fifty. He sees her buttocks and can't *not* think of her guy, how they throw him off with a single get-going once they've gotten what they wanted; and the calves, the calves skilled at kicking away a duvet when the night is too hot.

Over there, two girls are walking—he'd almost say they've avoided him. And what's with the reproving motion of that mommy over there, that her precious daughter not run away from her? That she might cut her off in front of him? – Yes, and the day before yesterday, those two girlfriends on the empty road who were fleeing from him all the way up to the first residential building? And that slacker high schooler who listened so knowingly when his father, upon realizing who was coming (him!), called out: "Get over here! Quit dawdling!" – The blindest of the blind are those who don't want to see. Yes, the landlady for example—how is it that it hadn't occurred to him before!—it's clear, after all, that she not only "looks the other way" (when she's paid), but that she even turns her head. There's a difference, sir, a difference! – And the postman, when he was delivering a registered package to him the other day: what was it he'd mumbled? And what was with that stubbornly lowered head? – And the waiter at the empty café, who was pouring for him as if in a hurry, God knows why...

"You silly, why are you against yourself?"

He was wont at times to stare into the mirror... Some of his features, after all, *must* reflect *that*! Were it not written in his features, it wouldn't be visible. But *they* see. For if they didn't see it, he wouldn't see it either... yes, and then he'd have no reason to cower before variations of this look, which was actually always the same... This look that we have suddenly inferred... This look like when a hand jolts away when it's touched cremains or filth unawares. – He knows this look well, as definitive as a tugged noose: the look of women seated nearby at a café, when out of the blue they call to the waiter to take their glasses elsewhere; the look of that mommy with whom he'd struck up a conversation late one morning on "lover's lane," when she was leading away her eight-year-old little girl, whose hair he had patted. – But when we get down to it, that's *just* how the Paris cops look at him, too, *brushing him off* when he's asked for a street (all he did was ask for a street!); and it was just like that, with the unexpected period at the end of the incomplete sentence, with which they all wrapped up, clearing off quickly—the baker woman, the owner of the tiny little café, the junk dealer, the mailman, the passer-by he'd greeted.

What's giving him away? He was looking, not flattering himself. He was looking with the slightly fearful animosity with which we look upon a stranger. He *knew* that he was seeing an unattractive face; he could go further: *judge what* was unattractive about it. But where might it be, the reason all those looks were like sentences broken by a sudden ugliness? The bottom lip? Is this the lip of a miser? The bags under his eyes? They hold the strangled cravings of sleepless nights; maybe it was visible—all those limp corpses? The gerbil cheeks? The runaway stubble and eyebrows? He was hiding his

rotten teeth: yes, such a perfidiously crooked-toothed smile . . .
But let's be fair! Heaping shame upon oneself, and nothing but
shame, reeks just as bad as self-praise. – That's not all there
is, there's also this here (and he knows it; for he has known
it): this exposed stringer of a forehead—disparage, if you can,
that *glacis*, the likes of which doesn't take the wicked into its
confidence! And the eyes: they look upon him as though into
an abyss they fear, but without despair. Why mightn't he at
least feel sorry for them? He pities strangers who've suffered
a wrong, too . . .

And now another nice about-face: hadn't he said a moment
ago that he was searching his features for what had been *giving
him away*? But didn't he just say that it was his eyes that were
being *wronged*? And that they therefore didn't take their own
side! And that he therefore doesn't brag as though he were
any better than what *they* take him for! What misery, not to
get out of this vicious circle. For every "guilty" there was also,
immediately, a mitigating circumstance. And what a mitigating circumstance! Ablutions, apology, exaltation. And when
it's still so simple to say, "They're moving their seats away, so I
suppose they have a reason; a person can't be litigant and judge
at the same time, isn't that so?"

But here was heard something so quiet that it might have
been a voice other than his, and it said, "And why would it be
that it's only the judge who is infallible? Because he knows
less than the defendant? Why would 'more' be less than 'less'?"

That's what he said, but to himself he concluded with this:
"So be it. *Surely* they're right." – He added: "This thought is
sinful." – But he held something back, and it sounded like this:
"But it's a sin that I delight in, for it's a sinful hope."

He bared his rotten teeth.

"The Church warns against excessive humility. It's right.

The Church forbids you from disdaining your own soul. It's right. Disdain your own soul?: too easy an alibi; and who knows, maybe it's laziness, and who knows, maybe it's pride in disguise?"

The worst thing was that the words "you silly, why are you against yourself?" were stuck in him like an indigestible morsel; worse was that they thwarted his equivocation; "jerk," he said, thinking of himself as if thinking of a stranger. "Jerk," which, to any personal question, keeps spouting the same lie: "Like I'd want something like that? Abstinence madness? Ach! Spiritual hunger, spiritual hunger!"; worse was that it reminded him not of hunger, but of denying hunger. Liars are disgusting. Not because they deceive, but because they fake. Faking is a synonym for ugliness. –

The following day, strolling on the ramparts, on top of which people lived—the only wise people in this petty-bourgeois town—who didn't even fake curiosity, he was suddenly handed—it had just gotten dark—a key: "*Qui veut faire l'ange, fait la bête.*" – Not words, not a thought. *Qui veut faire l'ange, fait la bête.* – Like a thing he grasps in his hand, a thing forged with care, with distinct, even somewhat exaggerated contours, a thing that has weight, and that unlocks. A key. To him it was like it was for the person who has already been working a big ring of keys in front of a locked door for a long time, so long that it's now just more for his conscience than out of hope that he might still finally arrive at the one that fits; without reveling in it—for he is so weary—only with dull surprise: "*Qui veut faire l'ange, fait la bête.*" And right there, a common denominator! For here we have a common denominator, and it comes out to: sex.

It's so simple!

It had begun—how? With the idyll with Zinaida. The

beast, which wanted to be an angel at all costs, adapted the idyll into a bucolic chant accompanied by bagpipes—*caritas*—and shawms—equality, liberty, fraternity. ("No, Zinaida, don't call me 'sir.' Speak to me naturally," his craving kowtowed, playing the democrat.) An unhypocritical beast would have grabbed Zinaida, who had wished for nothing else, grabbed her by the waist, seized the opportunity by the hair, and done what any country boy would—but yes, in mill-side meadows, in the willows past the pool! After noontime, in the scorching heat, when the whole house was having a siesta. – In the evening, in the yard, he would wait for his supper, a gratified little beasty, a benevolent little creature, a kind little monster. It was an evening so becalmed—he recalls—one of those evenings in which the gratified, and only they, can be innocents for a moment, with the mystical innocence in which love blossoms afresh like a lotus. – Gratified, refreshed, benevolent, kind. A car would have arrived, a car of swaggering upstarts; they would have motioned to him with a teaser's sprightly irony. They would have asked him for his room; he would have surrendered it to them grumbling, but grumbling heroically; no pedantry, no bachelor worry about "pardon the mess" he'd have been left in peace at his table; but no, he'd have gone upstairs; to help; let's say that even then he would have gone "to help"; let's say that it still would have come to a "misunderstanding"; and what then? It would have stopped at the misunderstanding, it would have dissolved the way mere misunderstandings do: with Homeric laughter, which opens the tears' floodgates and peoples' arms; for the male, when the satisfied female sets her gaze upon him, is cheerful, bold, and invincible; the female happy, and Zinaida, Zinaida *had, after all, been there*, she had been there from start to finish. She, his fair-haired, almost-new woman, heavy around the hips, with down on the back of her neck, with breath like mature rye... Move out of Benedictine Mill? Away from Zinaida, from the meadows and willows? Out of the question. He would remain there always, until the seductive September mists, when Paris's "happy hour" buzzes at those who know when they've heard it, even as far as mountain villages in the middle of nowhere.

Then, early one morning and in mist that stretches all the way to cities and arouses in them an atavistic, ephemeral memory of their country origin, Zinaida would have been helping him load up the carriage, and a swish of the driver's whip would have entwined the two of them and the simultaneous "until two weeks from now, in Paris," and this melodious ribbon would have become entangled in the looks of two creatures, boldly measuring themselves up, who had long since gone down that easy path from words of passion to words of reason, the path that the predestined couple are walking, and this melodious ribbon would then have been rolled up by the happy voices of boarders and landlords bidding farewell merely warmly, *but warmly*, and they'd then press her upon him even into the carriage, when it was already in motion...

"What a coincidence," someone said, grabbing him by the elbow.

At first he didn't really understand, at first he only heard, and then only that the words were directed toward him. And because it was precisely one of those now so frequent instances when he was meandering the merciless spiral that wound around his depraved thoughts, wherein drowned even the memory of his burning ignominy from Benedictine Mill, which he had to dig out from those sucking morasses again and again (for in his present humiliation it seemed to him so pure that he clung to it as to a treasure), because he was now once more on those humbling rambles, he jolted himself like a shamefaced man who's been found out, and who knows, maybe he wasn't shy about being addressed by a common cop, who was *also* sizing him up.

But it was Zinaida. She took him by the elbow and leaned over in such a way that she was both blocking his path and forcing him to look at her fully and slightly from above, for she was much shorter than he.

He recognized her immediately, even though she was wearing her enterprising Sunday smile, through which it was easier to get to her than it had been at the mill, where she carried a servant's lack of urgency, which one had to step around, and he saw Zinaida, in whom it was as if he'd wiped away the memory of everything that would have made him blush before her.

"What a coincidence!" she shouted cheerfully, and as if she were whispering to him the kind of accent with which to say "Zinaida, is it you?" so that the return of those dark memories would be exorcised forever. – But he said, "What do you want from me?" and in such a way that she turned serious and looked up toward the voice of a person accustomed to no one ever addressing him except to demand a justification, a handout, or a comfort in no way resembling the truth.

"What would I want from you? Nothing…just show me to the café. I'm waiting for someone. We can talk in the meantime."

"I'm waiting for someone," she repeated as they sat down, as though she were savoring it: "yes," she said, when he didn't respond.

She said "yes," not suspecting how timid that sheepish "yes" contrasted with the sticky thought within him, which at first only popped up, and then, as if in its own glue, got stuck and was rotting.

She was talking quickly and easily, radiating a chattiness

where, as though in rising water, her interest in him slowly drowned without her actually suspecting. He went from a being to an opportunity, some neutral vessel into which she was pouring scads of her excitement, joy, happiness, a little out of playfulness, a little out of need, and a little out of spite.

Yes, she has the day off; yes, of course she has a boyfriend (how could she not have a boyfriend?); yes, they go dancing; a tour bus driver (a driver! oh, a driver through and through!); no, he won't be here before eight; what time is it now?; half past seven; half past seven—another half hour; how will she get back to the mill so late?; she's used to it; for that matter, maybe she'll spend the night in town; why wouldn't she spend the night in town?; what's wrong with spending the night in town?; "Good heavens, what are you thinking?" At the inn, naturally; or possibly with relatives; but why worry your head over it?; how long?—till noon tomorrow; . . . yes; oh yes . . . What a card! . . .

"For that matter, if you want, you can wait until he gets here."

And if he's jealous? –Then he's jealous. – Oh no, he certainly won't be angry; "I'll introduce you."

At Benedictine Mill? – "The Steels? The ladies left for a spa." – And the gentleman? . . .

"Wouldn't you know it, he gives me his attentions . . . But no way . . ."

"About you? – Oh yes, they talk about you . . . Yes . . ."

She looked up, inadvertently stabbing him with her eyes, she felt bad, lowered her head, murmured.

"No . . . But no, what for? . . . What do you care?" She looked up again; she stared at him slightly askew, slightly from below.

"No . . . rather, no . . . don't go there . . . You wouldn't be able to do anything about it—you wouldn't. With a clear conscience . . . How could you with a clear conscience . . . ?"

"And what would you go back there for? – It's not like they would even serve you."

"What are you saying?"

"Really—they wouldn't serve you," and Zinaida's voice spilled out suddenly into a great and shame-inducing pity, and it was so thoroughly that humiliating pity that nothing else went into it.

"You wouldn't, either?"

"What can I do? I'm a servant. I do what I'm told . . . If they were to tell me . . ."

He grabbed her hand; he sank into it with his brutal fingers, as though he wanted to dig down to something. – But she broke free from him *like it was nothing*—yes, like it was nothing, and he was awash in shame at her having extricated herself so easily—and she snapped, not wanting to snap, but unable not to, "What do you think? I served you out of pity!"

The thought that had run aground in its own glue had long since given up hope of ever extricating itself. It had given up so perfectly that nothing of it remained but the smugly impoverished equivocation that it was hope itself that wanted it this way, and it was an equivocation so unavoidably necessary that it had maybe thus become true.

"It's not too late, it's never too late . . ." The stuck thought turned its hysterically loving eyes toward him: Of course it wasn't a coincidence; of course Zinaida had ambushed him; of course there's no tour bus driver . . . She was pressing him with a sales pitch as blatant as poorly-counterfeited coins . . . But whether she'll close the deal . . . Suddenly, like a bang—the dull "plink" of a fake five-franc coin on the marble countertop: a memory so indecently jolly that it was annoying, like genuine rejoicing at a funeral banquet: the memory of that fake five-franc coin that someone had once pawned off on him; of all the shameful failures in trying to get rid of it at the baker's, at the smoke shop, in cafés; and then the cash register at the art exhibition: the table laid with green cloth...The green cloth! The witness with his eyes peeled and tongue torn out...He threw down his five-franc coin with such bravado! The witness who caught him but could say nothing. – And following the reproach, no steps. He'd hit his mark, and his conscience had cleaned itself off in front of the mark. The mark: really, the sole autocrat, by the grace of God! You've passed off a counterfeit five-franc coin, so there is no longer a forged coin. Brass taken for gold is gold, and joy from a deception that's worked is an *agio*. – The thought rolling its hysterical eyes was a false thought, but it was his. So who is hurt, who is harmed, if he promotes it to the rank of a thought that is true? And anyway: who knows? Maybe everything is right after all. Perhaps he suspects it of wrong. It can't be helped: all it takes is something to belong to him, and already he's casting it mistrustful glances. – A right idea? Appearances, of course, attest to the contrary. Appearances! He, too, had been under suspicion, and appearances were against him as well. And anyway: wrong thoughts are merely lazy thoughts. This one, however, is lively; this one is prodding him. He's pleased by the thought that Zinaida had been lying in wait for him, *that she desired him*. It's a thought that is strong and positive, for it cheers him on. It is therefore not wrong; it's merely violent. Violent! Right is violence that's hit its mark. Zinaida had been lying in wait for him, Zinaida had been pursuing him: the wrong idea? Yes—if, like a weakling, he lets it go. But if he seizes it, if he forces it to be the thought he stands up for—as if Zinaida *had been* lying in wait for him, as if she *had been* pursuing him, as if she cared for him—he will magically transform it into a true thought, for it will be the thought of a person who wants. He'll be strong. And because he'll be strong, Zinaida has come for him, she's here next to him, offering herself. Fine; that's how he'll handle her. By the pool he'd allowed himself to get befuddled; once bitten . . . Now he won't be so stupid. – "She served me out of pity!" – Ha! A ruse, an indirect appeal for him to redress why he had seemed pitiful: when she pulled free of his hand? A ruse . . .

"What do you think? – I served you out of pity!"

He mustn't back down, not for anything; if he did back down, he'd lose. Dames don't get nuances: a violent man is strong, a tiresome man is persistent: boorish pestering in pubs—that's what they call strength. That'll do! He'd seen them, those raw youths who aren't put off by an elbow to the ribs or even a smack in the face; they know dames like the back of the hand. Zinaida's driver—and who knows, perhaps such a thing exists—he, too, got her only because he dared to take a shot. – "I served you out of pity!"? – And that she tore free from me? – That's it! I see, and I raise!

"Out of pity? Oh, you poor thing!"

Something was tickling him on the lips: Zinaida's tousled hair. Aha! He had already assumed an attacking position without knowing it. On the table, her hand like a bird on guard; his left hand has fallen beside it like a shot-down buzzard; his pinkie is creeping clumsily toward hers, his right hand, a soused, yet not blacked-out oaf, was lapping at her waist.

"No way! Just take a look at yourself!"

He saw her stand up; he saw her standing; he saw it a smidge before feeling the sting of a sprightly, dry, precisely-landed slap. At the same time, he reckoned, as though with the raking of a croupier's rake, what had actually happened. Just then he caught Zinaida's alarm as well, but an alarm morbidly erasing itself before the unutterable ugliness that was squeezing it violently from her features. (And he was stalking after this profligate alarm, which had dropped down suddenly as though through a chute, but was somewhere now outside of Zinaida, somewhere where she no longer remembered it, and it became clear to him that she thus *no longer remembered* him now, too); then, behind the girl, like an optical syncopation, there flashed the hurriedly unoccupied shadow of a young man, two automatically enflamed little lights in his eyes shining upon some side agreement between them both. Automatically? He was flooded with *such* certainty that he was *at least* the electrical switch that had made those little lights glow that he would rather seek refuge back in Zinaida's eyes, even though he was well aware what awaited him there. – No, he didn't know; it was something still much worse; Zinaida *spotted it and knew what it was*; he could immediately read that she had seen through him, that he was lying if he was pretending (and he was even pretending to himself) that he had cast a glance at those little lights only out of a contemptuous curiosity. Zinaida's eyes *laughed* with the irrefutable certainty that he had reached for those will-o'-the-wisps for some other, concealed reason. – And everything was as though it had hatched all at once in the middle of a very short sentence that had begun like an escape hatch (around which he was bumbling comically, as though looking for the latch) and ended like an insurmountable wall, from which he fell like a sack:

"Hilarious! I mean, hilarious! – But haven't you ever taken a look at yourself?"

She cast this at him as though it were a tight net, with no room to move; with this toss she caught both the cleverly probing noose he'd thrown after the fleet-footed ephebe, as well as the furious shrug of the shoulders, with which she confirmed for herself that the noose had gotten tangled.

"You pig, you!" she flung at him, God knows whether it was with her mouth or rather the grocer-like propping of her arms on her sides, and she vanished, God knows whether it was in the mist that had descended in the meantime, or rather in the sparse bunch of gawkers.

They were giving him a good going-over, exploiting the twilight that the pavement afforded them, whereas on the lighted terrace he was like a nudist in a display window. He saw them, not seeing them, but suffering through them; rather, he saw only something frighteningly languid, which was about to *dispense with him*. Dis-pense-with-him! He knew he was an object to them. An ob-ject! He reckoned roughly the kind of resistance that would be put to him should he wish to get away from them, not really understanding himself how he actually ventured *to reckon the resistance* (and according to what scale!), he gained the quite assured certainty that it would be an admittedly awkward resistance, but not too tough. He threw his money down on the table, stood up, and leaped out into the evening; he had a kind of unconscious impression that he was expending a certain physical effort, and an impression as though of an oversimplified satisfaction that he was not expending it for nothing. For he felt that he was outdoing something evil, thereby blazing himself a path toward something, not better, but toward something that was, perhaps though still worse, at least less artfully so. Something was troubling him: maybe the curses, maybe the clumps of desiccated muck—and out of the blue, a pitch-black and limpid silence; a solitude gaspingly encouraging a permissive acquiescence to his feeling his limbs. They were barely strained, nothing more. They started to stir; nowhere were they hindered; they started to walk, to turn the head, to thrash the arms; it didn't hurt; he tried to speak: he could; he stopped and listened: he heard, and he recognized: distant footsteps, the slamming of front doors, trees rustling somehow like Corot's trees. He was imbued with an immense gratitude to the world; he saw it as good. He knew that his gratitude was effusive, but there was nothing to be done about that—*péché mignon*—all he could do was be effusively grateful to it. He learned that beneath the terrace was a "lane for lovers." He was undertaking something along the lines of excavating a well, someone else would say: he went deep into himself. But wherever he climbed in his self-excavation, there were, everywhere, just the same cool and limpid springs. It seemed to him that everything was freshness. Somewhere the word "universe" leaped out, it had the quality of a roomy, trusted thing, even homely, in no way devastating, and he must have said to himself sulkily, but with a strained sulkiness, "the universe! Like it's now me and the universe." He couldn't help himself: he saw it, not with his eyes, but he saw it nonetheless, and as if in remarkably complete abbreviation. He didn't, however, feel like he was part of it: he was a spectator, an impartial, unprejudiced, undemanding, and undesiring spectator—perceptive, indulgently self-restrained, and compassionate. – He was digging, digging, and with a great scientific curiosity as to whether he might strike some wish: he didn't. As to whether he might strike some aspiration: he had none. He noticed that he had no right to anything, but at the same time he noticed that he was *therefore* the freest of all. He was looking, so that he might find someone he would hate; someone he would at least have a grudge against: he didn't. He was casting about as far as he could, so that he might find an enemy, a disparager, a slanderer: on the clean-cut and bright horizon, no one anywhere, nothing. And what if there were no him there, either? Oh what joy, what joy—not to be!

He stepped slowly, lightly, as though on cloudlets. The slightly denser form that crossed the path over there, what is it? Who is it? Never again would he encounter someone whose gaze he would fear. No one who would, upon encountering him, not meet his gaze. Who was it who had flashed across his path? Some young woman. Their eyes met. Why did she stop, why did she turn around? And this cone, upon the surface of which the woman's puffed-out skirt fell as she whipped around in flight; this cone, wobbling like a top after the initial spin. Where was she fleeing to? Why? The terrace's underpinning is entirely inviting nooks. It rustles, clucks, sighs. In one such nook, the fleeing woman vanished.

He continues down his path, slowly. His conscience is calm, even though he knew there was something still much calmer than his conscience: the *consciousness* that something has just happened; the calm, remarkably calm consciousness that, you would say, had exteriorized itself: it's walking by his side, a stone commander taking his time with his haunting. In the meantime, it's content to be suffered, making sure to keep up with him. Something's going on behind him, a betrayal; he sees, he sees, he sees a sinister cloud without having turned around. The commander—how very strange!—the commander has not changed, and still he's become spectral, as though a specter were a spectral wanting, not a being; he assumes terror, the terror grows, and the greater his terror, the more anxiously he's on guard not to quicken his pace. On the contrary, he hits the brakes as though he were counting solely on that foolish slowing; it didn't matter that he knew it wouldn't persuade anyone, that it wouldn't ward off anything. Such pure solicitude is a pointless solicitude. And now: the cloud has burst, and when it shoots, it hits; he doesn't see, but he knows, that the gun's barrel ends as a country boy's small, sensual mouth. God, who fell in love with its kisses even before He created it, has carved it beautifully and maddeningly.

"You say it's that one there? He rubbed up against you? Oh, the pig! Hey, you there, swine, we see you! Horny geezer! Leave the girls alone. Hands off, I say! Lecher!"

He looks around, not understanding.

"Swine!"

A rush of steel-toed boots, a jauntily jumped beating; he hears:

"Get out of here! But next time . . ."

Here is the looping staircase to the dark alley, to this coal-black alley. He takes them four at a time: only not a beating! Anything but a beating! – From six to eight there are several gas lamps burning here. Now they've already been lowered again. The darkness is so thick it leaves stains on clothes. – The steel-toed boots have forgiven him. But he's still fleeing. He doesn't know what's actually happening, but even though he didn't know what was actually happening, he knows he's talking to himself, without having heard himself: "Years! Years are passing!" – For he is surprised (hee hee, someone says, unpleasantly surprised) that he gets short of breath; till now he hadn't known he got short of breath; how does that happen?— so many years that he didn't once happen to drop his civilian gait (hee hee, someone says, a sensible gait). Now he can't. He collapses on a bench. It seats two; he's unaware: someone's already sitting with his back to him; he's unaware. He inhales; he's placed his hand on the backrest, withdrawn; his pinky has touched something alive; that living thing has not withdrawn: what is it? The pinky that had withdrawn ventures forth again, cautiously, like a snail's antenna; the living thing is still there the whole time. Even now, the living thing has not withdrawn; not only has it not withdrawn, it's spread itself out. It's a hand,

and behind it, a voice; one as cautious as the other. But, so far, all there is is:

"Ah!"

It's him.

He says it again: "Ah?"—only this as a question so illuminating that an exhortative smile leaps across his closed lips.

"I'm relaxing," says the man on the run.

"So relax," says the man run down, his hand resting on the hand of the stranger, and the stranger's hand says nothing, lingering.

"So relax," says the man run down, and the hand at rest gave the stranger's hand a little squeeze, then it pressed down, for that other one rose. He had shifted his seat with a movement that is God-knows-why like the quintessence of a military flanking maneuver.

"I'm relaxing."

The hand slides along the back of the hand caught off guard, it's tried the knuckle, it's found it to be an easy obstacle, it's scaled it, it makes for the forearm, for a while it sojourns guardedly on the elbow, having captured it gently; it examines the limp muscles: nothing; then a leap: it's behind the shoulder blade; it's slipped timidly along the nape; it's presenting itself to the throat; and because every door stands wide open, just an itty bit more and the entire arm is here. It's blackmailing the throat and the scruff, it's coaxing the chest.

"Silly, silly. Of course I'm rotten. But my rottenness smells of sweet reseda. You silly."

The head yields, the down cuddles and bribes. The torso follows. It had been expecting resistance; he's looking forward to it. But he's sinking into some invertebrate mass, beyond whose gluey non-particularity—he knows this—there is now only the egotistical helplessness of jelly.

And now it's his hands that are on the march. Literally, on the march. Like sworn and skittish spies on the front lines, they're looking out for whatever's eventually coming up against them; their fear is such that they long for a liberating clash: conquer! Even though what they're getting ready to conquer will eventually conquer them; his hands proceed; they've finally found a thumb; the defiant headland of the Adam's apple; what an enticing staging ground it is: the index fingers, ring fingers, and pinkies are suddenly granted access where they will: they bypass the throat; the unsightly pinky, which he had not anticipated, has pressed hard into the back of the neck and is reliably supporting this entire line of attack.

"You fool, you. What are you doing? Love is..."

"Love is..."

"Love is—what?" The hands were growing sordidly curious. The hands feel like finding out; they give free rein. They'll give for but a moment, to demonstrate that they haven't been bought off; they've given free rein, and the eyes, their proxies, in full armor over the words still rushing around in panic, though they are already assured:

"Love is love...Beggars can't be choosers."

The morning was dragging its feet. But so was his waking. – Oh, to pass away in that sleep, which he was devouring like a hungry man devours his first meager meal! – He half-rose, propped himself on his elbow, was careful. Don't wake anyone! And mainly, not him, the one lying here. The left arm bent under his head, the sealed eyelids; right now, at this moment, there is nothing behind them, neither thought, nor desire, nor illusion. A lockbox. A magnificently beautiful lockbox, because it's empty. In a while life is going to creep in there and besmirch it again. Nevertheless, right now it's beautiful, with an unsullied beauty. Where does *that* come from? Where does it enter? That which ravishes the mass that didn't recognize sin? If only he wouldn't wake up, this one. So that our fellow could take his leave honorably from this peace, which to him now seems, for the first time, to be a place where it is possible to live. And from him here, whom he could at least compensate for his ugliness.

A half hour later. The muted voice of the world, as the motor of the cab that has stopped is idling. It disturbs nothing and no one. It resounds to the point of incomprehension. It speaks only to him who, having closed up his luggage, is waiting, dwelling on the face of the person who was sleeping, the only person whose gaze he might have been able to stand, forever, in spite of everything. But just now the gaze of that one person bespeaks a world eternally fallen.

Some money on the table. – He opened the door, carried his bags out. When he got into the cab, he knew he was leaving. – What? – He's leaving. For he's on his way to nowhere.

"The Paris train," he said.

"I know," the driver replied. – Morning was dragging its feet.

The train of this auxiliary line ran daily, but it wasn't used to it. It was a homebody. Three hundred sixty-five departures a year, and each one as tediously awkward as the frightened excursion of an antediluvian aunt. Express trains, which make sense to everywhere and nowhere, carry people whose yesterdays have all been shed behind them; they take them to tomorrows, which are innumerable. On express trains, everything is possible, express trains bar nothing. – This little train, however, was shambling in vain: it was already far out of town, and yet it couldn't be rid of it. It drew it behind; the town was inside it, its presence petty, bespeaking sulkiness and hardship, and like them it lined the horizon, the little town calling itself importunately, pitifully to mind, like a dog barking behind a truck: nothing, but so puffed-up that what had been there could no longer find room for itself. Love, let's say, had boarded the train; love, which might alter the world's appearance; hatred had boarded the train, pledged to the same miracle; hostility toward life and death had boarded the train, or else it was a fidelity that depersonalized people into virtues—it was loaded with destinies, sins, and saintly deeds, invisible as atoms and heavy as worlds—but the train got the better of everything: it squeezed down everything that was within it, to the point of fussiness. A single chance remained: the transfer stop. The little train was carrying an impatience for the transfer stop.

There one awaits the express to Paris. The little train pulls into the station, still not entirely awake. Under a low, yet already promising sun, the chaotic optimism of a September morning, which befriends the sleepers returning to cities from their vacations. The tracks awaken to their infinitude with such enthusiasm it's as though they've discovered it today for the first time. It has dawned on the warehouses that they are significant and anonymous, they're even beginning to attain a barbarian beauty. A platform full of people. They marvel at the reassuring sense of their solidarity, but they marvel even more at the fact that they haven't discovered the reason for this sureness: yet it's as delectable as an ample vacation breakfast in the mountains. – So far, nothing has yet shattered this superhuman concord, but a spry inkling that there was worldly disorder nearby has already snuck in; it's imponderable and pronounced. Heads turned to the right as if on command. The train was still far away down the ruler-straight track, so far away that they guessed its arrival not so much by the black point into which it withered, but by the overbearing white plume with which it announced itself, and the immense din of this as-yet unheard announcement was such that it overpowered everything, everything and everything. It was the din of an obstinate and disciplined dominance that subjugates while reassuring and ennobling. You might think of the *Pax Romana*: that's sort of how it was rushing, at the head of proud and perceptive legions. A throng of latecomers descended onto the platform. Boys and girls. They were laughing and shouting. One, large, proud, with straight chestnut hair, is next to him, dancing, stepping back. He was dancing his courage, but he was dancing it for one of the girls (you could immediately tell), and you could tell immediately which one. It was the one who, being too happy, was the only one brooding: her conquest was still a flower unto itself; it had happened last night. The platform was now entirely subject to the onrushing train-tyrant, beside whose arrival there was nothing in the universe at this moment that would be "worthy"; and on the platform the shouting throng, for whom the only thing "that's worthy" was last night, because that's when the two had met; this was a cluster of the free within a crowd of the enslaved. They alone were not waiting. They were going to meet the emperor, who was coming to meet them. The carefree among the solemn, the unhurried among the bustling, they roared and skipped all the more provocatively for being oblivious. The train! If they miss this one, they'll catch the next. The nine-thirty train's as good as the eight. They cared about the direction, which is invariable, not about the trains, which are innumerable.

The locomotive was coming in on the first track; it was only inadvertently—for the rambunctious group fascinated him— that he'd caught sight of the train's eccentric, wheels, and rod.

A fleeting dissatisfaction: that the relationship between the dizzying speed of arrival and the nearness of the goal, where that speed would be impressively renounced, seems incongruous to him, as always. – He's lost sight of himself. The cluster dashed for the car it had arbitrarily selected; it dashed as though betting on a lottery number, knowing that there was no reason not to bet on any other number: that's why, by all that is holy, it won on just the number it had bet on. The train exerted all its will and worked itself down to a spare trot. He saw it all, waiting for the door that would stop in front of him. Why run after the car he's selected when there's one, when there's *surely* one that will stop right in front of him? Why bet if he knows for sure that he has to win *something*? He was standing here, waiting, disengaged, for it was to no purpose. And while he was waiting thus, that is, waiting while awaiting nothing, all of a sudden he discovered, just as we discover something that doesn't concern us, that he was unhappy.

No, he didn't discover his unhappiness so much as *that he was unhappy*. He *beheld* it with all his senses, each of which had as though assumed additional sight—perhaps to compensate for some enigmatic virtue of his.

He beheld it out of the blue, having anticipated anything but just this. It was a surprise for which amazement failed. He beheld that he was unhappy. He beheld it like a thing that is quite peculiar, though by no means awful; a thing apart from everyday reality, yet not at all imagined. It was a vision, but so cohesive that it outlasted even the shock of physical torpor, that is, the moment when he stepped forward to board. This thing—that is to say: that he was unhappy—gripped him, even though it accompanied him like a trusted friend, even though, like an atmosphere, it had became his environment, even though he carried it with care and respect.

The express had already departed again; with a tread each time more drawn out and pinioned. At last it took a shot at levitation, and a lucky one; it encouraged it with the bribes of intermittent bounces off its soles. The train became a self-confident gale. Now, once again, there was nothing besides the rumbling that had begun somewhere where individual destinies had ceased, and that would become somewhere where any destiny could emerge. The travelers' past had been obliterated, they had not yet arrived at the future that would sort them all out again: they were for the most part from among the favored, each one empowered by all the others, and their lack of skepticism was multiplied by their glee. – He, too, was aware of this, but only as information. Yet what he *knew* was that he was separate from that simultaneously destructive and unifying solidarity. There is no centrifugal force powerful enough to part him from the broodingly unexcited phantasm "I'm unhappy." There is no centrifugal force that would pull him back into that forgotten self, like a Segner sprinkler spouting from a spinning wheel of destinies that had ceased being destinies. He is apart, unsociable, monstrous.

These monotonous testimonies! He's asked his neighbor whether he might place his attaché on top of his thick rucksack. He has to depend on someone: he was coming off as affable, he even borrowed a smile (from where?); he sought his neighbor's eyes so obtrusively that he found them, but in vain: consent was mumbled; the eyes, averted. And the person opposite him, a lady whose lips prepared so many times to ask a question, which she finally took to the adolescent, though he was sitting so far away! (It was just the one who'd been dancing for that happy throng; he replied—astonishingly!—so politely, obligingly, and almost sadly.) And the talkative conductor who misheard his query, as though professionally; his query alone . . . Right . . .

That he's unhappy is a limpid phantasm, and it is also he: the two, inseparable. He's not scared of it. As a companion it is seldom encouraging, but that it would weigh him down: no! – It searches patiently, ransacks itself, digs into itself, thinking itself simultaneously both the soggy finger and the fisherman who wants to find earthworms in there, and the more, the better; it searches the worm-soil, and with so certain a certitude that it actually is wormy, with such sullenly sincere zeal for finding itself that it has to guard against self-congratulation for so great an ardor: well no, not really, as many worms as it seems it finds there, it's nothing against how many it won't find; not even close. It's just: where, where do they come from, all these misunderstandings, disagreements, losses? Where is it from, that unbridgeable hiatus between what he says and actually does and what can be heard and seen from his words and actions? Between what he's intended and what he's expressed? Between what he's wanted to do and what he's had to do? Where? From this thing that materialized so suddenly, transparently, and convincingly amid the screeching of the axles and the racket of cheerful country youths, from this thing so immaterial yet existing, from this thing shining with a kind of faint, stable, and interior moonlight, from this serious, real, calm, and collected thing. How to begrudge, how to bemoan an attribute so loyal, constant, and innocent! More and more he sees that he is unhappy. But no, that's not really how it is; the fact that he's unhappy—this thing made for his sake already long ago and decreed once and for all—he sees with increasing clarity, subtlety, persistence, and bitterness, but astonishingly he sees it bitterly without having experienced its bitterness, without a grudge, without bemoaning or lamenting.

That's how it is. It is neither weirder, nor more unfair, nor more hopeless than being happy, deserving, or famous, it's pretty much like being loved by someone. *That's how it is.* That's how it is: this is his world, his share, his reward. The sun of his day and the stars of his night. And because it is so, all he needs now is to make a rather slight effort: to say "yes," and *from the fact that that's how it is* something even more cosmically positive will emerge, something that could not and cannot be anything else... and that's all there is to say.

Benedictine Mill and its ignominy, and the spiteful and insidious town, and the frenzied circuit closed the previous night by that monstrous and unadulterated calm: to be compensated with money for a loved one's ugliness (how majestically foul this love is!)—what remains of ignominy, spitefulness, and frenzy if we know that we are under the protection of this eternally present, broody-looking attribute, next to this thing whose unwittingly evil eye no prank will cheer up, nor deflect from us? *That's how it is.* Why say that it could just as well be some other way if—and who cares if it is—we're the only ones who know, we and no one else, that now and then we maybe feel like something else? Perhaps something better? But if there's no choice, then what's worse, and what's better? – "I'm unhappy" isn't threatening, it's not scary; it simply is, and it's one of those rare things that doesn't go sit somewhere else. How loyal it is, how self-sacrificing this inscrutable and indiscernible thing outside us is, to which we have no obligations. It answers for mistakes and blunders, it shields from wrongs, it assumes failures and shame upon itself. It's the screen he is safe behind; and right away, again, the sacrificial lamb he redeems himself with; and right away, again, the confessor with absolution. That he's despised by them? But out of ignorance! That he's treated unfairly? But out of misunderstanding! That he's unappreciated and deprived? What does it matter, so long as there's this "I'm unhappy" of his, behind which and within which his innocence, his human worth, and his unrecognized right have found refuge? – "I'm unhappy" is broody, but not dismayed; poor, but tidy; weak, yet not cowardly. To him it imparted so suspiciously great a respect that he was awash in anxiety as to whether he might have started to love sinfully. He was seized with some puritanical fear that he might be flirting with incest.

They were alone; that is, he was alone. In the unifying whoosh of the express train, slavishly and proudly alone. The rest had already lent themselves out to each other; they deserved each other, they communicated, they understood each other. They understood, without talking it out, all the way to the point of collaborating on that circle with which they circumscribed the solitude they'd assigned to him. Each one did only a section, but it fit the sections entrusted to the others so precisely that a literal circle emerged, a circle in the middle of which were him and his exclusion and his "I'm unhappy," which he looked in the eye with suspicious pride. It was a circle of the spontaneously formed and colloidally diffuse tale of his leprosy, it was the guard of the healthy against the plague. He knew this, he didn't suffer for it; he asked his "I'm unhappy" questions; it answered him with a melancholic, yet encouraging, smile. He was alone, he was grieving, he was dejected but—no, he wasn't dejected; "I'm unhappy" was a sanctuary. What more can we ask for if we have a refuge?

A jolly, corpulent gentleman was telling a story; he was dumping it onto the person sitting opposite him (again, the inspiring youth from the platform). He began intimately; his neighbor added the punctuation with guffaws that, though sparing and concisely courteous, were getting longer and taking on an infectious virulence. The storyteller didn't take his eyes off them, he was sizing them up, and then, as though having judged that they had grown to a size worthy of a counterpoint, he encouraged them and himself, and the slapping of the neighbor's thigh became more frequent and substantial. The express train, too, finally eased off its enthusiastic levitation; it landed and dashed now only with attenuated, hulking strides. – The private joke was slowly being made public, admiring itself, reveling in its increasing gravity. And suddenly—as if it had remembered that it was actually that tiny crystal in which a helpless supersaturated solution had found its purpose—the sundry laughs ran to and fro like crazy shuttles and wove a net that no one wanted out of. But despite its having been woven with a speed that was utterly insane, it was careful not to miss *him*. The entire compartment had been as though gathered into a corner, where the overstuffed words were gushing, along with the youthful laughter that had been patronizingly surrendered: a fairy-tale prince, too happy to shy away from a graceless woodsman's joy. – He, the whole time alone with himself, he, the whole time sad and with a torturously senseless dignity, for he was boasting of something (and knew it) that hurt. He didn't surrender, not even when they started to dance the belly laugh, whipping into the walls like a downpour onto a slapdash rooftop, a shower as well as steam, both water and its benefaction. –

And just then, a settling down: a sudden, swift, noise-pregnant silence. He looked up: the dancer had stretched out his hands, on the fingers of which—like puppet strings—was the travelers' unbounded attention.

"He's going to sing! Attention!"

And a solo, as notarially somber as hushed laughter:

"Dans le jardin de mon père..."

The refrain and chorus buried the solo, as the masquerade procession buries the buffoon's monologue.

"Auprès de ma blonde..."

The refrain, a good-natured rascal, ruminated over what might be left of the individuals.

The people in this train compartment got along as no one had gotten along before, as no one would get along again: through words that were not the words of any of them.

And he suddenly understood that a great happiness had burst in here, that in which each would lose his trace, finding the trace of those similar to himself, and he is following it greedily.

His defiance broke into torrential relief: this is happiness! – Now he wanted it.

"Qu'il fait bon, fait bon, fait bon..."

He joined in, he felt like a fish in water.

"Qu'il fait..."

He shrieked into silence, into a silence ordered by the dancer's outstretched hands.

"Hold on! That sounded off... Who's spoiling it?"

The eyes of the entire compartment are simultaneously upon him; halberdiers clearing the way; and behind them, the dancer's finger, like the finger of a public prosecutor:

"It's that gentleman there! Please, don't spoil it for us..."

The song rolled out again like a ball in a steep trough; if only it could know what it was rolling through!

He, however, cast a timid glance to the side, where his encouraging "I'm unhappy" had still been sitting a moment before. Something shabbily diaphanous was sitting there. It had long, groomed eyelashes over ashamedly downcast eyes. It had the attractive and sticky-sweet smile of the fine-looking man from yesterday. It was only now that this yesterday was making itself manifest in its hidden truth. It was like a morsel that he couldn't get rid of, and that tasted like a purgative.

Boulevard Poissonnière is under the sovereignty of young men with lacquered hair, with manicured, slightly bar-blackened nails, with broad neckties under soft collars, with crumpled lapels, the responsibility for which falls to working girls taken to one-hour hotels; under the sovereignty of young men of the standard beauty of Languedoc brunettes resisted by just barely a fifth—statistics, please!—of the girls and boys they accost. – On Boulevard Poissonnière, there are marvelous shops with chic frocks—cotton garments whose finish weighs as much as the thing itself, with jewels for the most part cheaper than a single one of the light bulbs for their eye-catching illumination—public gramophone listening booths, vainglorious cafés with chicory coffee, half-blind display mirrors that go all the way out to the pavement.

Before a mirror stands a young girl; she has slight little hands, which please her. Her hands slide down from her bosom to her belly; it doesn't mean anything, and Boulevard Poissonnière doesn't ask about it: it's used to it. – Before a mirror stands a fine-looking man, he's tugging at the too-short sleeves of his heartbreaking Alba suit (heartbreaking, for it breaks the young ladies' hearts), he squints at his own Toulousian profile, which is his better side; he tightens his slipped tie. Boulevard Poissonnière doesn't ask what it means, for it's used to it; for that matter, it has long since known what it means: the tyrants of Boulevard Poissonnière hang around in front of display mirrors like this every time, by some unfortunate accident—which for that matter they don't whine about: *c'est la vie*—they've thrown themselves at one of those fifth of the girls they've accosted who is, with a nod to statistics, immune to them.

And right away there's this one here, whom we've had our eyes on for a while now, having our eyes on our hero, who noticed him where the boulevard meets Rue d'Hauteville. And how not to notice an idler hovering with that oh-so-familiar sham busyness, from which he makes a show of not seeing so as to assume the equally affected look of a wretch struck by lightning out of the blue a moment later, that is, when (if) the doe he's set his sights on reemerges, because he hasn't just set his sights on another he wants to get, because if a young man from the Boulevard Poissonnière says "she's the one," love becomes a matter of prestige, and the one that has popped into the shop over there . . . But this haberdashery on Rue d'Hauteville, it seems, has told her that the back room is still occupied. It so happened that the lightning's command, already rescinded, could be given after all, and just as the doe, walking in the direction of the Porte Saint-Denis, lashed the cunning huntsman with that look, after which, as they say, a prudent man loses his taste for it forever. But the dark-haired man was barely twenty-three; in other words, he was of a generation for whom the verb "to despair" is a synonym for the verb "to dishonor oneself." To them, everything is an encouragement: even the look "no, you're not worth it," which begins at the shoes—according to which everything else is unerringly surmised—and ends at the eyes, at which she hurls an apodictic "out of the question" that leaves no room for doubt.

Before phenomena by no means entirely unambiguous, the youths from the Boulevard Poissonnière are also likely to say "you never know." But their "you never know" is not so much dubitative as an affirmation of life, and the truism "dames are fickle" is, on the Boulevard Poissonnière, a mathematical postulate. It excludes the possibility that a woman would make firm decisions according to a principle, whatever it might be; it establishes that they only ever decide on a case-by-case basis, not suspecting that it is therefore assigning them a pragmatic posture; on the contrary, it holds that the most distinctive mark of feminine thinking is capriciousness; the Boulevard Poissonnière is an optimistic skeptic.

The idler, brushed off by the doe's look, has admitted to the universe and to the boulevard—and admitted without bitterness or embarrassment—that he has lost so far. He's slipped his finger under his collar, tilted his head to the side, and turned on his heels: such is the conventional speech of the Boulevard Poissonnière for expressing one's having been rebuffed, a defeat that is never sealed; it's a mere outpost skirmish, and the main detachment can christen itself with the name "outpost" as well, an opportunistic stratagem, to be sure: optimism's unconquerable bulwark. – So the idler turned on his heels: 360 degrees; behind them is the firm confession, through them the return to the point of departure: physically and morally: see the rebuffed man who's traced 360 degrees around his own axis! No longer is he rebuffed, he's just unattainable, he's once again a fine-looking man through and through, whom just a fifth of the girls and boys he accosts—statistics, please!—can resist.

See him before the mirror, and how he's raised his head! See him, how he admires his own image with such natural assurance, and say whether you can come up with a failure for him, a ruination that could hold a candle to this confidence! – He is so immersed in affectionate and deferential self-regard that the dense flow of passers-by has as if spat him out and forsaken him as punishment for his having betrayed the community of the street. He's been left alone, but then what is solitude to someone whose plethoricity is such that he is a community unto himself? The street has cast him out? He's brushed it off. He and his image have fallen in love with each other with so unfussy an ardor that it was actually the two of them, irresistible, invincible, who had been in control; he was in control. She there, the one who'd rebuffed him? There is no she; there is only the fact that the number of those who aren't worth the trouble has increased by one. One of that fifth for whom he's not their "type." But anyway, there are also people who don't like oysters. All the worse for them; he pities them, a somewhat contemptuous pity. For him, the problem of one-hundred-percent-ness is not a problem of the attainable and the denied; it's a question of eccentric idiosyncrasy.

New arc lamps were now flaring again in his eyes—three thousand degrees of heat. They've already forgotten the marginal happenstance that had extinguished them a moment before, they've honestly forgotten. He's raised his head so high, as if looking out for that impossible yoke under which he would have been bent, his fingers with their still-boyish knuckles—these fingers adapted to dry, unwieldy, painful, and sweetly punitive embraces—unbuttoned his overcoat, tugged a bit at his vest, buttoned it up again, gave his tie and the downturned brim of his hat an imperious flick, and with a snap these fingers said "good luck!" to him who was the only person he counted on absolutely: himself.

And now it's the snoop who is walking past the mirror; the snoop has cast a fleeting sidelong glance... Whom does he see? An elderly child. And this disastrous kitchen boy of moral petitions says: "That one there looks after himself; when we look after ourselves we become self-confident. Look after yourself!"

He recalled the mirrors at Benedictine Mill, the mirrors in town. Did they lie? They did not. They spoke the truth: but it was the truth of betrayal, for he betrays himself. That's how it is, he betrays himself! He's not quite thirty-five. So is the truth that he's ugly truer than the truth that he's not repulsive? And in particular, what's truer than the truth that he also has a right, a right I say, *to this here*? – Thirty-five, and how does he dress? Why does he dress like a man rebuffed? If he were to put some effort into it—like that other fellow. If he were to command himself to! The mimetic method of exercising one's faith: a proven mystical practice. –

The baggy knees, and the unironed coat, and the stupid habit of cramming his pockets with so many unnecessary things. And why skimp on underwear? Like you can't tell? Idiot! Neglect always begins where it can't be seen! And this disgraceful fakery with the threadbare end of his necktie . . . So who was the rascal who whispered to him that *all of this is of no consequence*? As though he didn't know his name: *his so-called soul*. – Of no consequence! – And he, who had obeyed him! Who'd repudiated himself for a sanctimonious stranger who thinks of nothing but how to leave him run-down, dilapidated, wrecked, in a lurch—his own foolishly accommodating shelter! His soul! The place where it's set its sights, this soul, his soul, what if he gets there too, he who knows *this place*, who is languishing and suffering? He won't, you say? So then who's it for? – But he's pointing at his soul. – It's a secure box, isn't it? The spurned substance besides which there is no *him*! It's enough to whisper sweet nothings to it: "Be on guard, don't work for free"—and then we'll see what the soul can do . . . What it can do against two.

"Ah," they uttered when he headed toward their table, which, feigning nearsightedness, he had recognized when he'd barely come in.

The café was skimping: the lights only went on at the signal of the girl at the register, and the exasperated girl at the register, hounded by the protests of the readers of yesterday's newspapers, was giving the signal, as they'd really gotten into her hair. – There were seven electric switches; the manager, pivoting methodically from one to the next, was unknowingly opening seven successive heavens. *He* was coming in only with the messy entrance of the seventh heaven's forgetful pathos. – Aperitifs, hardwired to the finest coils of the rheostats of the central office for the production of Paris's "happy hour" fever, glowed slowly from red to white: the café babble flowed like the red from the electric furnaces. The esoteric sense of the furious evening palaver shimmered over the heated trickles of words. It was moseying unobtrusively to and fro, without anyone paying it particular attention: a nonchalant, spherical flash to which they'd become accustomed, and which is effusive without inflicting harm. But from thinking of the not-so-likely possibility that it might pounce after all, and of what might happen afterward, heat was radiating and kindling the room to an infectious and unfounded enthusiasm. The pathological euphoria had deformed the world into untainted beauty, into purpose and order, and to those breathing it in, it indeed seemed a world of untainted beauty, of originary purpose and order. Troubles, difficulties, jealousy, envy, worries, destitution— these went on, but amplified, ennobled, dignified. The wretched microcosms saw themselves in the collective fever's artful mirror; they saw themselves there in heroic disproportion, and they grew as bold as notaries who've overindulged at funeral parties: in mourning coats, which they took for tragic togas. Flying words, sentences, proverbs, witticisms, the gossip spun a net; it was thickening into a more cogent reality than the actuality of those who, in talking, were unwittingly doing the weaving. They were getting tangled in it and growing into a familial form.

"Ah!" they uttered in chorus when they spotted him (and they spotted him immediately in the revolving doors), and they made a little room for him at the table—"ah!"—and they drew him in with their eyes, which were watching like eight examining magistrates. They surrounded him with looks, and those looks were merely the optical extension of the speech they'd only just been conducting about him.

"See who's . . . ?"

This "see who's . . . ?" in greeting had its own brief story. "See who's . . . ?" was an incomplete sentence, which the unsaid "here" fit like Cinderella's foot into the slipper. He noticed this "here?" What he noticed, that is, was the hand that passed just as though it were swatting a fly, and the fly it was swatting, yes, could be nothing other than a mocking "here," with a question mark that had, however, unfortunately—or else fortunately—slipped away. Yes, it had latched into the middle of the newcomer's head like a fishhook. He was caught on the question mark, literally, but it was an extraordinary question mark, for it was a question mark/answer, at which he blushed from his wounded brow downward. And he had been suspicious of himself for so many days already that he was, in his calculatedly chosen attire—the Boulevard Poissonnière had consequences, bad ones, according to the laws that governed them—like a crooked man in a straightening apparatus: convicted by the very thing he'd wanted to use to deceive. The question mark demonstrates to him that he isn't actually *dressed*, he's just funnily *dressed up*. What are you doing running into the labyrinth, you poor thing, when you can no longer afford a spool of thread?

Ordinary days, like bourgeois-starched Sundays—they constrict him like unweathered shirts.

The mocking "here" with the question mark put him at the level of a doleful subaltern bureaucrat, who, on Sunday night, puts on that cheap finery for which he'd saved up so much, and which *again* wasn't helping him. Nor would it help a week later, when he brushes it off again, when he, hoping against hope, puts it on again, again, and again *ad infinitum*, coming back *ad infinitum* on Sunday evenings, again and again, each time a little more deluded, but never so hopeless—each time, then, a little funnier—that he'd manage a corrective: "Never again."

He recognized himself, and, disgusted with himself, he exaggerated his own insignificance with furious and burning delight, until it was like the insignificance of a nameless corpse at the morgue, which not even grief notices. – And no "I'm unhappy" anywhere for him to hide behind. Now that's fair!

"Over so plucky a tie, one holds his head high!"

Someone had taken him by the chin and pulled him down. Right in front of him: two pressing eyes. Behind the encouraging smile, a malicious curiosity hunkers within them as to how it's going, and it's going badly.

"Well, and all the postcard allusions to vacation troubles . . . "

He'd come here for a prearranged meeting, the first autumn gathering with the gang. With his buddies, with his pals: both those eyes! – These eyes, already feasting in advance on what they didn't yet know but were already familiar with— this familiarity: how it dances within them—these *foreigner's* eyes. How is it that it's never occurred to him till now that he's foreign to them? And how is it that he's not amazed at this unexpected discovery?

He's appalled by the foxy correspondence between these eyes; with a horror thinned out by the café's radiant "happy hour" into a kind of noncommittal flirtation—so strained it was breaking—with dread. He sees eyes that are looking him over like those performing a dissection look over their subject: for knowledge and nothing else, but there was something still worse than indifference, there was the shame spun from the certainty (it was a very fine and biting thread of depleted horror that had spun it) that they weren't looking him over like this for the first time (and he hadn't known!). *That they had never looked at him; that they only ever looked him over.* They'd known him for a long time, he who didn't know them. They knew him better than he'd ever known himself. They'd prepped him with scalpels and tongs, which they availed themselves of remorselessly, and holding nothing back, just where it hurt most, while he only hacked away at himself, within himself, bypassing the painful spots. He had begun hating them, like a failed, faint-hearted experimenter hates an intrepid experimenter, but behind the magnanimous jealousy billowed the mindless malice of the robbed man who has suddenly arrived at the fact that, in his foolhardiness, he's left everything open for the burglar, even his most secret drawers, and not even out of fear, but out of a raving masochism.

And he who was coming here with a sealed promise that he "would give them a rest with these stories"! He who reads in the foxily imploring eyes that all they care about are his stories! That they don't care about anything else than the symptoms of "his case"! Their friendship? To his trust, a doctor's observant "ah, now that's interesting." – What advantage does this coalition of four have over him now that he recognizes that he has never been their fifth?

Three sentences: "Oh, see who's here?" – "Over so plucky a tie..." – "And all your postcard illusions?" – Three cleverly aimed blows, and beneath each a piece crumbled away from his fateful silence. So what if they then defame him. And the more dilapidated his demolished hideout was, the more eagerly he would oblige them, so that no stone would remain on another. They drew him in among them. It looks like a friendly chat, but it's a prison escort, cramped and compact as an asylum jerkin. The elbows are wide apart on the table, jovially wide apart, so wide you'd say: grateful listeners of the hunter's yarn. A trick! Indeed, *they* are not sitting; they're above, a conclave, they're looking down at him. Their eyes were passing through the café, measuredly measuring up this guy, that guy, saying hello, laughing at acquaintances. A trick! To mislead him that they weren't letting him down, that they were looking after him. Monosyllabic questions, easygoing words: clever investigating judges coaxing a confession. Stay away from these careless hands: that they're caressing the paper? That they've pushed the paperweight aside? A trick! – These are hands lying in wait, setting a trap for you. Absentminded words, futile questions: they've landed, and already it's as though they'd never been: look out for this synthetically woven net! Here and there, a skimpy burst of laughter; you'd say nothing more than a trickle spurting out because of an oversight, which you'll stop up with your heel: look out! it's a pebble calculatedly cast through a little window, into a lookout, into a dormer—like nobody's business, and the glass rains down: aha! Aha! So that's where it's from, that's where this frosty draft of non-participation is coming from! How it blows! His powerlessness is chilling. He's trying to warm up, he's rubbing his hands together, and right away it's a little warmer, right away this selling of oneself is easier again. – Really, as a matter of fact it's not so difficult, selling yourself for a hill of beans; being subject to little words, questions, and the rattling rain of laughter right in your face: child's play! On the contrary, it's somehow comforting and encouraging, like a pelican's acts of fatherly love: for what else would these scrawny kids of curiosity do against the brawny athlete, against his usurpation of misfortune, against this misfortune, as basic as rye bread?

He empties the drawers. What would he save, what would he withhold? In the drawers, it's all the same old junk. The goods, the goods are not to be found. They're his, his forever. –

He's drinking; drunkenness drags itself in from all sides; it's not drunkenness from drinking. What's intoxicating is this rapid alpine huntsmen's march banged out on that xylophone and its rather harsh tones. The harsh tones! Each of them so self-confident, so distinct, as though tipped out of a mold. With such sharp contours you'd say they'd been minted. Who's that playing the xylophone? No one. It plays itself. Red, white, yellow, opal glasses on the tables, like nobody's business: a sham! The blistering alpine huntsmen's march on the xylophone is their pied piper. It's the music of the spheres; and the music of the spheres is too substantial to be consumed by the ear. Or don't you see it? Or else wouldn't you see it if the colored quality of the aperitif glasses were to take wing? Listen! Don't you see the red, gold, brownish, and opal sounds, see them rushing, see them jostling on the glass bridges, so not to miss the rally? Look! Don't you hear the heads of their unfurled offensive lines twist suddenly, charmingly, skirting a kind of magnetic focal point, languidly and in vain? The eccentric courage of the spirals they've initiated is slowly mounting. Only that still higher, ecstatic self-confidence, and behold, from the spirals, unprotected and open to foreign incursions, delicate orbs. The alpine huntsmen's march had been straightforward, but now it's swerved angrily away from the straightforward. It's swerved into the voiceless quadrille of whirling milky orbs, do you see them? Do you hear the revolts of the seven lights breaking out within them, in long, unhurried intervals? The advertising globes of steamship companies.

A quadrille, hasty as mayhem and hurried as discipline. A quadrille of spinning orbs skewed toward a common ecliptic, along which they are sliding smoothly toward a still quieter and more spirited iridescent orb, which devours them. It rises charmingly, you'd say it was spherical lightning. Look, it's over their table, over the table of the efficacious vivisection. It floats neutrally, like an air bladder tossed in an evening dance hall. It spins every which way with nose-diving apathy.

His confessors are here: with carefree casualness, self-confidently composed people, whose metaphysical bread and butter had been confronted by the coziness of the armchairs at the club; theirs had patronizingly consented to start resembling the exceptionally iffy chairs of cafés: the discreet overtone of professional Spartanism suits these upper-crustily spoiled judges, and a judge's prestige awaits them. Their aloofness, the imperious sangfroid of their grudge, their icy and patient curiosity are as tidy as cultivated, though already domesticated, plants. He was encircled by the unwitting solidarity of the four researchers immersed in a common problem, they're keeping a close guard on him, like guards around a post-mortem specimen dearly acquired, and anaesthetizing him with a narcotic of alternating and rhythmic "dear friend," "friend," "oh!," "how very odd!," "really?," "can it be?," "how could you?" –

He, too, sees himself askew. He sees himself as a conjurer spinning an endless paper ribbon with signs of Morse code from his maw. The marks are voluminously concrete, and these concrete signs create a chain, and that chain represents an occurrence. It is an occurrence: that which has occurred—somewhere, somehow, to someone. This occurrence concerns him unintentionally, yet he is well aware that between the two of them there is a close relation, he'd happily pronounce it, now it seems to him that the quality of that relation is that of the words "I am responsible for everything that happens," but when he has these words already on the tip of his tongue he realizes that that's not quite it.

He pulls the sort of paper ribbon with its signs from his throat, but by now they're not written down so much as signs just now being written, the writing from Belshazzar's feast: written in bluish light like that which torments mercury lamps, and each mark was visibly impressed into a cartoon figure as well, but with a different light.

He hears himself talking, he's speaking the bluish words, and around each the tremulous and sparkling contour of a word of confession: in sum, a kind of moving electric advertisement trotting from darkness, where it lights up, into darkness, where it goes out.

He's looking at the current of confessional words which he hears, and he finds it strange that those who pronounce them are also looking at them, and also as though at foreign words; they're reading with the distracted interest of loiterers on the boulevard:

"A pronounced case of deficient will..." – "Passive tolerance of injury as an indication of subconscious criminal inclinations..." – The inscription, "The surest guarantee of moral depravity is approving of one's own ill treatment, it applies to everyone, present company excepted," flew by faster than the inscription that had preceded—somehow with a provocative shyness—but now we have the luminous question: "Who folds his hand when he has mostly trumps?" into the encouragement of which there spurted "A cheat in dire straits," and it drained away. "Or else a super-lucid Polycrates" passed with ironizing sluggishness, which courted the exhortation: "All of you who are suffering for a crime not committed, bring about justice by redeeming the crime after the fact..."

Here, however, the jotting's trotting was suddenly cut off, and with so sheer a suddenness that everyone, people and things, and even the trot itself, seized and chopped, shut down before an as-yet mysterious cause, almost irrevocably. For it had come right up to the slope leading toward the unsightly catastrophe, along which the town's ramparts crashed toward the little river, clinging to the bulwarks tailored to those two sycamore promenades, toward one of which, the smaller, he maintained an almost human amity. Where had this safety-memory come from? Safety, since it propped up his crashing presence of mind: he tugged at the reins, he tugged them with a strength he hadn't expected of himself, and which revived the pride within him. The café's "happy hour," which had reared so dangerously, settled back down and trotted as before.

"And why not?"—he heard himself—"and why not? He *was* beautiful."

It was a response (it half-rose), it was *his* response to some "no way! come on, no way!" which, having first taken fright, threatened some quiet sentence that he had interposed imme-diately before. The sentence died away in his memory; all that remained of it was the recollection that he had been saying it with his head lowered, as if he were reading from the light mahogany table where they were sitting.

And again those rushing aural figures with contours of tremulous light, except perhaps the slightest bit fainter, more personal, no longer sentention messages to EVERYONE, now just inquisitional questions to HIM:

"Didn't it occur to you that *that* event was the complement of the mishap at Benedictine Mill?" – "Since when do you have this magical attraction for wretches and lowlifes?" – "Maybe you exude *caritas*? Maybe it's predestination?" – "Then again, the dead do fear the living, and they're all over you." – "Like biting flies on rotten meat." – "Why don't you defend yourself against them?" – "Either you can, or you can't." – "The living can't *not* defend themselves—in your place, I'd have been afraid!"

After the word "afraid," the emboldened spiral intervened, and the trot, straightforward till now, broke into a whirl. And it was a smooth transition, through the sudden rotation of two quite disagreeable movements. The temporal divide between the two was a hair's breadth, and that hair sounded briefly, as though with the echo of something overheard somewhere and sometime before: "But see who's here? And why the long face?"

It was surely some kind of signal, after which he saw his confessors differently from how he *had been seeing* them just a second earlier. As if they'd passed from the realm of phantasmagoria into the realm of the real. Closer to the real, but not yet entirely there. For the whole time it still seemed natural to him, both that they were listening to him with so convincing an appearance of people who aren't listening, and that, though he was within arm's reach, they were addressing him as though from beyond so many mountains, not actually seeing him and not caring about his responses. He was drowning in incongruities, he knew it, but nothing in him opposed them: that's how he caught on that he was dreaming, or that he was in regions bordering on dream. He saw that they were taking his words in, but he saw just as well that there was no more of these words than there would be of a stone falling straight into an abyss. – He saw that they were speaking to him, but he saw just as well that the words they were saying to him, and which they were aware of, were sinking into their oblivion. But at the same time they were also banished words, words already prepared long ago. Merely an opening! Now he had finally provided one himself. – He saw the judge and the onlookers and their frayed condolence, for it was a condolence for a misfortune they were all secure from. And he knew that the originator of their superiority, which they find so flattering, which they don't brag about, but which they delight in, was him, and knowing himself to be that delight's unwitting creator he adopted a kind of frightened tenderness toward it, even though he knew that the bliss he had arranged for them was the high point of their jealous certainty that they had a reason to hold him in contempt.

A tenderness more than majestic, a tenderness aloft, but endeavoring to move him in vain. If he submitted to it, it was only as though upward toward the trap door onstage, carrying him up with a gliding lift without him realizing that he was ascending. And while he was emerging, dazed but sensible, the world around him turned so grimacingly, and was annealed with a rainbow oscillating so quickly that now it looked out, now it squinted, just as if some hand had grabbed it and let it go by turns, and all the sense of the world, it seemed, dashed from the matter of "I'm putting it out" to the matter of "I'm firing it up."

To him it seemed he had gotten up, with the one qualification that it was not him so much as his companions, in whom he now, for the first time, recognized foreigners, in no way foreign to him. He said that this was a subtle and fundamental difference, and he exhaled, deeply relieved. They were looking at him, calmly and blankly, and he, seeing this, leaped across the flexible permutation to the gossipy certainty, calmly and blankly, that he was the one looking at them; and now, in his jaws, he also felt the unpainful cramp of a person who, with immeasurable amazement or pain, has been left swallowing his saliva with mouth agape. But that gesture was without doubt merely a mimetic gesture, for he was neither amazed, nor suffering. So much had slipped between him and them, one thing after another, uncrossable spaces, thick and see-through sliding panels shifting along precisely tested grooves. He recognized that he was getting, if not farther and farther away from his companions, then ever more somewhere that was more and more "elsewhere" from where they dwelled, even though they hadn't lost sight of him. When quite close to the revolving doors—he noticed that this was quite close to the revolving doors—he suddenly fell into a rotation so powerful that he retained only as much consciousness as would fit into his abruptly cut-off knowledge that he had been seized by the swiftly swirling vortex, wherein he lost consciousness. All he still heard, as though behind manifold, unevenly-woven curtains of sound, was: "You'll get out of there somehow; carted off with the dead, no way...," and he awoke with a sober awareness that he was coming around from a rather brief, yet weighty, swoon. He passed through a door leading from one street to another, but the fact that the door leading from street to street was actually an extraordinary door struck him only when it had shut, hermetically sealing the street from which he had arrived from the street where he now found himself. There was a quiet so deep that, as though on an absolute scale, it was the sole means by which to measure how very demanding the racket had been on the street he had come from, of which he was still aware without actually remembering it yet. The quiet that had spilled everywhere rose from the earlier racket with contours as sharp as the drawings that, as you keep scribbling, will arise from coated "magic papers." – It was a long, monotonous, ceremoniously uninhabited, yet affably, if restrainedly, inviting street with ideal academic perspective, like in a simplistic urban design. Not that it was abandoned, but the passers-by—you could tell—were conscious of their own purely decorative nature. It was a commercial street, shop after shop, one like the next; but you could tell that all those shops were merely a guise of a *certain* shop that, it so happened, didn't differ from them, having more or less the appearance of a first among equals; it was quite far away. The entire street was somehow contrived, the specified shop as well, which seemed, however, the slightest bit less calculated, further testifying to the fact that this had to do with a shade that has a deeper cause. In the meantime, however, that shop's chosenness was in no way manifest except in that it sufficed to look at it (and it was impossible not to) for the thought that one might not head toward it to become absurd. Thus he headed toward it, fastidiously keeping to the sidewalk, which, despite the fact that there were people walking behind him, had the unerring quality of a sidewalk officially as yet "uncommissioned." When he arrived there, he encountered one of those decorative figures, several of whom, as in any perspectival plan, were scattered along the street. But the one in front of the shop was at the same time more calculated and more significant than the others, and the reality that the figurine was Tiemen was so natural—no, what am I saying—it seemed so inevitable that in speaking of its naturalness I'm not doing this naturalness justice.

Tiemen had the look of a person at an appointed meeting, and our walker the look of a person who, upon arriving at the appointed meeting-place, has found the one whose absence would have surprised him, if not discomfited him. Tiemen took him by the sleeve and led him to the display.

"Till now, I have never robbed a jeweler's," he said, "but your first time is worthy of something special. Don't worry, it'll go smoothly. You see the beautiful platinum bracelet with rubies? Your mission, as you know, is to steal that bracelet, that one there, and nothing else. That's what we agreed. If you fail ... But you know that everything depends on your not failing."

As he was saying this, Tiemen was pointing out a bracelet wrapped around a wax arm on a plush green pillow, where it was obviously boasting. *He* would have gladly nodded, and not only with his head, but with words as well, that it went without saying, but he couldn't, for again there was that unpainful cramp in his jaw, which made him salivate such that it wasn't enough to swallow, not being able to swallow.

All of a sudden, he sensed that Tiemen, behind his back, was surreptitiously slipping into his hand something that stood out for the striking disproportion of its weight (it was very heavy) to its dimensions, which were minute. And this disproportion taught him, without his needing to look, that it was a wooden club lined with lead.

"Make no mistake, the shopgirl is alone. What I gave you (after the words 'what I gave you' he became certain that Tiemen would never, ever pronounce the word 'club')—hide it up your sleeve. Yes, it'll fit, it's the right size. But don't you go using it before I give you the signal. I spill blood only if it can't be avoided. I don't like blood, you know, and I hope I succeed in making the robbery easy for you, so you'll find murder unnecessary. But it's not so much about avoiding the guillotine, but that it's more elegant without bloodletting."

All of a sudden a doorman approached them from behind, and in a manner that left not the slightest doubt that the word "guillotine" was the prearranged sign for him to step out onto that stage. He opened the door for them with a deep bow, saying:

"If I'm not mistaken, you're the two gentlemen who are supposed to steal the platinum bracelet with rubies. Right this way!" Tiemen nodded quite affably toward the doorman, and they went in. The saleswoman was, in all sincerity, Mrs. Steel.

But only for a few seconds. Before you knew it, the saleswoman, while remaining a saleswoman, ceased being Mrs. Steel. The fault lay with a hairy wart, about which our hero (and this annoyed him) was altogether incapable of saying whether it might have come about immediately, or whether he had simply overlooked it at first. A few seconds later, however, and here was Mrs. Steel again, and this despite the hairy wart, which went on as a hairy wart, but which the genuine Mrs. Steel—he was sure of it—did not have. He couldn't handle it, he lost his cool, he was already letting down the club hidden up his sleeve when this shopgirl, bowing gracefully, said:

"Oh no, I'm not Mrs. Steel. But what can I get you? Perhaps that beautiful platinum ruby bracelet that you, planning your burglary, have been eyeing for so long? I'll get it for you."

"Nowise have we a robbery planned," Tiemen responded, trying primarily to deceive those listeners, of whom there happened to be none, who might have known Old Czech syntax better than he, who hadn't the least notion of it, being almost illiterate, "and that bracelet, magnificent though it is, is not the bauble we wish for above all, albeit nowise excluding its purchase, should it come to that . . . First let's see the rings," he added in modern Czech, but apparently just to clear away—in vain, ultimately—the impression of that Czech which he took for the Czech of Chelčický's *Net of Faith*.

It's just as obvious from the retort of the hero, put off by Tiemen's chosen speech to the point that he exploded, "What's with this talk, now? . . . If you please!"

But Tiemen, as if he had expected the crotchety reprimand, already had a gesture prepared, which meant: "Leave it to me, alright? I know what I'm doing."

But just then the saleswoman returned with a velvet tray full of rings, which she very slowly placed on the counter. At the same time, she moseyed with a serene look over to Tiemen's eyes, then she moseyed with a serene look over to the other's eyes, thereby expressing that she was rebuking them, if only carelessly. When she had done so, she lowered her suddenly as-though-enamored eyes to the mat, saying, "Are you perhaps talking about the revolver...? Because if you are perhaps talking about the revolver...," and with her left hand she opened some drawer, into which she plunged her right hand, which she left there with a meaningfully threatening mischievousness.

"But it's too soon for that," Tiemen snapped at her, in a friendly way, "how many times have we rehearsed this, and you keep messing it up over and over."

"I'm sorry," Mrs. Steel said with prearranged mortification—now it was Mrs. Steel again—and she withdrew her hand. Hardly had she done so, however, than Tiemen leaped forward, dug into the half-open drawer, and took out the revolver. He stuck it into his pocket, and with a triumphant glance at Mrs. Steel he said to our fellow, "There—and now you no longer have anything to be afraid of."

"I can see that the rings say nothing to you (that is, she was speaking French, and she had literally said, '...ne vous disent rien'), so I'll show you something else. Perhaps women's cigarette cases?"

"Women's cigarette cases, after all, were not in the program ('I've never said a word to you about women's cigarette cases,' Tiemen muttered in the style of an actor's 'aside,' 'and it's unbelievable how forgetful you are'), but fine, bring them. But don't forget that nothing is going to appeal to us, not even among the things that will lead quite naturally to the bracelet."

"I'd rather get right to it."

"Right you are," said Tiemen, suddenly irritated by

God-knows-what, "right you are, at least we'll get through it faster, and why should I make so much fuss if I see that this nincompoop loses all the same, one way or another?"

"What nincompoop?" asked he who lived between two doors.

Mrs. Steel covered her mouth with her hand, and, brushing back her ringlets, she choked discreetly.

"Oh you!" and Tiemen, like a Gypsy cattle-rancher at a cattle-ranching Gypsy, winked at her, who was again no longer Mrs. Steel. "But let's move on," he roared, with his eyes following the saleswoman carrying the bracelet.

"Now," Tiemen moved on, settling into an armchair that the doorman had pulled up for him, "now, as you know, in no time it will come to the orchestrated confluence of people on the sidewalk across the street. The gunfire—at random—which will then break out will divert your attention." (Tiemen turned to the door.) "My comrade will use this distraction to swap the actual bracelet for a fake one."

Tiemen fell silent, he was gawking at the street, where there was nothing at all; a moment later he started pounding angrily on the armchair. This failure of direction was so infectiously awkward that it brought about embarrassment even for him who had come here to steal for real. An awkward pause came about: Mrs. Steel was wiping her mouth; Tiemen was pacing nervously; the doorman walked with an apologetic expression from the armchair to the door; and the virtuous thief, him there, was seized by the kind of feeling an actor has when his scene is cut short by an order to start all over again.

"Alright then!" an angry Tiemen mumbled. "And after all those rehearsals! Missing extras! . . ."

But just then, a sudden and deep relief: On the sidewalk across the street, from out of nowhere, there was a dramatically riled-up mob, and the mock gunfire started its rat-tat-tat. Tiemen spread out again comfortably and shouted eagerly, "Hurray! Attention diverted! Is your attention diverted?"

"It is," the saleswoman said with such affected intensity that it would have been an insult anywhere else.

"Good!" said Tiemen, and after nodding at the other fellow with the smug swagger of a virtuoso bandleader who, having provided the first couple of bars, leaves the rote-performing orchestra to its own devices, he said, "Now perform!"

Yet here there rang out such a dissonance that Tiemen, the bandleader departing nonchalantly, promptly returned to the conductor's stand.

"Perform!...But how? I don't have a fake. I don't have anything to replace the bracelet with! A fake! You haven't said a word about a fake."

"You haven't said so much as a word to me about a fake, not a word," Tiemen teased, while Mrs. Steel held her sides, "but of course I haven't said a word to you about it...Since when do we speak of obvious things?..."

"Idealist!" the saleswoman coughed.

"But how many times have I told you," Tiemen yelled, and for real now, "that I don't want any blood unless it's necessary. And when there's no blood, there's slickness and ingenuity, surely that goes without saying. – Idealist? A moron! He wants to steal, the hero, he wants to steal when it's already gone out of style. Or perhaps you've never even heard of deceit? Deceit, my little chickadee! So what's his business among thieves if he doesn't know how to deceive, what business does he have among people, the moron? *Why do you make everything so difficult for yourself?* My word—out with the fake."

"I don't have a fake. You haven't said a word about a fake. I'm not pretending, I don't know how to. I want to steal honestly."

"Steal honestly? Steal honestly?" Tiemen was dashing about rakishly. "Fine! As you wish. But don't count on me, eh? You have a club. So hit her with the club." And, solemnly, "Otherwise there's no bracelet for you. And you know how much depends on the bracelet."

"Too late!" And Mrs. Steel straightened up impressively; it was Mrs. Steel, the whole Mrs. Steel from Benedictine Mill, and her certainty that he recognized her dazzlingly was so banal somehow that she condescendingly uttered a "yes, it's me," not caring about how dangerously she was compromising the majesty of the appointed period with a familiar theatrical intermezzo: "Too late! Not only did you want to rob me, on top of that you were going to murder me. Rob me, murder me—a weak and helpless woman."

And she grabbed him firmly by the shoulder. – He looked around, they were alone: Tiemen, the saleswoman, and himself, for the doorman, though present, had assumed in the meantime the convincing quality of a permanent prop.

"Shoot her," he cried, trying to extricate himself. "Come on, you have her revolver! Shoot her, or don't you see that she's tricked me?"

But the saleswoman, having torn the club away from him, again burst into laughter; so Tiemen lit himself a cigarette and spoke precisely as though his words had but one purpose: to set to music the arc described by the tossed, still-burning match:

"Shoot her! But what are you thinking? Get my hands dirty... These days it's no longer done, in our circles it's no longer done... Tricked you! Tricked you! What was the poor thing to do if you weren't going to get on with it yourself?"

Some bell started ringing. Remarkably, you could tell that even the bell had been coached, "but," he said to himself, "credit where credit's due: it is *masterfully* imitating the bell of an impregnable cash register, roused by *unannounced* thieves," and at the same time this jangling also produced a darkness that swept down upon the street, drowning its as-though-green-house-grown traffic. But the bell also produced a light, erupting from the shop's hidden sources, that seemed to dissolve in the milky silence; and it also produced shadows on the partition between the shop and its back room. Those shadows numbered four, yet no sooner had he blinked than they materialized: Look, he was encircled by four policemen with martial mustaches and the expression of magnanimous bailiffs who have never inflicted more torture than the offender could stand before passing out. No! There were five of these individuals, but the fifth had the quality of a commander who never even resorts to torture, and it was Mr. Steel, with the heroically puffed-out chest of a man ready for anything life might throw at him.

Thereupon it turned out that the darkness in which the street was drowned was merely the lights going down on the stage so that the scenery could be changed without lowering the curtain; now, with the gradual drawing of the gauze drapes, the darkness was slowly fading, and when the last of them had lifted—the bell was cut off—the street turned out to be like so many others. On the street, there commenced a rectilinear motion that curved gracefully not far from there, craving the charms of the spiral, which it actually found quite quickly as well. It commenced along the street and slowly started spinning. Everything started spinning, notably the shop, as well as the saleswoman, Tiemen, the four policemen, and Mr. Steel. But not him: the fixed center putting his hands up in the melo-dramatic gesture of the penitent villain who is imploring them, for the love of God, to throw the cuffs on him. The policemen grew into a quartet, like soldiers carved into a single wooden slab, and it was a quartet so intricately detailed and of such hungry life force that, whirling, it sucked down everything else. At length, it passed into an undifferentiated and rushing blue—a preponderance of uniforms—where even the tanned whiteness of the policemen's faces came crashing down. And he was realizing what it is to get drunk on enthusiasm for one's own wretchedness when he noticed that someone had hit the brake: the blue turning was slowing down, and from the non-difference that hampered it there emerged, one after the other—like the drowned—what was left: first of all, and before anything else, the four policemen's faces, but faces no longer with martial mustaches, rather four lovely faces, cruel, but by no means evil, and they were the faces of people leaving, who wave gallantly and say:

"You'll get out of this somehow. *À un de ces jours*."

And they actually did say this. – "*À un de ces jours*" had transformed into a quite material obstacle, upon which all motion foundered because (he told himself): "*à un de ces jours*" is just a mockingly respectful "goodbye."

And that "goodbye" was the impact that no fall resists, and it, too, needed to be stopped, with a jolt so harsh that a brief and nasty cramp of "*non possumus*" ran through his calves.

The tall and flimsy stalk, to the tip of which he had been clinging till now by God-knows-what miracle, snapped, felled, and he, dreadfully sober, on a café chair behind a small mahogany table: emptied glasses and six theater tickets, scattered like a family of refugees in that place where they had been blown by the gale of impoverished misfortune, which howls for an echo that remains adamantly quiet.

And Tiemen is here with a dolefully fuming cigarette and the smile of an ashamed good Samaritan.

"Where are they going, Tiemen? After all, I was supposed to buy tickets to the cinema."

Tiemen was drawing in the strewn cigarette ash. "Well, you know what they're like."

"If I do know them … And they," he screamed, so that the people turned around, "and they don't know me?"

"That is possible only from this day forward," Tiemen said curtly; but just then he took the cigarette from his lips, leaned forward, and placed his left hand on the ashen hand of the nameless:

"Now then…"

"Teach me, Tiemen. – Tiemen, I've had something knocking around my head for a long time…"

"What's knocking around your head?"

"So many months already I've been chasing myself in vain. – That I might find myself, that I'd find myself, if only I dared to…"

"What?"

"Steal."

Tiemen's hand stopped him.

"Uh-uh, no, not that way. It's not something you can teach; you have to know how."

"To steal?"

Tiemen withdrew his friendly hand, sat sideways, and said, bitterly disappointed, "So you really are taking 'steal' literally? Steal! To hell with stealing. Take things easy, like a sneak thief in steerage—a sportsman-idealist. Can you do that? You can't. So suck it up."

The days grew so short that they weren't enough, they overflowed with milky futility and reeked of fermentation gone bad; then, even though they had begun at four o'clock, the nights could no longer accommodate all their specters: they protruded from those nights deep into rebellious, peevishly clouded daybreaks, which arrived as though only so the infinite nights would take pity on the people who hadn't fallen asleep, and because something has to replace the actual night. – Time's wound had been weeping for fourteen days already, and it still hadn't drained. The sun will come out here and there, a prefect sacrificing a scrap of stolen siesta to appease his conscience and see what the class has been up to in his illegal absence. But the sun, too, is merely rain gone wrong. It does the puddles on the embankment good, not so anyone else. But the puddles' satisfaction is as base as slime. They creep everywhere and behind everything. The only thing they don't venture through is the padded doors of bank directors; the puddles are also afraid of the garrulous lights of cafés, the false, cleverly arranged puzzles of small theaters, teatimes in ateliers with plank beds, and the standardized coziness of rooms in one-hour hotels. A hard-won reconciliation or a retraction as resolute as an exclamation point, which is a reconciliation divisible without remainder, is perhaps even better protection from a teary November stain. But he, having a choice between two equally unattainable things, has decided that his despicable poverty is from an insufficiency of what may once have been attainable: a room with a padded door, the encouraging chatter of café incandescents, the proxenetic dimness of chummy *salles de spectacle*, the literary pretexts of sex and their hurried stripping-down in discreet alcoves—he gave it up, as an ailing man gives up forbidden foods: with choked-down and renunciatory rage, which compensates not for one's hope in recovery, but for the triumph of one's unnecessary will, by which he recoups his damages. But the agreeable, calculating ascetic dressed with intentional slovenliness, so that he was two fingers away from hobo; he, with the greasy cap and the raggedy old shoes that the rag man didn't want to buy off him, looked down from embankments and bridges at the turbid, helplessly indifferent river, and looking into it he read, well, maybe not so much that there's no sure point at all, but that there's no sure point that would mean much to him. And the bit player, who toyed boorishly with the fact that he has nothing, spent his days lying to himself, with a violence bordering on pleasure, that what he doesn't have is just the thing that matters to him a great deal, and unhappily so. But one day, when, having caught a glimpse of his old "gang" from afar, he couldn't pull together hot or cold, when the thought that "there they go" was accompanied by neither sorrow nor revolt, he admitted to himself, with a clairvoyance we'll call heroic, that he had forgotten to suffer; he had even headed off the notion's correlate, that is, that that's why he's on the bottom.

That's why? On the contrary. He's on the bottom, and that's why he can no longer suffer. A nostalgia for misfortune, but so incidental: he didn't miss it, he just knew that there was a reason to. And at the same time he noticed how excruciatingly beautiful life was then, in those times when to him, too, the world seemed depopulated for no other reason than that one single being was missing from it.... He looked, and he found that he no longer missed anyone or anything. He was astonished to find that, but in no way petrified. And it wasn't a burning astonishment; it merely fumed. If he wanted—and he wanted this and nothing else—he found himself impressive, putrid, and swollen excuses to his heart's content: at intersections, on corners, under street-sweepers' brooms, next to bollards, and in church vestibules; mitigating circumstances proliferated like moldy mushrooms: in the neighborhood of Saint-Sulpice, in the window of stores selling devotional items, he spotted Him Who Was Crucified, and the blood sparkling on the tops of his feet gained a voice, and it implored: "See, you have been sold out as well." But his bankrupt ambition didn't abate: excuses that all you have to do is bend down for? He swept them into the gutter with his heel; the filthy mushrooms will get trampled, and the blood shouts out, "Heel!" – And all of this calmly, dispassionately, right? With an honorable prudence, he *naturally* refuses, because he knows that they're offering it to him by mistake: with a nasty, though not agonizing, feeling that he's playing without knowing with whom, cheating without knowing how, but that he's most certainly cheating.

The bright clock of the Gare d'Orsay reminded him that it was late—it reminded him fretfully, like someone he'd glued his eyes upon—and its circuit spun his eyes around a circuit much larger still, spun them around a horizon namelessly cut short, where—it came to him suddenly—he'd been wandering for a while now. But it came to him too late, that is, a second later than when he ascertained that there were no people, that there were no thoughts, that there were no things, that there was no desire, that there was nothing—and he was no exception—that would be worth death, much less life, let alone an irreparable—better yet—a sanctifying grief.

But that futility was not the downside of existence; it was more vindictive: people, thoughts, things, desires, he himself—and he above all—"were not" merely because "non-being" was the most essential of all their attributes. And not even thinking announced itself, that's just what was missing; what am I saying; nowhere was there even an inkling of the thought that any other way might have been *more natural*. He had an intense urge to want for something, but he couldn't make it out. He didn't feel a lack, he only remembered it from an earlier time, remembered the way one remembers objective knowledge. – It was despair; despair from things that are messianically absolute, from which only a single path leads, short and rushed like an indispensable vertical drop to somewhere, that is, anywhere. Anywhere—that is, toward the antipode of despair: toward cognizance. – The tendency's already there; already the overburdened "I want for nothing" was opening out to the abundance of the gossamer "then I've found it" when a pallid light shone upon him from that filthy darkness, illuminating his hunted face.

He was sitting on a bench; he lifted himself up, for he was seized by a promising horror, from the hope that that face was, after all, perhaps not the face of a prohibition on searching because finding had been denied him, that perhaps the opposite was the case, that it was the face of a prohibition on searching because he had already found. But just then he was already sitting on the bench again, not knowing whether he was relieved or rattled, for that face was a human face, and he knew it.

"I beg you, hurry," the person said, drawing in close, "if they ask you, you have to say you're with me."

She hadn't yet finished speaking, and they both already knew, but his "Zinaida" and her "is it you?" recoiled before the categorical plea, as astonishment awaits two who have collided out of nowhere in a burning house, until they carry out the thing they've flung themselves there for.

"Zinaida!"

"Yes," she said, breathless, "tell them you're with me. Afterwards..."

She fell silent. Two policemen on bicycles were approaching at a pace that boasted of the self-confident rhythm of studded soles; their heads swerved expertly toward the bench; they exchanged knowing looks, adjusted their holsters, tossed their shoulders, said *"Enfin!"* and walked on by.

"Zinaida!"

"Fancy meeting you here!" and she nodded until she finally leaped up. "But is it really you?"

He was staring with the belated shock of a person who has been denied the amusement of timely astonishment.

"What's this look? It's like you'd been expecting me."

"You? No."

"I only mention it because you don't seem surprised. You weren't anticipating this, after all . . ."

"So why should I be surprised?"

"The main thing is that they're gone."

They were sitting far apart. He twisted his torso in her direction; he had his arm stretched across the backrest. The visor of his cap was bent toward its top and raised comically. He swallowed, but his eyes, squinting and slightly crusty in the corners, were asking, though also already answering at the same time. The questions were answers, as though they were cut short; what remained of them was the neglected void of the cell they'd led the condemned man from *that* morning.

Because he wasn't saying anything, she twisted her torso as well. She kept her hands in her lap.

"I'm not registered yet. And I already look like I'm supposed to be."

He craned his neck. Not surprised so much as exasperated at her having been able to say *this* without turning her head away.

"Yeah, so—I'm not registered yet—what do you want? She just threw me out today."

"Yeah, Mrs. Steel," she added a moment later, as if he had asked, "Who?"

"How could you just run off like that? There—well, you did look different."

"I didn't run off. I only forgot myself."

"I know. With that boy. There was a rumor going round."

"You moron! Not with anybody. I forgot myself—I forgot my self—somewhere."

"Like me, then. – Like hell! It was different with me. Ugh!" She shifted.

"Actually, nothing's happened yet. I'm saying she only threw me out this morning."

"You're saying 'nothing's happened'—but now you're as sly as . . . ," and he stood up.

The grip with which she caught his hand was of the impatient and timorous kind, which people use to cajole when they no longer hold off any true disgrace.

"You're not leaving so suddenly—just like that?"

She pulled him onto the bench and so close beside herself that he shifted away involuntarily. But right away he fixed his eyes on her so compassionately—she thought it was compassion—as though he wanted to blunt the offensive point of that shifting. Zinaida saw wrong: he was not looking at her compassionately, he was merely on the lookout for a reason why Zinaida momentarily seemed so ugly to him. For she wasn't ugly, he clearly saw that this was the same Zinaida as the one back there. So then what was it? But just then it dawned on her, and she tore herself away.

"Right, that's enough! What are you looking at? Surely you can't see it yet, not today. Surely it's not possible that so quickly . . . It's not possible, see? Not at all—when nothing's happened yet."

Again he swallowed hard, and in his eyes the truncated void left by questions reappeared.

"I was thinking of you today."

She said it kindly, as though she were coaxing the rift where a dangerous silence had wedged itself between them.

"I was wandering the streets and thinking about you. I've been wandering for eight hours already. No, I haven't eaten. Not that I didn't have anything to buy food; I do. I have money, thank you very much. I haven't eaten...just because. And anyway, why am I saying that I was wandering? Only people who have nowhere to go wander. And I do have a room—in a hotel—that much is clear. So I wasn't wandering, I was strolling. I felt like a stroll; that's right! – Why aren't you saying anything?

"What was it I wanted to say? Oh yeah, that I was thinking of you. Because a moment ago you were staring at me as if you could already see it, and here it just occurred to me that while I was strolling about, it also occurred to me that one could already see it on me, even though nothing's happened yet. Here I recalled—forgive me—that one could see it on you as well, there—the robbery, the robbery that wasn't even your fault at all. If only I could say this better—I'm sorry...

"It's clear enough, you were innocent. There's proof, and so on...If only I could say this better: You're innocent, you were innocent—we get it—but you looked like someone who had to be the thief. By rights, the thief should have been you, and it was just your bad luck if it wasn't. – On my stroll it also occurred to me—on my stroll, I say—that one could already see it on me as well, even though nothing has actually happened yet. I swear to you. But what if it's just luck? Maybe you can see what a person is on anybody, were it not for the luck that he hasn't become it. – – – Hold on! Now I'm thinking that in anybody you can see what, only by luck, he isn't... For I—on my soul—nothing's happened. I went to the Steels for work—that's all—Mr. Steel took me in as a servant."

"When..."

"When what? That much is clear: when...But isn't that

why I don't have to run away from the cops yet?"

"You were saying something about being registered."

"That just really got away from me. I had it set up...so he'd have pity on me...I thought it was some tramp—how could I have suspected it was you? I needed him, this guy—like you. It just got so out of hand."

"But this idea of yours—on your stroll..." he said with wicked pity.

She turned her head away; only now did she turn her head away.

"I felt such shame, only shame, shame for myself; not that I would have felt sorry for myself. I was saying that I was remembering you. It was like I said to myself: maybe it was like that for you, too, back then, that kind of shame, but no guilt and no self-pity. Only shame...I'm telling you, it's a bad omen when we're incapable of foisting our misfortune upon others; when we tell ourselves that we have just ourselves to blame, just ourselves, just ourselves. A bad omen: because then it brings such harsh anger at ourselves. A person gets so sick of himself, and of nothing but himself, of himself and himself alone. It's a bit like suicide. But suicide is forbidden."

He raised his eyes, for the haphazard visor of his cap was bothering him; he fixed it with a flick.

"It's a skill—are you going to do it?"

She seemed to seize up, like she had shrunken in the shoulders.

"If you were perhaps going to do it...I have to tell you that when I was staring at you a moment ago, it's not that I would have been guessing at something or looking for it. No! It's that all of a sudden I saw how you'll be, when you become loathsome to me. When you become loathsome to me—you see? Watch! So far you're only taking a stroll—a stroll!—so far you're still as shapely, pretty, white-and-red as at Benedictine Mill—in short, a girl!—but I don't know: now, somewhere under your eyes, along your nose, in your double chin, one can already see it at work."

"Can see what at work?"

"I'll tell you what you can see at work: the loathsomeness, the aging, the whorish collapse into ruin."

And again he discerned that gesture of a person who's gotten unused to self-defense: her hand seized the hand on the backrest and set out along a path that he already knew from somewhere...

"Don't tempt me," he said, but he didn't shy away.

"Don't tempt me," he said, and he tolerated her embracing him around the neck.

"We have it lousy," he said when she drew herself quite close, "and you think so too, see?"

She didn't say "no," but a snigger had settled on her pleading, puckered lips.

"Oh, my darling," and he pushed her gently away, "I'm the first you've come across—on your stroll—if that's not enough to discourage you, you're an optimist. Just take a look at me.

"Just take a look at yourself!" he repeated, hardly mocking.

"I know what you're driving at. I remember," she answered swiftly, "it's weird: I had made up my mind, and so far everything's like nothing happened. Me too: I hear, I see, I speak as though nothing had happened—me, the one who'd made up her mind."

"About what?" he asked suspiciously. "Made up your mind to do what?" And he shoved her suddenly with his elbow.

"Oh, that's it! Now we're talking!"

"Let's stroll for a while; and then each can go his way."

"No."

"You'll come with me a while." She stood up, arranged the cloak that had slipped, and looked upon his crown. "Finally!" she said when he rose.

She walked along the retaining wall, so close that you could hear her scraping against it; on the retaining wall, inchworm-like, her fingers.

"If I've understood you right…But nothing will get solved that way."

She walked with her head lowered.

"Keep your learned words to yourself. Won't solve anything! What do you want me to solve? If it's a bust, it's a bust. I've had enough—*basta*. Won't solve anything! Solve! That's fine for you, the learned, or perhaps for people who have no courage. Who knows, maybe they're the same: the learned, and people without courage. Solve! What, I ask you? That which isn't there? You're not even telling me to have faith yet, like you. At least that's something."

She stopped, leaned against the retaining wall, and with the pride of the queen of the rag men:

"But if someone *had to*—like me… Like I had to serve a life sentence and amuse myself by reckoning the days served."

She started on her path again.

"I'm talking about that driver. He got married. A boy like that, such a beautiful boy.

"Are you still waiting for something?" she asked, but the tone in which she continued answered for itself: that what she was asking about wasn't worth an answer. "I'm just surprised that it can seem so normal: the most ordinary of ordinary days, as though nothing had happened.

"See here"—she'd set off along the ramp down to the river, but she had looked back, as though sensing that he had stopped, that he wouldn't follow her, and she repeated "see here" without changing her voice. And she went on, no longer looking back, since she was well aware that now he could follow her no further.

"See here, nothing like this even occurred to me this morning. See here, if Mrs. Steel hadn't found out that Mr. Steel hadn't left the house last evening—he went up to the fifth floor, to my chamber—everything would have been like it is, and all the same it would be different. Like about the driver, I mean. But she did find out, she took me to task—I don't know how to lie—so I left. First to his office, after the gentleman. Where I got the nerve—God only knows! Me!—and still I was proud of my daring, fool that I am. He gave me five thousand. That's nothing to shake a stick at. That's already enough to get something going with." (She turned around.) "You don't perhaps need a little money?"

They were walking along the water.

"A fool, I say, though it's really all the same. A fool, because who knows whether things would have taken this turn if I hadn't taken the money; I wouldn't have gotten . . . Because before that I was *merely* at a loss, I was merely desperate—desperate, let's say. What *really* happened to me only happened afterwards: a person would say it came my way from that five thousand . . . that is, my being ashamed of myself, my anger at myself. And who knows if it's anger, a sort of ugliness, rather . . . like this boy, like it was everything, and once he was gone there was nothing left, that's actually the thing that's really not worth it anymore."

Now she had taken his arm.

"I just find it strange that it only occurred to me today, and that it already seems so familiar to me, as though I'd been lugging it around with me for I don't know how long already. What do you think? Isn't it strange? – Really, it's not worth it. – A person would think that saying 'you'll do it' has to have some kind of effect; that afterwards everything would seem different to you, changed; and yet it's only something else than—well, yes—than something else; and, at the same time, not.

"And in the end I'll run into you—straight into you."

She laughed.

"I was startled at first, so much so that it gave me chills, the way you fell into my lap—forgive me. But to meet you of all people today—it's like it was *meant* to be . . .

"Forgive me," she added, so virtuous somehow, "but with you it seems so natural."

They were under the arc of Le Pont Royal.

"Throw me in."

He broke free from her and leaped back. She followed.

"I'm asking you to help me out."

She pulled at him; she was strong; still, he broke free.

"On the meadows behind the mill, you promised the moon and stars, and now nothing. I'm telling you I want it, I want it."

She circled him like a stray bitch; she grabbed hold of him. She hopped, she crouched, to make for him again.

It struck him "like the wrestlers at Le Bal Tabarin," and it's odd he didn't yelp with pain for having recalled so crude a spectacle for a woman who was wheedling her death out of him. Odd that he didn't yelp, but he was in no position to make so much as a peep, and perhaps you could read it in his eyes that he was rather calling for help, but that he couldn't manage anything unless mutely. For in his eyes she had hit her mark, and having hit her mark her own eyes lit up, as though victorious, that she would yet achieve what she'd wanted after all. And now they were grappling with each other again.

"Throw me in; I don't want to do it myself; the Lord forbids it; throw me in."

She was shaking him, pulling him toward the river. He was aware of it. And all of a sudden he sensed, not seeing, that they were on the very edge. He sensed it as though through the wacky notion that there is never an end to life, that hope is a virtue "and so forth," and from that "and so forth" he was suffused with the kind of strength he would never have anticipated. He didn't want to go there, he wouldn't go there. He extricated himself the only way he could: by giving her a brutal shove.

He heard a "Help!" but not the splash. And yet, right away, there was silence, silence more striking somehow than the yelp for help, and a silence that met no end. Until the ever-so-distant end of the roaring silence resounded with hurried, heavy footsteps. He stood there as if he were a host readying himself for the arrival of an esteemed guest. Now it's not only footsteps; hooves, a cavalcade, a cavalcade at first hard, then unexpectedly limber, majestic, and disciplined by a baton whose rhythmic taps could be precisely heard. A weight on the shoulder, a musty odor all around. And creatures tossed like fantastic boulders, strength flowed from them, a great strength, serene, occupied impassively.

"What's this then?"

Someone says, "She overpowered me... She jumped... I don't know..." and something tells him that it is he who is speaking.

"Fine."

That "fine" is just as great, serene, and impassively occupied as those as-yet inexplicably multiplied creatures. Something pliable is lying at his feet, you'd say it was a person, but it's somehow too small to be a person. It has a sandy-blond head; it's turned on its side, and oddly so. It's a clump that's suddenly, as though it felt like putting itself in order, become truly three-dimensional: a perpendicular has sprouted from it, if it weren't so skimpy it could perhaps be an arm, something came unstuck at the end. A finger? Isn't it pointing at him? If only it had at least enough strength to be able to stretch out completely, to point properly, to help him! But the perpendiculars are already collapsing again, hardly having waved. A massive, impassive voice has as if stood in for it:

"He hasn't had a finger in this pie? We'll see about that."

The voice that said "come here" was already a banal cop voice.

Just so we know: the authorities. Really? The authorities. – The slummocker! He pulled off his cap and flung it away; it described a well-trained arc and ended up on the bench. "To substitute for the luminous course of my Star of Bethlehem," but he was touching the scruff of his neck, for he felt bad that something like this had occurred to him. – He looked toward where his cap had landed, went there as if under orders, and sat down beside it. Right away he saw that things were fine: the police station hadn't come down on him; that was his version of praise.

He was in a strange locale: secure. A metal stove, and metal like plates of armor. Makeshift writing tables that had the timelessness of busted kitchen tables made from soft wood. On a peg in the lobby, askew, decorative cloaks and coats: they admitted that they were in contempt, that they were here because they were here: the police dressed differently.

And everything, all the rest, was soused in the miserable and imposing braggadocio of the grand and immune plenipotentiaries of human authority. With regard to this self-confident obduracy, all that remained for the apprehended man was a greensick apology, a red-flushed excuse, a fumbling, fast one.

He picked up his cap, held it between his knees. – A

sergeant was sitting astride a wobbly chair; he was smoking and staring at the ceiling. Performing his duty, he reached over his shoulder, took the evening paper from the table, spread it open, and read. Then he folded the newspaper into quarters and smacked it sullenly against his thigh. His boredom was flabbergasted by the innumerable anchor points all around him: which one do you hang yourself on?

"You there," he said.

"Yes?"

"So what really happened?" the sergeant barked into a hovering ring.

"Some whore. Apparently threw herself in the water."

"Her pimp. You're her pimp, is that it?" and he came forward.

"Not at all. – She wanted to."

So that something would jam up in him, nothing jammed up in him.

"Aha, she wanted to. *Ça va.* And you helped her out, eh?"

He didn't answer. And how was he to hear amidst this delectation? How was he to answer? He delectated in the immeasurable certainty, in the *bottomless fearlessness.* As though it were a satiny, barely rippled eddy of oily liquid oozing down the walls of an elaborate funnel. To somewhere. He didn't answer, because he was delectating in his admiration for an indifference as smooth as a jailhouse wall, but an indifference that was also so high that it was like the wall of a jailhouse without boundaries. He came to know that it's nothing, but his cell was the universe. He longed to be confronted with the most perfect, most noble, most exacting, most misdemeanor-proof being—God?—for he had an urge to look into the eyes of someone who sees more touchily than anyone or anything: he knew that he would hold out even against such as this.

Instead, there was the bailiff-like gaze of the policeman, who, not waiting for an answer, moved on quickly:

"I'm talking! You helped her, no?"

And he drilled in with his tallow gaze, which already melted on the first go-round.

"And don't be a wise guy, I'm telling you, we have methods for that."

He grabbed him by the chin and lifted it so roughly that his jaws rattled.

"We have methods for that," he chanted, holding the chin and drilling with his gaze, which had become enraged at not getting anywhere, "did you throw her in, or didn't you?"

In *him*, a resilient desire now sprang up to burst out laughing at the policeman, at least with his eyes. An even more resilient compassion swiftly jerked it back, however, and he, astonished by that brief encounter, which came off utterly different from what his will had prescribed, no longer had anything in reserve besides a vacuously fixed gaze. But just then the policeman's other hand stroked his face in such a way that it was as if they'd removed the fetters from his constrained astonishment. But the hand doing the stroking stopped, deliberated for a moment, then rose lightly and hit him ever so slightly. Then, seduced by the rhythm it had gotten going, it continued, alternately lifting away and falling back down, falling from angles that each time grew only slightly, but mindfully—quite like a differential proceeding toward its ideal sum, which is ideal because it's forbidden. And that sum was a slap.

The hand lifted up and fell down precisely to the cadence of its attendant words, like so:

"Her pimp—right?—Saturday—right?—your share—right?—not enough—right?—she didn't give you enough (two slaps, syncopated)—right?—the slut—right?—is that all?—I'm asking: is that all! (syncopation)—are you going to cough it up?—no?—got nothing?—got nothing?..."

The hand doing the shaming was putting on speed in this rhythm, putting on speed—but on the last "got nothing?" it recalled that the ideal sum is sacred, which is to say forbidden, and just on that "got nothing," where the irresolute slapping was supposed to collapse into determined smacking, the hand gave up, as if before the last dance, having infected even the other hand with defeatism, the one that was holding that differentially smacked face by the chin, which it now lifelessly released.

"So that's how it's going to be?" the policeman roared as reparation, nudging his prisoner so hard he knocked him over, "and what, you didn't throw her in?"

He answered quietly, resignedly, and with a word that you wouldn't cast aside:

"No."

"All joking aside," the sergeant protested, "one never knows."

The slapping policeman made a goliath of a gesture and walked off grumbling toward the table, where his colleagues were gambling as though seven mountains away.

He took his cap and held it between his knees. Thus it happened that his gaze slipped to the knotty floor. There he discovered a sort of vermillion line. It reminded him of a note on the general staff's map: the ideal offensive line "from there to here."

At this moment, however, he was suffused with a delightful indifference, toward both the "from there" as well as the "to here." A line—yes, but not an abscissa, not from there to here, merely a course, barely a course.

The Auer burners were buzzing like flies startled after a

great alarm. The sergeant puffed out a last ring, in such a way as to let it be known that it actually was the last ring for the time being: the ring had an air of ceremonial farewell. Thereupon he came back around and got himself together. The sergeant's torso and seat now made almost a right angle. He yanked at his pleated shirt, and the station became dignified.

"The report is the commissioner's business," he said, "but the commissioner won't be here before eight. Then he has breakfast—another half hour—which makes it half past. – We know him. – Either the *dépôt*, or release."

"What do you mean, sergeant?"

"What I mean is that we don't have much room. Keep him here till eight—and where will he lie down? Wait for the commissioner, who'll just sign everything I would have signed? Anyway, you know him, that heavenly nincompoop! So why wait for the commissioner! Either I hand down my judgment, or I let him off. And that's it. I'll judge whether he threw her in. If he didn't throw her in . . . Yeah, but I wasn't there. Which of you nabbed him? You? – Alright: did he or didn't he?"

"He says he didn't, that much we know."

"I, for one, haven't fallen in love with him," the sergeant said, "but to keep him here, going around in circles . . . ! And you know the commissioner: he doesn't like unnecessary work. And when there's a report, there are facts. Alright then: did he or didn't he?"

"Like I'm saying, he says 'didn't.'"

"He says; and she?"

"She! We walked right along the Pont Royal. Me and Durand. We hear 'help' and a splash. We're just two steps from the locker with the lifebelt. We toss it in, as you please, we run down the stairs. She grabbed onto it, we know that much. We untied the dinghy. She was floating five meters from shore. In you go! We put her down. Meanwhile, people had come running. They nabbed this fellow here. That's it: nabbed him!...Actually, he wasn't even running away. Actually, actually he was standing there like a pillar of salt. 'Are you the one who threw her in?...' But how did it actually go down, Durand?"

Durand: "'Was it you?' I says. He's like it didn't have anything to do with him: 'She overpowered me...She jumped...I don't know her.' Meanwhile, they've pulled her out. Well, what was she supposed to do? She's drowned! – To tell you the truth, I think she raised her hand—a pretty enough girl, but she was just throwing up water—yes, she raised her hand. I'd almost say she pointed at this guy and shook her head like it wasn't him. Then again, count on a drowning victim when you've only just pulled her out?..."

"Fine. She shook her head, or didn't she?"

"I'd almost say that she did."

"Like how?"

"Like I'm telling you. Like none of it was on him."

"Where'd they take her?"

"Wherever there's room."

"What was closest?"

"Saint-Louis...Or else Cochin."

"Ring them up."

The cards were upset. The perpendicular on the sergeant's chair went slack again. The shirt was unburdened; shirts take a breather by making creases across the navel. The telephone's bell rang so imperiously that the commotion eased back down like a whipped dog.

He, not having taken his eyes off the vermillion line, lifted his head without expecting anything. He was all the more meagerly astonished upon noticing that his despair was to no avail.

He caught sight of an aurora that was not so much an aurora that one caught sight of but rather a light laying siege. In the police station, it was the light of the Auer burners, but it was inside a kind of scattered light whose origin lay elsewhere. Because he then caught sight both of his dreadful poverty, as well as of his own raging inferno, he thought that it was from this.

Stop!

"What are they saying?" the sergeant protested, perking the sloppy perpendicular back up. "Well?"

"She's not at Saint-Louis."

"Cochin then."

The aurora was now so dazzling that he couldn't stand it. He fled from it, staring into the bowl of his greasy cap. There he found, you might say, something unbelievably precious, for he winced. But he didn't resist. He looked again. For us to say, after all, what was so monstrous—and what was so precious that it was monstrous—that it seemed he was seeing: it was something that looked like—but if only he knew why!—that looked like Mercifulness. He well knew that Mercifulness could not be seen. His disbelief that what he was seeing in the dirty underside of his cap could be Mercifulness was so sincere, so disbelieving, that he pursed his lips. And it was a peculiar image, seeing Mercifulness (for, in spite of everything, that's what it was) face-to-face with a person who makes fun of it.

"Cochin's answering. She's there."

"What?"

"But . . . really?"

"What?"

The fellow on the phone hung up.

"Apparently she keeps saying: It wasn't him, it wasn't him."

"Huh?" came the protest from behind the stretched-out evening paper.

"Huh!" and this time it was the sergeant's voice. "Well I'll be damned, Dusseldorf won."

The station clustered together. But the sergeant's arm dispersed them again. His chair groaned.

"You're in luck... She jumped in herself... Next time—next time—yes, people like you should know it's better not to get mixed up with strange dames."

"I do know her," he said, for the light was dazzling him unbearably. It was so quick that the entire station was on him like a swarm of mayflies.

"What's that you say?"

"I do know her," he said.

"There it is!" said the sergeant. "So it's for the commissioner to clear up. What a help."

One cop, quietly:

"You idiot. Why'd you say that? You could have been out already."

"But I do know her," he said grumpily, and he added by way of apology, "if I know her... don't I?" And he smiled a smile before which the station withdrew distrustfully. It was only there where the station had withdrawn that a bit of self-confidence accumulated, at just the moment when was said:

"If you didn't throw her in... if she says herself that you didn't throw her in... what do you know her for? Blockhead, why know someone who bothers us? You're the first person to acknowledge someone it would be better not to acknowledge. Now what's the commissioner going to say?"

"The commissioner is a friend of mine."

"Oh yeah? And now we might have some lunatic to boot."

"I do know her." And he said it as though he were placing an obstinate period.

"Fine," said the cagy Christian cop, "but if you know her,

there has to be somebody who knows you as well. In other words ... Someone other than the drowning victim."

"Yes."

"But who? – You know, it's a matter of having character witnesses—and for a person like yourself! Two witnesses, you know ... two, at least two."

"Our porter."

"Oh, porters! ..."

"Then there's this Mr. Steel fellow. A highly respected industrialist. Mr. Steel, Vesta gas heating system installation, 305 Rue Saint-Lazare."

"We'll see. – It'll be day in a while."

"In a while the sun will come out."

Day: that meant eight o'clock in the morning. It was another four hours to eight. Those hours were running away; you could see them running away. They afforded a diversion, and so it seemed they boiled down to too little.

At eight sharp, the commissioner, but before him something like an invisible footman who announced him, a footman so commanding that *our fellow* stood and straightened up. – With the commissioner a sandy-blond burst of light entered as well, a light more mature than accorded with the early winter hour. The commissioner stopped in the middle of the luminous room, which is like saying in the middle of that shimmering light (for it was shimmering). He was standing like someone who's promised to do so, or who's promised it *to himself*, but still like someone who couldn't do otherwise. He stood erect. In his drooping hand he held a hat. And one would say that the hat didn't belong to him, that he was carrying it only out of an affectedly sensitive courteousness, not wanting to stand out too much. For when he took it off, as he did now, his crop of hair was splendidly ruffled, and one would call it radiance.

The policemen formed a semicircle around him. The sergeant came forward and hastily buckled his belt.

"This is the fellow..."

"I know," the commissioner cut him off, collapsing into a small armchair. His morning hot chocolate was already steaming on the table in front of him. He dipped a scrap of brioche into it; he chewed. His eyes glazed over. But it was suddenly as though lightning got into them: an instant. – The flash of lightning shed light on the fact that the commissioner was in fact a commissioner, an officially appointed commissioner, nothing more, but in particular it shed light on the fact that the commissioner felt sorry about his rough response to the sergeant, whose eyes were just then sinking in the commissioner's curt severity. But the ginger-headed person in the small armchair ordered them to present themselves anew; he was looking into them again, and in such a way as to protect them from sinking.

"Cochin called, they say the drowned woman is blah-blahing, 'it wasn't him,'" the sergeant uttered, reading over the commissioner's shoulder the boldfaced headline on the first page of the morning paper (and still not done buckling his belt), "but then he claims he knows her."

"What a moron," and the commissioner, like it was nothing, smoothed out the crumpled page of his daybook. "And does he have papers?"

"None."

"Does he at least have references?"

"A certain Mr. Steel, central heating, 305 Rue Saint-Lazare."

"I'll take care of it."

"Good day, Commissioner, sir."

Eight in the morning is promising, even at police stations, and even in winter. It has so much potential that it attires even the naked, chilly, wearied light crumbling through its sooty transoms.

That fellow was kneading his cap, looking into it, not as though he were reckoning the broken possibilities within it, but rather as though he might spot reserve possibilities there, and in this way he wanted to entice them to speed up their development.

Eight in the morning has promise, but the thing is to wait for it lying down, rather than with one's torso vertical. At eight in the morning even the zeroes hold the rank of decimal places, and assured defeats dream of the microscopic difference that they've missed, having thus missed the opportunity to become an imperialist trump card. At eight in the morning, even homeless people might hope that by evening some of them will become the lords of the palaces that are only to be finished that day; at eight in the morning we calculate down to the millimeter where to go and when, so as to run into the dear people we've lost and miss and would encounter today by the grace of God, but for the fact that we were incapable of remaining innocent, that is, of avoiding ruses, fast ones, and the seductions of the wee hours, the marvelous hours that think of nothing else than of how to steer us so that we lose our way and miss our salvation. Eight in the morning is the hour of Good Advice, about which it is a given that no one will ever listen. He was kneading his cap. The sleepless night remained somewhere far behind him, so far it was as though it hadn't been at all. He was kneading his thoroughly greasy cap, looking into its underside, where a miracle happened: everything that was supposed to be was there, just as though it had been fulfilled, and more real than if it had actually been fulfilled. Only it wasn't welcome: a roll-your-own spit to the ground. He saw that things had occurred the previous night that one would be amazed by or that one would fear, but he had found neither amazement, nor fear. And yet, if there is amazement, then it's at the fact that his sojourn on this plank bed, worn down by innumerable, anonymous backsides, didn't mortify him. He knew he was the victim of puffed-up falsity, but his touchiness, otherwise so inflamed, didn't bristle. On the contrary: God knows where it came from within him, this patrician, self-confident certainty that freedom is near: so long as he makes a move toward the revolt that was germinating within him (but prudently, methodically, not with foolhardy impetuousness), so long as he gladly renders unto the devil what is the devil's, so long as he holds his breath one more time, swimming under the last low arch in the reeking sewer—and then, and then in no time he'll reach open waters, unrestricted, salty, stinking of primordial life.

He was looking into the underside of his greasy cap, reading there that life begins just when we have *sensed* (but sensed the way we perceive smells, tastes, or lights) that it is a spiral, which in the instantaneous point of the "I" is just beginning, and then—ever more vertiginously and centrifugally—it spins out into being without end and without beginning, and that we are wed to freedom just in the moment when we have no choice but *not to place* a pause between today and tomorrow, I and thou, here and anywhere.

He was kneading his cap with wondrous amazement (by now it had his trust) at how, just as he was fading in the disregarded scorn of the nameless and non-citizen crowd of Nobodies, he felt as though at the tip of that so perfectly annealed coil, from which that Nameless, which is the Unnameable, his neighbor and companion, is making up his mind to jump.

"So it's you then. – Your name?"

He told him.

"Your papers?"

"Left them at the hotel."

"You've resided there for how long?"

"Since yesterday."

"Your reference?"

"The hotel."

"You've only been there since yesterday. – Someone else."

"Mr. Steel, installation..."

"Fine...I know. – You were apprehended at the spot from which a certain hussy fell into the water. – Fell! You pushed her in. – Did you push her in?"

"On the contrary. I had to defend myself."

The commissioner stood, walked right up to him, and, chewing his brioche:

"Yes...Cochin...On the whole it squares with the testimony...with the testimony..."

All of a sudden he crouched down in front of him, looked him over from below, and, having done so, hopped up nimbly and landed his hand on his shoulder. It fell cop-like, heavily and rudely, but barely had it fallen than it gripped the shoulder, which it wanted to shake, gripped it in a quick and fervent squeeze that nevertheless swiftly went shamefaced and shy and had now let go.

The commissioner was preparing a word, but he said it only with his eyes, immersing them in the eyes of the man they'd caught. And it was an actual immersion, of blue eyes into black eyes, in which the sky-blue broke through.

"Right," said one.

"Right," said the other.

"You're innocent in all this, I know that," the commissioner stated, "but being innocent in all this is already wrongdoing as well. And anyway: all I know is the regulations."

"Yeah, sure," the other fellow said.

"All I know is the regulations; the regulations, and also the law," the commissioner insisted, looking at him timidly.

"No! That's all you're obliged to know," the delinquent responded, fixing his eyes on the commissioner's legs, which were trying in vain to remain planted on the floor. The commissioner was hovering, and upon noticing that this could be seen he tried all the more to make landfall (but still in vain), and he fell into a great embarrassment, absently holding it at bay. For he had, you'd say, still another job: keeping watch over the quiet, the great quiet that in the meantime was assuming the quality of a kind of third presence. At length the commissioner coped with his embarrassment by sort of swallowing (it seemed to the other fellow that he really was swallowing, and some extra-pure morsel at that), whereupon, still with that ever-so-incomprehensibly relieving hand on the delinquent's shoulder the whole time, he said, "I would like you please to look me in the eye, and nowhere else. It's fitting, and so: I'm well aware that your conscience is clean. But that doesn't matter. Here all that matters is evidence and regulations. If the only thing you have is a clean conscience . . . Fortunately, you were mentioning references . . ."

"Mr. Steel! Mr. Steel! I repeat: Mr. Steel."

"Mr. Steel," the commissioner said, "he's the one who . . ." But he broke off.

"Mr. Steel," the other fellow repeated obstinately.

"Because," the commissioner went on as though he hadn't heard, and now he was again in the little armchair behind the desk with the telephone, which he was fiddling with, "because I know how the world works. Mr. Steel. There isn't somebody else you know? Because – – think it over, whether you know someone who'd have no reason to go red in front of you..."

"Commissioner!"

"Because if he has a reason to go red in front of you—I know how the world works—and when you don't have anyone else, he'll deny you."

"Mr. Steel."

"Or else he'll say something that'll make me lock you up."

"Mr. Steel."

"What time is it?" the commissioner asked his watch, "ten to nine, let's give it a try."

He picked up the phone book.

"Steel, 305 Rue Saint-Lazare... Steel, 305 Rue Saint-Lazare... Steel... Steel... Ah, yes, 305 Rue Saint-Lazare... Provence 46-57..."

The telephone on the commissioner's desk was as pretty as a plaything, but when the commissioner lifted it, the plaything started to resemble a trap for martens.

He turned toward the plank bed.

"So you're sticking with it?" and he stood, not putting down the receiver. "The unfinished slap from Benedictine Mill isn't enough for you?"

"Mr. Steel," the other fellow said simply, and as though he had foreseen this.

Yet someone did marvel at the commissioner's unexpected statement: the commissioner himself.

"Eh?" he uttered. "I didn't know that one could know his way around these paths without me," and he sat back down resolutely.

"Hello. Provence 46-57."

"Provence 46-57? – The Steel Company, Vesta gas heating system installation? – Could I speak with Mr. Steel? –

Excellent, this is Louvre precinct headquarters—could I . . .
Excellent. Yes, please."

Between seven and eight, time just drags its feet; between
eight and nine, it walks; then it's already running; it's afraid—
and in winter especially—it's afraid of the prearranged
encounter with the prepared evening.

"Mr. Steel? This is Louvre precinct headquarters. Am I
speaking with Mr. Steel? – Oh, no, forgive the early call. It's
just that last night . . . But not at all . . . just whether you know
a certain . . . By the name of – – – I knew that beforehand. No
one wants a scene – – – Sorry? – But how could something like
that have occurred to me! I just wanted to say that someone
like yourself . . . so well-connected . . . memory fails so easily. –
Oh no! You've misunderstood: not that he'd be lying—far from
it!—it's just that perhaps it's your memory that's failed. He was
caught at the spot where a certain girl threw herself into the
river. That is . . . that's how they've both made it out, she and
him. It's for just that reason that I have certain doubts. What
good are doubts if they're both telling the same story? . . . Oh,
my dear Mr. Steel, one can see that you don't know how the
world works . . . The girl? O Mr. Steel, the girl is not the point,
you mustn't concern yourself with her. Because if you were
to concern yourself with her, we wouldn't have the honor of
looking forward to your visit—should it interest you. But of
course you're in no way obliged . . . We'd be most grateful . . .
Perhaps when you see him . . . You'd be doing a good deed . . .
Are the police capable of appreciating good deeds? No, Mr.
Steel, the police don't know what that is; the police know only
regulations and facts . . . but exceptionally well—you're most
welcome."

The commissioner let hang both the receiver and an over-
solicitous smile. He was the spitting image of a commissioner.

"Why do you appeal to people who don't know you?"

"Mr. Steel maybe doesn't know my name, but he does know me."

"We'll see as soon as he arrives."

"You know that Mr. Steel once wrongfully accused me of stealing."

The commissioner turned around sharply.

"What are you up to?...Appealing to someone who's accused you of stealing!"

"And who didn't ask my forgiveness; and who furthermore almost struck me for it."

"Almost?"

"I don't remember. – Perhaps you know better?"

The commissioner was drumming on the desk; you could see that this was his last weapon against the temptation to stand up.

"And what if he denies you? He wears a fur coat—so it'd be easy for him to deny any wrongdoing."

"Mr. Steel committed no wrongdoing. He suspected me because he had reason to."

"And he struck you . . . Did he have reason for that as well?"

The suspect was sitting up straight. His hands were pressed against the plank bed. He shrugged his shoulders.

"Aren't you a queer bird," the commissioner said, and he no longer resisted: he stood up and came closer. With short, intermittent steps, because, hovering, he couldn't do otherwise. But this time he no longer had second thoughts about his peculiar walk. His ruddy-blond mop of hair took heart as well: it stood up in impudent, sparkling spindles, and his youthful smile was confessing as well as commanding: it was commanding that this miracle must not be named.

Nonetheless, in that smile there was as though a residue of

consent, of consent allowing the suspect to say "you're not so much a commissioner like other commissioners" (and that fellow used this consent right away, too); one would say that the commissioner understood how greatly the delinquent needed to utter these words if he was to remain among the living.

They were now close, one in front of the other, and even the commissioner might have had the impression that their gazes were locked so firmly it was as if the two of them were faithfully holding hands. It was, however, but a brief moment before the fast and unspoken agreement by which the commissioner's look came loose again, floating along a graceful arc to the empty space on the plank bed, marking it meaningfully. The commissioner sat down there.

"And you were innocent?"

"Innocent insofar as I hadn't stolen from Mr. Steel."

"And insofar as something else?"

"I have never pilfered anything."

"So? – Then why say you're innocent insofar as that's concerned? It's a mental restraint. You know what a mental restraint is?"

"I know what it is. Quite. Restraint. – It's like tonight. I'm talking about Zinaida . . . how she fell into the water. All I know is her Christian name—Zinaida—nothing more. She chanced to run into me—why me exactly? . . . Why exactly was I the 'I' who *had to* perform this gesture ? . . . Just as I was the 'I' who . . . "

"Who what?"

"Who was suspected of that robbery."

"Strange notions."

"But I pleaded my case so poorly, Commissioner, sir," he started mumbling, speaking very slowly, "I was afraid, I shuddered, to all of them I was a laughingstock. Can someone be a laughingstock if he's innocent down to the marrow?"

"Strange notions. And what does it mean to be innocent down to the marrow?"

But the commissioner had shifted away so as to be able to see better. He leaned slightly away.

"What does it mean to be innocent down to the marrow?" he repeated. "I, who should know..."

"I don't know, Commissioner, sir. You said yourself a moment ago that an innocent accusation is already a misdeed as well. But then perhaps when we like ourselves..."

"What are you saying?"

"You mustn't take this the wrong way, I don't mean conceit or pride... But the living can't *not* plead their case, can't *not* apologize. Only the dead endure a wrong, only the dead revel in it. They have a right to... The dead are blameworthy."

"But you're here, you're speaking, you're answering..."

The commissioner's voice was more or less like a searcher who, for some unknown reason, obscures the fact that he's already hot on the trail of the one he's searching for.

"And yet, and yet the living are like that anyway, and are incapable of either detesting what's forbidden, or else of liking it—so how is that living?"

This is where an odd thing occurred: the commissioner placed his right hand atop the man's head, while with his left arm he gave him a brief hug, as though he'd wanted to really convince him of something.

"And now don't take your eyes off me," he said with curt speed, having quickly let him go, for they had both guessed that someone or something was approaching, before whom this harmony of law and conscience would come crashing down, in defiance of him who wanted it.

Mr. Steel entered, and it was as though they'd brought

in a bundle of self-evident and inalienable civil rights and responsibilities, which then lost a little heart once they'd seen our fellow sitting over there. But Mr. Steel's dignity, as ready-at-hand as reserves on alert, formed a defensive ring around him. His unbuttoned raglan coat wouldn't hear a word against it.

The commissioner offered him a seat, whereupon he sat willy-nilly with his back to the suspect.

"Naturally," Mr. Steel opened his raglan still more deco-ratively, and that "naturally" itself now testified that he was responding to the imploring inquiry of the commissioner's eyes, selflessly overcoming his outrage, "naturally, if I had only suspected . . . Of course: this man's face is familiar; or, rather, I do remember it."

"The suspect," the commissioner tactfully explained, "who doesn't look good in light of certain circumstances, but who it seems is innocent, albeit without identification, has indicated that you will vouch for him, you and nobody else. Thus it was our responsibility . . ."

"*Pardon*," Mr. Steel said, having made a curt turn toward the plank bed and just as curt a turn back again, "the matter is simple: this man came under suspicion for having pilfered my wife's bracelet, but there was no direct proof."

"For that I'm sorry," was heard from behind.

"Commissioner, sir, we'll have none of that . . ."

"For that I am truly sorry" (and upon turning around, Mr. Steel, not believing his eyes, noticed that the two of them, without having arranged it somehow, were looking into each other's eyes), "most truly," our fellow assured him mildly.

Mr. Steel's smile started trying to sever that offensive rap-port, of which he was somehow doubly ashamed, for both the impersonal authority and its personal representative, in whom it had been forgotten. And because this wasn't helping, he felt meaningfully for his brow.

"Back then it already seemed to us...To all of us, Commissioner, all of us...Why in fact is this person here?"

"Because of a woman who jumped into the water."

"I'm here because of Zinaida, Mr. Steel. I apologize to you for Zinaida as well."

Mr. Steel buttoned himself up, and Mr. Steel, having stood up, unbuttoned himself again. And that fellow had stood as well. They were facing one another. The suspect was holding his cap under his arm, which was swinging unnaturally.

"I called for you because I wanted to ask your forgiveness. I know that you won't understand, but it's not really for you that I'm asking your forgiveness, it's for me. So then, Commissioner, sir..."

"But what is it you're asking my forgiveness for? Did you steal it?"

"I'm asking your forgiveness for the iniquity of my not managing to give you a slap. It's a wonder that Zinaida didn't pay for this iniquity tonight—yes—wonder at it—but that's how it is."

The bundle of Mr. Steel's virtues were dying of shame for the fact that police stations don't have someone who plugs the madmen's mugs.

"Do you have any objections to our releasing this person?"

Mr. Steel indicated with a shrug of his shoulders that it wasn't even worth asking.

"Is there something you wish to add?"

"Oh, yes," Mr. Steel said with cheerful zeal. "Charenton asylum."

"You may go," the commissioner responded with a very polite gesture, but in a voice so stern that Mr. Steel, having initiated his own gesture, froze at the voice.

"Unless..."

"Unless?" Mr. Steel repeated, unsettled.

In a single leap toward our fellow, who was standing there with his arms hanging down, the commissioner seized him in a half nelson. At the same time he hunched over slightly, and hunched over in this way he turned his head toward Mr. Steel, who was walking away, and roared:

"Hold on! – Come here."

A livid Mr. Steel came over.

"What's the meaning of this?"

"The slap that you didn't deliver at Benedictine Mill ... finish it off, you scoundrel!"

"Finish it off, scoundrel," he stamped, as Mr. Steel was looking around helplessly. "That's an order."

And Mr. Steel's hand rose without his assistance, and it landed on the face of the motionless person, who didn't even blink. Who didn't blink, not even afterwards, when he sensed that the commissioner, having released his arms, had drawn himself up and nestled in close to him.

"You may go," he commanded Mr. Steel again, and when the latter made a move, the former attached himself to him like one soldier joining another in formation, and he accompanied him to the door, which he opened. There he turned to face him and repeated, "You may go," only a bit more tersely and as though put out.

Behind the slammed door, a few inches of light fell. It fell upon the point where even the false modesty of angels turns to ice.

Without moving so much as a step, the commissioner turned around, he had an enormous smile on his lips, he threw open his arms and called out:

"Come!"

Then the other fellow, having thrown his cap carelessly on, started running headlong, his head so hammered with joy it weighed it down, you'd say he was like a ram attacking an impossible rampart, but which he knocked down by faith, not suspecting that this was not enough.

And, in fact, there was this:

When he'd finished running and looked up in order to rest in those open arms, he spotted a young redheaded man with a tousled mop of hair and a hard look that, instead of open arms, showed him the door and said:

"All I know is the law—I have to—it's firm."

Our fellow threw himself into his arms; the commissioner shrank back:

"What's this now? Why?" he asked tenderly, but he swiftly straightened himself up and stamped:

"Get out!"

The day was dazzling, and it was having a laugh with the lustrous parts of Mr. Steel's car. A policeman was making his rounds as though he were looking after it, this car. His surprise at the arrestee coming out gave way to professional neutrality.

For the old-timer—for it was an old-timer coming out of the station immediately after Mr. Steel—this neutrality inspired such confidence that he stopped to revel in the bright day; never before had he stepped into such sunlight. At the same time, and if it were possible still more devastatingly, he was reveling in the astonishingly luminous certainty that he took no pride in himself. He didn't even know how he'd pulled off that little step beyond, that little step from there to a still newer certainty, though this time only darkly illuminated: that is, the certainty that he was invulnerable.

Mr. Steel was already sitting in his automobile; he was

stretching out his arm to pull the door shut. But that other fellow jumped forward and closed it with delicate courtesy and a bow:

"Votre serviteur!"

Had he perhaps forgotten his hand on the handle? When the car lunged forward he had a hell of a time keeping on his feet.

The policeman hooked his right hand to his belt and caught sight of him as he staggered.

"Pauvre vieux!" he guffawed in unstressed arsis, so it didn't really count.

The day was dazzling, and no longer having Mr. Steel's automobile to kid around with it took our old-timer by the hand and led him to the nearby embankment, down the platform, a little ways and a little more, along the row of tugboats meditating on winter ports and on the loves of the neighboring shipbuilders' teenage children. – And it was the waterfront where they sheared dogs. And there was one shearer whose exclamations had become the crystallization of the real, around which the crystals of the irrevocable things of life crowded of their own accord.

"You, old man . . . hold him for me."

It was walking there with weaned step. Some mutt. He was supposed to grab it head-on, and he had to crouch down. The animal held still. The muzzle was so close to his mouth that it cooled his parch. It was an oblique, black muzzle, all warty, but so tidy. How, dear God, is one to remain in this tidiness of the mute face and not move toward the eyes, toward the eyes with reddish pupils that didn't shy away? What am I saying, didn't shy away! Patiently, fervently, quietly, they were seeking other eyes, to speak with them mutely! They spotted each other, and they said nothing to one another, except:

"We live."

They were saying to each other, "We live, we live, we live," while that other fellow there was shearing.

At last they let the dog go. It shivered. The old-timer took his unlearned walk further along, not looking back. But because the call "here boy, here boy" didn't fade behind him, at length he did look back, and he saw that the dog was following him. He waited for it to catch up, and when it had, it squatted to crap in front of him. He tried to turn its head toward the customer; she was calling for it. The dog resisted. Again he saw its reddish pupils, beautifully starry and even more beautifully mute. They demanded no answer; there was nothing they would want to know. And their incuriosity was so colossal that there could be no doubt: only eyes that had already grasped everything could be so very incurious. The old man was gazing for the first time into eyes that showed no fear, for the first time into a gaze that *only* looked.

He turned its head, and in the end he turned the whole thing, that it might make up its mind to return to its owner. And leaving it this way, he set off more quickly.

"Here boy, here boy," he heard again.

He looked back. The animal was hurrying after him. The day was dazzling in its stone-like reality.

(August 1930–February 1931)